SEEK AND HIDE

AMANDA G.
STEVENS

SEEK AND
HIDE

HAVEN SEEKERS BOOK ONE

David C Cook®
transforming lives together

SEEK AND HIDE
Published by David C Cook
4050 Lee Vance View
Colorado Springs, CO 80918 U.S.A.

David C Cook Distribution Canada
55 Woodslee Avenue, Paris, Ontario, Canada N3L 3E5

David C Cook U.K., Kingsway Communications
Eastbourne, East Sussex BN23 6NT, England

The graphic circle C logo is a registered trademark of David C Cook.

The website addresses recommended throughout this book are offered as a
resource to you. These websites are not intended in any way to be or imply an
endorsement on the part of David C Cook, nor do we vouch for their content.

This story is a work of fiction. Characters and events are the product of the author's
imagination. Any resemblance to any person, living or dead, is coincidental.

ISBN 978-1-4347-0865-6
eISBN 978-0-7814-1175-2

The Team: John Blase, Renada Thompson, Susan Murdock
Cover Design: Nick Lee
Cover Photos: iStock, Shutterstock

Printed in the United States of America
First Edition 2014

1 2 3 4 5 6 7 8 9 10

090514

Now unto the King
eternal,
immortal,
invisible,
the only wise God,
be honour and glory
forever and ever.
Amen.

1 Timothy 1:17, King James Version

"It is well settled law that the First Amendment does not protect speech that incites violence. As we noted in *Jennings v. California,* the evidence considered by the California State Legislature was sufficient to support the Legislature's conclusion that the speech of 'archaic' bibles (as defined in *Jennings*) incited violence and thus that the California statute banning possession of archaic bibles was constitutional.

Similarly, we have long separated the social evil of hate speech and fighting words from protected freedom of expression, limitations of which do not 'creat[e] the danger of driving viewpoints from the marketplace.'

... And so we hold today that Iowa's Statute, which classifies attacks steeped in the philosophy of or quoting the text of archaic biblical translations as hate speech, not to run contrary to the First Amendment. Affirmed."

Carmichael v. Iowa [citations omitted]
Supreme Court of the United States of America

1

Booze behind the wheel could turn a sports car into a … well, wreck. No other word for the blue Honda that had rammed halfway through Keith's garage door before lodging there like a dud missile. Marcus pushed a shoulder to the door. It swayed a little, but the hole's jagged edges stayed wedged against the car. Trying to back out might take the whole door down. Not that Marcus would trust the driver to try it.

Murmuring party guests lined the garage wall. Nobody was doing anything about this mess, other than gaping at it. If the driver had kept his foot on the gas a second longer, the car doors might have cleared the crater. Then again, he might also have run somebody over.

"Brenner, man, you can fix it, right?" Keith hovered over Marcus's shoulder, and his beer breath wafted too close. "You can get Jason out of there, right?"

The driver hammered a fist against his door. "Keith, when I get out of this car, I'm going to kick your face in, you hear me? I'm going to—"

Marcus tapped on the car window. "Hey. Don't. We'll get you out."

"You shut up. You get out of my face, you—"

"That's no way to talk to the linebacker." Across the hood of the car, a woman wearing less than a tank top blinked at Marcus. She leaned forward and stretched a bottle toward him, spilling cleavage and beer. He tried to stare at her blue eyes.

"You're new. Best stuff that's left, right here in this bottle."

He could taste it. Yes. "No. Thanks."

The woman pouted and splashed the car hood with the rest of her beer. She sidled closer to Marcus. "You're so big."

And you're so drunk.

"Your eyes are like the sky."

Well, not unless the sky had turned brown lately. Marcus gently pushed her away.

Keith rocked from one foot to the other, his gaze shifting from Marcus to the trapped, cussing driver and back again. "See why I called you, Brenner? You build stuff and fix stuff. And I thought you could fix this. Or build it. Or yeah."

The garage door was beyond fixing. Marcus needed something to free the car. He let his eyes roam the four-car garage without resting too long on various available drinks. The half-finished side held a workbench in one corner. Garden tools hung from a dusty pegboard: rake and trowel and yeah, that was a pitchfork. But nothing helpful.

"Keith, got an axe?"

Fortunately, Keith only had one, or he probably would have tried to help. In the next ten minutes, Marcus widened the hole around the car. November rain blew inside, the kind that mocked fall jackets but sabotaged winter coats with cold, heavy saturation. The kind that Michiganders complained about until someone piped in, "Hey, it could be snowing." Likely would be soon. Still, at the moment, Marcus wasn't cold. Sweat dripped down his back and chest and dampened his shirt, then his jacket. He worked hard, not only to free the car but also to ignore Tank Top Girl's offerings of her booze and her body.

Once Marcus had verified the designated drivers, the last of the partiers dispersed. He was left with Keith and Jason for company, the two of them periodically hollering at each other through the windshield. At least neither one of them was drinking anymore.

As long as his hands curled around the axe handle, the other guys couldn't see his shaking. He angled his next swing, and the blade chomped into the garage door with a *thunk*. Splinters ricocheted off the arms of his jacket and rained to the garage floor. In another minute, he should be able to back the car out. Then he could get out of here and drive home and make coffee. He breathed through his mouth but could still smell the beer-washed garage. He tried to conjure the aroma of a fresh-ground roast.

A cooler stood open in the corner. Next to the keg.

The axe bit too hard, straight through the wood, and nicked the hood of the car. A silver gash appeared in the blue paint. Marcus winced, then shrugged. One more scratch in this paint job wasn't a big deal. From the other side of the garage, Keith raised his arms like an athlete on the Olympic medal stand and whooped in approval of the door's destruction. In the morning, the idiot would be sober. And ticked off. He hadn't changed one bit since their high-school partying days.

"Good thing the neighbors aren't home," Keith said. "They might've called the cops."

About time somebody besides Marcus had a sensible thought. He set down the axe. The car door should open wide enough for him to squeeze into the driver's seat.

"Jason, move—"

The guy turned the key and hit the gas. Marcus leaped back. The car backed down the driveway several feet, then skidded to a stop.

Jason stepped out into the drizzle with a grin born of braces. His blond hair dripped as he ducked back through the hole his car had left. "Neighbors wouldn't call the cops, because I don't need the cops. Because I am the cops."

Right. Of course he was.

Keith nodded. "Hey, Brenner, did you know Jason's the cops?"

"Uh, no."

"I'm MPC," Jason said.

He was?

The acronym had never rooted itself into civilian vocabulary, but everyone knew its meaning. Michigan Philosophical Constabulary. Marcus stepped back from the guy. Short, lean—Marcus could knock him to the floor without trying. He breathed. Slowly. Flexed his hands, opened them, flexed them again. Had Jason waited in the shadows last night outside a church meeting, a church like Marcus's? Had he handcuffed God's people and driven them away to re-education?

Keith stared from Marcus to Jason and back again. "Whoa, how crazy's that, for you to save the day for a con-cop? I mean, you don't like them much. Obviously."

"Keith, shut up." If he went to jail today, he'd go because he chose to hit this guy. Hard. Not because Keith had a big mouth.

"Hey, no worries. He never remembers a thing past his third or fourth shot. You could read a Bible to him, an old one, I mean, and he—"

"Shut up. Now."

"You guys aren't making sense," Jason said.

Marcus pointed at the car outside, still running. "I want the keys."

Jason seemed to gain height as Marcus watched. His chin lifted, and his forehead twitched above the left eyebrow. "They're my keys."

"You don't need them till tomorrow."

"Three cheers for Brenner, Garage Door Chopper." Keith hoisted Marcus's arm over his head, slapping the air with beer breath.

Booze made people say the stupidest things at the stupidest times.

"I'm leaving now," Marcus said to Keith. "And he's spending the night."

Confusion furrowed Keith's forehead. "You're not driving him home?"

Not a good idea. Marcus would end up wrapping his hands around Jason's neck and squeezing until ... Could a Constabulary agent arrest you for assault, or would he have to call the regular police? But that was the point—Jason wouldn't be arresting anybody as long as he wasn't breathing.

Right, because incapacitating one member of a government police force could make such a difference. Marcus might as well pull one scale off a rattlesnake.

"No," he said. "He's staying here."

Jason threw a splay-fingered gesture at the car still running in the driveway. Its headlights cut through the drizzle, through the crater in the door. "Car's still drivable. So I'm going to drive it."

"You're drunk, moron," Keith said. "I'll drive you."

Marcus squeezed his eyes shut. If he left them here, one of them would get behind the wheel. Even if they promised not to.

God, do I have to do this?

"Okay," he said. "I'll take him home." And try not to kill him.

Keith gave him directions although Jason insisted he knew the way. He also insisted he could get into Marcus's truck without help. Marcus let him claw at the door and hoist himself onto the running board, then inside.

As they pulled out of the driveway, Jason reached across the console to punch Marcus's forearm. "I'll drive."

"No." *Now don't touch me again. Or talk. Or breathe.* Marcus rolled down the windows halfway.

"We're gonna get cold."

"It'll help you sober up."

Jason laughed like a stricken hyena. "What makes you think I want that?"

Marcus turned the heat on high, but it couldn't compensate for the chill that rushed into the truck. Occasional drizzle hit the left side of his face. He merged onto the highway, and his senses began to settle, thanks to the wind that whisked away the clinging scent. Jason must have spilled beer on himself at some point. Why was the smell always stronger on somebody's clothes?

"I know that name." In the dark, Jason's silhouette had turned to face upward, to catch a green overpass sign.

"What, the road?"

"Somebody lives on that road."

No kidding. Marcus signaled a lane change and swept past an old silver car.

Jason's laugh bounced off the windshield into Marcus's face. "Somebody's gonna finally get put away."

An arrest, one that hadn't happened yet. A block of ice formed in Marcus's gut.

God, how much longer will You watch Your followers get locked up and spit on?

It had been six years so far. Six years of state Constabularies enforcing philosophical regulations that had been written into law, voted into law, signed by the president, and upheld by the Supreme Court.

God hadn't thwarted the US government. Just one more thing Marcus didn't understand about Him, but he would serve Him anyway.

"This young newlywed couple." Jason spoke to the side window. "Neighbor saw them on the back porch, reading an archaic Bible in broad daylight, like it was just another book. Gotta love it when these whack jobs get stupid."

Marcus forced his hands to relax on the steering wheel.

"You'd think they'd be easier to crack, you know? Whole lives ahead of them and all. But sometimes ..."

Deep breath. Ease up. Before his shoulder muscles twisted into knots.

"Sometimes younger ones are the most stubborn subjects you ever laid eyes on."

Subjects? Like lab rats?

"But we got them, man. Finally got us a warrant. Gonna get them off the street." The window reflected Jason's white smile.

Marcus changed to the right lane in preparation for the exit.

"I first saw their files and I thought they were black. Cole. Like Nat King, you know? They're not, though."

Jim and Karlyn. Married last year in the fairy-tale wedding she'd dreamed of, Jim's gift to her despite his weakening health. Now they lived on the first road on that sign. Until the Constabulary came to take them.

No.

Something jabbed at the embers deep inside Marcus, the chunks of himself that he'd thought cold, that now spit sparks and started to glow. When would the search be conducted? Tonight? A week? No, not that long. He had to get there first.

"That's my street," Jason said. "Told you I knew the way."

The house was a modest red-shuttered Cape Cod. Marcus tried to leave him at the curb, but Jason yelled and beckoned until Marcus joined him on the porch.

"Watch this." Jason pounded on the door. "Police! Open up!"

The porch light beamed down on them. The door opened on a petite brunette woman, closer to Marcus's thirty-two years than Jason's forty-something.

"Oh, that's brilliant, Jase, wake up the neighbors and have them call the police on you."

"They show their faces around my house, I'll pull rank on 'em."

"Come in the—" The woman's eyes snagged on Marcus. "Keith said Nathan was bringing him home."

"Change of plan," Marcus said.

Several rings pressed into his hand as she shook it firmly. "Pamela Mayweather."

"Marcus Brenner."

"Thank you for this, Marcus."

"Sure."

"If you'll excuse my abruptness, I should say good night and get my husband into the house."

"Sure." His feet already shifted. Move. Leave. If Jason had forgotten about the car by morning, his wife could get the news from Keith. "Good night."

"Thank you again." The curve of Pamela's mouth hinted more at relief than gratitude.

"Next time, I drive." Jason managed a quick, hard punch to Marcus's shoulder before shuffling inside.

Marcus returned to his truck while dangerous unknowns raced through his head. The Constabulary already had a warrant for the

Coles. And if they had a warrant, the landline might be tapped. He could text them, but if their phones were no longer in their possession ... if he was too late already ...

He'd have to go there.

By the time he reached their neighborhood, 3:00 a.m. had come and gone. He drove past the house without slowing. You never knew who was and was not working for the Constabulary. The smoke-colored uniforms everyone recognized were rarely seen. If Marcus had hoped for some sign or sense that they were watching the house, then he'd hoped for too much.

It didn't matter, anyway. No way did he plan to walk up to the front door and feign innocence. He parked two streets over in front of a gray van. Foot on the brake, he backed his truck until the bumper made gentle contact with the van's. Then he put the truck in drive for an inch or two and parked. Reading his license plate would now require more than driving by—or stepping between the cars, since that was no longer possible. If the Constabulary wanted to name him as a suspect, they'd have to earn it.

The chill cut through his jacket, but at least the rain had stopped. Marcus crossed the street halfway between streetlights and hurried up somebody's driveway—the somebody who shared a backyard fence with the Coles. *God, don't let them have a dog.*

The little half-brick houses crouched close together. Crossing this stranger's backyard took seconds. He paused a moment, avoiding moonlight, the trunk of an ancient oak tree rough against his back. Its leaves swished above him, and a car passed in front of the house. Now. Go. He breathed deep. Gripped the dripping chain-link fence. Stuck one foot into a space halfway up and propelled his body over and dropped to the other side.

Clouds drifted over the moon. He darted across the Coles' yard. The red door was more warning than invitation. Had the Constabulary beat him here? Had they raided the house, dragged the Coles away to re-education?

The weight of that possibility hunched his shoulders. His forehead rested against the door. *It's only been a few months. I've only had them a few months.* He hadn't even known about the family of Christ when he joined it. Those first two years of infant faith, he'd kept on belonging to nobody, responsible for nobody, which he'd figured was for the best—look at his track record. Then he'd met Jim and Karlyn and they'd opened their Bible and shown him. He had family again.

Marcus straightened, breathed in, and knocked.

2

After a minute, he knocked again. The deadbolt gave a sliding *click*, and a lightless gap appeared in the door.

"Jim, Karlyn." His whisper seemed to echo. "It's Marcus, let me in."

The door swung inward with a squeaking lack of caution.

"Marcus?" Karlyn's hand tugged at his sleeve, then shut the door behind him. "What're you doing here? It's three in the morning."

"I know," Marcus said.

Karlyn flipped on the light. She held a silver golf club over her shoulder, like a batter at ease. "It's a putter."

"Yeah, I see it. Karlyn—"

"It makes a great spur-of-the-moment weapon, especially combined with a purple belt in jujitsu."

"Right." Marcus followed her into the small kitchen. "Karlyn—"

"And I ought to use it on you. What could possibly be—"

"They've got a search warrant for your house."

The hand holding the putter fell to her side. The club end thumped against the floor. "A ..."

Marcus nodded.

Her eyes flickered around the room. "We've got to hide them—where else do we hide them? I won't burn them or throw them away or— Or ..."

"I know," he said. "Jim in bed?"

"He won't burn them, either."

The muscles in Marcus's neck threatened to snap along with his patience. "I need to talk to him. And you. Come on."

Karlyn all but ran across the ranch house to the master bedroom. She didn't bother to see if Marcus followed. Jim lay in bed, propped against the headboard, glaring at his walker against the far wall.

"Karlyn," Jim said, "I'm perfectly able to get the door my— Marcus?"

"There's a search warrant out on us, Jim." Karlyn sat down on the other side of their bed, which was lower than most king-size beds to give Jim easier access. She scooted back against the headboard and drew her knees to her chin.

"How do you know?"

"Long story," Marcus said. "I don't know when they'll come, but you've got to be ready."

"What do we do?" Jim said. "Everything's already hidden as well as it can be."

What *could* they do? Oh. Of course. Marcus stepped farther into the room. "Give it to me. All of it, whatever you've got."

The pause spread around the room, tight with the war on their faces. They wanted to let Marcus do this. Yet they didn't.

"No," Jim said.

"You have to."

"It wouldn't be right, Marcus."

"If you take anything illegal with you, you'll be ..." Karlyn's voice barely whispered over her bent knees.

Marcus paced the length of the bed and back again. "What? A criminal? We're already criminals."

"The crimes are misdemeanors now. But if you do this, then …"
She laced her long fingers together and turned them inside out, as if
to wring the words she wanted from her hands.

"Where is it? Just tell me."

"You'd be guilty of a felony. Of a lot of them."

Transporting illegal literature, removing evidence, obstructing
the prevention of philosophical crime … Quite a damning list.

"We can't let you do this," Jim said.

"The warrant's for your house. Not mine."

Fear and common sense were usually at odds in a decision, but
together, they were powerful. Etched into Jim's face was knowledge
of what he should do, and fear that wanted to do it. He tried to run
a hand through his hair, but it slumped back to his side. Multiple
sclerosis had attacked more than his legs.

"We're grateful you came, but—"

"Jim," Marcus said.

"My answer's no."

Screw his answer. Marcus wasn't leaving here without the
Bibles. Where would Jim and Karlyn hide them? He searched the
walls for a giveaway, but no, not in here. He headed for Jim's study.
More likely there than the kitchen.

"Marcus," Jim yelled after him.

He knocked his knuckles against the paneled study walls. The
sound thudded, nothing hollow behind it.

"Stop it, Marcus," Karlyn said behind him. "It's our decision."

He took a few steps, knocked again. Still a dense, abrupt sound.

"Hey, Pit Bull. Open those teeth." Her voice was closer now,
just over his shoulder.

The nickname wasn't fair. It tried to soften him, and he couldn't be soft with them in danger. His jaw clenched tighter, and his knuckles rapped the wall too hard. Ow.

"Let it go."

Marcus turned on her, and she stepped back, a reflex. "You'll come home believing you were guilty and the Bible's dangerous. Or you'll be all bruised and scarred and—hurt."

"The physical methods are rumors, and—"

"What do you think they'll do to Jim?"

Her face scrunched into a struggle not to cry. She hid behind her hands, then lowered them. Her eyes had hardened. "After the search, you bring them back."

"It'd be safer to let me keep them."

"Safer for Jim and me. That's the condition. I'll give them to you if you promise to bring them back."

All Marcus could do for now was nod.

Ten minutes later, he drove toward home with an opaque department store bag under the seat of his truck. Karlyn had insisted on layering dishtowels over the books. Jim had nearly fallen from bed, trying to reach his walker and stop them both. In taking the danger and the decision, Marcus had taken something else from Jim too, something he himself would never want to give up. But to make Jim and Karlyn safe, Marcus would do whatever he had to.

What if the Christians arrested last night had given up everybody's names? What if Jim and Karlyn were only the first warrant? No, Jason had said somebody saw them reading a Bible. He would've mentioned Christians betraying each other, a victory for the Constabulary.

Tonight, Marcus had scored a victory against them. Maybe his group shouldn't be limiting contact information. Had he never worked for Jim and Karlyn, he wouldn't know where they lived. The simple upkeep and repairs that exhausted Jim had been just another project for Marcus until his last day on the job, when Karlyn had handed him his check, thanked him, and stared at him.

"*What do you worship?*" she'd said.

If that was her idea of subtlety, she ought to look the word up in a dictionary. Not that Marcus was big into dictionaries. The question could have been a trap, but he'd promised God he'd never deny Him, and that meant a complete answer, not a vague one. She was asking what he believed about Jesus. He searched his memory, the few parts of the Bible that he knew, and finally found something.

"'*The Father has sent His Son to be the Savior of the world,*'" he said. It was a verse the government-sanctioned Progressive United Version would have cut. According to the PUV, people were supposed to save themselves.

Karlyn's grin had lit her whole face. Soon after that, she and Jim invited him to the Table, where he discovered a family that wanted to add … him.

He couldn't warn the rest of them. Phone calls, texts—too risky. And he didn't know where anyone else lived. His truck carried him and the towel-stuffed shopping bag homeward. *God, You gave them to me. Don't let the Constabulary take them.*

"*Doesn't it seem only right that what the Lord gives, He can take away? You have to open your hands, Marcus.*"

Almost two years since he'd last seen the man, Frank's voice still echoed in Marcus's brain at the oddest times, a hint of Indiana accent clinging to the vowels. Did Frank still believe that from inside prison? He'd die in re-education, forty-something years from now, an old man still asking guards and fellow prisoners and everyone else,

"So, what do you believe about God?" and then preaching the Bible to them from memory.

God hadn't taken him away. The Constabulary had.

With Bibles in his car, Marcus held to within three miles an hour of the speed limit and even braked for a late yellow light. He'd be on his way to re-education, and two Bibles—real Bibles, printed before the Constabulary's revisions—would be destroyed, if a regular police officer smelled the aftermath of Jason Mayweather in his truck and decided to search it. Or maybe the smell was only a memory.

He'd pass three liquor stores on the way home.

The neon clock on his dash read 3:43. Lee might be asleep. He shouldn't call. Well, maybe it would go to voice mail. He'd hold the phone to his ear and drive home without stopping. When she got a wordless voice mail in the morning and called him back, he could tell her the truth without shame.

Speed-dial one. It rang twice.

"Marcus."

"Oh, I hoped you'd be sleeping."

"Where are you?"

"This buddy called me around one, there was this party and everybody was …"

"You went to a party? With alcohol?"

"Some idiot drove his car through the garage door. I helped get him out."

When his words stalled, she didn't interrogate. He inhaled the silence that waited without pushing.

"And then the guy was going to drive home, and Keith was too drunk to drive him or stop him from driving, and by then everybody else had left, so ... I couldn't let him drive. Anyway. Now I'm on my way home."

"And how are you?" The warmth in her voice seeped inside him and blunted the claws of his thirst.

"I'm okay."

"Of course. Now. How are you?"

Eight years, ten months, thirteen days. Fourteen tomorrow. He tried not to swallow the phantom taste, but his throat contracted anyway. "I could use some coffee. But I'm okay."

"Nearing home?"

"Getting there."

"Are you passing anywhere significant?"

"One store down. Two to go."

"All right, then we'll talk."

"Lee, it's four in the morning."

"You drive fast."

A chuckle pushed through the gratitude that surged in his chest. But she needed to sleep. If he told her he was okay, she'd believe him. Not true of the early days. Lies used to spurt from his mouth without a thought, when booze was the topic. But he'd earned trust back, and she had to be tired, and ...

"Marcus?"

"I was going to tell you to go to sleep."

"If I do, will you get home all right?" Lee's voice held more caution now. Knowing.

"Probably. I just ..." He sighed.

"Then what should we discuss?"

"Um." He tried to roll his shoulders, but his neck felt like a steel rod. "How was work? Got a story?"

The pause evolved into hesitant silence. Lee needed to talk about something, but she hadn't decided if she wanted to.

"What happened?" He probably already knew. His hand constricted around the phone.

"One of my ER patients was a victim of ..."

Rape. He wouldn't make her say it. "Is she okay?"

"A vertebra in her neck was fractured when he drove her head into a wall. And she is unlikely to have children."

The needles in his shoulders barely registered compared to the knot in his gut.

"She could have been paralyzed." Lee's voice had become a flat-line of facts. "She told me she didn't know him. She was lying."

Words weren't enough. Silence wasn't, either, but he was better at that. He drove with the phone to his ear and listened to Lee's soft breathing. He passed the next liquor store, then the last one. He breathed deeply and imagined coffee and the smell of Lee's flowery shampoo. Finally, he pulled into his garage and sat in the dim glow of the overhead light. After a minute, it turned off. Time to go inside.

"Are you okay?" he said as he let himself into the house.

"I believe so. You?"

"I'm home."

Before he could free his key from the door, a clatter of toenails rushed toward him. Indy licked the back of his hand. Her tail lashed the air, swished across the wood floor when he motioned her to sit. Her tongue lapped between his fingers.

"Indy says hi," he said.

"Hello to Indy. And thank you for calling me."

He pictured her, curled against the arm of the couch, swallowed in fleece lounge pants and a size-large hoodie. Maybe her black hair was poking out around her face, damp from a shower. Maybe she'd plugged her ear buds into her phone and sat with her slim wrists crossed over her knees.

"Thanks for talking, and listening, and ... knowing."

A smile returned to her voice. "You're welcome."

The call ended. Marcus lowered the phone. They didn't need to say good-bye.

3

Sometimes, Aubrey would like a best friend who took no for an answer. She shifted the phone between her shoulder and ear to turn the crank on the old infant swing. "I'd rather not, Karlyn, really."

"Come on, girl." Karlyn's voice carried concern that she tried to mask as lighthearted persuasion. "I refuse to go alone to a baby shower for someone I barely know. And I hate to not go and make it look like I don't *want* to get to know her."

"I've never even met her." Aubrey set the swing in motion, and Elliott's pink smile opened wide in a soundless cackle. "You like that, baby boy?"

"Love it," Karlyn said.

"Hey, multitasking mother over here."

"You still talk to him?"

"Of course. I can't not, I guess."

"Does he look at you?"

"Sometimes." If she walked into his field of vision first. Aubrey stifled the sigh because sighing was such a shallow expression, anyway. As if air shoved from her lungs could smooth away the barbed truth. She focused on the less world-tilting topic. "Who ever heard of bringing a guest to a baby shower?"

"She knows I won't know anybody. It was nice of her to offer."

"We can sit in our own little corner and chat, and ostracize everyone else."

"Well, that wasn't *my* plan …"

Of course not. Karlyn's plan would include fluttering from table to table, meeting each woman there, and enthralling most of them with her genuine warmth. Nothing wrong with that, of course. If Aubrey possessed such a trait, she'd use it, too. She crossed her apartment living room, four steps on flattened ivory carpet. She sank onto the secondhand sofa and waved at her baby. That wasn't language; it was only a wave. She'd never known before that hand motions and sign language were not the same.

"I'm just trying to get my Salmon back," Karlyn said quietly.

Oh ... that. Aubrey tried to smile away the sudden weight on her chest. "Maybe I got tired of being pegged as a fish."

"It was you. It still is. We just have to get you out of hibernation."

"Salmon migrate, Karlyn. They don't hibernate."

"Will you come to the shower? Please?"

Aubrey leaned into the hard back of the couch and closed her eyes. Her fingers rubbed a mindless motion into the cushion beside her, as if she could massage the gold and brown tweed into soft microfiber. Maybe she could go. Maybe it would be right to mingle, however clumsily. To prattle with the moms about first teeth and diaper brands, pedicures and new purses (not that she'd gotten either of those things lately). Maybe it wouldn't be wrong to pretend she'd never lived three weeks of re-education.

But wouldn't she also have to pretend that she wasn't a Christian? And wouldn't *that* be wrong?

"I guess I can't make it any worse." The words slipped out before she could swallow them, slick and sour.

"Aubrey, listen to me. I don't care what anybody says. You're forgiven, girl. You. Are. Forgiven."

No. I'm not. But life should continue. Elliott deserved a socially functioning mother. Aubrey leaned forward, elbows on knees, and clutched the phone. "I get free cheesecake, right?"

Karlyn's soft sob caught in her laughter. "Goes without saying."

"Does the mom-to-be have a gift registry somewhere?"

"You're signing my card. That's all you're allowed to do."

"I'll see if Mom can watch Elliott. But she can always watch Elliott." Mom would adopt her grandson if she could. Get him away from his mother's dangerous religious beliefs.

"Fantastic. You're going to make it, Salmon. And someday—" Karlyn broke off as a muted pounding came over the line.

"What's that noise?" Aubrey said.

"Somebody doesn't see the doorbell, I guess."

"You need to go?"

"Hold on, I'm—" A gasp broke through the snap of rising blinds, faintly picked up by the phone.

"Karlyn, who is it?"

The second of silence felt eternal. "Con-cops."

Oh. No.

"Aubrey, it's okay."

Okay? *Okay?* "Okay?"

"I have to go, I have to let them in, they've got a search warrant, but listen—it's going to be fine, nothing's going to happen. I'll call you back when they're gone. Everything's fine."

"What are you—"

"I can't explain right now. I'll call you back."

"Be careful," Aubrey said, as if that would make a difference.

"I will. Don't worry."

The hand gripping the phone did not move from her ear, even when the dial tone turned to boisterous beeping. Don't worry? What was Karlyn talking about? They were at the door with a search warrant. They might wear gray uniforms, their cars the same color and topped with single green lights. They might wear navy suits, their car unmarked, dark and nondescript. When they came to Aubrey's door, she'd thought they were salespeople.

The illogical side of terror wanted to blame her for their arrival. They clearly had listened in on her and Karlyn's conversation, had probably listened in on many of Karlyn's conversations over the last few weeks. Neither she nor Karlyn had said anything incriminating, except … Forgiven? Karlyn hadn't specified God as the forgiver, but had it been enough? Or had association with Aubrey put Karlyn on the potential Christians list?

The phone was still beeping. Aubrey pressed the End button.

Oh, not Karlyn. Why had she sounded so inanely confident, as if she might not be arrested in the next few minutes?

The phone dropped into the cradle of its own weight, and Aubrey shuffled over to her fussing baby boy. It wasn't feeding time, but she nursed him anyway. Tears boiled over in her eyes and left marks like rain drops in his fine blond hair. She could not bear this role reversal. Karlyn had spent three weeks believing Aubrey was gone forever, but Aubrey would spend the rest of her life … knowing. Karlyn would never give in.

4

Marcus drove one-handed while the other hand kneaded his neck. He hadn't had a headache in days, so he couldn't complain. Besides, country driving was the best relief for a headache. Never mind the conventional wisdom about dark, quiet rooms. Blacktop spread a path in front of him, and fresh air rushed into the windows. Birds balanced on wires. Brown fields waited for winter's covering and spring's planting. He braked for a doe that bounded across the road about a quarter mile ahead, then coasted forward. The ten dining room chairs in the truck bed might not survive a collision with wildlife. Marcus had never damaged a piece of furniture in nine years of business. A streak he didn't want to end.

Out his window, the sun trailed streamers of pink and red as it headed toward the horizon. Wispy clouds twisted over the dusky blue in front of him. God had put some beautiful things in the world, but nothing beat the sky. Especially when it rolled with storm clouds the color of Lee's eyes.

After another few minutes, he turned right toward the Vitale house. Their dirt road was pocked with more dips and holes than he could avoid. The first mile of road passed only three houses. At the fourth, Marcus pulled up the crooked rope of driveway, backed his truck close to the porch, and walked around to the backyard. The Vitale property bordered on a forest a couple hundred yards from the house. A kidney-shaped pond occupied about one third of the yard space.

The house must strike awe in any first-time visitor. Marcus still paused sometimes to appreciate its vastness, girded halfway with a wraparound porch. It was even bigger inside. The layout included obsolete passageways and rooms behind rooms, which had housed the original owner's servants. The basement's tunnel surfaced out in the woods. The Vitales had owned it longer than Marcus had been alive, raised four kids here who now all lived out of state.

Belinda had told him last time he rang the front doorbell that he no longer counted as a guest and should knock on the back glass door. Marcus crossed the dusk-cloaked deck and triggered the porch lights. The sudden white flood made him squint. Ouch. He rapped on the glass. Soon the curtain was pulled away, and Chuck slid the door aside. His Italian complexion made his grin look whiter.

"Hey, Marcus. Come on in." Chuck nearly shook Marcus's hand off, a habit he'd taught his wife in their decades of marriage. Or maybe Belinda had taught it to him. He beckoned Marcus to follow and lumbered to the living room.

"The chairs are in the truck," Marcus said.

"We'll go get them in a minute. We're your last job of the day, right?"

"Yeah."

"Marcus." Belinda's Kentucky twang always sounded stronger when she said his name, but that was probably in his head. She rushed down the winding staircase in her typical stayed-home-all-day wardrobe—calf-length pink housecoat and oversized slippers. One hand grabbed onto his and pumped his entire arm, then yanked him toward her.

"Oh, never mind handshakes." She stood head and shoulders shorter, but her hug engulfed him along with her vanilla perfume.

"Hi, Belinda."

"You have time for coffee? There's some brewing."

"I can't stay long."

"You can stay a little while. 'Sides, I have that hazelnut creamer you like."

Coffee never hurt. "A little while. After we bring in the chairs."

While Chuck accompanied him to his truck, Belinda stood as the designated door-holder.

"You could've lost them on the way here," Chuck said.

You couldn't "lose" furniture from a truck bed unless you were an idiot. The tailgate pressed into Marcus's hands as he lowered it. He raised a foot to the edge of the bumper, then jumped up into the springy bed. "They're secure."

"You sure?"

Marcus nodded and handed each chair down to Chuck, watchful not to scrape them against the tailgate. The cherry wood was new and sturdy, smooth in his grip.

Belinda held open the screen door, and Chuck and Marcus carried the chairs past her, two by two, into the dining room. In a few minutes, they lined one wall. What would Chuck and Belinda do with ten chairs? People would sit in them, of course, to eat at the table Marcus was crafting. But ten chairs were a lot to fill.

"Oh, Chuck." Belinda clung to her husband's arm. "Aren't they beautiful?"

"I'll have the table done as soon as I can," Marcus said. "Do you want those pictures back?"

"I don't need them now, not with the real thing here in my dining room."

Soon the three of them sat at the kitchen bar. The latest news murmured from the radio under the counter. Marcus kept himself tuned to every few words and sipped from a mug on the verge of overflow.

"You still make the best coffee," he said to Belinda.

"Thank you, sugar. That's high praise coming from the Coffee Enthusiast of the Century."

Enthusiast. In his case, a euphemism. This was his tenth cup today, and the night was newborn. He took another sip, his hands enclosing the ceramic warmth.

"… local couple, James and Karlyn Cole of—"

The words pulled a fire alarm in Marcus's head. Belinda's latest bird-watching adventure morphed from calming small talk to obnoxious ramble. He squelched the impulse to glance at the radio, to ask her to turn it up, to hush her altogether.

"Pending further evidence, both may be charged with a philosophical misdemeanor. At this time, they have been detained for resisting a search warrant. Once inside the home, MPC agents were physically prevented from conducting their search."

A vise clamped onto his neck. Jim and Karlyn's Bibles lay behind the false back of the only bookcase he owned, but it hadn't done any good. Marcus hadn't protected his family.

Again.

The rancid bitterness of an old memory pushed up into his throat. He shoved it away, but another one took its place. Newer family, newer loss. Frank's wife Kay meeting him at the door with swollen, sleepless eyes.

"They took him, Marcus."

A voice in the present cut into the memory, underscored by interview static. "Both suspects became belligerent, and Mr. Cole physically struck out at one of the agents. It took two others to restrain him."

This story would never find the television. That would require a visual of Jim Cole and his walker. If they wanted a convincing lie, they should have emphasized Karlyn's putter and purple belt.

"Marcus? Did we lose you?"

Um. "You saw a kestrel."

"That's what I said," Belinda said. "A couple minutes ago. I'm talking about the Cooper's hawk now."

Did she really expect him to care about some bird right now? Marcus's thumb rubbed the handle of his mug, then pushed it a few inches across the dappled brown countertop.

"You know those people on the radio?" Chuck said.

"Yeah." Marcus raised his eyes to Belinda's worry-crinkled face.

Her fingers brushed his sleeve. "You're being careful, aren't you?"

Careful? What did that even mean in this situation? They knew he wouldn't deny his faith. But he wasn't shouting it from a busy intersection, either. He wasn't a preacher like Frank. He was just living, and people who got to know him usually figured his faith out for themselves. He drained his coffee mug.

"I think of you every time there's a Constabulary story on the news," Belinda said. "Worried it might be you until I hear the names."

Marcus pushed back the barstool and stood up. "I should go."

"You don't have to. We've got nothing going on."

"Maybe he's got work to do," Chuck said.

"Is it that kitchen you told me about? When you're done, you can work on mine." Belinda hugged Chuck's arm.

"No more remodeling, Pearl." Chuck's use of her middle name seemed to soften the scowl.

"We'll get back with you, Marcus. This kitchen's as old as my youngest, and he's thirty now."

They'd already forgotten the radio. "Okay."

"Regardless, I'll be finding you something else to do, since you're the only one who doesn't take my coffee for granted."

They both accompanied him to the back sliding door. Belinda gave him a sideways hug.

"Our door's always open to you, sugar."

"I know."

"Be seeing you." Chuck offered a half wave, half salute. And a wink. "She'll get her way about that kitchen, sure enough. Always does about stuff like that, you know."

Marcus nodded and headed to his truck. If he stayed on this porch one more minute, he would ask these people if they coped with the world by pretending it didn't exist.

"Thanks again for the chairs," Chuck called before he shut the door. "Your work's not half bad."

Marcus didn't turn to acknowledge that. He'd be gone before they realized what might be bothering him.

An hour later, he was running. Arms pumped, calves flexed and extended. Feet pounded, pounded, pounded, and legs drove him forward, down the unlit park path, past shadowed trees and fencing and weed-ruled grass. Run. Fast. Hard. Miles, maybe four now, maybe five. Just run, make the lungs work harder. Make the muscles want to quit and then don't let them.

He didn't stop until his body forced him to.

Then he bent double on the path, hands gripping knees, the wind in his ears replaced by long, controlled gasps. The sweat coursed down his back between his shoulder blades, soaked his shirt at the chest.

God.

God was here with him, while he grappled for air and answers.

"What could I have done?"

He'd done nothing for Frank. Nothing at all. He'd known the man burned for the truth of the Bible, for other people's need to know the truth. He'd known that one day someone would report Frank when he tried to convince them of that truth. He hadn't known it would happen so soon, a few months after Frank presented the truth to him. And he hadn't known a single thing he could do to stop it.

For Jim and Karlyn, it was supposed to be different.

What was being done to them now? How was the Constabulary trying to "crack" them? Was Jason in charge of the process? Marcus cradled his head as anger escalated the throbbing even more than the run had. *Don't feel it, fix it.* But he wasn't any less helpless today against the Constabulary than he'd been yesterday, the week before, six years ago when the Supreme Court had established a state-by-state agency to deal with "philosophical crime," or almost three years ago when he'd committed his head and his heart to the truth Frank showed him from the pages of an illegal Bible.

Reality battered like an unstoppable flood. Marcus was one man. They were many, and they were armed in every way.

"God," he said. "I won't let them do this. Not anymore. Help me stop them."

He hadn't found the way yet, but there had to be one.

5

Surely Elliott was awake by now. Aubrey headed toward her bedroom and tried to imagine the silence that immersed him. But how could she when she'd never experienced it herself, and when he was so … normal? His smile caused laughter from the elderly ladies who wandered stores without ever adding an item to their shopping carts. Before she'd had Elliott, Aubrey never knew how many of these ladies existed. Sometimes they seemed to trundle from every direction to greet him. Aubrey didn't bother to tell them that their *goo-goo*'s and *gah-gah*'s hit his auditory nerve and died there.

She leaned over the crib prepared for his shiny gaze. Instead, she stared down at his back.

"Elliott, you did it. You rolled over."

He wriggled and rocked. Aubrey raced to the kitchen, unplugged her cell phone from the wall charger, and dashed back to her room.

"Say cheese, baby boy." The phone clicked and captured. "Hey, it only *looks* like another picture of you lying on your tummy. It's really the aftermath of a stupendous feat."

She saved the picture, opened her contacts list, and skipped to K. Karlyn must know about this. Immediately.

Aubrey's thumb froze on the call button. The phone slid from her hand and glanced off the edge of the night stand. A new nick appeared in the walnut veneer, so she could walk past it every day and remember forgetting the loss of Karlyn. *God, what's happening to her, to Jim?* They were hungry by now. Exhausted. Scared. Wondering if they'd ever see each other again, if the person they loved most was being mistreated.

Aubrey reached for the fallen phone with a trembling hand. When the con-cops stole a person, she ceased to be a person. She became a flower in a windstorm. She could bow herself to the grass until the wind believed it had won, and then spring back up, stripped of petals but alive to grow again. Or she could stiffen against the storm until it snapped off her head.

Bzzzz.

Her apartment's obnoxious version of a doorbell. Mom? She usually called ahead, but who else would be stopping by right now?

Elliott was safe in his crib, so she snatched her keys from the kitchen rack—no, the door couldn't swing shut on its own, but just in case. She headed for the foyer. She never let someone into her building without knowing who it was, and the speaker system hadn't worked since she'd lived here. The main door was only feet from her own, but by the time she'd stepped out of her apartment, the buzzer droned again. Aubrey faced the foyer's tall glass doors ... and froze.

Two men, pinstriped suits, close-cropped hair. Two sets of eyes noting that she'd turned to porcelain.

Constabulary agents. They'd waited a whole day to pounce. How was she supposed to get through this—

This interview. That's all it was. An interview about Jim and Karlyn, not about her, not about old crimes.

Was she trying to comfort herself with that fact?

Aubrey crossed the foyer to the door, opened it for them, returned their smiles. At least, one of them smiled. The other seemed to try, but the result was more a sneer, a potential snarl though his eyes weren't unkind. Maybe his teeth and lips simply didn't match well.

Maybe she should try to curb the terror that made her analyze trivia.

"Aubrey Weston." Not a question, of course.

She cleared her throat of any residual sand particles. "How can I help you?"

"Agents Young and Partyka, MPC." Badges hung suspended from their hands, then disappeared with polish inside their jackets. "We won't take up too much of your time, ma'am. Just have to ask you a few questions."

"Go ahead."

"May we come in?"

No! "I guess that's fine."

Stilted seconds later, Aubrey had walked them through the foyer into her house. Her. House. She squared her shoulders and motioned them to sit on her sofa. The tweed cushions collided with their somber suits, either of which probably cost more than this couch brand new.

"We'll get right to the point, Miss Weston ..." Partyka said, sneering. Maybe it was an intimidation tactic, as if he needed one. Surely he'd read her file.

"Please," she said when he failed to follow through with his statement.

"You're acquainted with James and Karlyn Cole?" Agent Young spread long hands like doilies over his knees.

"I am, yes."

"You know they were apprehended earlier this week?"

"It was on the news."

"How long have you known Mr. and Mrs. Cole?"

A control question. They would already know the answer. A test, to see if she dared lie to them about something they could verify. An icebreaker, to lull her into believing all the questions would be this simple, this safe.

"Karlyn, about seven years," she said. "Jim, only a couple."

"And would you characterize your relationship as a close one?"

"I talk to Karlyn a lot."

Young's hands folded together in front of him while his eyes remained on her. "When was the last time you spoke to Mrs. Cole?"

"I don't remember the time exactly."

Partyka's lips pulled back further, exposing his teeth like a dominant wolf. He had to know he was doing that. "Miss Weston, I'm going to give you one warning, because you're not an uncooperative person, not anymore. But *if* you're thinking right now about getting out of these questions, or fudging the answers to them, that would be a very serious crime."

They wouldn't ask her if she'd relapsed into her original philosophy, not randomly during an interview about two other subjects. They wouldn't arrest her. They wouldn't steal her baby or hurt him. Logic told her all these things. But memory argued they could do whatever they wanted.

She should stand up and tell them that she was a Christian, that she'd never stopped being one.

"I talked to Karlyn the day she and Jim were arrested," she said.

Their faces were two masks of professionalism. Young nodded. "What did you talk about?"

"We were going to a baby shower. She invited me, I agreed to go."

Another nod. "And?"

"She mentioned there would be cheesecake."

"That's all you talked about?"

"We weren't on the phone very long."

Revelation sprang over Agent Young's face, patronizing, unreal. "What interrupted you?"

Aubrey's mouth turned to bedrock, and her pulse thumped a warning. How close were they to the question they couldn't answer? How close was she to betraying her friend?

"She said someone was at the door, and she had to let them in."

"Did she mention who it was?"

Aubrey nodded. This question was harmless. "Con-cops."

Partyka smirked at the colloquialism. "Did she say anything else?"

"She hung up before I could say good-bye."

"Miss Weston—"

A mewling sound, kittenlike from a room away, raised both agents' eyebrows. Aubrey's arms prickled as their focus shifted from her friends to her child.

"Meal time?" Young said.

She had to satisfy them somehow, right now, convince them to leave, but before she could open her mouth, an indignant wail burst from the bedroom.

"Hey, by all means, see to the kid," Young said. "We're in no hurry here."

"He's not hungry," Aubrey said.

Partyka crossed his arms and tipped his head back to look down at her. "Whatever he is, get him quiet, and then we'll continue."

Aubrey tried to rise on solid legs, like a mother lion, confident of her strength to protect her offspring. But she headed down the hallway toward Elliott with knees of mush. Why was she going to him at all? Complaining alone for a little while wouldn't hurt him.

She picked Elliott up under his arms. The soft bundle of him dangled contentedly before her, kicked out a random foot. Had she come to quiet him, to shift the con-cops' focus elsewhere? Or had she come because a con-cop had told her to? Maybe a person never escaped brainwashing, even nine months later.

"Hello, baby boy." Elliott's diaper was still clean, and he didn't need to be fed. She could take him into the living room with her, subject him to the eyes of the agents. Or she could set him back into the crib and hope he didn't howl anew at her departure.

"How old is he again?"

Aubrey spun toward the door. Her arms clasped Elliott closer.

"Sorry, I didn't mean to startle you." Agent Young leaned against the door frame as if he'd stood there a hundred times.

"Karlyn didn't say anything important on the phone."

"Then why don't you tell me what she did say, so we can head on out of here and check you off our list."

Yes. Tell them. Get them away from Elliott. But when Aubrey's mouth opened, a mutiny spewed out. "Jim didn't attack those agents."

Young's amiability cooled by several degrees. "That's not what I asked you."

"He couldn't have, and you know it. And if you had to make that up, then it means you didn't have any reason to arrest them but you arrested them anyway."

"If you don't answer the original question, I can detain you. Right now."

They shouldn't detain her. They should arrest her. *I'm a Christian, and I'll never deny my Jesus again.*

Elliott. She couldn't lose him. They must not be allowed to own him, to raise him, to scare him or hurt him. Or kill him.

"She said everything would be okay," Aubrey said. "That was all."

"And what did she mean by that?"

Understanding tunneled inside her. Karlyn's groundless reassurance was as cryptic to them as it was to Aubrey. Here, they wanted information. And here, Aubrey had none to give. She didn't have to betray her friends to save her baby. She could breathe again.

"I have no idea," she said.

"You can't explain to me how a person guilty of multiple misdemeanors would find Constabulary agents at her door with a search warrant, and not react in fear at all?"

"I'm—sure she was. Scared."

"You know, and I know, that she wasn't. She didn't believe we would find any reasons to apprehend her, or her husband."

"Maybe there weren't any reasons."

Agent Young narrowed his eyes. Elliott squirmed against her chest, and she relaxed her stifling hold.

"We have another theory," Young said. "She and her husband knew about the search beforehand. And once the evidence they removed is discovered and linked to them, they'll be guilty of a felony."

"How would they know about the search?"

"That's the question of the hour."

"Well, I don't know the answer."

Agent Young knew that she knew that he knew. She was telling the truth, and no further information could be maneuvered from her. The pause between them was an open one, because in this matter, Aubrey had nothing to hide.

He stood to his full height, apart from the doorway, and nodded and walked back to the living room. Aubrey followed him with

Elliott tucked in one arm. The baby cackled and waved from the shoulders, as if his elbow joints were still undiscovered country.

Both agents had risen and were heading for the door.

"Thanks for your time, Miss Weston." Agent Partyka backed the words with a sincere snarl.

Aubrey opened the door for them and tried not to lean against it.

"One thing to keep in mind," Young said, one foot in the foyer and one still planted in her house like a weed. "If you happen to hear anything useful, we'll expect you to notify us."

She nodded. Of course, they expected it.

"Failing to do so would be obstruction, which is a felony."

She nodded again.

"Have a nice day, Miss Weston," Partyka said.

The two agents crossed the foyer, let themselves out the main doors, and disappeared across the parking lot. Aubrey closed and bolted the door as if a lock could keep the Constabulary out. She wobbled to the couch and sank down on a cushion. Her body rocked back and forth. This rhythm calmed Elliott on colicky nights but couldn't calm Aubrey now. She held him to her chest and imagined Karlyn, an unsheltered flower, broken when she refused to bend.

"You're going to make it, Salmon."

"I'm not," Aubrey whispered. "And neither are you."

6

Pointless, that's what this was. Marcus should've stuck to his first answer when Keith called with that wheedling whine. Wouldn't be the first time he'd hung up on the guy in the last fifteen years. Then Jason's voice yelled in the background, "Nobody's driving me, I know my way home," and Marcus imagined other words tumbling out of the same drunk mouth that had warned him about Jim and Karlyn. God could be offering another chance to protect the family.

But after Marcus dropped Keith off, Jason's words had dried up. He slouched against the truck window and stared forward and didn't say anything. Marcus's playing taxi wouldn't rescue anybody tonight. He'd only bailed out two drunken idiots.

"Had this thing with names when I was a kid," Jason said to the windshield.

Then again.

"Probably 'cause of mine. I looked them up on the Internet, where they came from and everything, you know? Learned some weird crap."

No, this wasn't helpful information, but at least he was talking. "You've got a weird name?"

"Not really. Mayweather. Of course, kids can tweak that in a lot of stupid ways. I hated it, so I ran an Internet search on my name." The hyena's laugh was more subdued now. "Then I looked up all their names and lectured them when they made fun of mine. Believe it or not, most of them got bored and walked away."

Please say something useful. But interrupting might shut him up.

"Lecturing doesn't work on everybody, though. Some bullies just wanna be bullies."

"Yeah," Marcus said.

"Bullies like the Christians still out there, you know?"

So he got into the Constabulary because kids at school made fun of his name.

"They hide their hate lit from us, but it doesn't hide what they do with it. And it doesn't hide them. Sooner or later, I find them out."

Jason's head turned, and his beer-flavored breath hit Marcus's face. His eyes fixed on Marcus as if … as if he knew.

Marcus's jaw turned to concrete. Jason knew about the Coles, that Marcus had tried to save them. Had he threatened the information from them? More than threatened?

Jason's chin tilted up. "You believe in God?"

Not the expected question, but this one was no less a razor wire. Marcus worked his mouth till he could swallow again. "Yeah."

Jason nodded and looked back out the window at the guardrail that skimmed past.

No more questions? Maybe that one was random, had no connection to the Coles. Maybe Jason was too drunk to probe into what Marcus believed *about* God.

"How's work, Jason?"

"Just two streets away this time."

What?

"Sometimes it's unnerving, you know? How close they can be hiding to your own house."

Icicles ran a relay up and down Marcus's spine. Another chance.

"I pass this house every day I go to work, and every day I come home. When we got the tip and I saw the street, I couldn't believe it. And tricky, too, making a parked surveillance car blend in when the house is hanging on the edge of this hill, sideways to face the whole intersection—I swear it looks like somebody dropped it right out of the sky and left it where it landed."

Adrenaline spurted through Marcus's body. He could find this house. "Must be frustrating."

"Got 'em good now, though. Weed them right out of there, out of my neighborhood, away from my kids, get them behind bars where they belong."

Strangers would have no reason to trust Marcus. Well, he'd have to make them. Part of the job.

"Hey, don't miss my street, man."

Marcus braked hard and made the turn.

"You ever heard of a blinker?"

Marcus shrugged. Jason didn't say another word till they stood side by side on his porch.

"Watch this." Jason drew back his fist to pound his own door.

It opened, and he nearly gave his wife a bloody nose.

"What're you standing there for? I was going to knock."

Pamela nodded. "That's why I'm standing here. The kids are asleep."

"Oh." He turned to Marcus. "Wanna meet them?"

"When they're awake," Marcus said.

"Go on into the house, Jase," Pamela said with a wave of her bejeweled fingers. "I'll be there in a minute."

"G'night," he tossed over his shoulder at Marcus. He shut the door with enough force to wake his neighbors, not to mention his kids.

"Well," Marcus said before any silence could build between him and Jason's wife. "Good night."

"This is the second time in a week you've brought my husband home."

"Yeah." Did she want an apology for not leaving him to sleep it off?

"I do appreciate it."

If he'd been doing this out of kindness, maybe the words wouldn't have jammed behind his teeth. He mustered a shrug.

"But I know what you think of Jason." Then her words fell like dominoes. "You think he's a party animal, a loudmouth, and a belligerent fool, and when he's drinking, that's exactly what he is. But you think that's all he is, and you're wrong."

By the time she paused, Marcus's breathing had stalled. *"When you're drinking, you're no good to anybody. And you're always drinking."* Mom couldn't have known he'd prove her right so fast.

Pamela's gaze dropped to her stockinged feet, then rose again. "You have no right to judge him."

"I know."

"You do?"

Marcus nodded. Some men drank at parties and wrecked their cars. And some men drank every day and killed their mothers.

"Then thank you."

Another nod was all he managed.

"Good night, I guess," she said.

Yeah. Get out of here. "Good night."

⋄⋄⋄ ⋄⋄⋄ ⋄⋄⋄

"Two streets over" was surprisingly unhelpful in a maze of a subdivision like this one. The surveillance car probably still kept watch over this house, wherever it was. Driving under the speed limit to peer at both sides of the street would look suspicious. Given the time, so would parking the car and searching on foot. Maybe he'd missed the house. Maybe Jason's description was exaggerated by alcohol.

There it was.

He didn't brake as he passed the one-level piece of awkward architecture that looked down on the rest of the neighborhood from a sudden hill. *Left where it landed*—not a bad description. The porch looked ready to slide down into the street. Marcus made a right and parked between two houses.

Removing the material evidence against them wouldn't be enough. He had to get them to leave. Now. Well, first he had to get them to open the door. He stepped down from his truck and into the damp autumn night.

His body itched to leave the sidewalk. A passing car could easily spear him in its headlights. Decaying leaves crunched, dried and brittle, under his feet. He crossed the street and approached the house on the hill from an angle. Its back porch light beckoned, orange through the tinted fixture.

The brisk wind tried to make his eyes water. He swiped a hand under them. Not now, he had to see. No cars were parked on the street within three houses of this one. If agents watched, they'd holed up in somebody's driveway.

Marcus abandoned the sidewalk, slipped alongside the hill, and scurried up the incline into the backyard. A tire swing rocked in the wind, roped to an apple tree. He nearly slipped on a rotting apple, still round enough to roll under his shoe. Beside the porch sprawled a covered sandbox. Its plastic turtle head stared Marcus down with bulging eyes.

He reached the porch light as a brown moth fluttered into it and clung to the glass. Marcus lifted the brass door knocker…

If they didn't believe him, they might call the police.

Marcus would die in a cage, just like Frank. It was inevitable, though he didn't know how he knew that. Any day could be his last outside. Today could be.

He could walk away now, but of course he wouldn't. These strangers were his family as much as Jim and Karlyn were.

His hand shook as he lowered the door knocker firmly. Once, twice, three times.

Had he known this morning what he'd be doing now, he'd have driven west for hours, until he hit Lake Michigan. Wide open, endless water. Gritty sand under bare feet. And Lee. A picnic with Lee on the beach. She'd hunch into a roomy sweatshirt, and the breeze would toss her hair into her eyes. She'd glare at the autumn clouds over the water and point out the "absurdity" of spending a day at a Michigan beach in the last week of November. Maybe he'd have told her. *Last day, Lee. I wanted big space.* In fact, maybe he'd have told her everything and lost himself in selfishness. *And I wanted to see you one more time, and let's watch the sun set on the beach, and could I hold you?*

What would she say? If they'd never see each other again, if it didn't have to mean anything to her, would it be okay for his arms to feel her for just one day?

Nobody answered the door. Marcus knocked again. In a minute, it swung open, and light flowed from inside to make him squint.

The bearded man on the doorstep eyed him and frowned. "I don't know you."

"No," Marcus said. "But I've got to talk to you."

"Good night." He disappeared behind the door, and it swung forward, about to turn to smoke Marcus's only chance.

Marcus blocked the door with one leg and one arm. "They've got a warrant."

The man's face reappeared. The pressure on the door vanished. His dark eyes seemed to absorb Marcus, the way tar absorbed heat.

"Who?" the man finally said, as if he didn't know.

Marcus's whisper seemed to travel too far. "Constabulary. You have to leave. Now."

"You're insane."

"I'm not one of them. This isn't a trap. And even if you destroy the evidence, they can take you in anyway."

The man rubbed his nose, glanced toward the sandbox. "Where'd you get this stuff? Somebody's been yanking your chain. There's no reason they would come here."

The guy might as well be clutching a well-fingered script. *What To Say When Somebody "Warns" You About the Constabulary.* Marcus's feet grew roots that took hold within the porch concrete. This family wouldn't be safe till the man believed him.

"Time to move on, buddy," the man said.

"They'll take your children."

A storm cloud gathered over his face. "Game over. Get off my porch."

"I'm not Constabulary," Marcus said. "I'm a Christian."

The man's eyes narrowed in a moment of consideration, then—

Knuckles drove into Marcus's nose. He staggered back, wet warmth oozing from one nostril. Blunt throbbing radiated through his face from the center outward. The man dragged him from the edge of the porch before he could pitch backward into the sandbox. Adrenaline recaptured Marcus's tattered senses. His arm broke the man's hold from underneath, and he stepped back.

The man didn't attack again. "Won't work here, dirtbag."

"They don't know I'm here."

"Better get your Christian butt off my property then, before *I* call them on *you*."

Marcus pressed the back of his hand to his nose to catch the salty trickle. "Hide your family."

"You harass me again, I call them."

"Hide your—!"

The door shut quietly.

Marcus's head sagged forward, but he forced it back up. The guy could be calling the police, reporting a trespasser. *Go. Now.* He forced his feet back toward his truck.

He should have … Well, what?

He started to drive. Almost one o'clock now. He'd missed church. Tonight, his family had met in Janelle's basement storeroom. Chatted and prayed and studied Bible verses, written out on notebook paper in Abe's arthritic handwriting. No one risked bringing an actual Bible. They especially must have prayed for Jim and Karlyn.

The silence in the truck cab pushed an ache into Marcus's chest. His family's voices always filled him up inside, readied him for another week. Were they okay? Had the Constabulary identified anybody else? He turned the truck toward Janelle's store. Only a few miles from here. He'd drive past. Check for yellow crime tape. Just to be sure.

Ten minutes later, he coasted down a neighboring residential street. Almost there—wait a minute. A yellow street bike was parked up ahead at the curb. Clay's bike, which he rode without a helmet half the time and had been known to floor down the street after their meetings. Caution and Clay had never met. Farther down, on the other side, a red foreign car and a gray sedan. Phil and Abe's cars.

Church should have ended half an hour ago. Why would their vehicles still be …?

His heart seized. He parked half a block over and started to run. *God, my family, please, my family.*

7

No yellow tape. No circling green lights. No activity in front of the store, or in back. Marcus's head drummed in time with his heart. He forced himself to use the cover of the row of trees alongside Janelle's store. *God, please. God, please.* The words had pounded from his feet the whole way here. He should wait a minute, observe, be careful. But the strain of standing here, doing nothing, was going to wreck his head. He stepped out from the trees and dashed to the shadows alongside the building. He crept around the corner and faced the door. Were they still here? Why?

He knocked. Caught his breath for a minute. Knocked again. A sudden gust of wind pierced his jacket.

A whisper came through the crack in the wood of the door. "He prepares a table."

Marcus shut his eyes and swallowed the burning in his throat. *God, thank You.* "Before us."

"In the presence of."

"Our enemies."

The door opened halfway, and he slipped inside. Warmth and darkness and scent embraced him, that vaguely delicious mingling of every conceivable candle flavor. He breathed in. Home.

"You?" Janelle's voice sounded stuffy, as if she had a cold.

"Um, yeah, me. I mean, Marcus."

Five-foot-nothing, she all but bowled him over with her hug. "Oh, thank God. Thank God."

"What?"

"You're not in jail. Thank You, Jesus, that he's not in jail."

Oh.

"Come on, the others need to see you."

Marcus followed Janelle to the storage room, though by now he could find his way easily without the light. Her store was small, its layout simple, shelves of candles and figurines and random country knickknacks placed to allow a clear path from the front door to the back room. Janelle tapped on the storeroom door, and the light seeping under it disappeared. She let Marcus and herself into the room and shut the door, and the light sprang back on. Weathered, cautious routine. They hurried down the half staircase.

At the bottom, Marcus glanced toward Janelle, and every muscle in his body turned to stone. Tears stained her cheeks, reddened her eyes, left damp marks on her light blue shirt. Her cropped salt-and-pepper curls stood up as if she'd been pawing through them for hours.

"Janelle, what—?"

The rest of them sat in a circle on the cold white tile, or at least they had been sitting. Almost as one, Phil and Felice, Clay and then more slowly Abe stood and crowded around Marcus.

"What happened to you?" Felice's voice wobbled worse than Janelle's.

Phil fiddled with his eyebrow ring. "Seriously, bro, we thought you were—"

"We've been praying," Abe said quietly. "For you."

Marcus trembled from the inside out. "I'm okay, I—I couldn't come, but I had to—I had to check the store, to make sure—and then I saw the cars, and—"

Janelle swiped at her cheeks. "You've never missed church. Never. Everyone misses sometimes, but not you."

"I ... I."

Felice pushed past her fiancé and didn't pause when Phil patted her shoulder. She marched straight up to Marcus and hugged him. Something eased around them, a breaking of tension, a snapping of restraint. Phil grabbed Marcus's hand and shook it while Felice still hugged him. Abe shuffled forward and rested a hand on Marcus's shoulder.

He was hemmed in. Surrounded. He wrestled the ache before, oh heck, before his eyes could start to burn. No. He bowed his head, but they didn't step back. He pushed the ache down deeper in his chest, but the way they wrapped him up, the way they cared. He would protect them, all of them, whatever he had to do. It was what he had to offer.

Abe's hand tightened on his shoulder. "Dear Father, thank You for Your protection over Marcus. We're out of words tonight, Father, but we want to thank You for answering the prayers for our dear brother. You heard us and You shielded Marcus and You brought him here to us tonight. We love You, we trust You, and we thank You. Amen."

"Amen," everyone whispered.

The huddle loosened and backed away. Felice raised her hands to her cheeks, hiding tears. Her nails were electric blue tonight. Phil circled his arms around her. Abe's hand stayed on Marcus's shoulder.

Clay stood to one side and grinned. "Let's just say we're glad to see you."

"Don't ever do that again," Janelle said.

Marcus nodded, swallowed the leftover soreness inside, and offered a prayer to accompany Abe's. *God, for my family. That they're safe. And here. And that I have them. Thank You.*

They must be ready to leave. He should let them. Look at the time. "What'd I miss?"

Felice giggled. "Don't tell him. He'll flip out."

"What?"

"Oh, for Pete's sake, Felice." Janelle hustled around the room straightening boxes of inventory that were already straight. "It was nothing."

Felice smirked at Janelle's back. "So, Marcus, you know the crack in the front door …"

"I told Janelle I'll replace the door."

"It has character," Janelle said over her shoulder without a pause in her straightening. "It's the original door."

"Anyway." Felice huffed. "Like I was saying. You know the crack in the door …"

"We want to go home before tomorrow, babe," Phil said.

Clay propped himself against a man-sized box—what was in there?—and crossed his ankles in front of him. "Summary. Janelle thought she saw a light through the door, before anybody got here, and convinced herself it was a Constabulary raid and intercepted all of us as we were arriving and told us to run for our lives."

How could any of them be amused by that? But only Abe wasn't wearing a small, tolerant smile. Well, Abe and Janelle, who hid her blush by walking down an aisle of shelves to sort already sorted candles.

"What was it?" Marcus asked.

Janelle raised her voice from the other end of the aisle. "The night light I leave on when the store's closed. I guess the crack in the door got wider over time and made it look brighter."

"Janelle, let me replace the door. I'll do it for cost."

"Not a chance," she called.

"Family discount."

"Ha-ha."

He'd convince her later. "Prayer requests or anything?"

"Mostly for Clay's family," Phil said.

Clay nodded. He pushed a fist against his palm, cracking the knuckles. "Obviously, they're still not here. And they're still going to Elysium on Sundays."

"Con-cop hole." Janelle emerged from between the candle shelves smelling like them. "And get this, Marcus, Elysium used the s-word the other day. Clay's daughter learned all about it."

What ...?

"Sin," Clay said. "Self-Imposed Negation. We're all too hard on ourselves, and we need to quit it and get with God's program of a rewarding lifestyle."

Not surprising, really. Elysium Fellowship of Believers was all about government-sanctioned spirituality. Still, Clay had to feel helpless. He couldn't force his family to come here, though Marcus sometimes wondered why not. But Clay's wife was so afraid of the Table meetings, she'd begged Clay not to reveal her name or their daughter's.

"I'll keep praying," Marcus said.

"Thanks, man." Clay lounged against the box.

The conversation drifted. Maybe everybody else was more affected by Janelle's night-light scare than they wanted to admit, or by thinking Marcus had been arrested. Whatever it was, nobody hurried to leave. Marcus breathed in the scent of candles, and his family's voices trickled around him. He thought of the rest of the psalm, the one they used for their passcode. *My cup overflows.*

8

By the time she reached her mother's house, Aubrey would have all the details of the morning's top local news story, interspersed with infant wailing from the car seat behind her.

"... recovered eleven copies of various banned Bible translations from—"

The howl neared a scream. Elliott's face was as red as the fuzzy blanket waiting for him at Grandma's house. Aubrey didn't have to see him to know.

"... charged with multiple—"

"Take a breath, baby boy," Aubrey said, as if the content of this story didn't threaten to shut down her own lungs. She didn't know these people, but she didn't have to.

"... including possession with intent to distribute—"

Yeah, eleven Bibles signified that. She pulled up the incline to park in the driveway that circled a Japanese maple. She killed the radio. Deep breath. Had to calm down before she faced Mom.

She wasn't sure if Jim had a Bible of his own or if Karlyn's served for both of them. Two Bibles between two people would be unusual, excessive. Either way, though, the reports of their arrest hadn't mentioned any illegal materials found. Where had Karlyn managed to hide even one Bible from the comprehensive search?

Aubrey rounded the car and opened the door. Elliott's flushed face went still when she unbuckled the car seat and turned it toward her.

"I haven't been ignoring you, baby. I talked to you all the way here."

She carried the car seat up the steps to her mother's front door. A wooden snowman grinned from one corner of the porch, half his face obscured by a straw hat. A sign between his cotton-puff hands bore painted red letters: "Deck the halls, y'all!" For a woman most proud of her doctorate degree, Mom had interesting decorative taste.

The doorbell echoed throughout the house just as Elliott's hiccups began. Aubrey swung the car seat to her other hand, and seconds later the door opened.

"Hi, honey." Her mother stepped aside for her to enter, her black cat called Hareton under one arm. According to Mom, that Brontë character warranted a feline namesake more than Heathcliff did.

"Hi, Mom."

"I heard about Karlyn on the news. I'm so sorry, honey. Hopefully she'll be out soon."

"You mean hopefully she'll deny everything she believes in? Do you want me to hope that along with you?"

Mom shut the door and set Hareton on his six-toed white feet. "Considering the alternative is prison ..."

The time for their courteous war wasn't now. "I haven't heard back from the doctor yet. About the implant for Elliott. By the end of the week, I should know if he qualifies."

"Tell me if I'm wrong here, but it seems like Karlyn's arrest could renew their interest in you."

"Mom, I'm late for work."

Her mother blinked at her. Aubrey blinked back. Calm. Stay calm. Distress fueled the blaze of Mom's agenda.

Her mother sighed, not a retreat but a redeployment. "I'm making your father some beef and barley soup tonight, if you'd like to join us for dinner."

By "making," she meant adding water to a packaged mix. Aubrey hadn't inherited her mother's enjoyment of the kitchen, because none existed to inherit. She smiled away some of the tension between them. "I can do that."

She kissed her fingers and rested them a moment on the curve of Elliott's nose. Then she hugged her mom. "I'll see you tonight."

"Good."

Aubrey swallowed the tightness in her throat and hurried out to her car.

She'd been trying for the last month to prepare for confrontation. The notorious anniversary approached like a hurricane offshore, invisible from the beach but a mass of red and orange on the radar. Six months since her breakup with Brett. For six months, she'd dodged her parents' poorly veiled attempts at drawing her out.

But the discussion of Brett, of her decision to leave him, would be delayed for now. Instead, Dad and Mom would want to discuss Jim and Karlyn. The arrest was ammunition against Aubrey's "religious obstinacy." Really, what remained for them to oppose? She didn't own a Bible. She no longer attended her church. But they'd find some way in which Karlyn's arrest heightened the danger to Aubrey and more importantly, it sometimes seemed, to their grandson.

Aubrey drove toward work and tried to formulate a script in her mind for use at dinner tonight—a script that wouldn't hurt or marginalize anyone, including herself. She had to face her parents down, to "swim upstream," as Karlyn would say. But that waterfall-leaping woman had been someone else, someone who would never cower in an interrogation room.

9

Who would have thought a single punch could make you look this beat up? Marcus had slept most of the night with a cold gel pack over his face. The sealed plastic edge ended at exactly the right place to poke his eyelids, but it numbed the leftover throbbing. More important, maybe he'd wake up with less of a bruise.

Talk about wishful thinking.

The face in the mirror looked ridiculous. The blow had landed on the left side of his nose, possibly the only thing sparing him a break. Blue pooled from there into his cheek and the hollow beneath his eye. The eye wasn't swollen, but he had no way to conceal the aftermath. He looked … well, like he'd been punched.

Over the next several days, clients would ask, but he could lie to them. His plans *after* work today were the source of the dread that settled in his gut. Lee.

She would read him like one of her books. Whatever he told her, whatever his clients swallowed whole—she'd chew it into tiny, transparent bits and spit it back at him. And she'd want to know why he was lying.

Marcus showered and dressed in the time the coffee took to brew. He downed one cup while he fried his eggs and fed his dog, and he was working on another by the time he tied his steel-toed work shoes. He checked the mirror one last time before leaving, as if in the last half-hour, maybe God had decided to erase the evidence of last night's failure.

Nope.

He drove to Keith's great-aunt Penny's house. The woman's condominium had flooded due to an upstairs neighbor's toilet malfunction. The job wasn't his typical work. Her homeowner's insurance had already sent a restoration company to replace, mud, and sand the drywall. In the meantime, Keith had gotten his hands on the estimate and thrown a fit over what they were charging. He'd asked Marcus to do the priming and painting and ordered the insurance company to cash out the estimate's remainder. Marcus couldn't remember the last time he'd gotten paid to paint. Most people only paid him for jobs they couldn't do themselves.

The first step of this job, though, wasn't priming the ceilings and walls. It was deciding what to tell a brand-new client about the fiasco of his face. Maybe she'd have the tact not to ask. In case not, he invented an explanation while he parked his truck behind the rust-gnawed, maroon Corsica in the driveway.

The scrawny woman answered her door wearing a paisley blouse and white cotton pants.

"Hi. I'm Marcus, Keith's—"

Her veined hand reached toward Marcus's cheek. "You do that on the job?"

He stepped back in time to avoid the stiff claws of her fingers. "It won't keep me from working."

"Don't tell me—a big board came up and smacked you. And you can't even get worker's comp from yourself, can you?"

"Um, no, but it's not—"

"Oopsy-daisy, I've forgotten my manners. Come in, young man. I'm Penny Lewalski. And you're here to paint my house."

"Yeah." He followed her into the tiny kitchen.

A well-used foam roller tumbled from her white hair. Marcus scooped it up. Who had advised her to lay carpet in her kitchen? The stuff was the color of mud, at least twenty years old, and stained in various shapes and colors. Tearing it out should be his next project.

"Here's some of it, those gray spots on the ceiling. That's where the other young man fixed the holes they had to drill to let the water out."

She turned back to look up at him, and he handed her the roller. "Why, thank you. You're doggone courteous. Like I was saying—" She stopped to eye his face again. "You know, looks an awful lot like somebody popped you one. Weren't in a brawl or anything, were you?"

"Ladder fell and hit me in the face," he said.

"You must be one unlucky son of a gun."

He smiled. "I'll get to work."

"You do that. I'm ten years off a hundred, and I want a lot more days with this place looking good."

Penny gave him a tour of the other damaged rooms, a bathroom and a guestroom. Marcus stood under the patched spots in the guestroom ceiling and ran his fingers over rough ridges.

"He sanded this?" Marcus said.

"'Course he did."

Like heck.

"Ready to prime," she said, "that was how he was supposed to leave it. Is it not right or something?"

It was fine, if the guy wanted her ceiling to feel like tree bark. "I've got to sand this again."

"You go right ahead. You need anything? Tea, soda pop, coffee? Cookies? Spinach pie?"

"Spinach? Pie?"

Her parchment hands sprang to her hips. "Now what kind of a look is that? It happens to be tasty, and I happen to have some left over."

"No, thanks. But coffee would be good."

The crags of her face tugged at each other, and the smile lit her pale eyes. "You tell me how big a pot to make, and then you get to work. Keith said you do an excellent job."

Good to know. "Four cups." She'd save him a Starbucks run.

Hours later, he'd learned about Penny's forty years of work as a teacher and fifty-three years of marriage to her late husband, Roy. He'd also discovered patch screen under every bit of mudding in the house. A few swipes with the sander had revealed the lousy workmanship. He'd have to re-mud. Everything.

Penny questioned his every move. Maybe she saw him as one of the fourth graders she'd taught in decades past, though the top of her head barely hit his shoulder. The questions and sideways glances continued throughout the day as reliably as the supply of coffee. It was no match for Belinda's gourmet blend, but he'd tasted worse. Gulped worse, if he couldn't get hold of the good stuff. Addicts weren't choosy when a fix was at stake.

By midafternoon, he had finished re-covering the patch screens. He couldn't do anything else today. Mudding was one job that couldn't be rushed. Penny had disappeared in the last half hour, so he followed the blaring voice of the news anchor into her living room. Did one elderly woman really need three coffee tables, two overstuffed chairs, and an L-shaped sectional? He squeezed between a table and chair and waved an arm to get her attention.

"Leave the tarps down. I'll be back tomorrow," he said over the TV.

She looked up from her perch on the edge of the sectional. "If you stay longer, you could finish painting."

His mouth tugged upward. "Not today."

"Priming, at least."

"I've got to come back and sand everything."

"I told you, the other young man did that."

"He didn't do it right. I'll be back tomorrow to sand, and then probably patch some spots again. It's going to take a few days to—"

"What if I don't have a few days left? You never know, at my age."

"Penny," he said, but her attention had drifted back to the TV.

The house behind the anchorwoman, squared off in yellow tape, squatted on its hill. *"Left where it landed."* He'd heard about the arrests on the radio this morning, but the visual reminder clenched his gut.

"... recovered eleven copies of various banned Bible translations from the home, some behind a wall in the bedroom of eight-year-old Enrique ..."

Oh, that was brilliant, something to make the public really shudder—hate-filled books just inches from a helpless kid.

"How old are you, Marcus?"

He met a gaze that suddenly bored into his, that seemed to care about more than primer and paint.

"Thirty-two," he said.

She nodded. Her eyes left his for a quick moment of calculation. "When you were born, I was fif—when's your birthday?"

"June."

"I was fifty-eight. How about that?" Her fingers encircled the TV remote, and her rigid thumb pressed the mute button. A quiet, rhythmic *swish*, unnoticeable before, reigned over the sudden quiet. It came from the pendulum tail of a bulbous-eyed cat clock that hung over her front door.

"Well," Marcus said. "I'll get the house fixed as soon as—"

"Do you know how all this got started?" She waved her hand at the TV.

"The Constabulary?"

She didn't nod, just raised her chin, as though trying to look up at him and down at him at the same time.

Marcus forced a shrug. "Officially? Springfield."

"Oh, sure, officially, after the Springfield tragedy. Six years ago now, wasn't it?"

She waited for him to nod. Was she just making conversation? Or was she trying to figure out something about him?

"But that's obviously not when everything started," Penny said. "It was a couple years before, when they found Bibles after those crazy cultists opened fire on those government guys—liquor, tobacco, and whatever else they regulate."

"ATF. And the cult was in Bozeman. Montana."

"Right. Got the whole country scared of freedom. But that's not when everything started. It was ..." Penny shifted, then pulled herself up on the arm of the couch. "It was the schools, and the courts, and the media, and things."

"I know. I'm not that young."

"Oh, you're definitely young. Maybe we'll talk more tomorrow."

"Okay," he said.

He walked the few steps to her front door with curiosity nibbling at his brain. Her words stopped him with his hand on the cold doorknob.

"Remember, young man, if a ladder starts falling, make sure you duck. Avoid a lot of scrapes that way, and if there is bad luck, you'll avoid that, too."

"Right."

In his truck, he turned the ignition as his phone vibrated in his pocket. He shifted his weight to pull it out. An unfamiliar number.

"Hello," Marcus said.

"Hey, is this Marcus Brenner?"

"Yeah."

"Jason Mayweather. Don't think you know me, but I got your number from Keith. I was wondering if you've got time for another client."

Didn't know him? The guy really didn't remember anything when he was boozed up.

"Well." One hand on the phone, one hand on the wheel. He couldn't knead the tension from his neck.

"If you're booked, that's cool too. It's mostly handyman kind of stuff, but I don't have the time to deal with it, and my wife's been putting up with it long enough, you know?"

"Sure."

"I'd rather hire you than a complete stranger. Think you could swing it?"

Why couldn't he get away from this guy? Was God giving him a third chance? Certainty landed on his shoulders. "I've got some open time this week."

1 0

Aubrey's fingers danced over the keys, seventy-five words per minute, as she navigated the billing software. Enter patient's account number, click on Post Charges, enter procedure codes. As she set the final patient's chart on the finished stack, Mary-Beth's face sprang into the doorway like a stressed jack-in-the-box.

"Hey, I've got two insurance companies to call and three patients on hold. Could you take the next patient back?"

Aubrey nodded and hurried to the front. They ought to stop hiring part-time high school girls who called in sick more often than they worked. She snatched up a patient's chart from the ordered stack, opened the door, and stepped into the waiting room with a practiced smile.

"Gina?"

She had hoped Gina would be looking up as the waiting room door opened, but her head was turned toward the magazine rack. Aubrey stepped forward. Would she have to tap the woman on the shoulder? Did deaf people consider that rude? As she reached the center of the room, Gina looked up with eyes that seemed too wide.

"Hi," Aubrey said. She was pretty sure Gina could read lips but motioned to her anyway. "You can come with me."

Gina smiled and stood to follow. Aubrey led her down the hall to an adjustment room and motioned to a chair in the corner.

"You can have a seat. The doctor will be with you in a minute."

"Thank you," Gina said. The expression was missing its *k* and proper inflection but was unmistakable.

"You're welcome."

Aubrey filled the other rooms with patients, sorted charts to file while listening for Dr. O'Shaughnessy's cue, and finally heard, "Okay, Aubrey's coming back to give you a quick massage."

Gina's head was lifted to watch Aubrey enter the room, unlike other patients who lay facedown on the table to wait.

"You can lie back down," Aubrey said. "This will take about a minute."

She ran the massager up and down the woman's spine, into her shoulders, exactly enough pressure. When she turned it off and hooked it back onto the wall, Gina sat up.

"That thing vibrate your hands, bother you?" she said.

Aubrey's surprised blink was less at the clarity of the voice despite a few slurred letters, and more at the question itself. Countless other patients had asked it too. Well, of course. A lack of hearing didn't change how one saw things, or felt them, or tasted or smelled them.

"No," she said. "I don't even notice it, really."

"Oh." Gina turned to gather up her purse and a purple water bottle, then turned back to meet Aubrey's eyes.

"My son is deaf," Aubrey said.

A smile lit her round face. "You sign?" Her words were now accompanied by hand movement, first pointing at Aubrey, then moving her hands in rhythmic circles in front of her body.

She was smiling at the handicap of a baby. "No, I don't, no. I—I just found out. Two weeks ago. He's four months old."

Gina's brow drew down, and she nodded.

"He's seeing a specialist. There's been a lot of tests. They want to give him something called a cochlear implant."

Before the last word was out of Aubrey's mouth, Gina was shaking her head. "You don't do that to him."

"Do that *to* him?"

"Cochlear implant means they drill his skull. They put metal in his head."

"I know." An electrode array in his inner ear. A receiving unit under his scalp. Permanent damage to his cochlea. But in the confounding realm of technology, intentional damage to biology could restore its function. Sometimes.

"You can't do that to a child only four months old. It should be his choice, if he wants it."

"He's too young to choose," Aubrey said.

"Right. Too young."

"I'm his mother. I have to choose for him."

"No." Again the firm shake of the head. "It's not your choice. It's his. If he wants to have it, he decides when he's older."

Internet searches had sealed the grotesque images into her mind—incision diagrams, operation photos of exposed tissue, post-op photos of children with wires protruding like alien growths from a shaved section behind their ears. The specialist called it "minimally invasive," but he didn't deny that it was irreversible. He didn't deny that if it failed, no hearing aid would work for Elliott.

All those things, she understood. What she didn't understand was the woman in front of her. The specialist's voice crowded into her thoughts. *"This ought to be done as quickly as possible. He's already lost several key months of language development."*

"I can't wait," Aubrey said. "If the procedure's going to be done, it has to be done now, while he's learning how to communicate."

"You can communicate with him now. You don't have to wait for a surgery."

"You mean sign language?" That option had been laid out for her briefly but was hardly the doctor's first choice. Talking to her son with her hands. Admitting he wasn't normal, never could be. Learning how to squash the English language into gestures.

Gina was nodding with conviction. "Learn sign, talk to your son in his language."

"It isn't his language." Judging from the quick furrow of Gina's brow, the sharp points of the words must be visible on Aubrey's face. "He's just a baby with a ... a—"

"Handicap?" Gina said. "Impairment? Disability? You saying I'm disabled?"

Yes, of course she was. She couldn't hear.

"You see your son disabled, you *make* him disabled. You see him a smart, strong baby, then that's how he grows up."

If Aubrey continued this conversation, her words would cross the professional boundary. "I'm sorry, I should let you go. I'm sure you have places to be."

Gina's face was a wide window to feeling that most faces never unveiled. Right now, disappointment and frustration peeked from her eyes. "You talk to other Deaf, too. See what they say. Don't make this choice for your baby."

Well, maybe deaf people lived in mass denial. "Have a nice day, Gina."

Before Gina could answer, Aubrey fled down the hall to her workspace in the back and sank into the leather computer chair.

Mary-Beth's voice came through the door. "Okay, we will see you Monday at four. Bye, Gina."

The front door squeaked closed, and Aubrey stepped back into the waiting room with a plastic smile. She'd spent hours in the almost-ten months of waiting for her baby talking and humming and singing to nobody but herself. A womb must be lonely when swathed in silence as well as darkness.

Please, Father God. Don't punish Elliott for his mother's sins. Let him hear. She couldn't resist throwing pleas to heaven sometimes, though God couldn't possibly be listening anymore.

"Medicare's on line two for you," Mary-Beth said as Aubrey approached the front desk.

"Thanks." She ducked into her office, picked up the phone, and pressed the button. "Thank you for holding. This is Aubrey."

The explanation for rejection of the claims bounced around Aubrey's mind without processing. Only after she'd hung up with the representative did she notice the blank Post-it note stuck to the desk in front of her. What had she been told to do, again? Rebill the claims with ... what?

A knock sounded, too timid to be Mary-Beth, but her head was the one that poked around the door. "You okay?"

"My son's deaf. I'm perfectly fine."

The glossy pink bow of Mary-Beth's lips tugged downward. "Did Gina say something inappropriate?"

"It's nothing, Mary-Beth. I mean, it's not nothing, but it's not something to talk about in the middle of work."

"I'm taking you to lunch," Mary-Beth said. "Not today, I've got a hair appointment, but soon. My treat, and you can unload whatever you need to, okay?"

Mary-Beth wasn't even a mother. Her showers of sympathy, however well intentioned, would only scald. "Maybe. I've got … a lot of stuff going on right now, but I'll let you know when."

As if Aubrey had given a true yes, Mary-Beth smiled, then held out a driver's license and insurance card. "Great. Meanwhile, if you could scan these and return them to the new patient in room five, that would be great."

Aubrey accepted the cards and shoved them into the scanner's card slot without bothering to look at them, then clicked the Scan button on her screen.

The enlarged images coalesced moments later. An unmistakable face, up close and in color.

Oh. No.

His presence could be a coincidence, didn't necessarily mean he'd been assigned to shadow her. Mary-Beth had taken the call this morning and said he'd hurt his back in a tennis match, and—who played tennis in Michigan in November?

Her fingertips had gone cold along with the plastic cards they clutched. She'd seen his name on the appointment screen—Jeff Young. But he'd never mentioned his first name, and his last alone was too generic to resonate.

She had to face him at some point, and nothing about her job would concern the Constabulary. She was on their radar only as a re-education success story, and they'd already grilled her about Jim and Karlyn. She breathed in, out, in, out, then pocketed the man's cards and headed for room five.

"Here you go." Aubrey offered the cards back and forced herself to meet his startled eyes.

"Small world," Young said as he inserted the cards back into his wallet. "How's the kid?"

"The doctor will just be a minute." She turned to leave.

"Aubrey." When she turned back, his pale hands were settled on the arms of the chair.

"Did you need something?"

"I wanted to let you know that I leave my work at the office. I'm just another patient here, okay?"

"Of course."

"Good." The smile warmed his eyes.

She nodded and left the room, mind spinning. He was a very nice man, or he was pretending to be a very nice man. He had no intention of collecting information on her while he was here. Or he'd been sent here to do exactly that.

Her back office had become a haven. She was being irrational and childish.

"Aubrey?"

She fumbled with a random stack of papers as if she'd been sorting them all along. "Yeah, sorry, I got distracted. Be right out."

Mary-Beth's green eyes darted from the pile in Aubrey's hands to her averted face. Her foot nudged the worn doorstep under the door, to keep the waiting room in sight. Then she stepped into Aubrey's alcove. "Who're you hiding from?"

"Nothing, nobody, I said I'm on my way out."

"Look. Elliott's one thing, but you can't get all paranoid on me here. If anyone ought to be cool with the con-cops, it's you. You've already been through their stuff, so—"

"What?" The word jolted out of her.

"Worst case scenario, you go and tell them everything you told them last time, and they let you go again. Right?"

Aubrey's lips froze half open.

A blush seeped into Mary-Beth's cheeks. "I've actually known for a couple months, I overheard you talking on the phone … to your mom. When you first started. You thought I was out to lunch."

Talking to her mom? More like yelling. Aubrey couldn't recall the argument, verbatim, but it had involved her mother's judgment that she was "paranoid" and "self-absorbed," and her own (yes, paranoid) accusation that maybe Mom was working for the con-cops herself.

"Aubrey?" Mary-Beth said. "Wouldn't you do what you did last time?"

She shook her head, and Mary-Beth's gaze narrowed, more confused than condemning.

"Wait, are you saying … you're a … a …"

Her mouth snapped shut, and she turned toward the hallway. Before she could say a word, another voice drenched Aubrey like a plunge over a waterfall, over and down toward unforgiving rocks.

"Hi. Where's your restroom?"

"Um, down the hall, back the way you came, last door on the right," Mary-Beth said too quickly.

Young had heard her. He must have. No one had ever taught Mary-Beth how to lower her voice, much less whisper. No, she hadn't said *Christian*, but with the context he knew, Young would have no trouble interpreting her question.

She met Aubrey's eyes with humiliated apology. "I didn't mean … I thought you … I'd better go back up front."

Aubrey didn't answer or nod.

11

An hour after leaving his last client's house, Marcus had devoured a sandwich, showered away the workday, and put on black dress pants and a mustard-colored oxford shirt. For this occasion, he'd even added a tie. No suit coat, though. Suits were for funerals, and funerals were for mourning people who needed comfort from other mourning people. He'd gotten rid of his suit coat twelve years ago, after the last funeral he'd ever attend. His shoulders had never fit, anyway.

He stepped up onto Lee's porch and tugged at his black tie, though it was already straight. He could not turn Lee into a criminal. She had to stay out of his new work—all of it. He sighed and pressed the doorbell. The subsequent silence tugged his mouth down. She really should have a dog.

The door opened. Her gray eyes iced over at the sight of him.

"Happy birthday," Marcus said.

"What happened?"

"I'm okay."

"Marcus. What happened?"

Marcus took a silent breath and stepped out onto the tightrope of her questions. "I got hit."

"By whom?"

Not *by what*. Lee knew a sucker punch when she saw one.

"Some guy at the park," Marcus said. "He was trying to get into my car, and when I went to stop him ..." He shrugged.

"Did you call the police?"

"It was some drunk idiot, Lee. I startled him, he hit me, and then he ran off."

The wrinkle between her eyebrows might be suspicion. *God, she has to believe me.* She stepped forward and eyed the bruise, and Marcus breathed in the fresh scent of her hair.

"You're not easily outfought," she said.

"Took me off guard. Anyway, it wasn't a fight."

"You're fortunate he wasn't armed." She stepped outside and locked the door behind her, and her thin lips rose at one corner. "Shall we?"

Marcus nodded again and walked her to his truck. His hand lifted halfway before he forced it down to his side. A hand on her back, light and guiding—simple, but to Lee, it wouldn't be. She would flinch. He flexed his hand, then opened the truck door for her and offered a hand up, knowing she would ignore it. He closed the door and pushed down the rusty frustration.

Lee didn't mention his face again, and relaxation stole over him as he drove them to the concert. The venue was smaller than he'd expected, a steep-roofed building painted drab brown. Inside, the last beams of sun illumined stained-glass side windows to betray the auditorium's former life. Maybe a cross had hung on the wall behind the stage that now held a single piano and various sound equipment.

At least the building hadn't been torn down.

Marcus had purchased second-row seats. He followed to Lee's right as she found them, removed her leather jacket, and settled it over one chair.

"You look nice," he said.

Those three words never received acknowledgment, but he was still compelled to say them. The black sweater fit the lines of Lee's body with just enough emphasis, and the gray pants were cut to flatter her narrow hips. Of course, if he mentioned a detail like that, she'd never wear those pants again.

"The seats are perfect," Lee said.

He shrugged. "A little far to the right."

"Ideal, though, given the position of the piano."

Okay. "Have you seen her in concert before?"

"No." After a moment, her eyes left the stage to meet his. "Thank you."

"For what?"

Her mouth quirked upward on one side. "My birthday present."

"You're welcome." He squashed the desire to encircle her shoulders with his arm.

When the first song began, he leaned closer to whisper against her ear. She smelled light, fresh, a breeze of blossoms. "The songs have words."

"Of course," she whispered back, then understood. "You were expecting classical?"

"I thought that's all you listen to."

"With exceptions."

"Oh." He tried to refocus on the singer, but Lee turned to face him with a full smile, the curving lips unrestrained though they didn't show her teeth. They never did. Marcus turned to experience this phenomenon head-on, never mind the concert.

"You didn't research the artist before buying the tickets?" she whispered.

He shrugged. "I recognized her from the CDs in your car." And classical music was dull but not intolerable. Besides, she'd watched *Die Hard* with him. Once.

An hour later, Marcus had rediscovered three things. First, anyone who could pull those sounds out of something made of wood and plastic and strings was talented beyond his limited imagination. Second, he simply didn't connect with music—not the way the people around him did, eyes rapt on the slim Asian girl's hands as they strolled or scampered up and down the piano keys. Third, emerging from the short layers of her black hair, Lee's neck was a slender, graceful, ivory snare for his eyes.

Another song ended, and Marcus added to the applause around him. Behind him, a woman sniffled. The same woman who'd sniffled over the last song. What was he missing?

The pianist looked out over the seats, appearing to see each audience member, though with those lights on her, she probably couldn't see any of them. "This song came about because I was tired of playing the piano, but it's all I know how to play. So I thought maybe I could use it as a drum."

Laughter rippled over the audience, then melted to silence as she began to tap on the side of the piano. The rhythm continued throughout the song, woven around the piano notes.

The music fell away and didn't return for a long moment. When it did, the audience's mood switched. Again. Marcus never knew an instrument could create so many feelings in people: joy, excitement, peace, anger. This song, mostly pictures, seemed to build up their emotions with each verse: *"The fallen pedestal, the broken vase, the overturned glass, the down-turned face."*

It all meant something. Marcus stretched his mind for the answers to the songwriter's riddle.

"Tell me what's the worst in me, that keeps you from safeguarding me?"

Well, that was ridiculous. Nothing about a woman should keep a guy from protecting her. And if he failed to, she shouldn't blame herself. His foot scuffed the smooth wood floor. One hand drew into itself, a loose fist.

Lee turned her head to catch his eye, then raised her eyebrows in question.

"Nothing," Marcus whispered.

The self-directed anger that washed over him sometimes—no, it didn't make sense, not when you really thought it through. Lee was eighteen when it happened. He hadn't met her yet. What had he been doing while she screamed for help and nobody came? Twenty-one years old, a man, no excuses, probably not sober enough to protect anybody even if he'd known. He drew in a deep breath and opened his hands.

The music of the next hour blended into what he'd already heard, though Lee would probably say each song was unique. Maybe Marcus's ears didn't catch the nuances. Or maybe the soloist had no chance to keep his attention, not when Lee sat beside him, absorbed by the music, her eyes reflecting the subdued stage lights, her hands laced comfortably on her knee.

When the encore ended and the house lights came on, they collected their jackets and left only footsteps ahead of the little tide of people. Lee waited to break their silence till Marcus pulled onto a main road.

"What was your opinion?"

He glanced at her profile, refocused on the road, and shrugged. "She was good."

"You don't sound certain of that." Was that amusement?

"Well … just because I didn't completely get it, doesn't mean she wasn't good."

"What specifically did you not 'get'?"

"You know, the usual. Why people get so into it. Like that woman behind us. And the ... candles-underwater, fallen-pedestal-overturned-glass stuff. I know it all means something. I'm just never sure I've got it figured out."

She turned her head to smile at him. Again. Did she have any idea how easily he could drive them over the yellow line when she did that?

"What?" he said.

"For someone who doesn't 'get' music, you retain lyrics surprisingly well."

A gas station's green-and-yellow logo lit the north side of the upcoming intersection. Marcus could get her home without stopping, but this place was cheaper than most. His tank was down to an eighth. He made the turn and pulled up to the first pump.

The display told him to remove his card quickly and begin fueling. Maybe his card had actually scanned this time. The pump allowed him to fill up before changing its digital message. *Please see cashier inside.*

Hopefully, the new card he'd requested would come soon. He could barely see this one's swipe stripe, and only certain machines were able to read it. Still, it looked better than his health insurance card.

He opened the car door and leaned inside. "Be right back. This card's shot."

"Ah, fate." Lee got out of the car and followed him toward the tiny, brightly lit building. "There must be a freezer inside."

"That stuff'll kill you," he said, as if he'd never said it before. The grin that pulled at his mouth knew her response before she said it.

"When you give up your daily consumption of fast food, I'll consider renouncing cheap ice cream."

"What we need right now is a sundae bar," he said.

"So you can play with your food."

Marcus opened the door for her and followed her into the blast of heat. "So I can build a project and eat it while it melts."

"Construction, entropy, demolition."

"Rules of life."

"I'll settle for a meaningless Klondike bar." Lee moved away from him, toward the freezer.

Marcus stood in line behind the only other customer. Some metal band gagged and screamed from the overhead speaker. Probably not the station that played during busier hours, but would the guy behind the counter actually choose this stuff? In his midforties, he'd gelled his hair straight back to conceal a creeping central baldness, like stiff grass blades trying to camouflage a bird's egg. His musky cologne was no youthful scent, either. The woman in front of Marcus left the store, and he stepped up to the counter.

"Wow." The guy gaped at Marcus.

What—? Oh. Yeah.

"You get that in a bar fight?"

"No."

The man laughed. "Pump one? Want a receipt?"

"No, thanks."

"Excuse me," Lee said from halfway across the small snack store. "Your freezer is locked."

"Closing up the place soon." He snatched a pair of keys from under the counter and tossed them to her. "Had some kids come in here and swipe half the drumsticks the other day."

Lee unlocked the freezer, leaned inside to pluck out a silver-wrapped bar, then joined Marcus at the counter. She peeled away the foil and took a small bite. The guy leaned toward her, and a meaty hand reached to reclaim the keys.

Lee's gasp ripped the air. The man froze, keys jingling from his fingers.

Her face had blanched the color of new drywall. Her eyes had stopped seeing. The ice cream bar dripped a vanilla tear over her thumb. What was wrong with her? It wasn't dark. She only panicked in the dark.

"Hey, is she okay?" The man rounded the counter.

Oh. Him. It … was … him.

Something hot and red seized Marcus's brain. His body surged forward. Shoved between Lee and the attacker. Pushed Lee away from him, safely against the wall. She stumbled, and Marcus caught her. The Klondike bar splatted onto the floor and caved in beneath her heel.

Her breathing was too fast, too shallow. In a minute her legs would give out and she'd curl up in the corner, wrapping arms around herself. As if smallness was the only way to be safe. But she was safe now. This animal was going to die, now, finally. Marcus had found him, and he was going to break him into tiny, shredded, bloody pieces. Marcus was going to kill him, here and now, take out his eyes so they could never look at her again, make the monster beg for a chance to ask her forgiveness and then not give it to him. Marcus would break him, hands and nose, ribs and teeth—

"No." A voice he knew.

His hands were curled into the bright green polo that bore the gas station's logo, and the monster inside the shirt was cowering against the wall Marcus had shoved him into.

But somebody had said, "Marcus ... No ..."

Yes. Yes, yes, yes. Kill him. A growl slid between him and the monster. His own voice now.

Fingers on his arm, clawing, digging deep, straining the fabric of his jacket. Lee. *Oh, God, look at her, are You looking at her?* The eyes that pled with him were dilated almost black.

"Not," she whispered.

Not ... not him.

Marcus's hands unclenched. The blaze inside banked to that old, feeble flicker. No justice, no finish, not today. The monster still prowled somewhere, and Lee still ... Lee. His arm tried to take her weight. She stepped back. She could meet his eyes. She was still with him. But she didn't let him support her.

The man—not the monster, just a man—scrambled around the counter, stared at them both.

"You get out, now, right now. Get out before I call the cops."

Already the plan. Marcus walked beside her, out the door, to the truck. He opened the door. She stared at it.

"Lee." Her shoulder went rigid at his touch. "It's Marcus. We're getting in the truck, my truck. You're okay." Her legs shook too much to step up into the cab, so he lifted most of her weight and tucked her inside. He closed the door, hurried around to the driver's side, turned the key, pulled onto the road. He had to get her home.

"Lee?"

Nothing now. She couldn't hear him, couldn't see him. He turned on the dome light, but the weak glow might not be enough. Her breaths came nearly on top of each other.

"Lee, it's Marcus. I don't know what happened. But you're okay. I'm here. Nobody's hurting you. Can you hear me? Can you say something?"

Nothing.

"Listen. You have to slow down. Your breathing. Slow breaths. Lee."

He kept up her name as he drove, a one-syllable chant. He said other things he didn't fully hear. If only he could cradle her through this, absorb the shaking against his chest, give her his body heat. After a minute, his hand ventured across the little space. Of course, holding her was out of the question, but maybe a touch would help to bring her back. Maybe her convulsing fingers would be able to open. He wouldn't confine her, not even her hands. He brushed his fingers along the back of her cold satin hand.

Lee jerked backward, and her head knocked into the window. A whimper escaped through her teeth.

"No, Lee, it's Marcus. You're okay."

He kept on talking till he parked the car in her driveway. Safety within her own walls would help: familiarity, warmth, light. He rushed around the truck and opened her door.

"We're home, Lee." He took her shoulder again to ease her down. Her arms were frozen to her sides, her back was a wooden beam. She recoiled from his hand.

If he tried to remove her, he could make this worse. Going inside should be her choice. But the darkness and the cold out here weren't helping her. He'd try, once.

"It's Marcus. I need to get you into the house. It's light in there, Lee. This is my hand on your arm, okay? And this is, too—"

She cried out as if he'd hurt her. She hugged her body and curled tighter into herself, knees pulling up, heels of her shoes digging into the seat.

Marcus yanked his hands back. Right. No touch. He forced himself to shut the door, then ran back around the truck and got in. He turned on the individual bulbs to add to the automatic dome lights and pulled down the lit passenger mirror. He cranked the heat, and then he sat facing her. His own lungs constricted as she struggled for air.

She blinked. How long had she been like this, an hour? The clock said only seven minutes.

"Marcus—"

"Shh. It's me. Nobody's here, just you and me. Nothing's happening to you."

"Marcus."

"Yeah."

"Talk."

"I am. It's okay. You got scared of something. We're home, you want to go inside?"

"Marcus," she said. Her hands unclenched, cupped in front of her mouth. Relief flooded him in a dizzying wave. She knew she was hyperventilating. The flashback was over.

He kept talking for another few minutes while she worked to calm her breathing. Finally, her hands fell into her lap, and she met his eyes.

"Was ... it ... dark?"

He shook his head. "The guy at the gas station. You remember anything?"

Her expression shouted a sudden yes. "I thought …"

"You said it wasn't—he wasn't—"

"I thought … he was … at first."

Marcus swallowed. "Why?"

"It was … something … the … the smell." Her hands opened in front of her, one clean, one smeared with ice cream and chocolate. She scrubbed it against her black pants. Her breaths began to snag on each other.

"Lee. Hey. Stop." He grabbed her slim wrist before he could think not to. She pulled away. She stared at her fudge-stained fingers while Marcus scoured his memory. "What smell? Was it … was it his cologne?"

Her hands clenched and withdrew against her body.

Marcus's gut was a tight, sick ball. His thoughts were splintering into images he had to squash. Quickly. Before he drove back to that gas station and his bare hands committed murder.

"Lee. Are you sure? It wasn't him?"

"No tattoo."

On the attacker's wrist, a staring eye in red ink. The only glimpse she'd gotten before he nearly suffocated her with the black hood. Marcus hadn't even looked for the tattoo. He tried to gulp calmness from the truck's heated air. More than one man wore that cologne. No justice. Not today.

Lee looked toward her house. "Inside?"

"Sure," he said.

He opened the door for her and offered his arm. *Come on, Lee. It's okay this time.* She sidestepped him. Even up the two garage stairs, her shaking legs made each step alone. Marcus shadowed her, ready if she stumbled, but not too close.

At the door, her trembling hands jostled her keys. She couldn't find the right one. Marcus let her try for several seconds, then held out his hand. She went still, stared at him as if he could be a stranger, and finally let the keys fall into his palm.

She'd marked the head of her house key with a stripe of green Sharpie marker. Marcus unlocked the door and motioned her in ahead of him. She didn't move.

"It's okay. You're home. We'll turn on every light in the house."

She stepped inside, then turned sharply. Keeping him out. She shook her head.

"What?" he said.

"You need to go."

The words were a hard, hollowing punch to his gut. A barrier sprang up between his brain and his tongue. He shook his head.

"Please," Lee said.

"What if it happens again? You could need a doctor."

"It won't."

"Because it's not dark? It wasn't dark before."

"I simply need some time to myself. I'll be fine." Her hand crept to the doorknob.

Their gazes clung. *Let me in, Lee.* He waited. A long minute. She stared back, the gray lakes of her eyes washed in weariness. The door inched forward. Marcus's hand shot up, stopped it with a dull slap of palm against wood, but didn't push it back.

"I would like to ..." Lee shuddered.

What? ... Oh. "Take your time. I'll wait."

She darted a glance over her shoulder and rubbed her chocolate-stained palm against her thigh.

"Lee. Hey. Look at me."

She didn't. Heck, this wasn't her, except it had been twice before. After the power outage, the first time he'd seen one of her panic attacks. And years before that, when she'd finally told him everything about her and then stood up from their park bench as if the only thing left was to part ways forever.

"I did lie to you before, when I implied you were ... the reason. I wanted to rectify that."

He braced a hand on the door trim. "Go take a shower."

Surprise widened her eyes, probably that he remembered what she'd needed after the blackout. As if he could forget.

"It's okay. I'll stay out here. You can lock the door, if you need to."

"I won't force you to wait in my garage while I—"

"You're not forcing me. Come open the door when you're ready."

"Go home, Marcus. Please."

He shook his head and dropped his hand. Lee shut the door with a sigh, inches from his face. The deadbolt slid into place. Marcus paced until the lava cooled from his veins, until the pounding outrage in his skull muted to a throb he could ignore. She was inside right now trying to get clean, as if that monster's dirtiness had transferred to her. The quiet of the garage magnified Marcus's growl.

An hour passed. The deadbolt clicked. The door opened. Lee stood in sweat pants and a hoodie, both so big they hardly touched her. She held a blanket around her shoulders. When Marcus stepped inside, she didn't flinch or look away, but no warmth resided in her eyes. This was an easy Lee mode to recognize. Coping and cold.

You'd think by now she'd give up on that one. She should know he couldn't be repelled by glares. Or panic attacks. Or, well, anything.

Marcus locked the door and let her lead him to the living room. They each switched on a lamp. She picked a book from her shelf and curled up in her chair. He sat on the couch opposite her, clicked the TV on and surfed, volume low. Hopefully some channel was playing a Spielberg movie.

If they talked at all, it would be about the book or the movie. Eventually, he'd drive home. Tomorrow would come and go. And moments from tonight would stay cocooned in knowing silence. Marcus leaned his head back and closed his eyes. This was Lee to him, and him to Lee. The place safe enough for silence.

12

The day after Agent Young's appearance at the office, Mary-Beth didn't speak to Aubrey all morning. She left for lunch, then charged back in before Aubrey had a chance to lock the front door. "I'm sorry."

Aubrey turned the lock and tried to shrug. "You didn't mean anything."

"All this stuff with Elliott—the last thing you need is time in re-education, away from him and work and everything."

As if re-education were a governmental inconvenience, like jury duty or an IRS audit. "Don't worry about it."

"I might've thrown a huge, stupid curveball at your whole routine and schedule and life. And if you were serious about that—about not going along with them—"

"Did you think I was joking?"

Mary-Beth froze with one arm in the sleeve of her red peacoat.

"Look, Christians don't bomb things or kill people or—" The words froze half formed on Aubrey's lips. She couldn't discuss this.

But Mary-Beth stood in front of her, dangling a coat sleeve and wearing lost confusion behind her eyes.

Aubrey felt a coward's shiver and tried to abbreviate the truth. "Being a Christian means I believe in the Bible. The real Bible, not the PUV."

"The PUV *is* the real Bible."

"Oh, come on, Mary-Beth." Aubrey sat down in a padded waiting room chair. "Does that make any sense? The Bible's supposed to be from God, isn't it?"

Mary-Beth nodded, tugged off her coat, and draped it over her crossed arms.

"But you think a bunch of elite academic people get to decide after all this time that the Bible's screwed up, and *they* have to fix it?"

"The old ones *are* screwed up," Mary-Beth said.

"So a thousand years ago, God looked down at the translators of the originals and went, 'Uh-oh, they're biased and incompetent, I guess My message is ruined.'"

A pensive frown tugged at Mary-Beth's face. "But you're saying God's a Person outside us, and that's— Oh, I've got to go, meeting Dom next door for pizza. I wanted to apologize, that's all. I don't think you're going to go kill someone, or anything, and I'd feel really bad if that con-cop heard me."

"He probably didn't." The words had to be true, that's all.

Mary-Beth's lips curved into a ribbon of relief. "I bet you're right. He would've said something if he'd heard me, right? So, um—forgiven?"

"Yeah, of course." Aubrey headed toward the back kitchen and took her sandwich and apple from the fridge. Mary-Beth trailed her, shrugging into her coat.

"Thanks, Aubrey. And remember, I'm still buying you lunch. I was thinking Friday?"

"Sounds good."

"Great. I'll see you in an hour."

"Enjoy your pizza."

When the office's back door closed on her babbling coworker, Aubrey leaned against the counter and closed her eyes.

She'd only tried to explain to Mary-Beth, tried to make her think. But accidental blabbing was no safer than deliberate reporting, and right now, Mary-Beth had no serious reason to keep quiet. She couldn't know how the Constabulary procured compliance.

Over her head, the bulb too bright to look at, sharpening her shadow that stretched across the ivory tile.

Aubrey opened her eyes to the irritating, reassuring flicker of a fluorescent bulb well into its last days. If she worked through the stack of documents on the back cabinet, she could stay punched in through lunch. She chomped down on her apple and got to work.

Jeff Young's paperwork leered from the top of the stack. She flipped through it, then settled all five pages into the scanner and clicked the green button on her screen.

"Did you hear her, or not?" Aubrey said to sheets as they whirred out the other side. She labeled and saved the scanned documents, then closed the computer window as if the face on his scanned license might answer her. A memory did instead—not Agent Young's voice, but a voice from that sharply lit room, all glass windows with shut blinds.

"What are you waiting for, Aubrey? Fire and brimstone to finish me off? An earthquake to shake the walls down and set you free? Or a white knight, maybe? Brett's already been released."

"And they were singing, 'Bye-bye, Miss American Pie ...'"

Her mother's ringtone. Aubrey hurried back to the kitchen and retrieved her phone from her purse. "Mom?"

"Aubrey—" The voice choked on a sob.

"Elliott. Is he okay?"

"They took him, honey."

"Who—" Her whole body froze solid. Only a whisper managed to escape the ice. "Con-cops?"

"They barged in and took him. They said I could get him back after they approved our home with the state. I thought they'd already arrested you, the way they were talking. I had to warn you, in case they hadn't. Aubrey, when they come for you, you have to tell them what they want to hear."

"Like Brett did?" *Like I did, nine months ago?*

Her mother's tears came louder over the line. "Don't you want your son back?"

"Of course I—"

"If they take you a second time, they might never let you out, for the rest of your life."

"Mom, you know I can't."

"Honey, you absolutely must cooperate with them. For us, for Elliott."

She could. For Elliott, she could. Her body shook. *Father God, they have my baby, those people have my baby.* But she could lie again, and they would give him back, unhurt, if she acted now.

No. God saw her. She'd shamed Him once, maybe forfeited His forgiveness, but she would let the con-cops kill her before she denied Him again.

And Elliott? Would she let them kill him, too?

"Aubrey?" Her mother's voice quavered. "Please, honey. I don't want to lose you."

"Mom." She swallowed. "Did you hear where they took him?"

"They didn't say."

"I've got to go. I'll call you later."

"Aubrey. I love you."

"I love you, too." She closed the phone and shoved it into her purse. They knew where she worked. She sat here, a pathetic statue, a stationary target. She had to go. Somewhere.

Like where?

Her breath came in a sharp antirhythm as she turned on the answering machine, changed it to the lunch message, and scrawled a note promising a quick return. Leaving in a panic would trigger her boss's suspicion. But a ruse was worthless. The con-cops knew her face, her car, her workplace, her house. They knew who watched her baby, and they must know now she had been warned. Letting Mom call her must be one more move in the strategy of their game.

Aubrey locked the door behind her and jogged to her car. The wind at her back pushed a parade of dead leaves over the blacktop toward her. She got into the car, turned the key, and took illogical pleasure in the click of the automatic locks. As if these locks were any more effective than the deadbolt on her apartment door, on her mother's door.

She braked at the driveway to wait for traffic to clear. Right or left, it probably didn't matter. Where could she go to hide from the Constabulary?

Where can I go to hide from Your presence?

"Father God," she said. "I'm scared."

The traffic cleared for a right turn, and she pulled out. Any of the cars behind her, in front of her, passing from the other direction—she was hemmed in by possible con-cops.

"I don't know if You're listening or not, and if You're not, I don't blame You, but please—not for me, for Elliot—please help me."

Karlyn would have tried to help, but there was no one else on her entire list of friends and acquaintances. Not one, and she couldn't blame them. Every friendship had its lines in the sand, and a felony charge was a universal line.

Nonstop checking out the cars in her mirrors threatened to distract her from the road. She had to focus, or she'd wreck her car and have only her legs to flee with. She tapped the brakes until she was no longer tailgating. She glanced in the mirrors again.

Dormant green lights topped a car, three behind hers. Trying to see her license plate, or knowing already who she was. Maybe they waited for her to speed along the dirt shoulder in panic, so they could add resisting arrest to her charges.

"Please don't let them catch me," she said. "Please, I have to get Elliott back."

Her ramblings might qualify as a psalm, but she had no right to compose one. Space widened between the cars ahead. Aubrey accelerated with nowhere to go.

"You saved David from all his enemies. You can do anything."

The cars behind her held their position for the next two miles, through several traffic lights, past plazas and gas stations and restaurants that bordered both sides of the windblown road. A squat blue vehicle directly behind her, then a longer red one, then smoke gray with green lights. This must be a game to the agent in that car. *"Where Will the Cornered Suspect Go Next?"*

Crash.

Aubrey jolted. She'd hit somebody. No. Her car was still moving. As was the SUV in front of her. In her rearview mirror, two halted vehicles faded to the far background: the con-cop car, and the red sedan that had braked without warning.

"Oh, God," she said. "Did You do that?"

She had minutes to disappear. The agent would radio his position this very second, report the direction she was headed, send others to converge on her. If she could trade cars with somebody ... but that solution would die young. She couldn't use her credit cards, couldn't show her face in public if they flagged her for a most-wanted news blurb.

First things first. Disappear for now, figure out later how to disappear for good. And how to find Elliott. They expected her to flee somewhere familiar. Or maybe they expected her to drive until they stopped her. Maybe they would station cars at her aunt and uncle's house, her grandmother's. Maybe they would interview old friends from college.

She was tailgating again. As she braked, the SUV signaled for a left turn into a small plaza. Aubrey's heart misplaced a beat.

They would not expect her to go shopping.

She signaled the turn as well and accelerated through the yellow arrow. She should enter a store to complete the act. Her choices sprawled in a line before her, stores of various sizes and specialties. Electronics was out. She'd probably step through the door as someone tested a home theater system with a news channel broadcasting her description. The shoe store and the bath-and-body store huddled between electronics and home improvement like two petite sisters holding hands. Those doors probably held jingling bells. Those buildings probably held helpful associates who would flock to her the moment she walked in.

She'd been inside a home-improvement store maybe three times in her life. They were vast, and in Aubrey's experience, a person who wanted assistance had to search out the employees. She pulled around the building and found the employee parking, backed her car into a space framed by others, and headed for the store with hunched shoulders. She'd forgotten her jacket. Cold wind stung her cheeks and drew water from her eyes. She blinked it away. Any form of tears right now would undo her.

1 3

Marcus was headed for the checkout line, carrying sanding screens and a bucket of mud for work at Penny's, when two men stepped into the main aisle, not a hundred feet in front of him. Badges beamed from the chests of their smoke-gray uniforms. Constabulary agents in a home-improvement store? They were after somebody.

They were after him.

Marcus meandered past and threw them the same superficial glance any innocent person would, before the bill of his hat cut them from his peripheral vision. He'd worn it to shield the black eye from double-takes, not to hide his face in general from the Constabulary. Well, whatever worked.

Behind him came a burst of static, then a radio voice whose words he couldn't make out. One of the agents quietly spoke back.

Maybe Jason's drunken memory lapse was an undercover role, and the guy really held his liquor like a rock. Or maybe the father with eleven Bibles behind his walls cut a deal so his kids could go back to their sandbox. The bruise on Marcus's face had transitioned from blue and purple to purple and yellow. The man would recognize him in a lineup.

Instinct veered him off course. Heading to the front of the store might look like fleeing. He turned a corner and faced the cabinet hardware display ... and a young female shopper.

She was a few years younger than Lee, shorter and curvier and bearing a brown leather purse over one shoulder. Not the first woman her age he'd observed in a home-improvement store, but they did tend to stand out, especially when they shopped alone. Maybe she was holiday shopping.

He'd kill a minute or two here, then head out. Plenty of cabinet pulls to gaze at. Actually, those were similar to the Vitales' cabinet knobs. Satin nickel finish, rope edge, thirty millimeter. He'd ask before buying, of course. Belinda might want a change. But good to know they were here if he needed them.

The woman to his left hadn't moved. She didn't even seem to breathe. Her head should tip from one product to another. Her fingers should graze over display knobs. Women shoppers touched everything in the store—light fixtures, flooring, countertops—as though feel were the most important gauge of quality. Marcus angled his body to face her.

Her hand was shaking.

"Are you okay?" he said.

She jolted. Her eyes caught him, unable to mask a shimmering fear. "I am, yes, but thanks for asking."

She stood before the display like a soldier before a firing squad … or a Christian before a squad of Constabulary agents.

He couldn't ask, but he didn't have to. The two agents weren't here for the sale on bathroom hardware. Or for him. He took a deliberate breath, and the scent of raw construction eased the strain in his neck.

"Having trouble finding something?" Marcus said.

"No trouble." No eye contact, either.

"Okay." She couldn't really expect him to leave her here, frozen and alone. "You need to hide in here, or get out?"

She pivoted to face him as if he could be some dangerous animal she had to keep in sight. Maybe he was wrong about the

Constabulary agents. But if somebody else threatened her, why try to blend in here when she could go to the front of the store and ask for help? Not that battered women always did the sensible thing.

"I'm perfectly fine, thanks. I just needed some—um—"

"Kitchen tiles?"

"Tiles, yes." She turned back to the display.

"Then you need to go five aisles that way." Marcus pointed.

She bit her bottom lip. "Go away."

"No."

"I'm—"

"You're scared of somebody. And this"—he jerked an arm at the display—"isn't hiding."

"I'm not scared."

"Is it your boyfriend?"

Her mouth opened, closed, and opened. "Can you get me out of here? Without being seen?"

"What's he look like?"

"I mean, by … anybody."

The seesaw of his thoughts crashed down with certainty. But if he mentioned the two uniformed agents, she'd deny it and close up again. To get her out of this, he had to pretend to believe her.

"Stay here," he said. "And … here. Read this." He grabbed a cabinet knob from the rack and handed it to her. Tiny text covered the plastic bag: contents, installation suggestions, warnings not to let your three-year-old eat this bag.

Her forehead wrinkled.

"Look like a shopper," he said. "In case somebody else walks by."

"Oh. Right. Okay."

Marcus walked to one end of the aisle. He gazed down the main walkway as though searching the hanging signs for something specific. He turned enough to lower his eyes and capture a view of the shoppers.

Gray uniforms, straight ahead, half the store away. Their heads turned. Their eyes roved. In minutes, they'd reach him. He rounded the corner, sprinted down the empty neighboring aisle, and re-entered the previous aisle from the opposite end. The woman jumped, startled.

"Come on," he said. He shoved the sanding screens into her hands. Then he headed toward the front of the store, toward ground the agents had already covered. He swung the blue-lidded bucket of mud from his right hand.

Wait a minute.

He turned, and her forehead almost hit his chin. She jerked back.

"How many?" he said.

"What?"

They didn't have time for pretense. "Two? Four? Six?"

"I don't know what you're—"

"They're in uniform. One's got kind of red hair. The other one's a little taller than me. Are they the only ones you've seen?"

"You know what? I think I'll deal with this myself."

Her wooden steps backward would send her right into their path. Marcus dropped the sanding screens to seize her arm. He should pull her along behind him. "I can't avoid them if I don't know they're here."

"Like I said, I'll—"

"If I'm one of them, you're already made."

The next three seconds nearly killed his patience. Her hazel eyes stared into his. She stopped trying to free her arm. "I don't know for sure, but I think there's only two."

Marcus resumed his path toward the front. Right angles down aisles took him and the woman gradually east. Less traffic at that exit, and usually no greeter. The agents had probably given employees a description of their prey.

"Where's your car?" he said.

She fast-walked alongside him. "The employee lot, almost behind the building."

Smart. "Theirs must be unmarked."

"Maybe, but there was a squad car earlier. It hit a car behind me."

A Constabulary agent hit a car? The east exit appeared ahead of them, and only a few customers cluttered their way. No gray uniforms, and no orange employee aprons. But a vise still squeezed his neck.

"They know your car," he said.

"Oh, yeah, they know it. They were tailing me. And then they called those two in."

Time for clarification on that later. He and the woman could step through those automatic doors and get shoved against the building and handcuffed. She wasn't safe till she was at least away from here. At best, she had a safe place to go.

Did the description include her khakis and pink shirt? Marcus gestured her to stop and set the bucket on the floor. He stripped off his jacket and handed it to her, probably futile but better than nothing.

"Put it on."

She shrugged into the jacket and resumed walking only when he did. He swallowed a sigh. The jacket's sleeves fell past her fingers. As if reading his thoughts, she pushed them up to wrist level.

Her pink shirt still showed through the jacket's opening. "Zip it up."

Again, she complied without comment.

"Wait," he said, and they halted two steps before the end of the aisle. Marcus stepped out into the open checkout area and wandered to an impulse-shopper display before one checkout line. He tugged a blister pack of batteries from a rack and searched the vicinity while pretending to scan the rest of the display. The agents weren't here. If they had followed the same general path as before, they were now on the other side of the store.

Marcus replaced the batteries and half turned to catch the woman's gaze. He tilted his head toward the doors. She pointed at herself, then at the door, her eyebrows arches of question. Marcus gave half a nod.

She was at his side in a few seconds. He rested a hand on her shoulder and guided her to his left. When they stepped through the doors, he would block her from the camera mounted above this side of the door, but that was only one. She'd still show up on the feed from the parking lot. Well, maybe the teenage cashier with the comb-over had meant it last week when he said the cameras were never turned on.

"If I get back in my car, they're going to follow me again," she said.

"You're not getting back in your car."

"Then ... what are we doing?"

"I'll take you where you need to go."

Marcus angled his face as they passed through the door, revealing nothing but the back of his neck and his hat's faded Red Wings logo. They walked outside freely. The wind whipped her hair around her face, long, loose curls the color of oak stain. If only his jacket had a hood. He could hope the cameras were off, but he couldn't assume they were. He kept his hand on her shoulder as they crossed the parking lot to his truck. If they thought she was alone, maybe his presence would throw them when they looked at the security footage later—or if they were looking at it now. You never knew with the Constabulary.

"I don't have anywhere to go," the woman said. "They're already watching my parents' house, my work ... and my best friend's already ..."

Her steps lagged. Marcus propelled her forward. He'd get her into the truck, out of here, and then ... What then?

"So ... we ought to part ways." Wind or desperation brought tears to her eyes.

"I could drive you ... away. To Ohio, if you want."

"No."

"At least you'd be dealing with a different Constabulary, one that doesn't know you."

"Well, this one took my son. I'm not going anywhere without him."

Did they drag him screaming like a kidnapping victim? Had he even realized what was happening? She wasn't old enough for a kid more than a few years old, unless she'd had him as a teenager. Marcus shepherded her to the passenger side of his truck. He opened the door and offered her a hand up, as much for courtesy as for appearances. The cab was a step up for Lee, and this woman stood several inches shorter, not much past five feet.

Her gaze welded to his hand, and she shivered inside his jacket. "Come on," he said.

Her hand was chilled silk in his as she gripped the door frame to slide inside. Marcus shut the door and kept a leisurely pace as he got behind the wheel.

Rather than wait for a green left-turn arrow, Marcus left this parking lot for the larger one beside it. A right turn here would save time, depending on their destination. Wherever it was.

He pulled into traffic when he shouldn't have and accelerated quickly. The car behind him still had to brake. "So they tailed you, you lost them, and you hid in a store."

She swiveled in the seat to watch him drive. "I thought I should do the last thing they'd expect. Not that it worked. They found me again pretty much right away."

"Does your car have GPS?"

A grin without a smile darkened her eyes. "My car doesn't even have AC most of the time."

"Then how'd they find it?"

"How should I know?"

His hands squeezed the wheel as his mind sorted options. They could have tagged her car weeks ago, been trailing her all this time, but it seemed melodramatic, even for the Constabulary. Somehow, though, they'd gotten an instant location on it. Or … they'd followed something other than the car.

"You have a cell phone," he said.

Her forehead scrunched at the significance in his voice. "Pretty much the whole country—"

"Take out the battery."

"You think—?"

"Now."

She pawed through her purse and snatched up the phone. An intersection lay a hundred feet in front of him. The light turned yellow.

"Wait," Marcus said.

Her eyes shot him more confusion, but she cupped the phone in one hand and waited. He braked and swung a hard right as yellow climbed to red. He jammed the gas pedal. Not yet, his intentions would be too obvious. Wait ... a long plaza zipped past on the left, then a medical building ... wait.

"Okay," he said.

She held down a button long enough to trigger the good-bye tone, then popped the battery from the back. Marcus turned left into the next driveway, made a tight loop, and pulled back into traffic, back the way they'd come. He gunned the truck through another late yellow to take them past the light where they'd just turned. All this was futile, though, if they were tracking *her*. Her body. Lee's voice unfurled in his head, recounting every detail of the patient she'd seen a few months ago, in a hospital room guarded by Constabulary agents.

"The person may feel only a twinge as the device enters and think nothing else of it. They intend you to continue with normal life while being monitored."

No matter how Marcus asked, this question would sound crazy. "Have you gotten close enough to them to get shot with something?"

"Um ... I'm not shot."

"With a tracking ... thing. I don't think it feels like getting shot. You might not notice."

"I'm pretty sure I would."

Except that most people didn't know about the trackers. But for now, he'd have to take her word.

Her eyes drilled into the side of his face for a long moment. "I'm Aubrey."

"Marcus," he said.

"Marcus, you just committed a felony."

"Just?"

Based on her tight smile, she must think he was making light of this. "I'm wanted by the con-cops."

"Yeah." And ... con-cops? She might be younger than he thought, based on her choice of slang.

"Thank you for your help."

The taut muscles of his neck barely allowed the nod.

"But you're going to want to let me out of the car now. I'm kind of dangerous company." She faced forward again, and her hand poised on the door handle as if he'd pull over and throw her out.

"Where'll you go?" he said.

She looked out the window at the myriad stores flashing by. The speedometer read ten miles over. He eased off the gas.

Finally, an answer leaked from her, faint, beaten drips of words. "I don't know yet. I have to make a plan ... to find my son."

"But where'll you stay? While you plan?"

"I ..."

She couldn't sleep outside somewhere in subfreezing weather. "You can't use credit cards. Or an ATM. How much cash have you got?"

"I ... eleven dollars and some change."

"Eleven dollars."

"And some change." She barely reached a whisper now.

His wallet held about forty bucks, but that wouldn't even get her one night in a hotel. Sure, he could use his own credit card. But if the Constabulary watched her home, her parents' home, and her workplace, they'd done some digging. They would know to search the hotels. She needed to stay somewhere they could never guess, somewhere without any connection to Aubrey before … this moment.

No wonder he'd been subconsciously heading southeast.

"Okay," he said.

"Okay what?"

"I'll hide you."

Aubrey bit her lip.

"You don't have a lot of choices right now."

"I don't know you."

"No, you don't." He turned right and merged onto the highway, the path home. She needed help. His help. He'd have to earn her trust.

14

"It's not that I don't trust you," Aubrey said, but that must be a lie. She knew absolutely nothing about this man. Getting into his truck had to be one of the stupidest, most desperate choices of her life. True, a con-cop undercover would have delivered her straight to Young and Partyka, but her brain suddenly reminded her of other ways a man could endanger a woman. She could see the headlines now. *"Serial Rapist Found His Victims in Home-Improvement Stores." "Police Nab 'Handyman Killer' after Victim Aubrey Weston Found In ..."*

Marcus removed his Red Wings cap and tossed it onto the dashboard, ignoring a flattened section in the short brown ripples of his hair. The bruise under his left eye looked deeper without the cap's shadow. He drove in silence.

"Are you a Christian?" The words popped from her mouth.

He nodded with barely a glance at her.

"Oh, that was convincing," she said.

"Well, I can't prove it."

Actually ... his simplicity *was* convincing. Maybe he was for real. *Father God, is this Your doing?* Guilt stole her breath. After she denied Him, God had provided her with a job to feed herself and her newborn. Half an hour ago, she'd considered denying Him for the second time, yet He'd still sent her a haven in the form of this stranger. She burrowed against the leather seat and breathed in the wooded scent from Marcus's jacket.

"Okay," she said quietly.

His shoulders caved slightly. He actually seemed to care what she chose to do.

"But once I know how to get Elliott back, I'll be leaving." As if she could go for a walk and trip over the knowledge.

"I'll help you," he said.

"How?"

His hands shifted on the wheel, big and knob-knuckled. "I don't know yet."

"What happened to your face?" Her trivial question seemed to surprise him less than it surprised her.

"A ladder hit me."

"It looks like it hurts."

"I'm okay."

She didn't deserve the gift of this man's willingness. "Thank you for offering to help, but you shouldn't get involved."

"Too late now."

She'd thought his voice deep at first, but it wasn't very. More like ... solid, each word an arrow that knew where it headed. And clipped. The syllables never lingered.

"Those two agents," he said. "You know them?"

"They questioned me about my friends, after they were arrested."

His nod was short, almost a jerking movement. He didn't seem the ignorant type, but if he understood the risk, he wouldn't hide her in his home. He wouldn't offer assistance at all. Apparently nobody ever told him about felony charges, about lines in the sand. A draft from the cracked window caught Aubrey's face, and she bunched the jacket's surplus fabric in one hand.

"If they connect us in any way, they can take you in, maybe even arrest you."

Again, the jerking nod.

"I don't mean if they find me at your house. I mean if they realize you've even talked to me."

"I know."

No, he didn't, and she couldn't accept help from him when he lacked a full picture of the danger. She had to paint it for him. *"They'll keep you awake for days. They'll say things you know aren't true but sound like they are. They'll find out who you most want safe and threaten to kill him."*

When none of those words would come, her mouth supplied others. "Last week, there was a couple arrested, James and Karlyn Cole."

He nodded again.

"Karlyn's the friend the con-cops questioned me about. I've known her and Jim for years. And that news story was a pack of lies."

Did the silence mean he didn't believe her, or he was listening?

"Jim couldn't attack the con-cops like they said. He can't get around most days without a walker. They made it up, because somehow Jim and Karlyn hid their Bibles too well to find."

The wind-whipped quiet tunneled into Aubrey's mind. He'd pull over now and tell her to get out.

"I know," he said.

"What do you mean?"

"Jim's got MS."

Marcus ignored her stare. The seconds stretched until they tore on words she didn't expect to hear from herself. "He prepares a table."

Marcus's face tightened in surprise. "Before us."

Residual doubt washed away. He was a Christian. A stupid Christian. "You're taking me to your house, to—what, hide me in the spare room?"

Another short nod. The motion made her want to scream, to grab his Atlas-sized shoulders and shake him.

"That is completely crazy," she said.

"Nothing else to do."

"Hand me a twenty and wish me luck, like a normal person. Marcus, they will lock you up and throw away the key. They'll—"

"I know." One hand leaped up to his neck and clenched his knuckles white. "They'll lock me up. I'll die locked up. I know."

The grip on his neck didn't ease for a long minute, and they drove onward without further conversation.

Time stretched into moments of illogical ecstasy at how long she'd managed to evade the con-cops, then moments of terror that they were gaining behind her, or lurking before her, around the next curve in the two-lane road. Maybe this was hysteria. She had to keep swallowing the demand that Marcus let her out of the truck. She had to find Elliott, to hold him, soft and trusting, his head nestled in the crook of her arm. She had to babble at him, even though the words couldn't reach his mind or heart. She had to know the con-cops hadn't harmed him to get to her.

By the time Marcus pulled into a serene, tree-lined subdivision, Aubrey knew she had to tell him thanks and good-bye.

He pulled the truck into the attached garage, turned it off, and hit a button to lower the hefty wooden door behind them. Horizontal blinds on the garage windows completed Aubrey's feeling of fortress. Nobody could see her in here.

"Okay," Marcus said and opened his door.

Aubrey did the same, then jumped down to the concrete floor. The impact smarted through her ankles. Marcus headed for the back door with his house key already in hand. The few other keys bobbed and clinked against the Swiss army knife that dangled in their midst.

"I've got a dog," he said, shoving the key into the lock, "but she—"

"I'm not staying."

His hand froze to the doorknob. "You don't have anywhere to go," he said as if she might have forgotten.

"My son wants his mommy back."

"You can't go looking for him."

"I have to. I'm his mother."

He stepped away from the door, closer to her. "Aubrey. You can't go looking for him."

"You don't understand."

"Anything you try to do, anybody you try to contact—it'll be traced."

"Hiding in your house will not get him back."

"Neither will getting arrested."

"Marcus, thank you, for everything. Here—your jacket." He didn't take it, so she draped it over the truck's hood. A tremor zipped down her spine at the idea of abandoning these secure walls for exposure outside, but she headed for the door on the side of the garage.

"Wait," he said.

Listening to him another minute would puncture her scant courage. She grasped the cold doorknob and turned it.

"Aubrey." His fingers closed around her forearm.

"Let me go."

He did, only to plant himself between her and the door. His warm hand pried hers from the doorknob. She tried to sidestep him, but he blocked her. The powerful arms and torso, first noticeable in the store when he removed his jacket, transformed from protection to threat.

"You can't keep me here," she said, though he could.

"I'll find your son."

She turned her head toward the wall.

"Nobody can get him back overnight," Marcus said.

"He's four months old, and old ladies in Kroger love his smile, and he likes this jack-in-the-box Mom bought him, and he was born deaf, and he's ..."

Marcus didn't move. "Stay for now. It's the safest thing. Please."

"You're going to help me get him back. Away from them. Soon."

"Yeah."

"Okay," she whispered.

The nod didn't madden this time. He eased away from the door as if she might lunge for it and bolt.

Aubrey followed him to the back door and waited for him to push the dog back inside. He didn't touch it, though, simply thrust an open hand, palm out, under its nose. It backed up quickly, toenails scraping tile.

"Okay," he said to Aubrey, then closed the door behind her. "This is Indy."

"Can I pet him?" The German shepherd eyed Marcus as if for instructions.

"Her," he said automatically. "Sure." He dropped a hand onto the dog's head and rubbed between her ears while Aubrey stroked her sleek back.

"Would she hurt anybody?"

"If they tried to come in without me." Indy licked his free hand.

Aubrey stepped back. Vigilant eyes gazed at her from the dog's black face.

"Don't worry," Marcus said. "She knows you're accepted now."

"Would Indy happen to be short for Indiana?"

His mouth didn't smile, but amusement creased around his eyes. "No, actually."

"Not short for anything?"

"For, um, *Indutiae*. It's Latin."

"No kidding."

"A friend named her," he said. "It was too much to call her all the time, so I shortened it."

"What's the translation?"

He looked down at the dog for a moment, then met her eyes again. "Truce."

"Sounds like there's a story behind it."

He nodded.

"A … personal story?"

Another nod, and then he led her from the laundry room to the small kitchen. A few crumbs dotted the counter, but the sink was clean and empty.

"Well." Marcus's quick glance traveled past the end of the kitchen into the living room, then back to her. "I'm late for my last job. If you get hungry, help yourself. I don't cook, but there's stuff you can throw together."

"So the fridge isn't crammed with beer and leftover pizza?"

"No beer," he said. "Maybe some pizza."

He was opening his castle to a stranger. Aubrey smiled to battle the resurgence of tears. "Thanks."

15

Nosiness was not to blame for Aubrey's self-guided tour of Marcus's house. He hadn't given her permission to explore, but as the hours passed, idleness bred images until she'd either scream or flee: her son wailing, gripped in gray-clad arms, dumped into a cold crib and left to cry.

Marcus's dog wasn't really lying down, merely sitting with bent elbows. She may have her stomach to the floor, but her head was poised erect over her paws. Her eyes tracked Aubrey's every move. When Aubrey ventured from this room to the next, Indy pushed to her feet and followed.

"You don't mind, do you?" she said. Indy didn't blink. "I'll take that as permission."

Aubrey couldn't bring herself to trespass into his bedroom beyond a peek from the doorway. The rest of the house held a clean, steadfast simplicity. Every room's walls unfolded beige and bare. A woven afghan was tossed over the back of the living room couch, but the room held not a single throw pillow. Remotes for the TV and DVD player lay parallel on an end table that ached for a doily. The entire house was paved in solid, shining hardwood, and every piece of furniture, from kitchen table to bedroom nightstand, announced itself genuine as well.

"I guess Marcus likes wood," Aubrey said to the dog at her heels. Veneer seemed sacrilegious within these walls.

What her mother would find sacrilegious was the single book-shelf in his living room. His DVD collection spanned a wall, but his books numbered no more than a couple dozen, and that was only if she counted the handyman and carpentry magazines lining one shelf with their ragged spines. She tugged one out and flipped it open. Dog-eared pages, highlighted pages, missing pages, spilled-on pages. He also had a book on film theory, but it looked brand new. His copy of the Constitution was not as abused as the magazines but was clearly read. Sandwiched between them sat a worn leather address book, which she left unopened, and a children's illustrated hardcover *Treasure Island*, the only fiction book in his shelf. How random.

She completed her tour before Marcus called to question her on clothing sizes. She'd give him her remaining cash when he got home. She tried to appreciate his thoughtfulness, but why did it matter if she wore her work clothes threadbare? Not that he would listen, of course. In fact, he sounded perturbed that she dared protest.

When she finally hung up the phone, her stomach grumbled. Well, he'd told her to eat without him.

The fridge was hardly crowded. Carry-out pizza and a carton of Chinese occupied the top shelf. Beneath that stood a battalion of pop cans and flavored coffee creamers, half a loaf of slouching white bread, deli lunch meat, eggs, condiments ... and on the bottom shelf, two glass containers. A baking pan covered in gleaming foil, and a small lidded bowl of green salad.

Aubrey opened the salad first. Sliced tomatoes, carrots, green peppers, purple onions, egg whites, bacon bits—all decorated a variety of greens. So Marcus didn't cook, but he labored over salad.

Removing the foil on the glass pan shattered that theory. An inquisitive meatball peeked from the white cheese slathered over homemade spaghetti. Truly homemade—Aubrey would bet her last eleven dollars that was no prepackaged meatball. If Marcus "didn't cook," what on earth did *she* do?

She tucked the foil back around the spaghetti and pressed the plastic lid back onto the salad bowl. The sight of it all increased her stomach's complaints, but she'd wait for Marcus.

The key didn't rattle the lock until almost 8:00. Indy abandoned her guarding of Aubrey to rush the door like an excited child, her tail beating the air for the first time since Marcus had left.

"Hi," he said from the laundry room, and Aubrey headed over to answer him, then realized he was talking to the dog.

Marcus crossed into the kitchen with Indy's head pressed into his hand. A fine gray dust salted the top of his hair. "Hi," he said, this time to Aubrey, and plunked two strained plastic shopping bags onto the counter. "Clothes."

"Thanks." She lifted the first article from the top of the crushed pile, a heather-gray sweater with peasant sleeves and a modest key-hole neckline. Aubrey dug to find two identical tops, one in brick red and one in dark chocolate, and beneath that, two pairs of jeans. Did he want her indebted to him?

"Did you eat?" Marcus said.

"What is all this?" She unearthed yellow thermal separates from the bottom of the bag. "I told you not to buy pajamas."

"You've got to sleep in something."

"And I told you I could sleep in anything."

"It's no problem. You need clothes."

She dumped the rest of the bag onto the counter. He'd purchased everything but a bra, even a four-pack of white ankle socks. "I can't believe this."

His frown seemed knit from real confusion, but he said nothing. He crossed the kitchen to hang his keys on the wall rack.

"Marcus, why did you buy this stuff? What do you want?"

He shrugged out of his jacket to reveal a brown T-shirt a shade darker than his eyes, covered with the same dust that coated his hair. He removed his wallet from his back pocket and tossed it onto the table. "I want you to wear the clothes. And not worry about the money. They're from Wal-Mart."

As if quality was the point here. Right now, Wal-Mart was as unaffordable to her as Nordstrom's. He tugged off his scuffed work shoes, and his foot pushed them against a wall. Disquiet still crinkled between his eyes. Maybe he simply wished to take care of her for as long as she hid here. Logic reasserted itself. Wearing the clothes would not jeopardize her son any further, would not signal disregard for where he was.

"Okay," she said.

Marcus gave a short nod. "Well, did you eat?"

"I couldn't dig in. You haven't even cut into it yet."

"What?"

With a *snap*, Aubrey jerked a plastic tag from the pajama bottoms. "I take it we're having spaghetti and salad."

"You made spaghetti? But I don't have noodles and stuff."

"What are you, a sleepwalking chef?"

Marcus strode to the refrigerator and yanked it open. "Oh."

"The sauce is homemade, isn't it?"

He slid the glassware onto the counter. He half removed the foil, and an edge of it tore. "Yeah. But I didn't make this. It's from a friend."

"And you forgot you had it?"

"It wasn't here when I left for work."

"So somebody delivered it to you, straight to your fridge."

The stove's controls beeped with each press of his thumb. He crinkled the edges of the foil back in place, slid the whole pan inside, and closed the oven. "Yeah."

"And Indy let them waltz right in?"

"It was Lee," Marcus said as if the name explained itself.

"So …?"

"She's the only other person Indy would never attack. I had Lee help me train her, so Indy would obey her, too."

Hm. "Did Lee name her?"

He nodded, pulled out his phone, and dialed. He paced to the living room as if Aubrey couldn't hear every word he said from the kitchen.

"You brought spaghetti. … You didn't call me back. … It—it didn't happen today, did it? … Well, thanks for the food. It looks good. … Indy says hi. … Okay. You're sure you're okay. … Then I'll talk to you later."

Wow, so they weren't a flirty couple or a bantering couple. What kind of woman was she, Lee the Latin-Speaking Chef, who preserved Marcus from a diet of pure fast food and held a key to his house? She must have a high-maintenance side, based on Marcus's worried tone and the name she'd given his dog.

His head popped back into the kitchen—"I'm going to take a shower"—then disappeared again.

He reemerged in minutes. The black T-shirt clung to his chest, and his hair almost curled when damp. Probably would, if it were longer. Aubrey broke off her stare before he could notice it, but he seemed oblivious. He pulled the dishwasher open and stacked plates without regard for the clatter, then moved around the kitchen, shoving them and glassware into cabinets. He waved off her attempt to help.

"So how often does Lee bring food over here?" Aubrey said when he'd finished restocking the silverware drawer.

"Once or twice a week. She likes to cook."

"So do I let her in?"

"No," Marcus said, too quickly. "Lee doesn't know you're here."

Of course. "She'd turn me in."

"No. But she has to stay away from all this."

The blaze behind his eyes required no guesswork. He didn't distrust Lee, and he didn't anticipate misinterpretation or jealousy. He simply wanted her safely behind the line in the sand that he ignored for himself.

"What happened to Elliott's dad?"

Aubrey ought to be able to answer while meeting Marcus's eyes, but her gaze lowered to Indy, stretched on the taupe throw rug in front of the sink.

"We're not together anymore," she said.

"Did he leave?"

"Um … in a way, he did, yes." By showing himself to be a person she couldn't stay with.

The blaze that had subsided only seconds ago revived in Marcus's gaze. He opened the oven. Checking the food? The timer wouldn't go off for another five minutes.

"What?" Aubrey said.

"Nothing."

Right. Did he think …? "It wasn't abandonment, Marcus."

The oven door shut with a forceful *click*.

"It wouldn't have worked."

"You should've been given a vote on it." He balled up a stray paper towel and thrust it into the trash.

Aubrey buried the easy way out of this, the way that let Marcus think the best of her and the worst of Brett. "I broke the engagement. Not him."

Marcus's quiet, tense activity ceased. "Did he hurt you?"

"Physically? No. Not in any way, really. But he let me believe he was somebody else, and when I finally got wise, I ... I couldn't pretend it was okay."

"So it wasn't about Elliott?"

She hugged her middle against the sudden, illogical longing for Brett's arms. "It wasn't, no. But he never wanted to be a dad. When I told him we were fine without him, he was happy to believe me."

The fire banked again with a taut nod of Marcus's head. He could grill without regard for tact, then permit the return of silence when he had only a patch of the convoluted quilt. But he probably thought the whole quilt was in his hands.

"It was ... beliefs," she said quietly. "I mean, it was faith, and ... nonfaith. But everyone has faith in something, right? So it was faith in different things."

Marcus didn't nod again, didn't blink, simply absorbed her words.

"He told me a few months after we met that only the Christian God could be the true one, based on all his studies of religion. Then the con-cops ..." She couldn't say it.

But Marcus wouldn't fill the taut silence. He watched her, waited.

"We didn't share ... what I thought we did." Aubrey's finger traced a *B* over the smooth countertop. "And it kind of fell apart."

He nodded. He didn't ask any questions. She'd said too much. Her face had betrayed the truth. Wouldn't be the first time. The timer couldn't ring soon enough.

While they ate, Aubrey attempted normal conversation between bites of spaghetti and salad, as much to occupy her mind as to discover something about the man across from her. Marcus worked for himself as an independent contractor; this was the only thing she could draw out. He wolfed down the food more with single-mindedness than with hunger. He had turned on a news station that Aubrey first considered background noise, but he must have intended it as a shield against small talk. The only polite thing to do was to oblige him. Even in the quiet, he probably didn't hear the newscaster.

"And now the latest on fleeing Constabulary—"

Marcus's head snapped up. So much for not listening.

"—suspect Aubrey Weston, who is still at large despite increased Constabulary patrols in the area. Ms. Weston's parents were apprehended earlier this evening after they broke Constabulary prohibitions against aiding and abetting suspects. Her mother Sharon called Ms. Weston's cell phone to warn her after the suspect's four-month-old son was taken into protective custody from her mother's home. Aubrey Weston is described as five-foot-five, medium build, with long brown hair and hazel eyes, and was last seen wearing—"

"Marcus."

He glanced her way, but most of his attention remained on the radio.

"They arrested my parents."

He nodded. "Wait."

"Did you hear what they said, they *arrested* my—"

"—abandoned car has been recovered. She may be traveling on foot, hitchhiking, or possibly driving a stolen vehicle."

"Stolen vehicle? How dare they—" She quashed the rest of the tirade.

The news story moved on to legislative chaos in the state of Texas, an anticlimax after the exploits of a local escaped criminal. Marcus met her eyes.

"How could they arrest my parents? They're die-hard humanists. Mom only did what any mother would do."

He nodded.

"I was right. They're not giving Elliott back to them. They're keeping him. I knew they'd keep him." The food that had delighted her tongue moments ago now nauseated her by resting on the plate.

"Yeah," he said. "They'll keep him."

"That's it." Her legs propelled her toward the door without logic, without a plan, without anything but the knowledge of what kind of people had her son. *Father God, if You're still listening to me, please don't let them hurt him.* She could go to the Constabulary building she passed every day on her way to work, stake it out, determine the difficulty of entering undetected.

Marcus stood in her way before she'd gone five feet. "Sit down."

"You're part of this, aren't you? It's a new con-cop mind game, seeing if you can get people complacent enough to stay in jail as long as they don't know it's jail. No wonder you bought me three sweaters."

"You don't believe that."

"Prove me wrong. Let me leave."

"You weren't listening to everything."

She shut her eyes, though she should be shutting her ears.

"Aubrey. Look at me."

She obeyed the solidity in his voice. Honesty burned in his eyes.

"They didn't mention me. They still think you're on your own. They still think you're running."

"What about Elliott?"

"I said I'd get him back."

"You have no idea how to do it."

"I'll find out."

Aubrey's hands came up to curtain her face, and her body doubled over in defeat. She straightened and shuffled back to the table, groped for a chair, and capsized her glass of water. She lunged for it and missed. It rolled off the table's edge, kept rolling across the rug instead of breaking.

"Sorry."

"It's okay." Marcus picked up the glass and set it on the table.

"I'll get a towel." Aubrey crossed the kitchen to the multiple drawers and tugged them open—silverware, household tools, random junk. "What's wrong with you? Don't you put towels in a drawer like a normal person? Don't you do *anything* like a normal person?"

Marcus's voice came close behind her. "What?"

"You don't even have a roll of paper towels."

"Under the cabinet."

"Oh. Yeah." Right in front of her face.

Don't cry, don't cry, but the counter blurred, and the flood she'd kept dammed since this morning broke free. When she gulped away the last of the tears, the hard support of a wooden chair pushed against her back. Marcus had steered her to the table. She scrubbed her palms across her cheeks. Yesterday, she'd have cared that her makeup was long gone.

"Sorry," she said.

He stood over her, one hand on the back of the chair, and shrugged. "It's just water."

Her laughter fractured into a gulp against more tears. "Yeah."

The radio still droned from under a corner cabinet. "And now the latest on Constabulary suspect Aubrey Weston ..."

She couldn't help the sudden stiffness of her spine. Marcus strode across the kitchen and silenced the radio, then returned to her.

"You didn't eat much," he said.

"Well, gosh, I can't imagine why I wouldn't have an appetite right now."

He rubbed the back of his neck. "Yeah. Okay."

He resumed his seat across from her and twirled his fork in the cooling spaghetti. A minute passed while he ate and Aubrey matched stares with his dog. Clearly, Marcus had nothing else to say.

Aubrey fidgeted in her chair. "Are you expecting me to stay here? In your house? Indefinitely?"

"It's the safest place for you."

"What if I'd robbed you blind today and set your house on fire?"

He set down his fork and cocked his head. "Set my house on fire?"

"Not literally, I just— I don't understand you. We're strangers."

"We're family."

Um ... "What?"

Confusion furrowed between his eyes. "You know. Family. Christians."

Oh ... oh. Around her heart, a steel band cracked and fell away. Her sins weren't known here. No disownment. He stood up from the table and reached for her half-empty plate as well as his own, but she intercepted him. They didn't talk while they loaded the dishwasher.

"I've got some work to do," he said when the kitchen was clean. "But I'll get the bed ready first. When I'm woodworking, sometimes I lose track of time."

Sleep might be a wise attempt right now, though she might never achieve it again. But ... "Bed?"

"Sure. I sleep on the couch half the time anyway."

"Do you at least grab a pillow from somewhere?" And the couch didn't appear to pull into a sofa bed.

He shrugged. "Pillows screw up my neck."

Ten minutes later, the master bed was stripped, and Aubrey had helped him put on fresh sheets. The pillow he produced from a closet somewhere was flat as a rug, but he didn't seem to notice.

"If you need anything, I'll be in the basement."

"Thank you," she said, lost to other words.

"Good night." Indy followed him from the room.

Aubrey reached for the brand-new happy-yellow pajamas, but her hand froze halfway there. Lie here in this unfamiliar bed, in this dark, unfamiliar room? She'd never sleep. She left solitude behind and crept down the basement stairs.

Marcus stood behind an L-shaped workbench, head bent over his tools. Indy sat beside him, leaning her head on his leg. To his left sat a long natural-finish table, probably for a dining room. The wood was smooth and pale. Raw.

"Marcus?"

He looked up. "Everything okay?"

"Um, sure, I ..." Heat flooded her face. "I thought I'd watch you work, but if I'll be in the way ..."

His brow furrowed, but he shrugged. "No, it's okay. I'll be staining the table. The smell's kind of strong."

"That's fine. I just don't really feel like sleeping."

He nodded. Aubrey perched on the only seat available, what must have once been a barstool, legs cut off and reset to match the height of the workbench.

Marcus produced a blackened rag and a can of stain, and soon the stain left his fingertips as dark as the rag. He was left-handed. The knuckles of that hand bore old scars Aubrey didn't notice until she'd been watching his hands for several minutes. Broad and sure, they worked the stain into the wood, up and down, over the same section until he approved of the color.

"Marcus?"

"Yeah?" His hands didn't pause.

"Did you know them a long time—Jim and Karlyn?"

His hand faltered, then kept rubbing at the wood. "No. I'm still … Well, they all—Jim and Karlyn, and Janelle—they say I've got a lot to learn. About family."

Aubrey swallowed the ache Janelle's name brought. So Marcus was a new Christian. No wonder he still saw things like church family with such simple purity. He might accept Aubrey even if he knew everything. Not that she'd take the risk.

"I …" She shifted on the stool. Drowsiness was setting in. "Would you pray for them?"

Now his hand stilled. He looked up. "Out loud?"

She nodded. *I would, Marcus, but it needs to be someone God is definitely listening to.*

"I, um … I pray, but not …" His face reddened.

In any other circumstance, if anyone else was at stake, maybe she would back off. She lowered her voice. "Please?"

Marcus's fingers slackened around the stain rag. He stood back from the table and bowed his head. Maybe only half a minute passed, but it could have been an hour. Aubrey glared at her feet, tucked under the barstool's single rung. She shouldn't have asked. She didn't know him. Maybe he had a phobia of public speaking, and in his brain, this qualified.

"God," Marcus said.

The blush had seeped down his neck, all the way to the crew collar of his T-shirt. His fingers curled at his sides. Aubrey ducked her head before he could glance up and catch her staring.

"Jim and Karlyn." The pause didn't last as long this time. "They're Yours."

Yes. If God somehow still listened, her prayer would join Marcus's. Two or more, gathered together. *They belong to You, Father God.*

"Please keep them safe."

Don't let the con-cops use the MS to hurt Jim. Or to threaten him, or scare Karlyn. Don't let them break my friends, Jesus.

"Please bring them back to—to us, their family."

She'd done enough crying for one night, but tears dropped onto her folded hands. *Please.*

"Um. Amen."

By the time she wiped away the tears and dared to lift her head, Marcus had resumed working. His lips pressed together as if he didn't intend to speak again until next year. The motion of his hands quickened slightly. Agitation? But if God heard him and listened, Aubrey wasn't sorry. A minute stretched out, twisted tighter. Maybe she should go upstairs. She could sleep now, probably. His prayer had washed away the burning behind her eyes.

"Thanks," she whispered.

He looked up, his eyes a mirror. No tears, but a bleakness like the hole inside her. The Elliott-shaped hole. Marcus knew loss, too. But he was fighting back. An ally who didn't stand idle in the face of threats, who counted her as family. *Father God, did you send Marcus to get my baby back?*

16

"Can you say hello to Mr. Brenner?"

The boys stood side by side, size-ordered. Their sand-colored heads resembled a three-step staircase. The smallest one's attempt at Marcus's name sounded sort of Spanish. *Misto Bwenno.*

"I don't mind if they call me Marcus," he said.

"I do." Pamela Mayweather smiled. "This is J.R.—" she gestured to each of them, starting with the tallest—"Dirk, and Kyle."

"Hi," Marcus said.

"Hi, I'm five." J.R. left the lineup and poked at Marcus's toolbox. "You going to fix some stuff around here?"

"Yeah."

"Good, because when stuff don't work right, sometimes my mom says bad words."

Pamela's laughter hit the air with a splash. "Let me give you the tour of our problem areas, Marcus, before my son asks for a tour of your tools."

"I'll come, too." J.R. trotted behind them. The two toddlers wandered back to a plastic mat of black racetracks and blue rivers and green trees, dotted with one-piece plastic cars and spread over the living room carpet several yards from the real holiday tree. Revving engine noises burst from Dirk as he created a two-car collision in midair.

Most of the Mayweathers' home "issues," as Pamela called them, shouldn't require a handyman. Some people simply didn't make time to deal with things like this themselves. It was good for business. From realigning a closet door to replacing a few loose bathroom tiles that Jason had purchased months ago, Marcus would complete the whole job in maybe three hours.

Which was fine with him. Walking through a Constabulary agent's house hurt his neck. Even with a houseguest, he didn't need this job to pay the bills. Why had he agreed to work for Jason?

He tackled the bathroom first. His pads buffered between the cool, hard floor and his knees. He pried away the loose tiles that served as the room's baseboard.

"Whatcha doing?"

J.R. knelt at the threshold. His chin jutted out as he leaned forward to eye the two stacks of tiles, one worn and graying, one shiny and white.

"Putting in new tile," Marcus said.

"How come?"

"Because the old stuff was coming off."

"How come?"

"Because … it was old." Marcus peeled away the adhesive backing from the first tile and lined it up with the edge of the floor.

"I'm the oldest." J.R. stood and walked around Marcus to kneel on his other side, closer.

"That's good." What did you talk about with a five-year-old?

"I'm not a baby like Dirk and Kyle," J.R. said. "I go to kindergarten."

"Why're you home today?"

"Because I got sick, except I'm not really sick, except Mom says you got to treat people's kids how you want people to treat your kids, so she made me stay home. I just got a cough sometimes." His breath was warm in Marcus's face as he demonstrated. "See? And Mom says it's bad to cough on kids."

Not bad to cough on adults, though. Marcus's mouth twitched. He pressed the tile and held it.

"I'm glad," J.R. said. "You wouldn't be here when I was here, if I didn't get sick."

"That's true."

"Want to hear about my names? Mom told me yesterday I got lots of names. There's Ronan, and J.R., and Mayweather, and Jason. And sometimes people get mixed up and call me R.J. Then I tell them what's my real name."

"So you're named after your dad?"

J.R. crinkled his nose. "No. My name's *J.R.* Dad's name is *Dad.*"

"Oh," Marcus said.

Did you explain that kind of stuff to kids, or did you let them figure it out on their own? He couldn't remember how old he was when he watched the original *King Kong* and asked Mom why there were no colors. *"That movie was made a long time ago."* For the next few years, he believed color must be a recent addition to life.

He reached for another tile. J.R.'s spine rounded as he leaned closer to the floor to inspect Marcus's work. Finger and thumb of one hand pinched the middle knuckle of his other hand like a stress ball.

Marcus pressed another tile against the wall to meet the floor at a right angle.

"Is that a vein?" J.R.'s pudgy finger hovered an inch away from Marcus's left hand.

"Where?"

"On your hand, in the middle. Nana has one of them, on her arm, right here." He poked the crease of his own elbow. "But her vein's stuck out and purple. Your vein's skinny."

Oh, that. Marcus's hand flexed. The old vertical line over his middle knuckle stretched whiter. "It's not a vein."

"What is it, then?"

"A scar."

"Like from chicken pox?"

Not really. "Sort of."

J.R. jabbed at the mark. "Did you sort of get chicken pox?"

On Marcus's hands, nine years of work had recorded themselves in nicks and slices and scrapes, in the occasional stupid gash or concrete burn. But yeah, the knuckle scar stood out the most. The only one Marcus couldn't explain. *My best friend finally told me she was raped, years before I knew her. I couldn't stop hitting things. Including a porch beam.* Definitely not the way to talk to a five-year-old.

"J.R., are you being a pest?" Pamela's face popped into the doorway.

"No way, Mom." J.R. straightened and lifted his face to beam at her. "I'm talking to Mr. Brenner so he doesn't get bored."

"Mr. Brenner, is that true?"

"Yeah."

Pamela folded her arms. Shiny, pink nails tapped above her elbow. "Would you like to be bored for a little while?"

"It's okay," he said. "I don't mind kids."

"See, Mom?"

She smiled. "Don't touch any of Mr. Brenner's things, or get in his way."

"I know. You making bread today, like you said?"

"Yes, I am. And if Mr. Brenner tells you he'd like to be bored, you come play with your brothers."

"He won't want to be bored." J.R. hunched again to study Marcus's tools, hands behind his back. "He likes me already."

Over the next half hour, the yeasty aroma of baking joined the house-pervading scent of pine, and J.R.'s words pumped like a full-blast hose. His best friends at school were Mike and Mike, who didn't actually have the same name, since they were Mike O. and Mike S. His favorite thing to eat was pizza, after he'd picked off all the toppings but the ham, but he only got to eat it on "special days."

Probably a nutrition thing. Probably normal in a house where the mother baked bread from scratch rather than giving the kid her credit card and a collection of takeout menus. Well, Marcus probably hadn't been ordering dinner by kindergarten. More like second grade. A year before he learned how to work the washing machine.

Some people might question her skills as a mom, but she'd been a good one, overall. He'd learned to be responsible, not only for himself, but for her, too. And responsibility was a thing every man should learn, as soon as he was old enough to understand it.

Marcus shoved history away and focused on J.R.'s favorite toy, a Lego pirate ship that he set on the bathroom counter.

"Don't you have to go to work soon?" J.R. said after reciting his holiday wish list.

Marcus pressed the last tile in place. "I'm at work."

"No-o, you're at my house."

"Your dad's paying me to work for him. This is my job."

"You going to come every day now, since it's your job?"

Marcus leaned back on his heels and removed his kneepads. "I'll only be here today. Tomorrow I'll work at somebody else's house."

"You go to a different house every day?"

"Well, I stay till my work's done. I'll be done with your house today."

"My dad's a Constabulary agent." The word fell easily. J.R. must have heard it a thousand times.

"I know." Marcus stood and hoisted his toolbox. Next up, the closet door.

"Know what he does? It's real important. He stops people when they got hate stuffed in 'em, so they don't hurt no one. And he takes bad books away, and he takes the people to a place, and other people at the place teach 'em that hate's bad. You know hate's bad?"

Marcus fought to keep his balance in this conversation. "Yeah. I do."

"Me too, but guess what, some people don't know that. What're you called, Mr. Brenner?"

"Um, I'm a contractor."

"That's important, too," J.R. said. "If you didn't come, people's doors would keep getting stuck, and they'd keep saying bad words. Know what Mom calls me?"

Besides J.R. and all the rest?

"I'm her hoarder." J.R.'s grin showcased a dimple. "Know what that is? It means I'm good at finding stuff. I'll bring you some stuff I found, okay?"

"Okay. I'll be in your brothers' bedroom."

"You going to fix the door that won't shut?"

"Yeah."

J.R. nodded, suddenly somber. "That's the bad-words door."

Tiles and a door weren't the only issues with this house. Marcus washed his hands in the bathroom sink, and the water's reluctance to drain gave away a clogged trap. Halfway up the stairs, he bumped the banister and it wobbled. Hadn't anybody noticed this stuff?

The bedroom door couldn't possibly have been installed by a professional. The slope of it caught at the top of the frame when it was only three-quarters closed. Marcus had barely started to adjust it when J.R. blew into the room like a dwarf tornado.

"Here's some of my stuff! I keep it all hid, in different places. I even got some stuff buried outside, but don't tell Mom. I'll set it all out, and then you can look, okay?"

"Okay," Marcus said.

"Don't look yet, or I'll take it all back."

Marcus pawed through his toolbox for the electric screwdriver. These hinges would have to be reset. "I'm not looking."

"Okay!" J.R. said half a minute later. "Turn around and see my stuff."

Marcus turned. The shaggy green rug was littered. Two bird eggs and a nail file. The tail of some glass animal, probably a horse. A square yellow scrap torn carefully from a phone book. What looked like the back of an earring. And a photograph.

That wasn't what it looked like.

Yeah. It was. Marcus snatched it up.

"You like it? I call her the Red Face Lady," J.R. said.

His fingers threatened to crinkle the picture. A four-by-six glossy, not something printed from an Internet search. The girl's extinguished blue eyes seemed to look at something over Marcus's shoulder.

"Mr. Brenner! Where're you going with my picture?"

In the kitchen, Pamela stood over the counter, sleeves rolled up, hands and arms caked with flour. She added some to her dough and worked it in with the heels of her hands. "How's ev— Marcus?"

"J.R. gave me this." His voice was like wire.

Her face jumped in recognition before Marcus turned the photo toward her. She knew where it had come from, who this young woman was with her face half lifeless and half obscured in blood. A storm cloud rolled into Pamela's eyes as she snatched the picture from Marcus. Her thumbprint smeared the corner with flour.

"How did he get this?"

She posed her question to the air, not to Marcus. He couldn't have answered, anyway. What kind of people kept a photograph of a brutalized corpse?

J.R. jumped over the threshold of the kitchen and barreled into his mother. "Don't be mad, Mom, I just found her. She's the Red Face Lady."

"Where did you find her?"

"In Dad's office."

"J.R." Pamela set the photograph facedown on the granite counter and knelt to meet her son's eyes. "Did you go into Dad's desk?"

J.R. tucked his chin.

"We don't go into Dad's desk."

He balled up his hands and pushed them against his clenched eyes.

"If you do this again, you'll be in big trouble, Jason Ronan. You understand me?"

J.R. nodded.

"It's time to go play with Dirk and Kyle for a little while."

The boy dashed from the room. Pamela remained on her knees for a long moment, then stood. She turned back to her bread dough and thumped the heel of her hand against it.

Marcus took a step back. The yeasty smell soured at the back of his throat. Enemy territory. He should go back to work, collect his check, and get out of here. He shouldn't say another word that Pamela could construe as suspicious and report to her husband.

He rounded the counter to face her. "Who is she?"

Not *is*, though. *Was.* The sudden violence of the woman's death flashed in front of his eyes. And Jason kept a picture of that where his kid could find it.

"I don't know what you're thinking." Pamela pressed a thumb all the way through the dough to the countertop. "But it probably is as bad as you're thinking."

A trophy. One less dangerous Christian on the streets. *God, did he—?*

One hand ruffled her curls and left behind a streak of flour. "I'm sorry, Marcus. All I can say is that Jason has … plenty of incentive to take his work seriously. And hopefully the future is safer than the past because of him."

"Safer?"

"Obviously, he hasn't fully succeeded yet, but statistics show improvement." She shrugged and leaned her elbows on the counter.

She assumed Marcus was pro-Constabulary, of course. The sour taste crept into his mouth. How many more pictures did Jason have in his desk? Marcus had to search that office. Not to count the dead, but to protect the living. Jason must store information there, too, not only trophies.

Pamela straightened and stepped away from the counter. Understanding glittered in her green eyes. "It's upsetting, I know. I had this friend in college who called herself a Christian, and ... of course, back then, it was still legal. 'Freedom of religion.' Gosh, we were naive, weren't we? Less than a generation ago."

"Pamela, I—"

"But re-education is snowballing into a success. Maybe within my kids' lifetimes, you know? I hold onto that."

"Not everybody wants that." He'd be under arrest by the end of the day if he didn't shut up.

She dusted some more flour onto her hands and kneaded the dough, this time wearily. "You're right, unfortunately, but it doesn't matter. We'll look back at our generation and say, yeah, there was resistance for a while, but they were always going to fail."

She looked up at him and smiled.

Words would achieve nothing. Heck, she'd married a Constabulary agent. But that was okay. He didn't need words. He had actions.

"I'll get back to work," he said, and Pamela nodded. "Oh, and you've got a loose railing halfway up the stairs. It could come off."

She waved a dismissal. "I don't think so. It's been like that for a year."

He could argue, but that would require more words. He'd run out. He returned to the closet door and attacked the job while her voice ricocheted in his head. *Always going to fail.*

No, he wasn't.

He hadn't failed Aubrey.

Not yet.

He finished in an hour. He packed up his tools, left them in the bedroom, and slipped down a carpeted hallway to the only room that could be Jason's office. From the other side of the house, J.R. and his brothers reenacted a demolition derby with vrooming engines, screeching tires, and occasional shouts of, "Crash!" None of them would be sneaking up behind him. Or telling their mom what he was doing.

The French doors' decorative glass blurred the room behind them. He could make out a desk, a painting on the far wall. Nothing else.

If the Constabulary really was executing people, who would know? Not like re-education prisoners were allowed visitors. If you never saw someone again, you assumed they were choosing a life in custody over a denial of faith. But what if ...

His shoulders locked into a spasm. Jim. Karlyn. Frank. They could all be dead.

God, no. Please.

He had to know. He had to get more information, something on the other side of this door that would help him stop Jason. His hand gripped the door knob.

Locked.

What? How had J.R. gotten the picture? Pamela must have done this only minutes ago. The doors locked from inside, easy to pick with a paper clip. Too bad he didn't have one. Or enough time to find one. He tried the other door, as if Pamela might have overlooked it. Locked, too. He ran his hand along the door trim.

No key, only dust.

17

By six o'clock, the thirst had become an ache in his throat. He parked the truck and marched across the parking lot to the automatic doors and into the grocery store. A bar would have been more ceremonial, but he didn't care about ceremony. Anyway, the drive home passed this store first.

Almost nine years without a test of willpower. It was time.

He hadn't come in on the grocery side. He walked down the main aisle between the greeting cards and the baby clothes, cut across through the shoe department. He passed other shoppers but didn't see them. Didn't see much of anything but the hanging red signs marking the grocery aisles, overhead and across the store, flags on his horizon. Especially aisle 6. Liquor.

This was better than a bar. He couldn't order one drink here. He'd have to buy a bottle and pour one glass. Then he'd have to be strong enough to pour the rest out.

Call Lee.

He froze and almost got run over by a cart.

"Sorry," muttered the cart's owner, a spectacled kid in flannel pants and a beater shirt.

Call Lee.

What, did some part of him think he needed her permission? He didn't. He started to walk again. His throat closed around the thirst and held onto it. His hand dug into the worn pocket of his jeans, pulled out the phone, and dialed.

"Marcus?"

His mouth opened, but no words came.

"Marcus, are you there?"

"Yeah."

She waited, then, "Did you mean to call me?"

Not really. "I'm going to have a drink tonight. Then I'll come over to your house. For ice cream or something. And you can see that I had just one."

Yeah, this was a good plan. Should have done it a long time ago. His strides ate the distance to aisle 6. Soon, he'd hold the bottle in his hand. Ring it up. Drive home. Open it. Smell it and taste it.

"Marcus. Tell me where you are." Her tight voice hit him like an open hand to his chest, pushing him back.

No. He wanted this. One drink. "I'm at the store. I'm going to buy some whiskey."

"In your car? Or inside the store?"

"Lee, stop it. I didn't call you so you'd talk me out of it."

"Then you shouldn't have called me."

Good point. He closed the phone and shoved it back in his pocket.

Without her voice in his ear, he picked up his pace. He crossed another main aisle and entered the grocery section. Against his thigh, the phone buzzed. And buzzed. He let it.

Pick it up.

No, dang it. No.

Pick it up.

He pulled it out of his pocket and barked into it. "What."

"You need to listen to me and do what I tell you."

"I'm okay, Lee. This is good for me. A good test."

"Stop walking."

He halted at an end cap stocked with frozen pizza. "Okay, talk."

"How many days?"

"I don't need—"

"How. Many. Days?"

He rubbed the back of his neck, but the pain was somewhere else. "Eight years, ten months, sixteen days."

"True or false: you are an alcoholic."

His lungs shut down. He reached a hand to the frozen food case. "T-true."

A sigh bled over the line. "All right. True or false: when you're thirsty, you call me."

"True."

"Why do you call me?"

He should hang up. He was three aisles away from the goal. Did she think he was so pathetic he couldn't handle one drink? See, this is why he needed one. To prove to her. He was strong.

"Marcus."

"I ... I call you because ... because I'm an alcoholic."

"Yes." The tension still gripped her voice, but something new held it too. Something gentle. "You are."

"Lee." He turned his back to aisle 6. His whole body shook.

"You need to walk out of the store, immediately. Focus on the door and don't stop until you're through it."

He forced his feet to move. They were heavier now, as if he'd shifted from walking with the wind to walking against it.

"Marcus?"

"Yeah. I'm walking. Out. I'm getting out."

"Good. Then you're going to drive to my house, without stopping anywhere else."

A last setting sunbeam hit his face as he stepped through the doors. His feet weighed less. He reached his truck and started driving.

By the time he pulled into Lee's driveway, night had settled. She answered the door clad in a slate gray sweater and jeans. Fuzzy green house socks adorned her feet. She motioned him inside and locked the door behind him. Her eyes reflected the hint of blue in her shirt. They appraised him up and down, the way they probably scrutinized a trauma victim at work.

"Come into the kitchen," she said.

A tub of chocolate ice cream, squeeze bottles of fudge and caramel sauce, and two deep bowls cradling spoons sat at one end of the counter. Miniature bowls formed a flawless line across the island. Chocolate chips, Oreo crumbles, nuts ... everything but sprinkles, because she knew he wouldn't eat them.

"Where'd you ...?"

"The Kroger on the corner," she said. "I shop the way you drive."

"Lee."

"Marcus." Her mouth curved.

The mouth that would taste so right. He flattened the feelings before they could scrawl across his face for her to read. Lee. The things she gave him.

"Can you tell me what happened?" She pulled out the bar stools and motioned him to one, then perched on the other.

He let his body sink onto the stool, and everything hit again. He blinked against the images of Jim and Karlyn, shot or beaten or whatever had been done to that woman in the picture. A drink wouldn't fix anything, but ...

"Marcus, what happened tonight isn't ... typical, for you. Not anymore."

The belligerence. The pitching feeling in his chest, like he was tied to the top of a ship's mast in a storm, and the only way to hold on tight was to toast his own strength and down the glass. Lee had heard it all in his voice, no doubt. He bowed over the counter and held his head.

"I ... Lee ... I'm sorry." Heck, he hadn't hung up on her in years.

"I wasn't soliciting an apology. We need to know what triggered this."

"My family could be dead."

The silence hung between them, and he lifted his head. Lee's mouth drew down with confusion. In her mind, his family was already dead.

"Not Mom. I mean my church family. The ones that got arrested."

"Why do you think this?"

He stammered out the story. Lee listened without interruption, her eyes darkening at his description of the photo. While he talked, she put the ice cream back into the freezer, then sat on the counter across from him, feet dangling in her fuzzy socks.

When he finished, she laced her fingers and propped her chin on them. "This doesn't necessarily mean that agent killed her. We're not even certain she was a Christian."

"I know. But if ... and his wife, she was so ... and I can't ..." *I can't do anything.*

"I understand."

Well, he didn't. Nothing excused the thirst that still gouged his brain with need. And not for one drink, either. For the whole bottle. He went to the freezer and pulled out the ice cream.

One side of her mouth tilted up. "Yes, you need a construction project."

"You didn't get vanilla. For you."

She pushed off the counter and joined him at the line of topping bowls. "I'm having chocolate. Behold my boldness."

In this moment, anything was possible. Someday soon, her hand would reach across her space into his and hold on. She would stand in front of him, rest her hand on his chest, and decide it belonged there. She would let his arms wrap her up, his hands mold to the curve of her back, his chin rest in her hair.

He tucked them inside, the things he could have someday. He let himself lean on the things he had now.

18

Marcus's keys slid across the washing machine in a jangling dance. He washed his hands in the laundry room sink, scrubbing off the workday and only half-expecting Aubrey to come say hi. She didn't.

She'd actually waited up for him last night, expecting news of her baby. He shook his head. What would it be like if your child was held prisoner by your worst enemy? He shouldn't be frustrated, but she was so scared, so convinced of nonsense, yelling at him last night that her son's life could be in danger. Since seeing that picture yesterday, he understood better, but not even the Constabulary murdered four-month-old babies.

He shouldn't have shared his intention to get her son back. He'd raised her hopes too high, too fast. Her anger made sense. But lifting somebody from the Constabulary's grasp required a different blueprint than warning them of an impending arrest, especially when the somebody was a baby. And he also needed a reason to return to Jason's house and a way to search that office. If the Constabulary were murderers, he needed proof. And a plan of protection.

One way was obvious, for his church at least. They'd be meeting again next Tuesday night, but Marcus wouldn't be there. Couldn't be. What did a church do when someone became a criminal? Vote on whether to keep him? Surely they'd want him to stay away. But no matter what they wanted, he had to sever himself. He shoved away the sting of … loss.

They'd worry as they did last time. They'd pray he wasn't arrested. But the lack of his name on the news would reassure them. Maybe, eventually, they'd assume a loss of interest on his part and let him go. He had no other options.

He shut off the water and dried his hands on the threadbare towel looped over the faucet. "Hi," he said to Indy, who crossed the kitchen with him.

He halted in front of the fridge, and something cold zipped through him. He snapped up the folded sheet of paper scrawled with purple ink, and the magnet clattered onto the floor ahead of a ten- and one-dollar bill, held in the paper's fold. Aubrey's writing was relatively large, full of loops like shoelaces.

Dear Marcus,

First of all, I'm sorry for last night, for acting entitled. I certainly don't have any right to ask more of you.

Second, thank you. You gave me time and a safe place to forge a plan, and you did this at huge risk to yourself. You did more for me than most would do who have known me all my life. I don't think you realize how much courage you have.

Third, I want you to know why I'm leaving. I have a responsibility to my son, and I can finally see the way to fulfill that. If they have me, they have no more reason to hold those connected to me. You don't have to fear for yourself. I would never, ever reveal your role in these last two days.

Again, thank you. I'll never forget what you did for me.

God's blessings to you through Jesus.

Aubrey

P.S. I took the black coat in the closet. I know it was worth more than $11. I hope it was abandoned.

Marcus crushed the letter and hurled it to the floor. *"Don't fear for yourself?"* She was the one banging on their doors and begging to be let in. And what kind of idiocy convinced her they would release her child, whether they had her or not?

He had to stop her. He swiped the ball of paper from the floor and smoothed it out. He read the note twice more. No clues. She said she would exchange herself for her son. She did not say how she'd contact the Constabulary or where she'd go.

Marcus quickly searched the house. She'd left the Wal-Mart clothes and taken only her purse. And her phone.

The nearest Constabulary building inhabited the corner of Hall and Schoenherr, less than five miles away. She had to either walk there or call to have them come pick her up. They probably already had her. An image struck him—blood on her face, her eyes staring over his shoulder, lifeless.

No.

He scooped up his keys, grabbed a hat, and dashed back out to his truck.

19

This must be one expensive coat. Aubrey's legs were chilled Jell-O, but her arms and torso felt as warm as the indoors. Her brisk stride down the sidewalk kept her legs and her bravery from buckling. She dialed the purple numbers she'd penned across her palm.

"Hello."

"Is Jeff Young there, please?"

"Speaking."

I can't do it, I'm going to hang up. Her teeth dug into her lip. "Agent Young, this is Aubrey Weston."

In his silence, cars rushed by on the busy road to her right. A horn beeped, more greeting than annoyance. Now he knew she was near a road. Then again, his knowledge of her whereabouts no longer mattered. She kept walking, squinting into the sunset.

His throat cleared. "What can I do for you, Aubrey?"

"I want to make a deal."

"How'd you get this number?"

If she told him, Mary-Beth could be charged with giving out confidential patient information, not only to someone who no longer worked at the office, but also to someone on the con-cops' most wanted list. "I want to turn myself in, but I have conditions."

"You've got my attention."

"Did you release my parents?"

"You know, I've got to hand it to you, however you got my cell number. I can't trace your location."

A gray-haired man jogged past, wearing an orange sweatshirt and blue workout shorts. Ear buds bobbed around his neck. Aubrey returned his wave and let the distance spread between them for a moment.

"If you still have them, let them go, and release my son into their custody."

The jogger never glanced back. Her hand trembled at Agent Young's silence. His voice finally came, nearly bored. "It's sort of interesting, your hostage-negotiation approach."

"I'm the one you want," she said. "They have nothing to do with this."

"You're very sure about that."

"Philosophically speaking, they're on your side. And you know that. You've already talked to them."

"Where are you?" he said.

"Headed for the Constabulary admini—" Why had she told him that? "Are you saying it's a deal?"

"Three for one? I think I'm getting the short end here, speaking as a kidnapper."

Seemingly someone else's nerve pushed words out of her mouth. "I'm sorry, I guess I'm wasting your time, then."

"No." His voice nipped the word like a snap of fingers. "You want this, then I'll make it happen."

"You have to call them, the building on Hall Road, make sure they know we have a deal."

"I'll be there personally."

"Okay. Me, too." She closed the phone with a snap that made her jump.

A shiver wrapped around her, unconnected to the weather. She tried to square her shoulders, to thank God for this plan. Elliott would be free of them. Not free of their philosophies—his grandparents would try to raise him with a "safe," legal belief system—but free of them. She would let some cannibalistic jungle tribe raise her son before she let the con-cops keep him one more day.

She couldn't think about what they would do to her, or she might stop walking. She tried to pray.

A few miles from the intersection where the Constabulary building lurked like a sleeping dragon, the traffic thickened and slowed. Several con-cop vehicles poured themselves down the street, mired in the congealed soup of cars, trucks, vans, and SUVs.

Would one of them recognize her? Her lungs skipped a breath. They might arrest her before she could reach Agent Young. But even if they did, that wouldn't negate the deal. She intended to be arrested. Which agent got to her first made no difference.

"Aubrey."

Her gasp sucked in an extra dose of the cold air, and her body spun to face the voice.

Oh no.

Marcus.

From under the bill of a black cap, his gaze scorched her to the sidewalk. She couldn't move, even when he broke eye contact to scan the traffic. What was he doing?

"My truck's parked a block over."

"You've got to be kidding," she said.

"Come on."

"Back to your house?"

His glare said that was the stupidest question she'd asked since they'd met. "Your son goes to state foster care whether they've got you or not."

"He gave his word." Oh, brilliant, give away more information.

Marcus's eyes shot from their surroundings back to her with fresh sharpness. "Who did you call?"

"Did you even read the note? I'm done complicating your life."

"On your cell? Is it still on?"

Why had God let him find her? She tried to walk away. His hand clamped onto her wrist. She jerked her arm, but he didn't let go.

"You," he said, too close to her, "are making a scene."

"*I'm* making a—? If you don't let me go in three seconds, I scream."

"This isn't the way."

"Two ..." His fingers relaxed, and she stepped back. "Go home, please."

She might as well hurl words at a brick wall.

"They *want* kids," he said.

"He told me he'd honor the deal."

"They told the media Jim attacked them."

"And you said you'd get Elliott back." *And you obviously did nothing yesterday to keep your word, stumbling home at two in the morning after an evening with your girlfriend.* The homemade soup he'd brought back gave him away.

His knuckles dug into his neck, below his skull. "Aubrey. Think. They're rebuilding everything. The future. They won't trade a kid. And the government doesn't make deals with terrorists. Or with Christians."

She shut her eyes.

"He's looking at you."

Her glance couldn't help itself. A con-cop car crept toward them, hindered by traffic, no different from the others that had passed ... except for Aubrey's millisecond of eye contact with the agent driving it. He glanced down to the likely location of a computer console.

"Maybe he'll arrest me right now, and I won't have to walk another three miles," she said.

The muscles in Marcus's face drew tighter. If not for the parade of drive-by witnesses, he'd probably haul her back to his truck. The con-cop car inched forward another several feet. The agent inside still watched her. Now his lips moved.

Maybe Marcus was right.

If he was, she'd be offering herself up on an altar of futility, throwing away her real chance at freedom for both her and Elliott.

"I leave my work at the office," Young had said, which made the timing of the Constabulary's pursuit one mammoth coincidence. Or it made him a liar.

And that made Marcus right. Marcus, who stood here on an open sidewalk beside a wanted woman and didn't flinch. She stared at him, and he stared back, his feet rooted miles beyond that line in the sand.

She stepped forward and linked her arm to his. They'd act like a couple. It had worked in the store parking lot. He shifted to block her from the con-cop's sight.

Father God, if I'm making a mistake here, will You show me?

No nudge, no voice. Aubrey walked beside him, her hand nestled in the warm corner of his arm. After only a few steps, his body stiffened, and a quiet breath hissed through his teeth.

"Marcus?"

"Walk." He steered her left, down a side street.

She obeyed in silence, but something was wrong with him.

20

Who else would have recognized the momentary pain for what it was? Marcus maintained an even stride. But this sidewalk stroll was a ridiculous ruse. Any moment now, a car door would slam behind him. A sidearm magazine would *click-click* into readiness. Somebody would yell, "Freeze!"

His truck sat waiting a hundred feet away. "Turn off your phone."

Aubrey did what he said for once, but this was futile. All of it. He could break into a run, carjack a dragster, stow away in the landing gear of a plane … and he would never, for a single second, be hiding.

Instinct commandeered action. He thrust Aubrey into the truck and found himself behind the wheel, maneuvering through traffic. He had to put some distance between himself and the enemy. But distance was all he could achieve now. He wasn't invisible anymore.

The intention must have been to tag Aubrey. Did the Constabulary use some kind of dart gun? Marcus had blocked the agent's line of sight at the last moment, so they had to know their target was foiled. Maybe they'd planned to wait and watch her, but now they'd probably move faster. They'd also rush to identify Marcus, but he was likely still nobody for the moment.

A pinching soreness gnawed the right side of his back, below his shoulder. His hands choked the wheel. The Constabulary hadn't cuffed him and shoved him into a patrol car. They had latched onto him instead, and now they lurked here, in his own truck, under his own skin.

Last day.

Not yet, God.

"Are we going back to your house?"

Aubrey. He had to think of her, not just himself. "No."

"Not now? Or not at all?"

"I don't know yet." He'd never seen a tracker, but he tried to picture it—like a bullet lodged in his back, silently screaming to the Constabulary, reporting every inch he drove. He had to get it out. Now.

21

By the time Marcus merged onto the highway, hands firm on the wheel, gaze sweeping, Aubrey *wanted* the silence to snap. If it didn't soon, every rigid line of his body would break instead.

"Where are we going?" she said.

The quiet continued to coat them. Marcus didn't glance at her until he took a tight loop of an exit, switched on the high-beams, and came out on a wide rural road heading north. He jerked the truck to the gravel shoulder without brake or blinker, then skidded to a stop and jammed the gear shift upward.

"What're you doing?" Aubrey said.

"That coat'll keep you warm. And here." He pulled a pair of black ski gloves from the glove box.

"You're leaving me in the middle of nowhere, in the dark?"

"In case they catch up."

"But I'm the one they're after."

"Get out. Now. I'll come back if I can."

"I'm not going anywhere until you explain yourself."

His glare nearly scalded her into taking those words back. "There's a tracking ... thing. In my back."

Trackers were real, then. She'd thought him paranoid when he mentioned them days ago. So at some point while they were walking, he'd been shot. He might be bleeding.

"Now," he said.

She wrapped her arms around her middle, fingers clutching at the filched jacket. "What're you going to do?"

"Aubrey, get out of the truck."

With every argument, the con-cops drew closer. She should listen to him, get out and get away from that awful thing ... in his back. While he scowled at the danger to Aubrey. Her heels dug into the truck mat. "You might need help."

"You want me to drag you outside?"

Aubrey's hand curled around the door grip. "You want to waste time trying?"

His mouth tightened till the narrow line of his lips disappeared.

"I know it's a switch, but you're stuck with me for now."

"I don't need help."

"Shut up and drive, Marcus."

He threw the truck back in Drive. Gravel shot up behind the tires. About ten minutes later, he turned onto a dirt road, which led to another dirt road, which led to another one. The truck jostled them at fifty-five miles an hour, and he made no attempt to miss washed-out dips or outright holes. Aubrey's hold on the door grip was no longer a show of stubbornness.

About the time she contemplated asking him to pull over and let her throw up, Marcus turned onto a new road, slimmer than the last one, newer, or maybe less traveled. She never thought she'd consider anything made of gravel a smooth ride, but at least this was level. Wait a minute. ... This wasn't a road. It was a driveway.

Marcus parked the truck behind a farmhouse whose wood siding had warped and peeled. The back porch drooped in the middle, and spider webs had replaced the glass in the door, woven into the spaces as if to ward off intrusion.

He took the cap off, dug a flashlight and cigarette lighter from the glove box. "Got a mirror?"

"Um, yeah. A little one."

"I need it."

She dug the square cosmetic mirror from her purse, and he snatched it from her hand.

"Just the one?"

"Yeah. ... What're you going to do with it?"

He reached past her and wrenched off the sun visor with a *snap*. "Come on."

Aubrey shadowed him up the weathered steps but hesitated at the deck itself. The far left section had rotted and collapsed.

"It's stable. Just don't walk over there." Each word wielded a spike of impatience. He jerked a nod toward the missing boards.

Aubrey tried to step forward without her full weight, then settled for placing her feet as close as possible to where he'd placed his. Marcus used body weight to turn the rusted doorknob. Inside, his flashlight beam punctured the darkness. The place was bare of furniture, but not of cats. A white-chested tabby and a bony calico blinked with green-glowing eyes and didn't bother to flee.

Only Marcus's silhouette was visible between Aubrey and the flashlight beam as he shifted it from one hand to the other and removed his jacket and shirt. He pulled out his keys and worked the Swiss army knife from the ring.

Surely he wasn't planning what she thought. "You can't."

Marcus barely spared her a glance. "Here. Hold the light in your mouth, and tilt the mirrors so I can see."

"Marcus, you can't."

He yanked open the blade, and it gleamed silver in the flashlight beam. A blue flame clicked to life in his other hand. He submerged the edge of the knife in the flicker, glided it up and down until he was satisfied.

"There has to be another way to do this," Aubrey said.

Marcus knelt on the pale tile floor and held the now blackened knife away from him so only air would touch it. "Find the place it went in. Point one mirror at it, and the other one at me. I'll tell you when I can see."

"Maybe I should do it."

"No."

The floor gnashed cold and hard against Aubrey's knees, and she clamped her teeth around the flashlight end. Dried blood smudged his right side, between two ribs, under the sturdy wing of his shoulder. After a minute of tilting the mirrors first one way, then another, Marcus finally nodded.

"Good. Don't move."

His back arched slightly, and his left hand reached across to press the sharp edge of the blade against his skin. The knife drew a reluctant red drip.

"See it? The tracker?"

"Uh ..." she said around the flashlight. What would it look like? Surely she couldn't miss it. But the slice in his skin revealed no secrets. "Uh-uh."

The knife pressed harder this time. His breathing amplified, and the flow of blood grew steady.

This wasn't a good idea. Blood without gloves, without bandages.

"Aubrey. Hold still."

He angled the point of the knife, not the edge, toward the slice in his back.

"Wait," she said, but the tip sank in.

His hand shook and dragged the knife in a dip between his ribs, then upward and out. A growl shoved through his teeth. Something clinked onto the floor. Marcus's hand skimmed the tile as Aubrey angled the flashlight downward.

"Here," she said. Tiny nettles projected from the surface of a piece of bloody silver.

Marcus took it, rolled it around his palm. "Where's my shirt?"

Aubrey swung the flashlight toward him and gasped. "Marcus, you're bleeding."

"I'm okay."

"No, I mean you're bleeding a lot. Oh, God, help." Spotless white bone. It had to be a rib. Marcus flinched as she pressed the shirt to the wound. Warmth oozed against her hand.

He pulled away. "Not now."

"You should've let me do it! You couldn't see well enough. Why didn't you let me help you?"

"Aubrey." He took the shirt from her quaking hands and stood. "We have to go."

"Right. To get you some help."

Marcus struggled a moment to raise his right arm but soon got the soiled shirt over his head and shoved his arms into the sleeves. "This thing needs to keep moving."

The tracker. As long as it traveled, the con-cops would chase it. A purring tabby sneaked into the flashlight's circle, or maybe it had been standing there for a while.

"The cat," Aubrey said.

Marcus looked down at it, his forehead creased with a frown.

"It has a collar."

"Oh," he said and crouched, one hand shooting out. The cat skipped backward into the darkness with a hiss. Aubrey aimed the flashlight and joined the chase. If it escaped the house, they'd never find it. After a few minutes, they managed to block it into a corner. Aubrey hoisted it up in one hand, and stinging claws gouged her arm.

"Got any gum?" Marcus said.

"There's some in my purse, in the truck. I'll be right back."

While she chewed two minty sticks into a moist blob, Marcus's knife dug a depression inside the leather collar. He stuck the silver ball into it, then sealed it with the gum.

"That animal will be cleaning itself for a year," Aubrey said.

"Here." He all but shoved it at her. "Hold onto it."

They left nothing in the house but a few drops of blood, which Aubrey tried to scuff away with her shoe but merely smudged across the tile. Back in the truck, Marcus took the road at an uncomfortable but less lethal speed. Aubrey released the cat onto the seat between them, and it clung with panicked claws. Marcus turned off his phone and turned on the radio.

"How'd you know about that place?" Aubrey said when the weather report began.

"I've got some clients that live farther down the road. I noticed the house, and it looked vacant, so I walked around the property a little. Old houses are better. More brick and wood and … Anyway, it's been open for the last couple months. There's nothing inside, but still, whoever owns it should lock it up."

Had Marcus ever used so many words at once? "So was this a one-time thing? Or are you a pathological trespasser?"

His mouth quirked. "Well, we had a picnic on the porch. Me and Lee. We were out driving and I wanted to show it to her, and then we realized, why not eat right here?"

Aubrey laughed. "Sure, why not."

He might have kept talking if not for the radio. "In local news, the fugitive who MPC agents nearly apprehended earlier this week may not have gone as far as they thought. Aubrey Weston was spotted on foot this evening, south of the M-59 expressway. An anonymous source speculates she may be aided by an unidentified man. Details are sketchy at this time, including the description of this possible accomplice—Caucasian male, medium height."

"Accomplice," Aubrey said. "Like we robbed a bank or something."

Marcus's scowl was louder than words.

"On the bright side, they haven't ID'd you. We can go to a hospital and get you stitched up."

"No."

"Don't worry, I'll stay in the car. You can check yourself in. We'll have a story put together by the time you get there."

"No hospital," Marcus said, refusing Aubrey even a glance.

Too many people? "Fine. One of those walk-in clinics, then."

"I'm okay."

"I saw your rib cage, Marcus. You're not going to magically stop bleeding."

He wrenched the truck to the shoulder and braked. "Open your door."

"You think I'll get out now, while you're all sliced open?"

"Aubrey. Let the cat out."

"Oh," she said. The moment her door swung outward, the cat streaked over her lap and outside. It disappeared from the headlights' range in seconds. When she slammed the door, Marcus resumed driving. The minutes dragged along. Five, now ten, now twelve, now twenty-three. The high-beam headlights bounced off a deer's luminous eyes, but the truck maintained its speed. The dirt road bent and straightened and collided with its narrower cousins. The dark stain on Marcus's jacket crept outward.

"Marcus," she said, when biting her tongue one more time might amputate it.

No reply, no glance. She was as acknowledged as the beaten, dusty floor mats.

"You're staining the back of the seat."

A sigh leaked from his lips. "Check under your seat."

"For what?"

"A rag. Or something."

Now he told her? She scrounged behind her feet, and the borrowed coat pulled tight across her shoulders. Her fingers found … well, something, but to call it a rag was flattery. The tattered cloth had mopped up a lot in its lifetime, including grease, sawdust, and was that wood stain?

Marcus reached for it.

"You can't put this on a wound. It'll get infected."

"I'm not. Give it to me."

She surrendered the thing that had probably been white about five years ago. Marcus jammed it between the seat and his jacket, both of which appeared slick with moisture. Germs could still find their way from the cloth to the gash on his back.

Twenty silent minutes later, he nodded at the floor. "Get down. So nobody sees you. I have to stop at the next light."

"Stop for what?"

"Gas."

Was now really the time for this? She glanced at the gas gauge. Low fuel.

No way. What if they'd run out, on some dirt road in the dark? She released her seat belt with a click and crouched between the seat and the dashboard, knees to her chest. Minutes later, Marcus pulled up to pump 8, the furthest from the store's windows. He pulled out a credit card, new and shiny.

"Shouldn't you pay cash?" Aubrey said.

"If they haven't ID'd me, the credit card's safer than being seen inside. They might have a sketch on the news by now."

"And if they *have* ID'd you?"

He shrugged. "It won't matter."

True. They'd be screwed regardless of how he paid. "You can't go out there. Your jacket's too bloody now, and your shirt has to be worse."

Marcus twisted to look. "It's dark. Nobody'll see from a distance."

"You'll be standing under very bright lights."

"I mean the jacket. And I can't sit here talking to myself." He half glared, then got out of the truck.

His face had paled in stages as he drove. Right now, he was about the shade of cheap copy paper. Without medical help, sooner or later, he'd drive them off the road. Calling 911 was out. She couldn't slide into the driver's seat and refuse to move, either. She couldn't even sit up. And trying to talk some common sense into him would be as effective as singing to Elliott. If she'd ascertained anything about Marcus, it was that he listened to no one.

Except.

Her hand snaked upward to the cup holder, and her fingers curled around his cell phone. Lee. The woman had named his dog. He would listen to her.

22

The back of Marcus's head was barely visible from Aubrey's handicapped vantage point. She monitored his position as the phone powered up to brighten her little nook against the passenger door.

Contact list. She typed an L. Surely Marcus's list was as prosaic as he was. If it resembled Mary-Beth's—"Dumpling" for her boyfriend and "Random Chick" for her sister—Aubrey's scheme was sunk.

One L. *Thank You, God, thank You, thank You.* Lee.

The line rang twice, followed by a calm voice. "Marcus."

"Um, no, but don't hang up, I'm, um, a friend." No click, no dial tone. A good sign. "This is Lee?"

"Yes. Is he hurt?"

"He won't go to the hospital, and I'm hoping you can talk some sense into him before he passes out."

"Can you describe the injury?" No panic. No reaction at all, really. At least she wasn't one of those stereotypically dramatic women.

"There's a gash in his back. It's bleeding. I need you to tell him to swallow his pride and get some stitches."

"How long has he been bleeding?"

"Look, Lee, let me give him the phone, and you—"

"I'm a nurse. How long?"

A nurse. Oh, that man needed his neck wrung. "Almost an hour."

"Give him the phone."

Marcus shifted from Aubrey's line of sight and withdrew the pump nozzle with a muffled *thunk*. Seconds later, the gas cap clicked.

"Just a second," Aubrey said. "He's coming."

Marcus ambled to the front of the truck as if his back weren't sliced to the bone. The driver's door opened.

The cell phone was some kind of magnet. His eyes jumped there with uncanny immediacy. Then they ignited. "What—"

She deposited the phone into the cup holder without closing it. "It's for you."

Marcus leaned inside, snatched it up, and snapped it shut, then pulled himself into the truck and lost another degree of color. He started the truck and pulled into traffic. For the moment, he was too angry to faint. That didn't make him okay. Aubrey reached for the phone.

He grabbed it first. "It was off."

"I turned it on."

"What were you thinking?"

She propelled herself back into the seat to face him at eye level. "I was thinking of the one person I could come up with that might get you to listen to reason, and I find out she's a nurse. You're bleeding all over the place, and she's a *nurse*. You complete, absolute, utter idiot!"

Marcus's eyes forgot the road in front of him. They stared at her, blazing with disbelief and something else. The phone display lit up, and his hand convulsed around it. Incoming call.

"No," he said.

"What did you expect me to do?" She tried to gentle the words, but they still grated. "This is stupid, Marcus, it's completely stupid."

"She's not—" His words were crushed by the clench of his jaw. "Not supposed to—"

"To know what you're doing, helping fugitives? She doesn't. I asked her to talk you into getting some stitches. That's all."

The phone vibrated in his hand. If his teeth gritted any harder, they would crack.

"Pull over and talk to her."

"Shut up." The phone darkened. "Did you tell her where we are?"

"Of course not."

The truck veered into the next parking lot and jerked to a stop outside the spread of the lights, away from the lighted sign: Dr. Ralph Walton, DDS. Brightening Smiles since 1999.

Marcus left the truck running and bent to scoop up the phone. He opened it and dialed, and Aubrey didn't try to withhold her relieved sigh.

"Don't go to the house, I'm not there," he said, then listened. "No … Leave. Right now."

In the pause, Marcus's forehead furrowed, smoothed in comprehension, and then crinkled up again. His shoulders buckled. Lee said something that started with his name, and he closed his eyes. Aubrey huddled on the floor and hugged her knees, suddenly no longer inclined to glare at him.

"Lee, no," he said. "Go home."

Again, silence, and Aubrey could read this one. Refusal.

Marcus's teeth refused to unlock for a long moment. When they did, they released a growling sigh. He closed the phone, dropped it into the cup holder without bothering to turn it off, and pulled out onto the road. If he was going to meet Lee, then mission accomplished. But given the resentment that radiated toward Aubrey from the taut lines of his body, from the sharp edges of his face, maybe she should have considered the mission's cost.

23

The last thing he'd told Aubrey was to shut up, and she actually listened to him for about twenty minutes, while he drove as fast as he dared toward home. If he didn't come, Lee wouldn't go. Stupid ultimatum. The Constabulary might identify him, might show up at his house. Failing to report his criminal activities—and obviously from their conversation, she knew about them—made her a criminal too.

The traffic light traded green for yellow. He should brake. He accelerated. *God, You can't let them take her.*

"Marcus?" Aubrey's voice quavered. "Look, if you want to yell at me, go ahead."

He didn't want to yell. He wanted a punching bag.

"Would you say something, please?"

He never should have left the phone in the truck. He never should have told Aubrey that Lee existed.

The glowing yellow lines on the road blurred past. He ought to slow down before a cop pulled him over, but he couldn't. His neighborhood finally came into view over a little hill in the road, and he jerked a nod toward the floor. Aubrey crouched down a minute before he made the right turn into his subdivision. The truck cab seemed to shrink. They could be watching.

If they were, they'd found camouflage somewhere he couldn't imagine. Lee was right. They didn't know him. He was a profile masked by a baseball hat, not a name, not even a face.

Lee's silver car sat in his driveway, unhidden and unsafe. Marcus pulled past it and lowered the garage door again before shutting off the truck. Aubrey sat up.

"No," he said.

"What?"

"Stay."

She blinked, and her lips froze, half parted to argue.

"Lee hasn't seen you. The less she knows, the safer she is."

"Sure you don't want me to start walking now?"

"No," he said, and Aubrey slumped against the door of the truck. Oh. That could be taken two ways. "I want you to stay here. Till she's gone."

After a searching pause, she sighed. "Okay."

Marcus nodded and left the truck, then let himself into the house. Indy met him at the door with dancing. Lee met him in the kitchen with a frown. Her eyes found the stain on his jacket in seconds, but she was looking for it. Marcus matched her scowl. Aubrey had probably told her he was bleeding to death.

"Remove the jacket," Lee said.

Yeah, nurse mode. She wouldn't leave or relax until she'd examined his "wound." Okay, fine. Marcus brought his hands behind his back and tugged the sleeves down, trying not to move his right arm.

"Come sit." Lee's strides flowed toward the table with customary poise.

Her eyebrows arched when he didn't argue. On rubber legs, he crossed to the closest chair and sank into it sideways, giving Lee a clear view of his back.

His green tackle box squatted on the table. Lee had found the box buried in his garage almost a decade ago, verified he wasn't using it, and filled it with first aid supplies, then stowed it under his bathroom sink.

"You criticize my movie collection, while you have nothing to treat injuries but a random Band-Aid. Which collection is more vital?"

Blood had slicked the shirt to his back. His right arm wouldn't lift high enough to shed it. Lee's cool fingers wrapped above his wrist, and his pulse leaped. *Get a grip.* He was her patient right now, not her friend. Definitely not more than her friend. She raised his arm above his head. The spurt of fresh pain restored his ability to think.

Lee eased the fabric from his back and then, before he could try himself, stripped the shirt off over his head. By the time his vision cleared the fabric, she stood behind him again. He swiveled on the chair to face her.

"See, I'm okay."

Lee's eyes darted up to his, then away. "Yes, I see."

Uncomfortable? That didn't make sense. In the ER, she saw things like gunshot wounds and car accident victims. And she'd patched him up a few times, mild work injuries mostly, but this one wasn't much worse. He barely heard her clear her throat before facing him again, cold detachment in the line of her mouth, but something else in her eyes.

Something not cold at all.

"You're still bleeding. Turn around." But her gaze slipped from his face. Down. To his chest.

Whoa.

She'd already regained focus. "Marcus, please."

He took the shirt from her hands. She glared.

Kiss her.

No. However she'd been looking at him, this was Lee. Touch had meaning—they both agreed on that—and she didn't want what it meant. Did she? If she'd changed her mind, wouldn't she tell him?

If she leaned a single inch toward him, he would …

She sighed almost without a sound. The flicker between them went out. She walked behind him, he dropped the shirt onto the floor, and Indy poked her nose at it.

An icy liquid was sponged over his back, and then something sterile crushed against the cut. He bit the side of his mouth. No wincing allowed.

"This is self-inflicted, I assume with your knife. Did you remove a tracker?"

"Wh … at?"

"And where is Aubrey? Waiting for me to leave?"

What? No. "Aubrey?"

"Weston."

"The fugitive on the news?"

"Marcus. She called me with your phone."

But Aubrey said she never used her name. "How …?"

"I know you. The pieces weren't difficult to put together. And you hardly allayed my suspicion by turning off your phone."

"What pieces?" He tried to rise.

The gauze shifted as one of Lee's hands weighted his shoulder. "Relax."

He replayed the news story in his head. "They said it was a white guy, that's all they said."

"Medium height. An overwhelming giveaway."

"Come on." He glanced over his shoulder in time to catch the curve of her mouth.

Silence draped them as she cleaned the wound with something that made his eyes water. Then came the burning pull of the skin as she drew the sides of the slice together. After three butterfly bandages, Lee stepped around to face him.

"Water, or fruit juice, especially if you feel shaky. No caffeine."

"I'm—"

"Yes, you will be fine. I don't believe you would have passed out. But you need to be hydrated for twelve hours, at least. Coffee won't help."

He checked his watch. He had to last until 11:26 tomorrow morning. "Okay."

She stepped nearer, and he breathed the herbal scent of her shampoo. "Where are you planning to take her?"

"Don't know yet."

Lee stilled. Her eyes combed the room and beyond it, down the hall, as if she expected Aubrey to lurk in a corner somewhere. "How long will she stay?"

Marcus half shrugged. No way to guess.

"Is she the only fugitive you've sheltered?"

"Yeah."

"The only one you've aided in any way?"

He turned his head, as if silence and breaking eye contact could conceal anything. Besides, according to the "passive accomplice" law, Lee was as guilty for failing to report Aubrey as she would be for failing to report a dozen more fugitives. Still, on principle, his jaw refused to unlock.

Lee shoved the rest of the gauze package into the first aid case and shut the lid. "Don't attempt to change the dressing. I'll do that."

"Okay. Please go home."

The nurse's look raked from his eyes to his feet and back again, no pause, followed by a nod. But he hadn't imagined the heat from before. She latched the supply case and headed back to the bathroom.

"I can put the stuff away," Marcus said.

"So can I."

He followed, then shifted his path to block her from the bathroom. The plastic sides of the case pressed his palms. Lee would let go. But his pull was rougher than it should have been. She didn't have time to release the handle, was tugged forward three steps. The giant bubble she maintained between them punctured with a silent *bang* that resounded through Marcus's chest and downward. Lee's body jostled against the case, and the case bumped against his chest. Surprise parted her lips, turned her for one brief, lingering moment into a frosty-eyed sculpture.

If he dropped the case, he could touch her. His fingers loosened.

She stepped back.

The plastic box crashed to the floor and sprang open. Out gushed bandages and gauze and medical tape and little scissors and tubes of medicine. Lee knelt, righted the box, scooped handfuls of things back inside. Her back curved over the tackle box. Her thighs and calves made an acute angle.

"Lee," Marcus said.

She sorted the tape and bandages into the different compartments.

Marcus squatted in front of her and thwacked one hand against the tray she'd set into the top of the box. Her hands leaped back into her lap. Her eyes met his.

"Go," he said. "Now. They could come. Any minute."

She nodded and rose and headed for the front door, like any innocent guest. Like any friend whose body did not cause a throb of delight and desire as it moved away.

24

Aubrey sat in a hard chair, in a sparse room with a long window. People stood on the other side of that window, people she couldn't see, people in gray uniforms, like the agent who rounded the table between them and leaned over her. The scent of his cinnamon gum turned her stomach. She tried not to cower against the back of the chair.

"Let me level with you," he said. "The pregnancy hasn't helped our cause. If anything, I think it's given you a boost of courage. Not sure how that works."

He took hold of her hand, the one pressed against her belly, and tried to pull it away. Aubrey pressed harder, gritted her teeth with the effort as he began to pry her fingers off, one at a time. She gripped the curve of her belly so hard that the baby shifted in protest. Then the agent's stronger fingers slid beneath the palm of her hand and forced it away, grabbed and didn't release it.

Aubrey met his eyes and settled her other hand over her belly instead.

After a brief battle, he held both of her wrists in a painful grip, pinned to her sides.

"The pregnancy's over, as of today."

Her sleep-deprived brain couldn't follow. He didn't make sense. She wasn't due for three and a half months.

"Someone will be coming to transfer you. After the procedure, you'll come back here, and we'll talk again."

The procedure? No. Oh, no, no, no.

"Yes," he said. "Unless you want to answer my question correctly."

"I'm a Christian," she screamed into his face.

"Then you won't be a mother."

"Please!"

"Which would you rather be?"

∘⦂∘ ∘⦂∘ ∘⦂∘

Air rushed into her lungs, and darkness cloaked the room around her. She lay, coverless, on Marcus's bed. The pillow rested beside her. Her body quaked.

"Aubrey."

The voice startled a cry from her sore throat. She wrapped the pillow in her arms. "Elliott."

Marcus's weight shifted the mattress. "Are you okay?"

"My baby, my baby."

His hand lighted on her shoulder.

"They have him," she said. "They have him."

He didn't understand, so he would pitch platitudes into her face. But the silence settled in. His hand stayed as if to lend its warmth. Aubrey's words poured into the darkness.

"Oh, Jesus, I'm so sorry, forgive me, please forgive me, or send me to hell—I know I deserve it, but please, my baby, give me back my baby, it's one thing, just one thing, please, Jesus, just my baby."

The quiet remained for long minutes. Her shaking eased, and Marcus's hand shifted once but didn't withdraw.

"Marcus?"

"Yeah."

"I'm sorry for calling Lee."

A long, quiet sigh spilled between them. "She knows."

"Well, like I said, not my name."

"She figured it out." Beneath the accusation, defeat weighted his words.

"I won't involve her in anything else."

"No, you won't."

The ghost of his trust ran a finger down her spine. Not that he'd trusted her on a personal level before, but now he never would. A tear dripped down her temple, into her ear. She shifted to her side, curled her body around the pillow she held, and stared into the dark, at the outline of his face.

"I'll go. I'll leave in the morning, if you want me to."

"No."

"You'll still help me?" Why would he? Her fingers curled into the pillowcase.

His hand came up to rub his neck. "Sure."

"Elliott. Am I … Am I going to see him again?"

"Yeah."

"You promise?" Her whisper almost didn't dare to exist.

But he didn't hesitate. "Yeah."

25

When he'd checked the TV news for a sketch of his features this morning, Marcus had opted for subtitles to avoid waking Aubrey. Penny, on the other hand, blared the news channel from her living room so she could hound Marcus in the kitchen without missing anything. You'd think she'd have something more interesting to occupy her morning, but for four hours, she followed him with the loyalty of his dog. Loyalty that would probably evaporate fast if his face did show up on the news.

"Young man, you look like a volcano survivor."

He brushed at the gray powder caking his shirt, but his hands were dustier than his clothes. "Yeah."

"I already made a pot of coffee for you. Are you absolutely, one-hundred-and-ten-percent positive you don't want some?"

"No, thanks." He'd honor Lee's compromise. He could resist the mouthwatering scent for a while longer, though withdrawal split his head and muddied his brain.

The bathroom ceiling finally looked and felt smooth enough to prime. His right hand's grip was back to normal, but lifting his arm above his head still strained the cut across his back. Well, he'd sanded all morning with one hand. He could prime the same way. Penny should go do something else, though, before she noticed him favoring his arm. This was the first day she hadn't commented on the fading bruise under his eye. If she knew his back was held together with butterflies, she'd probably send him home.

The blaring news channel restarted its loop the same way it had eighteen minutes ago.

"No news isn't good news in the case of Aubrey Weston and her accomplice, who evaded MPC apprehension yesterday evening and continue to do so this morning. Agents have declined to offer ..."

"They sure do make the news a lot," Penny said from behind him, "now that they've got what they want."

Marcus grabbed a screwdriver and pried at the primer can's lid. "What do they want?"

"Power, of course. Look what they can do now, and everybody agrees with them. Used to be, they had to do things sort of secret-like."

"How far back is 'used to be'?"

"You really want a history lesson, or are you humoring an old lady?"

Her knowledge wasn't worth the risk of showing interest. Nobody cared about Constabulary history. And how could knowing the past help him fight now? The lid popped off the can, and Marcus stirred the primer.

"It's not that big, the area you had to patch up," Penny said. "You could paint it now and save a step."

"Paint won't stick to mud," Marcus said. "You'd get bubbles."

"If you say so." The pout drew wrinkles into themselves till they almost obscured her lips. "I'm only trying to be helpful."

"I know what I'm doing." Marcus dipped his paintbrush and wiped the excess on the edge of the can.

"Oh, I know you do. Keith said so."

The watch digits that had tugged at his attention all morning glowed with a sense of freedom. 11:20. Close enough. "That coffee still hot?"

About an hour later, caffeine began to clear his thoughts. Armed with a full travel mug, he left Penny's and drove to Chuck and Belinda's. Today, even the rural scenery couldn't relax him. Lifting a paintbrush over his head seared his back, and he was about to wrestle Belinda's old countertop out of place. Or try to.

He managed it. When a drip of sweat ran down the side of his face as Belinda served him his fourth mug of coffee, he let her turn down the thermostat rather than clarify.

Marcus drove home feeling old. Halfway there, his cell phone buzzed against his thigh, not for the first time that day. He worked it from his pocket and recognized the unstored number. They really had missed him at the Table last night. Well, Janelle wasn't stupid. Nothing would be said that could catapult them both into prison if overheard. Marcus opened the phone.

"Hello."

"In the flesh?"

"What?"

"You're really not in a morgue somewhere. Okay, let me process that for a minute." The voice that tossed out those carefree words betrayed the faintest wobble toward the end.

"Hey," Marcus said. "Everything's okay."

"You don't sound sick or anything."

"I'm not."

"Flat tire?"

"No."

"Death in the family?"

His gut tightened. No way to answer that one for sure, but he couldn't tell Janelle that. "No."

"Okay, then. Coffee shortage? Dog ate your homework? Alien abduction?"

"Janelle." He had to distance his voice, or she wouldn't buy his words. He swallowed. This was a lousy way to say good-bye to them. "It's just time for me to ... move on."

Silence. When she spoke again, her voice had thickened. "Absolutely not, Marcus. Meet me at the Rochester Starbucks in fifteen minutes—you can get there in fifteen minutes?"

Geographically, he could. "No reason for that."

"You'd better believe there's a reason for it, and you'd better be there."

Maybe he shouldn't have picked up the phone.

"Marcus? Come on. Please."

Coffee with Janelle didn't hold the potential for danger that the Table meetings did. And in a way, she was right: the little group did deserve an explanation. A truthful one. If only safety didn't mandate lies.

Marcus guided the truck to the left turn lane, no longer headed home. "I'm on my way."

The customary college crowd hadn't yet gathered when he entered Starbucks at roughly 6:30. In fact, only two customers lingered there. The first was a plump redheaded girl engrossed in her laptop and clacking fake fingernails on the table to a rhythm her headphones broadcast only to her. The second, nursing an iced cappuccino at the corner table farthest from the entrance, was Janelle.

Marcus stepped up to the counter half expecting the spike-haired kid behind it to bolt for a silent alarm button linked to the Constabulary.

"What can I get you?" the kid said instead.

"Grande Americano." Minutes later, his hand around the steaming cup, he crossed the café to Janelle's table for two. "Hi."

"Needed something to chew on?"

He tilted his back against the chair without fully touching it. His mouth found the energy to curve. "Sure."

"You ever wonder how much of that stuff you've consumed over a lifetime?"

"Some people start on it when they're five."

"You didn't?"

"Nope." He hadn't needed it till about fifteen years after that.

Janelle eyed him with a birdlike head tilt. She gyrated her plastic cup till the ice cubes made a sluggish circle. "You had to know how terrified we were. No word from you at all. Nothing."

He'd constructed a reasonable explanation on the way here, but the protective lies fizzled in his mouth. He washed them away with bitter, bracing espresso.

"I'm not being melodramatic when I say this. We waited for hours." She shook her head. "If you think I was a basket case last week ... All of us, Marcus. I think even Clay was shook up. We were sure we'd never see you again."

Marcus raised his eyes from where *Jack + Samantha* had been carved into the tabletop, framed by a lopsided heart. "It wouldn't have been safe. To call anybody."

"You shouldn't have needed to call. You should have been there."

No. The lie he had to tell crept back up from the pit of his stomach. Janelle had to believe he didn't want to go back.

"You need to tell me what's wrong."

"Nothing's wrong. I'm just not … I don't …" Words. Stupid, evasive words. How did other people collect so many, pour them into each other like creamer into coffee, smooth and easy?

"What, you think you don't fit in? You think you're not needed? Haven't we proved otherwise by now?"

Marcus let the silence hover. He needed the words that would make her stop fighting to keep him.

She twirled her straw. "You want to know what Phil said last night? Felice wants a ceremony when Abe marries them, a little celebration among us, and Phil said he was going to ask you to be his best man."

Don't feel it. But deep inside, a river rushed and roared. Janelle might see too much. Marcus glued his gaze to the table. Another heart, more symmetrical and pierced by an arrow, had been gouged below Jack and Samantha's.

"Marcus."

In the deliberate breath before he met her eyes, Marcus dammed the river. His mind's eye saw Phil and Felice and Janelle hauled off in handcuffs, saw Abe and Clay and their families shoved into prison cells after the Constabulary finally identified and followed Marcus. And until he knew otherwise, he couldn't help seeing all of them dead.

"Please listen to me," Janelle said. "When—when I lost my little niece, everybody tried so hard to say the right thing, except you. Your hand on my shoulder meant as much to me as words from somebody else."

Marcus looked up. Her face crinkled with care around her lips.

"I'm not coming back," he said.

Now it was her turn to stare at the carved hearts.

Marcus sipped his Americano.

"You know God doesn't want us to forsake 'the assembling of ourselves together,'" Janelle said.

God didn't want him to endanger his family, either. They might accept him no matter what, even if they knew the whole of him, the days of wringing thirst, the fact he'd failed every family he'd ever had. Jim and Karlyn. Frank. Mom.

"Jesus wants us to be His body. You know that. All different parts, all with a purpose, all connected. I'm betting I'm the mouth." A smile drifted over her face but didn't stay. "You're a hand, or a foot."

"Janelle," he said. "I'm not coming back."

She jabbed her straw into the bottom of her cup. "I hope you don't mean it. But you've never said anything to me that you didn't mean."

"If you ever need anything, you know my number."

"Ditto that. And listen, if you've decided to run the race alone for a while, whatever your reasons are ..." The straw twirled again, and her voice fell to a whisper. "Do what you can to get hold of reading material."

A Bible. At least he could reassure her in this. "I've got some."

Understanding glistened in her eyes, brightened into awe. "You have?"

He nodded.

"Oh, Marcus. Then you've read it."

"Not all of it."

"Read it, read every word. Oh, Marcus."

Of all people to own her own Bible, Janelle would have been one of Marcus's first guesses. "What happened to yours?"

"I was a coward."

He took another sip. She leaned nearer, although nobody in the café could overhear her brittle whisper.

"When the ban passed, I ... I got rid of it, told myself I'd always have the words in my heart. Every day since, I've asked God for another chance to hold His Word in my hands."

She'd prayed for a Bible for six years.

"Read First Corinthians, Marcus. It's toward the end, I think chapter twelve. Read about the body of Jesus, change your mind, and come back to us."

His hand flattened on the table and covered the hearts. Against his palm, they pressed as meaningless scratches.

Janelle's hand crept over the table, wrapped around his, and squeezed. "You'll be back. I can feel it."

The warm pressure on his hand nearly brought out the words he couldn't make on his own. That the little group had taught him so much and given him so much, that they meant so much. That they were too precious to risk holding onto.

His hand withdrew. "No."

2 6

Aubrey ladled out a second serving of soup when the lock rattled and Indy rushed toward it. Perfect timing. She listened for Marcus's routine "Hi," but only Indy's ecstatic panting broke the silence from the mudroom. That, and a muted jingle of keys set onto the washing machine.

She took a deep breath and rehearsed. *Hi, Marcus. How was your day? By the way, I want to apologize for the emotional outpouring last night. I promise to be levelheaded from now on.*

"Soup's on," Aubrey called. "Looks even better than the spaghetti."

"Thank you."

A gasp jumped down her throat as her body jerked around to face the voice. The female voice.

"Aubrey Weston." The black-haired woman stood at the kitchen doorway, erect but comfortable.

"Y-you must be Lee."

The nod was as measured as the posture, as measured as the voice Aubrey recognized from yesterday's forbidden phone call. "Marcus isn't home?"

"Um, no."

Indy nudged close to Lee's leg but didn't shove the way she did against Marcus. Lee didn't pet her, but the dog's tail didn't miss a happy beat against the door molding.

Lee's body flowed through the kitchen on liquid strides, the kind of body that could deliver triplets one day and slip into junior-sized jeans the next. She poured herself into a chair with-out touching the back and ran one thumb over Indy's black ear.

"You've stayed here since the original news story?" Lee said.

"Um, yeah." Okay, that was enough. Aubrey straightened her spine. Two could impersonate ramrods.

"I assume Marcus initiated this."

"He did, yes." Much better.

"And he intends to retrieve your child."

She didn't have to fake the stiffness now. "My son is not a Frisbee or a stick."

Lee's eyebrows arched. "I apologize if my choice of words was offensive."

A vague shock rippled through Aubrey's brain as the blurry picture finally focused itself. This was Marcus's girlfriend, poised, articulate, and aloof. Somehow, she had expected a woman less ... less funda-mentally the opposite of Marcus. The apology held sincerity, though.

Might as well be on good terms with the woman. "I'm think-ing he'll be back anytime, so would you like to eat with us?"

As if Lee needed an invitation to stay for dinner with him, to eat food she'd prepared herself. Maybe Aubrey would do better if she stopped trying.

Lee walked into the kitchen—yes, as if she owned it. "I'm here to examine his wound."

Again? "It's that serious?"

"His job involves physical labor."

"Oh, you mean he could tear it open? Wouldn't he call you, if he did?"

Lee's head barely turned to angle her gaze. "You've observed the answer to that."

"But last night was … different."

Silence claimed the room. Maybe Aubrey's conversation annoyed Lee. But indifference, not irritation, encased each line of her posture. Eye contact alone distinguished her from a sculpture of herself, harder than stone, colder than bronze. Steel, maybe.

"I'm sorry," Aubrey said.

"For?"

"Well, I ruined your chance for plausible deniability."

No response to that, either. Aubrey must have offended her, after all. Stupid, stumbling self, inviting the woman to dinner as if Aubrey owned something here.

Oh. Of course.

"Lee, I'm not … I would never try to … I know you and Marcus are …"

Aubrey was pinned by Lee's gaze like a collected butterfly to a foam board. "Are what?"

"Um, are … with each other. Together." She couldn't sound more adolescent if she tried.

"Where is his father?" Lee said.

"I'm sorry?"

"Your child's."

The question wasn't unfair, and the implication was impossible to miss. But Aubrey couldn't lie to Lee, couldn't reassure her that Brett waited on Aubrey's horizon like a rescue ship.

"He's living his life," Aubrey said. "He was living his life before my face hit the news, and I was raising our son. It was mostly a mutual decision."

Lee nodded.

"That's irrelevant, Lee. Really."

The steel eyes disagreed. Aubrey turned to the bowls on the counter, now barely steaming. Her stomach muttered with hunger despite the discomfiting silence. *Marcus, please hurry home.*

As the only sound in the room, the scrape of Aubrey's spoon against her ceramic bowl nearly drove her to start humming. Instead, she finished the bowl almost without chewing, then poured the second bowl back into Lee's glassware and deposited her dishes in the dishwasher, as all the while silence thickened. She found a niche for the glassware on the middle refrigerator shelf between cartons—one of coffee creamer, one of eggs. Even the seal of the refrigerator door was loud.

"I am not 'with' Marcus," Lee said.

Wait, was she kidding? She didn't sound like it. Aubrey turned to face her. Lee's expression remained flat. The back doorknob rattled.

The bull in the china shop had nothing on Marcus. He charged into the kitchen. His eyes found Lee in seconds, and the glare that tried to char her where she sat met only an incomprehensible lift of her eyebrows.

"I told you to go home," he said.

"I did."

"I didn't mean come back later."

"Your paranoia is no longer justified."

Indy butted her head against Marcus's hand, unresponsive at his side. Aubrey did not exist right now either. There were only Marcus and Lee, irresistible force and immovable object, fire and ice.

"No," Marcus said. His body propelled itself across the kitchen on strides that needed more room, then reached the far wall and whirled and paced back. Lee's eyes followed him.

"Marcus, they can't identify you."

He halted, but his glare didn't cool one degree.

"Resist your impulse to shut me out, and listen." Lee waited, and finally Marcus jerked a nod at her. "They've had nearly twenty-four hours. Had they composed a sketch, they would be using it. We've seen nothing. What do they gain from feigned ignorance?"

His left hand contracted into a fist, then loosened. The knuckles dug into his neck.

"They're reporting only vague details because vagueness is all they have."

Behind Marcus's eyes, the flames flickered down. His hand dropped to his side. He gave her one more short nod, then stood still.

Lee flowed to her feet. "Sit. I need to examine the wound."

"It's okay."

"Marcus, please."

A sigh seeped from him. He tugged a chair away from the table and dropped into it sideways. He started to pull his shirt over his head but froze with his right arm only halfway there. "Lee, just … lift it."

"Your arm?"

"No," he said quickly. "The shirt."

Lee rolled the shirt up his back. The black fabric crept up in front as well, baring half of Marcus's torso.

He could advertise for a gym. The thought had barely formed when Aubrey's eyes met Lee's, over his head. The woman didn't have to glare. She simply held eye contact with flat frankness that brought heat to Aubrey's face for no reason whatsoever.

Aubrey ducked her head and turned her back to both of them. She should clean something. How about this nice, shiny counter?

"You won't consider canceling tomorrow's clients," Lee said.

"I'm okay. It's just a cut."

"A strained laceration. Have you taken anything?"

The sudden quiet nearly infused Aubrey with the nerve to turn around, but before she could, Lee spoke again.

"Acetaminophen is not an anticoagulant."

"I know," he said, as if he'd heard those words from her a thousand times.

"Marcus, there is nothing … unsafe in Tylenol." Like his, Lee's words plodded a worn path, but in her hesitation, Aubrey's neck prickled.

Had that been a glance her way? *Gosh, Lee, sorry I'm in the room.* Not like there was anything intimate about treating a knife wound. *Oh, and obviously, you're not with Marcus. Not at all.* Aubrey tossed the sponge into the sink.

The chair scraped the wood floor. "I don't need Tylenol."

"No," Lee said. "You don't."

Aubrey turned to face them. The tightness around Marcus's mouth eased, as if Lee had handed him some kind of gift. He nodded, but with more than agreement. His eyes glimmered, and Aubrey stood on the other side of the counter, noticeable as a molecule of air. Just when she thought these two did nothing but clash.

Both of them took a step toward the back door, then kept going. Neither followed, neither led. They could have been two legs on one body, headed in the same direction without conscious thought. They could have been two bodies with one mind. Now they would say good-bye.

But no. The door opened, closed. They'd gone outside together.

Within Aubrey, something broke free and let itself ache. Had she and Brett ever looked that way to observers, as if their thoughts raced along one circuit, as if spoken words were superfluous to communication? Had anyone ever seen the appreciation in Brett's eyes that shone out of Marcus for Lee, simply because she stopped arguing with him over *Tylenol*?

Aubrey had promised to live her life with Brett, dragged him away from his studies when his eyes burned, kissed his tears when he lost his beloved granddaddy, tunneled with him under the covers of his bed without regard for what God said was wrong, exposed and offered her body and her soul, carried and cherished his baby. She had done all these things and never basked in a beam from his eyes that saw nothing in this moment of life but her.

And Lee stood in a light like that without realizing it.

27

Halfway across the closed garage toward Lee's car outside, she stopped walking. The frosted slate of her eyes studied Marcus, not as a nurse's patient, but as a reader's book.

"Why is she still here?"

"She's got nowhere else to go."

Lee crossed her arms. "Family, friends, acquaintances? A hotel?"

"She's got eleven dollars."

Did Lee just roll her eyes?

Couldn't have. "And yeah, I could give her money, but it's safer—"

"I was not suggesting you give her money."

"I can't take her to Ohio. Not without her baby."

"She doesn't belong in this house."

Where was this coming from? The chill of the garage seeped into him, and he crossed his arms. Now they both stood the same way, as if shielding against each other instead of the cold. "It's my house. And I'm not putting her out in the street, if that's what you want."

"I'm merely pointing out the absurdity of an adult woman, a mother, so unable to deal with her problems that she's willing to impose on a stranger."

"She's tried to leave twice. And offered to leave again last night."

Lee flinched at the end of his sentence. The silence enveloped them until Marcus had no idea how to break it. Well, he had nothing to say, anyway. Lee was being ridiculous.

"You're determined to do this," Lee said. "Protect fellow Christians, even those you don't know."

He'd done hardly anything so far, but he nodded. No stopping now.

Her arms lowered to her sides. "All right. I can assist you."

"No." The word punched through his clenched teeth.

"Indirectly. I know someone with information. I'll give you the means to contact him."

"No."

"Sam Stiles."

"I said no."

"He's worked for the Constabulary nearly two years."

"What are you doing?"

"He isn't a field agent, Marcus." Conviction edged into her voice. "He works in data management."

The significance left a flashbulb impression in the flurry of Marcus's thoughts. Every day, this man could get to information that Marcus could secure only when Jason Mayweather was too drunk to shut up. Not that it mattered. Lee wasn't allowed to help him, even if she could shove a truth serum into Jason.

"Stop," he said.

Her mouth hardened.

Marcus had stepped into the damp garage with hardly a nudge of energy left. Now his legs pumped, up and down the center line in the cement floor. Sam Stiles. He'd managed Lee's inheritance since before it was hers. From financial adviser to Constabulary agent? Well, there were weirder things.

Lee's eyes marked his repetitive path. "You don't appear to be reconsidering."

"No."

"I expected you to credit God with this arrangement."

He shook his head. "There's no 'arrangement.'"

"I've known him twelve years. I'm a capable judge of his character."

"I know."

"Then why the stubbornness? Besides the fact it's your routine state."

Marcus's feet halted. "The charges against you wouldn't be passive anymore."

Her eyebrows rose. Surprised at his worry for her, though by now she should have learned to expect it. She wandered away from him, to the random tools propped in a corner alongside plywood shelves.

She fingered the handle of a snow shovel. "It's unlikely they would be able to establish a connection."

"They might."

"I accept that risk."

"No," he said.

"You act as if this choice belongs to you."

To protect her, no matter what he had to do—that choice did belong to him. The stare-down crystallized, then shattered against the concrete in Lee's voice.

"It does not." She headed for the side door.

"Lee," he said. "Stay out of it."

From Lee, no response meant no promises. Her hand grasped the doorknob. He rushed forward, and his left arm barred the door closed over her head.

"If someone else offered you this information," Lee said quietly, "would you use it?"

He tried to separate them, the information and the source. Tried to imagine that Janelle, or Clay, or Abe knew Sam Stiles instead. But they didn't.

"Marcus."

"You offered it," he said. "Not somebody else."

"I'm speaking hypothetically."

Hypotheticals were meaningless. Lee wanted to throw herself into the dangers of his work, and she wanted him to approve. Nobody else would do that.

"You're not certain?" Her gaze was unwavering.

"It wouldn't happen that way. Just stay out of it, Lee, all of it."

"All right."

God, did You do that?

"You do the same," she said.

Hope vanished. "I can't."

Lee nodded. "I know."

"This is mine now. But it's not yours."

"Reverse the situation, and tell me you would agree to that."

His knuckles dug deep into his neck. Convince her to stay away. Come on. Get the words.

"Move, Marcus."

"Lee. Please."

Her hand abandoned the doorknob. Smooth, unhurried strides headed back across the garage. Of course. He could have darted after her again, physically hindered her again, but he could do that for only so long. The idiocy of his actions finally sank in and drained everything left inside. Lee pressed the garage door opener, and the rumbling pulley raised the door. Plenty of space for her to step through.

Her eyes locked onto him. "Take care of yourself for a few more days. Try not to overexert. Don't subsist on coffee."

"This fight isn't for you," he said.

"And consider searching the Internet for the lack of addictive properties in Tylenol. Several thousand articles exist."

Of course, she had to repeat that point. She wouldn't if she'd ever been in his head. He was pretty sure he could get addicted to anything. Lee walked to her car and backed it into the street, pulled away from the curb, shrank, disappeared. Minutes multiplied. His feet decided to go into the house. Indy's nose shoved between his fingers and through the fog of his thoughts.

"You look like you need to eat," Aubrey said from the doorway.

Marcus lifted his gaze from the wood floor. Aubrey leaned against the door frame, her eyebrows wrinkled with thoughts. Her face might have lost color since he found her four days ago, staring at a display of lightbulbs as if she could wish the Constabulary away.

"I warmed up some soup earlier, but you weren't here. I'll throw it back on the stove, if it sounds good."

Marcus shrugged past her into the kitchen. "I can do it."

"I don't mind."

"I don't need help. With anything." He yanked open the fridge door.

"Literally? Wow, okay then."

Marcus brought out the half-empty glassware, a steel pot, and a spoon to stir the soup while it heated on the stovetop.

"I wasn't questioning your kitchen abilities," Aubrey said from behind him. "Look, I've been pacing holes in your floor all day. Six times today, I had to talk myself out of getting on your computer to check my email. Not because anyone important emails me—it's mostly spam—but that's how desperate I got. Desperate for spam. So … soup warming would be a great diversion. But then, so would jury duty. A root canal. A zombie attack."

Marcus turned on the burner, then met her eyes again. One hand tugged at her earlobe, and the other hung at her side. Had Marcus never really looked at her before? How had he missed the emptiness that dripped off her like too much paint off a roller brush?

"The house looks good," he said, something he'd meant to tell her sooner. Her forehead gathered more wrinkles. "I mean, clean."

"It kept me busy for a little while."

"Well. Thanks."

Halfway through dinner, his cell phone buzzed. The number looked familiar. "Hello."

"Hello, this is Pamela Mayweather. Is this Marcus Brenner?"

"Yeah." He tilted his shoulder against the phone.

"Oh, good. That banister you told me about—you were right. It came right off. It's not broken, just needs reattaching. I was hoping you could squeeze us in sometime tomorrow."

A railing repair wouldn't take long, but the Mayweathers lived half an hour from Chuck and Belinda, whose kitchen was going to consume his time for the next few days. He tried to shuffle the locations in his mind and couldn't make it happen.

"Pamela, I'm sorry. Tomorrow's booked. I could do the day after."

"Oh, no, that's fine, I'll call around and see if there's anyone that can do tomorrow. If there's not, I'll call you back."

"No, don't." He was crazy to risk this, but he had to. *God, don't let her be suspicious.* "I can be there in fifteen minutes."

Aubrey shot him a questioning look as he swiped his keys off the counter.

"Aren't you off work for the day?" Pamela said.

"Guess not."

"What's your after-hours rate?"

"I'll charge you regular time."

He dug through the junk drawer. There. A paper clip. He shoved it into his pocket.

2 8

The railing job was half finished before Marcus figured out what was missing. Not what, who. He kept working, wondering, until Pamela started up the stairs, carrying the littlest boy and keeping herself between the middle one and the gap in the banister.

Marcus moved to the top of the stairs to clear their way. "Where's J.R.?"

Pamela inclined her chin toward the far end of the hall. "He's in his room. After I called you, he confessed. You never know what your kids are overhearing."

"What?"

"Came to me ducking his head. 'Mom, I wanted to see if Mr. Brenner was right about the rail coming off. So I tested it, and he was. He's real smart.'"

A chuckle lightened the weight that had sat on his chest since he walked through Jason's door. If anybody was smart, it was J.R.

"Don't laugh, Mr. Brenner." Pamela's half grin disappeared into a frown. "He'll hear you and think what he did was fine. He could've fallen eight feet."

True enough. Marcus nodded.

"If you need anything, let me know. It's bath and bedtime for these mini monsters." She bounced the baby on her arm.

They disappeared around the corner, into the bathroom. The middle one started to whine but was cut off by Pamela's voice. The faucet came on, and Marcus's heart pounded. She wouldn't notice that he wasn't hammering anymore. She wouldn't leave kids that young for any reason, not in water.

He waited half a minute, then stole down the steps, down the hall, to the French doors. He tried the doorknob and sighed. Unlocked this time, no paper clip needed. Jason must use the locks for privacy while he was inside working. Well, he was too arrogant for paranoia, and a man's house wasn't supposed to be infiltrated by his enemy. A finger of cold traced Marcus's spine. He slipped into the room.

Sage green walls, bookcases, a gilt-framed painting of a volcano at sunset—the details of the room blurred as Marcus focused on the L-shaped mahogany desk. It stood centered on the back wall, spread with manila folders, phone, laptop, and fax machine. Beside it sat a printer-copier.

Okay. Work fast. Touch as little as possible.

He crossed the room and stood behind the desk to open its drawers. Not much in them, until he opened the top right one. But these were personal items—cinnamon gum, nicotine patches, a few ballpoint pens, and ... the picture. Marcus's hand trembled on the back of the desk chair.

Only one picture. Did that mean Jason had only killed one person?

He couldn't stop to think. He shoved the drawer closed. The computer was probably a gold mine, but far too risky to touch it. Instead, he poked at the papers on the desk. The clutter might be ordered, or Marcus might move a piece of paper without Jason ever noticing it had moved. But maybe nothing here was helpful, anyway. An arrest report, half complete. Transcription of a few phone calls, but the callers talked about things like box office totals for the latest movies and which fast food place had the best French fries. What, did Jason think Christians talked on the phone in code? "French fry" for "Bible" and "McDonald's" for "black market distributor"?

Marcus's hand stilled on four pages of copied driver's licenses. Two dozen of them, or more. Handwriting in thick black ink scrawled all over the sheets, right over the copied images sometimes. Abbreviations, dates, a few of the licenses boxed in orange highlighter. Shorthand everywhere. He flipped to another page. *God, help me figure this out.*

From the top left, a woman smiled at him through a thick black X. He didn't have to read the license, but his eyes did anyway. *Karlyn Elisabeth Cole.*

His fingers left creases in the page. He fought to relax his grip. Jim's license was copied below hers, also crossed out. Pain clawed Marcus's chest. What did the X's mean? That they were in custody? Or that they were dead?

Stop thinking, stop feeling. Get out of here. Most of these licenses were scribbled on but not crossed out. He set the pages into the top tray of the copier, but it was asleep. He hit the green button, and its face lit up. *WARMING UP. PLEASE WAIT.*

He dug his knuckles into his neck and shifted from foot to foot. *Come on, come on.* Finally, the display changed. *READY.* He hit the green button again, hoping it was the right one. He hadn't used a copy machine in years.

The whir sounded more like a roar in the silent room. Marcus paced two steps while the paper fed through the tray—oh heck, face up or facedown? But a few seconds later, the machine spit the first sheet out, copy complete.

He folded the four warm sheets into quarters, then eighths. He slid the originals back under the other papers, pushed the chair back into place, and scanned the desk. Unless Jason had positioned things deliberately, he'd never know.

Marcus slipped from the room, back upstairs, and buried the pages at the bottom of his toolbox. If you looked hard enough, bright white paper peeked through a few gaps in the tools. He shut the lid and breathed.

He'd done it.

Jason, you should've bought a deadbolt for those doors.

Jim and Karlyn's crossed-out faces kept imprinting on his eyes. He finished his job only a minute before Pamela exited one of the bedrooms and shut the door behind her. She approached Marcus with a smile.

"They're all tucked in. And it looks like you're wrapping up?"

"Yeah. It's solid now."

"Thanks for coming so fast. You'll be getting referrals from me."

Trust was such a weird thing. She had no real reason to assume Marcus hadn't raided her husband's office. But she also had no reason to assume he *had* raided it. So she didn't. He latched the toolbox and followed her downstairs.

They were halfway to the kitchen when the back door crashed open and banged shut. His every muscle coiled to fight. Jason must have some kind of silent alarm in his office.

If Marcus bolted now, he'd make the front door.

But wait. Pamela didn't look shocked or even worried. She threw her hands up in a gesture that wasn't aimed at Marcus. She stalked past him with a huff.

"Wait here a minute." Her voice came from the kitchen a few seconds later. "Do you have to treat doors like—"

"I'm getting a work fax," Jason said.

"A work fax is what finally brings you home from work?"

"I was out, closer to home, I need this right away and my cell phone's not accepting the attachment. I have to take that stupid thing in and—"

"You could simply shut the door, Kyle will be screaming like a banshee in—"

"Whose truck is that?" His voice clipped around the corner less than a second before he charged into view. Marcus stepped back to avoid a collision.

Jason's blue eyes widened. He glanced over his shoulder at Pamela. "What's he doing here?"

She twisted one of her silver thumb rings. "The railing broke, going up the stairs. J.R. was leaning on it."

"Oh. Thanks for coming by, Brenner."

"Jason." Pamela reached a hand to his shoulder before he could vanish down the hallway. "J.R. didn't fall, but he could have. He was leaning on the railing on purpose, to see if it would break."

Jason turned to face her, but his hand twitched and impatience stiffened his shoulders. "Why would he go and do that?"

"I just put him to bed. I told him if you got home before he fell asleep, you'd be up to talk to him. He needs to know what he did was dangerous. I think he'd take it more seriously, coming from you."

From the office, the fax machine started ringing. Jason's eyes darted to the closed doors. "I'll talk to him tomorrow."

"He—"

"Pam, I said I'll talk to him tomorrow." Jason headed down the hall. "Catch you later, Brenner."

The doors shut behind him with a quiet click. Pamela cleared her throat. "Let me get the checkbook."

Oh. Right. Marcus trailed her into the bright kitchen, which smelled like homemade cookies. While she wrote out the check, he counted seconds. A minute. Jason would have noticed the intrusion by now, if he was going to.

Pamela signed her name with a sweeping flourish and tore out the check. "The picture you saw, the girl."

His heart misplaced a beat. "Yeah."

She ran her thumb over her signature, then met his eyes and handed him the check. "It's Rochelle. Shelly. Jason's sister."

Marcus folded the check and stuffed it into his pocket. "Why are you telling me?"

"That picture's nearly ten years old now. She was working at Springfield. You know, at the clinic."

Of course he knew. The whole country knew.

"She was a receptionist, Marcus. Collateral damage. Or maybe not, to them." Bitterness tiptoed into her words. "After all, she was making appointments for abortions. That definitely deserved a death sentence."

Marcus swallowed, tried to work his jaw.

"Jason requested a copy of the photo from the case file. I asked him once to get rid of it, and he said when his work is complete, he'll bury it in the plot with Shelly."

Not a trophy. A mission statement. Jim and Karlyn, Frank, everyone else—the images of them, bloody and lifeless, washed out of his head in a tide of relief that squeezed his chest and almost knocked him over. He reached one hand to the counter. *Get a grip, before she notices.*

"And I'm telling you because you've just seen my husband in a negative light, again. He *is* his worst self, but everyone has a worst self, and—and I didn't want you to leave here seeing only that."

"Okay," he said.

Pamela ruffled her hair and paced to the other end of the counter. "That Christian friend I had in school—when Springfield happened, we talked about it for weeks. She said she was appalled and that no true Christian would do what those people did. At the time, I believed her."

Injustice gripped Marcus's shoulders. Janelle lived in fear of owning a Bible, Aubrey woke up screaming because her baby was gone, Jim and Karlyn and a thousand others were imprisoned because some sociopaths blew up a building filled with people and took the name of Christ in vain as their battle cry.

He shoved his hand into his pocket and rubbed his thumb against the edge of the check. "The people who *did* it should pay for it."

"And the people who *would* do it, if they could?"

"That's not how it works." If he'd crossed a legal line with that sentence … well, then he had.

"It is now, fortunately."

No. Now, it was whoever the government decided *might* commit a crime like this one. But Pamela's lips were forged down with resolve. Still not listening. He edged toward the door, toolbox in hand.

"I should go."

Pamela sighed. "Thank you again for coming."

"No problem." But time to get out of here.

"I'd better go talk to J.R. Have a good night."

Marcus nodded, but halfway to the door, something weighted his feet.

Five years old, waiting up in bed for Dad to come home. A rusty, long-forgotten spear jabbed his gut. It wasn't the same. J.R.'s dad hadn't been gone without a word for three years. J.R.'s dad lived here, and if Pamela was right, Jason was a decent father most of the time. Still, the ache didn't let go. If right now, a floor above Marcus, a little boy sat with his spine against the headboard, knees up, counting minutes on the glowing clock …

He turned to Pamela. "Um … do you think it'd help if I talked to him?"

Her eyes widened a moment, green brightening in the kitchen light. "Would you? He thinks you're a superhero."

"Sure."

"Mom doesn't carry the same weight, you know? Jason will talk to him tomorrow, like he said. But since J.R. did this to prove your smartness …"

Marcus followed her upstairs, into a darkened room brightened in one corner by a night light of some caped cartoon character. Sure enough, J.R. was sitting up in bed, covers pulled over his knees to his chin.

Pamela sat on the side of his bed. "It's way past sleep time, young man."

"I heard Dad's voice downstairs. He coming up?"

"Not right now, and I want you to go to sleep for tonight, okay? Dad's still got a lot of work to do."

"Oh. Okay."

"But someone else is going to say good night." She motioned Marcus past the doorway.

J.R. jolted up to his knees and shoved away the covers. "Mr. Brenner! Did you fix that rail?"

"Yeah." Marcus stood at the foot of the bed and rubbed his neck. "And you got your toolbox!"

Oh, heck. If J.R. asked to open it, he'd have to say no. Better detour the topic. "I'm going home, J.R., but I wanted to talk to you about something."

"Mom said I couldn't watch you working because I was bad, but I didn't mean to."

Marcus stepped closer. "I know. But listen, J.R., from now on, if you want to test if something's broken, first ask your mom, and she'll tell you a safe way. She doesn't want you to fall or get hurt. And I don't want you to, either."

"We're friends, right?"

"Right."

"How about you come over sometimes and play?"

Pamela's smile carried through the near-dark. "We'll see, J.R. Now it's time to go to bed."

"Okay, Mom." J.R. lay down and pulled up the covers. "G'night, Mom. G'night, Mr. Brenner."

By the time Marcus climbed into his truck, the old ache had disappeared. He left Jason's subdivision and didn't stop driving till he was halfway home. He pulled into an empty parking lot, turned on the dome lights, and dug the crumpled pages from his toolbox. One was now smeared with a stripe of wood oil and sawdust.

Ten minutes later, he'd deciphered enough of Jason's writing to know who on this sheet had been arrested, who had a search warrant, and who was under surveillance. Search warrants were the most urgent, of course. Those homes could be raided at any time. Good thing this list contained addresses and not just names. Marcus chose one randomly, the only way he could choose, mapped it with his phone, and started driving. He'd warn them. Help them plan. Drive them to Ohio, if they couldn't get there themselves. Whatever he had to do.

The Constabulary was about to lose. *And, Jason, you're helping me win.*

2 9

Aubrey should've gone to sleep in bed, so she didn't have to drag herself upright on the couch when Marcus returned. It was 1:42. How did he function on less than six hours of sleep? Well, some people could. She just wasn't one of them.

He lumbered into the living room without switching on the light.

"Hey," Aubrey whispered.

He didn't jolt at her presence, but he didn't answer, either.

"I was getting worried." Until she fell asleep, that is.

He sank down on one end of the couch. The middle cushion lay between them. "Too late."

"For what?"

Indy had followed him and now began the knee-nudging routine. Marcus leaned forward, and his palm rubbed the top of her head. A minute of silence said he wasn't going to talk, but he didn't get up to leave, either.

"Marcus? I thought you'd be back in an hour or two. Where'd you go?"

The silence tightened. Even in the dark, Aubrey could picture the tension that must have seized his jaw.

"Tape," he said.

"What?"

"Police tape. Yellow. Crime scene."

"What? Where? Somebody we know?"

His hand abandoned Indy's head, clenched around his neck instead. "No."

"Then who are they, how'd you find them?"

No answer. *Father God, please comfort those people.*

"Marcus? Were there ... kids?" Babies, wailing for their mothers, dislocated from arms of love.

"Just at the one house."

"Wait, how many houses did you go to?"

He locked his hands behind his head and pulled, a slow, steady stretch of his neck. A long breath filled him, then released. "Three."

"And they were all ... gone?"

"No. Just one." His jacket rustled as he worked his right hand out of the sleeve and let it slump to the floor.

"But the other two—you got to them? You helped them?"

"Yeah."

"They must be so grateful. You saved them." She skimmed her fingers over his shoulder, but he stiffened. Why the defeat? What did he expect—that he'd never lose?

"I'm sorry," he said.

"What?"

"I don't know what to do. About your baby."

"You're doing everything you can."

Sometimes, the automatic trigger of her words spoke truth she hadn't understood until it entered her heart in her own voice. What this man was attempting was brave, was insane. She'd accused him of a lack of effort. Her cheeks burned.

"I'm trying to find a way. To find him. He's got to be in foster care. If I could get a list of the homes ... but he could be anywhere."

That fact pelted her heart. "It's been four days."

"I know."

"Are you a father?"

He darted a startled glance her way. "No."

"Then you don't know."

Quiet wrapped them up again, in a blanket too thin to keep out all the cold truths. Aubrey shivered and hugged her aching self. Minutes dripped away, and he said nothing. She should leave him alone.

"Okay, well, good night." She was halfway to her feet before his whispered words skewered the darkness.

"It won't be your fault. If she gets hurt."

A lurking weight lifted. He did forgive her. Then the subtext caught up with her relief. "You think it'll be yours?"

As soon as the question left her mouth, she knew he wouldn't answer it. He laced his fingers above his neck again and pulled his chin to his chest.

"Marcus," she said. "Lee decided to help you. As a mature, intelligent adult."

She dropped back onto the couch, but he didn't seem to notice.

"That whole 'carrying the weight of the world' thing doesn't work for anyone but God, you know."

"Go to bed, Aubrey."

"You actually believe the well-being of ... everybody ... is up to you?"

A harsh sound broke from him, not a laugh. "Everybody? No. My family, yes. And Lee."

He'd said that before, about Christians, but she hadn't realized ... "Marcus, seriously, who made you responsible?"

He turned his head, barely enough to meet her gaze, and frowned as if she'd asked a meaningless question. From the kitchen, the refrigerator cycled on. At Marcus's feet, Indy yawned and sighed.

Aubrey angled her knees toward his. "Come on. Let it go."

He lurched to his feet. "Good night."

He trudged toward the hall that led to the basement, one frail man trying to be more, shoulders bowed under the weight he wouldn't relinquish. Aubrey closed her eyes. *Dear Father God, don't let him be crushed before he gives it up to You.*

3 0

Cabin fever didn't creep up on a person. It tackled when another nightmare chased her awake to stare at someone else's ceiling, to realize this ceiling, these walls, this floor, were boundaries without a foreseeable end. Aubrey stood to one side of the window to raise it, struggling a moment with the awkward angle. The December sunrise slanted a chilly, red-tinged light into the kitchen. A hair-raising current rolled over her arm, but at least the air was moving. Her fingers ran along the wood sill. She wouldn't even have to cross the house to the back door. She could pop the screen out, hop up there, drop down to the other side. Outside.

Better stop tempting herself. She reached across and up to slide the window back down. As her fingers wrestled the stiff lock, joyous toenails sounded from the other room. That was Indy's Marcus-dance, but Marcus was already gone. The couch was empty; she'd checked. Aubrey padded toward the living room.

She rounded the corner and yelped. Facing the bookshelf, Marcus jolted. Some kind of figurine plummeted toward the floor, rescued by his left hand a second before impact. He straightened and whirled to face her.

"You weren't here." Her words shot out like an accusation. "I looked. Where were you?"

"Oh," he said. "Basement."

"Working out?" She hadn't missed the gym equipment across from his workshop.

"No." His mouth drew down. "Tomorrow, maybe."

Oh. His back. But he wore the same navy shirt from yesterday. "Um, did you sleep down there?"

He gave a short nod and looked away. A few steps farther into the room shifted Aubrey's line of sight. Part of the back of the bookcase lay across the shelf like a lowered ramp. The rectangular hole in the wall gaped only a foot across and maybe half as deep.

"Quite a piece of work there," she said.

"Yeah." Marcus set the figurine inside the space. A whole throng of them clustered atop a leather-bound book. He'd cut a hole in the wall to hide his Bible. Kind of extreme, but she shouldn't be surprised. If Marcus did something, he did it to the hilt. And the figures ... Aubrey came closer. Not resin as she'd first thought ... wood. Smooth, some of them, but others barely represented people. Or animals. That was definitely a sheep.

Ohhh ...

"You're making a nativity scene," Aubrey whispered, as if his neighbors could overhear.

Marcus nodded.

"Why?"

He shrugged. "I wanted one."

"But why? You can't put it out."

Another shrug, and he turned to raise the panel over the little trove.

"Wait," Aubrey said. "Could I see them? Would you mind?"

He looked surprised. "Sure. I mean, I don't mind."

Wood in various stages of roughness grazed her fingertip. Some hadn't been sanded yet at all. Each piece revealed its role as she studied it, though. The still faceless shepherds announced themselves by the hooks in their hands and the worship in their poses. One of them knelt. Joseph and Mary appeared finished, right down to the fingernails.

"This is amazing, Marcus."

He shrugged again, but a satisfied light crept over his face.

She drew out baby Jesus for a closer look. He was fashioned separately from the manger, a half-curled infant wrapped in detailed strips of cloth.

"I started with Him," Marcus said. "It made the scaling a little harder. But He was the reason everybody else was there."

"No halo?"

"Well, it's not in the Bible. And they didn't need a halo to know Him."

"Sounds reasonable to me." Aubrey turned the tiny figure between her fingers. Marcus's baby Jesus slept with the slightest wrinkle between the eyebrows, caught up in a newborn dream. One hand lay open at His side, and one curled beside His head. The realness breathed from the wood. This could have been any baby, could have been Elliott, yet at the same time, His identity was carved into Him, something somber but peaceful.

Aubrey set him back inside the wall's space. In her fascination with the figures, she'd missed that more than one book composed their foundation. Marcus had three Bibles.

"You distribute?" On top of all his other Constabulary crimes.

Marcus's gaze followed hers. "Oh. No. I don't."

"Then—" Aubrey's lungs paused. A braid of ribbons peeked from gilded pages. That wasn't just any Bible. She tugged it from the middle of the stack before Marcus could stop her. "This is Karlyn's."

In the moment of silence, Marcus's face weighed options. Aubrey didn't give him time to choose one.

She yanked the bookmark farther into view. "There are eight ribbons, two each of burgundy, magenta, rose, and baby pink. Karlyn's crazy about pink, every shade of it. I made this for her when we were in high school."

"Okay," Marcus said.

"Okay? How'd you—" Wait ... surely he hadn't ... "Did you get these after the arrest?"

"No."

Forgotten fragments fit together, but Aubrey's brain stumbled over the complete puzzle. Karlyn hadn't concealed her Bibles in a brilliant place. She'd gotten rid of them altogether.

"I thought it'd make them safe." Cynicism serrated his words.

His hands, warm and rough in their momentary brush against Aubrey's fingers, closed around the Bible to take it, to put it away. Aubrey held on.

"This is Karlyn's," she said.

Marcus nodded.

"This is the Bible that—" Her throat closed around the past. "I found it. In Karlyn's locker. I told her I was going to turn her in, and she said—my boyfriend's name was Mark, and she told me, read Mark's book first, and then if you want to turn me in, go ahead."

Barely a smile drifted over Marcus's face. "That sounds like her."

"She called me Salmon sometimes. She said I wasn't afraid to swim upstream."

Marcus nodded as if the name still fit.

"It was a thing with her," Aubrey said. "Animal nicknames."

"Yeah."

"Wait a minute, she gave you one?" He'd been more than a church acquaintance, then. Karlyn and Jim had been close to him.

"Um." Marcus broke eye contact, rubbed his neck. "Pit Bull."

"You gnaw on small children at unpredictable moments?"

"Once I latch onto something, somebody's got to pry my jaws apart. That's, um, what she said, anyway."

Pit Bull. Yes. And of course, Karlyn would see it. Sometimes, she saw people better than they saw themselves. Aubrey's hands trembled around the Bible. "God used her to save me. I always wanted to be used like that. I never was."

"Not yet," Marcus said.

God would never give her that kind of privilege now. Aubrey thrust the book at him and thrust the feelings to the back of her mind. "You can put it away."

He slid it inside the hole in the wall, tucked the ribbon back inside, and pressed the wood panel upward. The hole disappeared, even the seams. He had created a perfect fit.

Marcus swiveled toward her as if seeing her for the first time. "Why don't I know you?"

"Why would you?"

"If you're Karlyn's best friend, if you've been a Christian since high school, why were you never at the Table?"

A flood of memories seared her cheeks. The dear people she'd disappointed. The verbal grenades Janelle had lobbed at her. The way Abe refused to meet her eyes.

"You're new, I take it," Aubrey said.

Marcus watched her and waited.

"I ... left. Before Elliott was born."

"Oh," he said. "But you could've brought him, if you were careful."

"I was …" *I was Judas. I was a coward. I was asked to leave.* "I was really busy when he came."

After a weighing moment, he nodded. "Well, I've got to get going."

"Okay," Aubrey said, but he was already halfway from the room.

From the muted beating of the water, the man showered for less than five minutes. He then claimed the kitchen with more clatter than usual. If this was how he typically made breakfast, he'd been diligent in regulating the noise level the last few days. Aubrey chose the brick red sweater for today, got dressed, and ventured toward the aroma of eggs and sausage.

"Want some?" Marcus said without looking over his shoulder.

"I do, yes." She peered around his arm into the frying pan. She preferred an omelet to over-easy, but if he wanted to cook for her, she wouldn't complain. Five eggs. The man must crave cholesterol.

The spatula flipped each egg without perforating the yolk.

"I can never do that," she said.

"What?"

"Anything I try to flip goes everywhere. Those things would be bleeding yellow by now if I was making them."

Crinkles formed around his eyes, somehow a deeper smile than any mouth could make. "Just takes practice."

Could she get his eyes to do that again? "Pancakes flop over and leak batter out the sides. Grilled cheese loses the cheese."

"Come on."

"I am a terrible, horrible, no good, very bad cook."

"Hmm."

"You didn't read that book when you were a kid?"

"Um ... about a bad cook?"

"About Alexander's bad day. I thought every kid read that book."

"I didn't read much." He shrugged, then delivered the first egg onto the waiting plate. It still didn't break. "More?"

"No, thanks."

"Sausage? Or there's bagels."

"This is fine." She wasn't that hungry, and she'd rather not swallow another bite of bagel after eating one four mornings in a row. She grabbed two forks from the silverware drawer and set one on the other plate. After a sprinkling of salt, she took her first drippy bite. Hmm. This wasn't a bad way to eat eggs, after all.

Marcus turned his sausage one last time, then shut off the burner and joined her at the table with a heaping plate.

"So," Aubrey said before he could revisit the topic of the Table. "You didn't like to read? Even at four, five years old?"

"Nope."

"*Goodnight Moon? Where the Wild Things Are? The Little Engine That Could?*"

He shook his head to each title.

Pity surged, though he clearly didn't understand what he had missed. "Didn't your parents believe in reading?"

Marcus's fork impaled a sausage link, and he bit off half and swallowed it before answering. "Books are expensive."

"That's why there are libraries."

His mouth curved. Why was that funny? "So books were important in your house?"

"My mom's degree is in literature."

"Oh." He pushed his chair back from the table, then paused. "So ... she could get a Bible. If she wanted one."

"Well, not 'get' as in own one, of course … but yeah, she got a pass to an RRR when she was working on her dissertation."

Marcus nodded and headed for the dishwasher, a hint of awe behind his eyes. Only those holding doctorates—or, in her mom's case, working on one—could gain access to a library's Religious Reference Room. Among other legal religious literature, these rooms housed multiple old Bible translations. If one's thesis was state-approved, one could use banned books to develop that thesis. Mom had written something about philosophical contradictions in the original parables. Aubrey should have made time to dig up that old thesis, read it, discuss it with her.

"Do you think they're still in custody? My parents?"

Marcus looked toward the silent radio, as if the news might come on spontaneously and announce her parents' fate. "I don't know."

"They probably don't know I haven't been caught."

He shook his head.

"I wish I could let them know that I'm okay, and that we're working on getting Elliott."

Marcus nodded.

"Marcus, does your family know about all the things you're doing? Or would they turn you in?"

He retrieved his shoes from the laundry room and his keys from the hook on the wall. Had she overstepped again?

"My mom wouldn't have turned me in," he finally said.

"But she's safer not knowing." Like Lee.

He shoved his feet into his shoes without unlacing them. The slight hunch of his shoulders seemed to bear a sudden physical burden. Oh … *wouldn't have.* Long past tense.

"Or is she … did she pass away?"

He seemed to stop breathing. His head bowed.

"What happened?" She shouldn't ask, but she couldn't ignore such a visible pain. If he tried to clam up, she'd change the subject. After all, he'd let her avoid one.

As she concluded he wouldn't answer, his voice trickled out. "Her heart."

"You were really young?"

"No."

"It must have been hard for—for your dad." *For you.*

"He left. When I was two."

"That's heinous," she said, the first word suited for that magnitude of abandonment.

Marcus's left hand rose to his neck.

"I'm sorry, Marcus."

His gaze jerked up from the floor. "Don't."

Okay, that qualified as clamming up. "She was a good mother, the way you talk about her."

"She read *Treasure Island* out loud. From the library. I was about seven or eight. I liked it. I kept asking her to borrow it again, and she kept saying no. She'd bought it for me for Christmas." His hand lowered to his side and unfurled slowly. "Well. I've got to go."

"I'll clean up," Aubrey said.

"Okay."

When he was gone, she scoured the kitchen, ending with the egg-caked frying pan she'd set to soak. What kind of father deserted his family? He had to know his two-year-old would ask Mommy when Daddy was coming home. She rewound time thirty years or so and imagined the man she still barely knew, a toddling soldier with coffee-cake curls and caramel eyes, thigh high to his mom and vowing to be responsible. For his family. The way his dad refused to be. *Oh, Marcus.*

Did every child need a father, barring outright abuse? Or was a baby better off without someone in his life who would even consider discarding him?

She was scrubbing a perfectly clean pan.

She shut off the water and dried her hands on a worn but clean towel. Now her options were more pacing, more jabbering to Marcus's dog. Surely it wouldn't hurt anything to step out onto the deck for a while, to breathe in the outdoors even if it was damp and cold out there.

The minutes of contemplation finally found her staring at his bookshelf. Of course. When inactivity is ready to send one over the edge, a book is always helpful. But no good mother would distract herself with a book as if all was right with the world, as if her baby slept safely a room away. She'd be no different than a father who complied with a breakup and never asked, "What about the baby?"

Stop it. She'd told Marcus that Brett hadn't abandoned her, and he hadn't. The decision rested on her as much as Brett. He was nothing like Marcus's father, and she'd make sure Elliott knew that.

She needed to look at something other than these walls. If only she could tug down that panel and bring out Karlyn's Bible, but no. Those books, those figures, were invisible for a reason. Maybe she was cowardly, but she couldn't make herself expose them.

Her other choices were limited in topic. Carpentry or film theory or the abridged classic that Marcus's story had given new significance. She tugged out the shiny paperback film book. A book this thick, with a binding this tight, would bear evidence of reading. This one had barely been opened.

Aubrey forced herself through the first chapter. Flicker fusion, beta movement, persistence of vision. She didn't care. No wonder Marcus hadn't read this, if he didn't like to read in the first place. Why did he own it? Oh. She'd already read this paragraph. Twice. She turned the page, not wanting to. Great, chapter two. A history of Hollywood, starting with the Motion Picture Patents Company.

She swapped it for the children's book. At least it was fiction.

By the afternoon, Aubrey had finished the exploits of Jim Hawkins and returned to the film book. At some point, she set it aside and stared at his dormant computer on the corner desk. Of course, she couldn't touch it, not even to browse online. If the concops got hold of it and saw Internet history logged while he wasn't home ... which would mean they had already entered the house with a warrant, but ... still. She browsed his movie collection instead, which would take her at least a month to get through even in her current idleness. The cluster of silent films at the front of the first row gave away the chronological organization, so Aubrey worked her way backward. Hours later—having escaped into the Old West, pirate-infested seas, and a bank heist—Aubrey stretched her lazy limbs and jogged a few laps around the house. Indy kept pace for half a lap, then stopped to watch her.

The key in the door jolted her every cell to attention. Marcus hadn't said anything about coming home early. Maybe Lee had done some more cooking. Well, Indy could be the welcoming committee. Aubrey burrowed into the couch, picked up the film book, and pretended to read. The door opened.

Her baby cried.

Chest seized. Feet flew. Not real, couldn't be real, oh God, oh Jesus, make it real.

Infant carrier on the counter. Not Elliott's. But the music in the air was his fussing. His hiccups, his gasping, his indignant voice demanding the location of his mommy. Elliott.

Her socks slid around the counter. His soft cheeks, the blond fluff on his head, his nose, his moist eyelashes. The buckle slipped between her thumb and finger, then clicked open. The safety belt lifted away. Elliott in her arms, and another sound louder than his fussing, a sound that heaved from the depths of her body. Time melted into saltwater that ran down her face and all over her baby.

When the crying faded, Aubrey stood like a bent tree, and Elliott's tiny hand filled itself with her sweater, and Lee stood watching them.

"You?" Aubrey said.

Lee stood with her arms in a loose fold. Her eyes held no more warmth than two frost-encrusted windows. But she nodded.

"H-how?"

"The method is immaterial."

Elliott thrust an arm past Aubrey's clutch, and the nails of his open hand grazed her nose. "Where was he? Did they take care of him?"

"He appears to be healthy."

"But where ...? How did you ... Lee, how?"

The arch of Lee's eyebrows deflected Aubrey's questions without even a second of consideration.

"Thank you," Aubrey said, the two most inadequate words she'd ever spoken. "I ... You ... I don't know how to thank you."

"Gratitude isn't necessary," Lee said.

"Of course it's—you don't understand, this is the greatest gift you could—my baby ..."

Lee nodded as if she could possibly understand.

"Why?" Aubrey said. "You don't know me, why did you do this for me?"

"I didn't."

"You didn't do this?"

"I didn't do it for you."

So she'd done it for Elliott? By default, anything done for him was done for Aubrey, too. Oh … of course. "This was for Marcus."

Lee's gaze lowered to Elliott and assessed him with the same detachment she'd used to clean and bandage Marcus's back. "I was in a safer position to achieve this than he is."

"Not to mention he's coming home to me every night. Now I can move on."

Lee flicked a dismissing glance and gathered up her keys.

"But listen, I don't care why."

Lee nodded and moved toward the door as smoothly as a stream.

"You should think about it, though—him and you. You didn't do this because he's just a friend."

Elliott fussed into the silence, while Lee opened the back door and started down the garage steps. Aubrey hurried after her with her son's warm, chubby form clutched close. His cheeks were flushed with distress, not illness, and his weight in Aubrey's arms was unchanged. But the reassurance of a nurse wasn't something to ignore.

"Lee, wait, please. You looked at him? He's fine?" Aubrey said.

"Yes."

"Thank you."

Another nod. Another turning away.

"Wait," Aubrey said. "What do I tell Marcus?"

Lee faced her, expressionless. "The truth."

3 1

"This is Marcus's bedroom. You'll sleep in here, with me. I won't have to hug a pillow tonight."

Elliott arched his back, and one of his fists beat the air. Aubrey shifted his weight from the crook of her arm. His squirming ceased once he could see outward, and his back settled against her chest.

"This is a hallway. It could use some artwork, don't you think? And this is the living room. Marcus sleeps on the couch there, without any pillows. He's probably never been to a chiropractor in his life."

Elliott's body erupted in a hiccup.

"Exactly. And this is the kitchen. It's very ... well, I don't know what it is, I guess it's just a kitchen ..."

Tears rained into Elliott's hair. She'd try to contain them if there were any point. Elliott's blue eyes sparkled up at her. At least her spells of weeping didn't scare him. That he couldn't hear them probably helped.

In a few minutes, she swallowed the rest of her tears and rubbed a finger over his tiny knuckles, then returned to the living room. She pushed aside tattered magazines to nudge the back of the bookcase. Nothing moved. Under harder pressure, the panel swung down like a rusted hinge.

Wooden figures wobbled as Aubrey eased Karlyn's Bible from beneath them. She couldn't do this one-handed, but when she tried to lay Elliott on the rug, her hands refused to let him go. Finally, the hand under his back withdrew, then the one that cupped his head. His blue-socked foot punched the air above him, and his smile showed off his gums. Aubrey scrambled up and grabbed the pink-bookmarked Bible without losing Elliott from her peripheral vision. She scooped him up again and settled on the couch.

"You're not going to have that operation, baby boy," she whispered. "We have to hide, I don't know how long. No more medical records for us, anywhere."

Her baby's eyes trusted her, blinked slowly. Sleep fogged his gaze.

"We can't go back, Elliott. So we have to go forward." Yellow down caressed her lips as she bent over his head. "Forward is Ohio. And then maybe farther, I don't know yet. And forward isn't an implant. It's our lips and hands moving."

She didn't know what sign language could do for her child. She didn't know more than five words of it. But something inside her drew itself up from its former curl of silence, stood taller than she'd thought it was. She'd find a way to communicate with her baby.

Elliott's eyelids closed.

"Go to sleep, Mommy's got you now."

The reminder didn't birth tears this time. Her hum existed only for herself, but it bolstered this something inside her that had reawakened with the return of Elliott. After a minute, the hum gained words.

"What a friend we have in Jesus, all our sins and griefs to bear! What a privilege to carry, everything to God in prayer ..."

Elliott's breaths left his body with wisps of dreams inside them, like Marcus's carving come to life. Aubrey opened her best friend's Bible, and the pages rustled between her fingers.

"This is why we can't go back, baby boy," Aubrey said. "Because this book is true, no matter what."

She should ask Marcus if she could keep the Bible. Karlyn would want her to have it. How she'd hide it while on the run, she couldn't imagine, but she couldn't leave it here. She had nearly finished the book of Luke when Indy lifted her head and rushed to the back door. Marcus was an hour earlier than usual. Then again, he didn't punch a time clock.

In a minute, he appeared at the entry of the living room. "Aubrey, I've—"

The air held the taste of his shock.

"I'd like you to meet my son," Aubrey said.

He lurched forward two steps, then more. "I ... I don't ... how?"

"I don't know exactly, she wouldn't tell me, just brought him here."

"Who?"

Aubrey tried not to shrink into the couch. "Lee."

Emotions flashed across his face too fast for distinction.

"She's fine, Marcus."

He snatched his cell phone from his pocket and speed-dialed. "Where are you?" His bark didn't give Lee more than a second to answer. "Park. Now."

He was halfway to his truck before Aubrey could catch him. Elliott fussed at the jarring passage through the kitchen. "Marcus, wait—"

His strides paused, but he didn't glance back.

"Elliott needs diapers."

Slowly, he pivoted to face her.

"And baby wipes. And I had to go back to work, so I don't, um, make enough milk for him. Lee brought a bottle, from wherever he was, but he needs more formula. Baby formula."

And baby powder, baby soap ... But for now, Aubrey stuck to the most immediate necessities. The moment lengthened, and then Marcus nodded.

Her hand was pulling her earlobe. She dropped it to her side. "I think I've complicated your life all over again."

"I'll take care of it." He headed again for his truck.

"Don't you want to know his size?"

"What?"

"Diapers. He's in size two. Whatever formula you get will be fine, I don't buy organic or anything. It's expensive."

"Okay." Then he was in the truck, and then he was gone.

3 2

Marcus shut off his truck and jumped down to the gravel parking lot. Why had he picked this place? The little park was secluded compared to most public places, especially on a snow-sodden evening. Still. They could only say so much on a park path owned by everybody. Homes weren't safe, though, if the Constabulary had identified her as Elliott's … kidnapper. Really, that's what she was. Maybe an agent planned to watch her, tail her to work, follow her into the hospital … Marcus's strides lengthened as his neck muscles shortened.

Limp snowflakes landed on his hair, seeped into his scalp, dribbled down his neck. A white-haired woman passed him, hurrying toward the parking lot, tugging noisy twin girls by the hands.

"Going to turn into rain any minute now," she said without slowing.

"Thanks for the warning," Marcus said.

In a few minutes, he reached the garden. Lee sat amid the flowers, of course—or at least, where the flowers would be. Every spring and summer, this was her favorite picnic spot, surrounded by a rainbow of blossoms. She told him the name of each without expecting him to keep track of them. He did know geraniums on sight, ever since she'd called them her favorite. *They grow regardless of conditions, Marcus.*

Lee's back didn't touch the wood-and-iron park bench. Her head barely moved to track each passerby—the cluster of female joggers, the guy power walking with a mutt on a leash. When nobody was nearer to her than fifty feet, she rose and fingered the snow-sprinkled needles of a blue spruce. *God. She's here, and okay. Thanks. Keep her that way.*

Did they have a sketch of her? The outline of the face, the cheek-bones, the chin ... if an agent saw her, would he know?

Lee stood, turned halfway, and saw him. Her head angled, and a shaft of sun fell across her hair. Marcus halted outside her space. A cardinal trilled.

Lee didn't speak. Of course. He'd called her here; he'd have to start the conversation. Her hands hung at her sides, each bone so fragile, like every other line of her that hid beneath her slim coat.

"How'd you do it?"

"Sam was able to locate the foster home. He also informed me of the baby's deafness. I told the foster mother I was a social worker and that Elliott was being placed in a home with other deaf children."

"And she didn't ask for ID?"

"I was well-dressed and knowledgeable, and I was removing a responsibility she didn't want in the first place. She already has three foster children."

"Lee, if ... if she'd called to verify anything, or ..." His hands cupped his neck. "Why'd you do this?"

"Surely you know why."

"I told you no. I told you—"

"And I told you the choice was mine."

"You have to stop."

"I will, if you work with Sam."

The power walker cruised toward them from the other direction and tugged on the dog's leash to keep it from jumping on Lee. Marcus stepped away from the center of the path, but his legs wouldn't stop there. He paced over a patch of mushy brown grass, then whirled to tread it again.

"Marcus," Lee said when the guy was out of earshot, "he obtained the child's location in an hour. He verified that the foster home was temporary, providing me an ideal story. He reduced the risk of—"

"There shouldn't have been a risk." Not to Lee.

"Your stubbornness created it. I asked you to work with him."

"And if I don't, you will?" What kind of idiocy was that?

"Exactly," she said.

"You can't do this."

"You desire to maintain my safety. Working with Sam is now the best way to do so."

She ... was right. He couldn't try to keep her involvement passive. It never would be again. The knot in his gut grew cold. "Why."

"If I aid you directly, your obsession with my welfare will cause a blunder, and you'll be arrested."

"I don't want 'aid.'"

Her gaze didn't warm or waver.

"If." The rest of the words thickened in his mouth like a lump of old paint.

Lee's eyebrows asked how long he planned to make her stand here in the snow.

"If I let him give me information, you'll stay out of it."

"Yes."

"All of it. For good."

"Yes."

One hand dropped to his side, but the other wouldn't release his neck. "Okay."

Lee's head dipped a smooth nod. "Dinner."

"Dinner? You can't live like things are normal."

"You do."

"I didn't kidnap a kid."

"You're merely harboring criminals and committing felony obstruction on a daily basis."

He'd never match words with her. He growled.

"I didn't exactly disguise myself, but I did bleach several strands of my hair, and I wore uncharacteristic clothing and makeup."

Bleach. So she'd dyed it back, then. He shook his head. She'd probably been plotting this since she'd met Aubrey.

"I don't look like the woman who took Elliott," she said.

Not enough, but all they had. Marcus started toward the parking lot, shortened his strides so she wasn't forced to trot beside him. He waited for a couple to pass on the other side of the walkway. They swung their scarf-smothered toddler between them and punched the air with laughter and an off-key rendition of "Rudolph, the Red-Nosed Reindeer."

Lee walked beside him, calm in her silence. The path emptied into the parking lot. Marcus headed for the west corner. The snow turned to spitting rain as they walked. Her car stood out, but only because he knew where to look—beneath the floodlight, safe from shadows.

"What if they have a sketch of you?" he said.

They halted at her car. Lee unlocked it with a muted click and a blink of the lights.

"This is done now. You can't go back."

"I don't wish to," she said. "Do you have a restaurant preference?"

The ice in his stomach was on its way to a thaw, but his shoulders couldn't shrug. "Somewhere dim."

Lee's lips lifted.

"In a corner. And you keep your back to the doors."

"Marcus."

He opened her car door, and she slid inside. The slenderness of her frame made him want to hold her close. Stand as a shield between her and them. Between her and everything. The car roof froze his hand almost instantly. He kept it there anyway.

"Mexican." Her face turned up to his. "That place on Van Dyke."

"Okay."

"However, murky lighting is usually accompanied by a bar."

"That's okay."

It was. Had to be, despite how often the thirst hit him lately. He was slipping backward somehow. Last night, he'd slept in the basement rather than risk walking past his keys, grabbing them, going for a drive, stopping at that tavern on—

Lee nodded. He closed her car door and walked to his truck. He cracked the windows, cranked the heat, and switched on the windshield wipers. It was raining, after all.

33

Babies required a lot of stuff. Not like Marcus hadn't known that already, but wandering the infant department ... Heck. Strollers and car seats and high chairs and baby gates, and that was just one aisle. The easiest aisle. Then there were the rows and rows of softness. Apparently, they needed separate cloths for multiple functions. And so many blankets. He imagined the small form of Elliott in the crook of Aubrey's arm and understood. Babies were so helpless and so ... well, valuable. Why had Aubrey asked only for formula and diapers? Elliott should have more than that.

He threw three packages of size-two diapers in his cart and searched out the baby formula. Aubrey had said the brand didn't matter. If he could buy the wrong thing, she'd have specified. He grabbed a can, then three more. Maybe he'd call the landline and make sure she didn't need anything else. Oh, baby wipes. He had to get those, at least. They'd be with the diapers, right? He started back.

"Mr. Brenner!"

A five-year-old whirlwind gusted down the aisle and stopped only a foot before crashing into Marcus's legs. He grinned upward as if he was meeting a celebrity. Or a best friend.

A quick look down the aisle didn't show Pamela or Jason. Where ...? Oh, heck. Jason.

Marcus couldn't leave J.R. here alone. "Where's your mom?"

"At home."

Great. "Where's your dad?"

"He said I could come with him to get the pizza! But first we got to buy some stuff for Kyle's bottom."

Okay, then. "Let's go find your dad."

"Oh, we don't got to. Hi, Dad."

From behind Marcus, Jason's voice snapped with panic. "J.R., don't you ever—"

Marcus turned. Surprise smoothed Jason's face, followed by relief. "Brenner. Okay, the don't-talk-to-strangers lecture won't work here."

The guy wore jeans and a smoke gray sweatshirt. Did he wear that shade of gray all the time, even out of uniform?

"Da-ad." J.R. rolled his eyes. "Mr. Brenner's not a *stranger.*"

"You do not leave the aisle I'm in without telling me. And you do not go running after people." Jason passed a tube of ointment from one hand to the other. His tone seemed caught between explanation and tirade.

"But Mr. Brenner's my friend, Dad. I got to say hi to friends, or they won't be friends anymore."

"You always ask me first, always. Otherwise, I don't know where you are."

"And you think some hate-stuffed guy grabbed me?"

"That's right."

Marcus's arms prickled as if he stood in a draft. Before he could bid them good-bye, Jason's eyes skimmed over his cart.

"Diapers, huh?"

His pulse jolted into overdrive. Crap. He couldn't say the cart wasn't his. J.R. had seen him pushing it. *Okay, get a grip.* No reason for Jason to connect dots. No dots for him to connect. Marcus nodded.

"You've got a kid?"

The nonchalant *yeah* almost made it out of his mouth. But no. You couldn't lie to a cop, not about something he could check into later. Marcus shook his head.

Jason's head tilted, considering him. He was just being conversational. Right? "So, whose kid you buying for?"

"A friend."

"Friend who can't do their own shopping?"

"Yeah."

"Sick or something?"

"Something."

Jason nodded, but his mouth narrowed at the edges. Probably used to everybody spilling their guts to him whenever he demanded it. Well, Marcus's shopping cart was none of his business.

J.R. darted to Jason's side and pulled his sleeve. "Dad, come *on*. Let's get the pizza, and Mr. Brenner can come over."

"I can't, J.R. I've got work to do. But maybe I'll see you later."

They couldn't part fast enough. Marcus pushed his cart back to the diapers and found the baby wipes. Tomorrow, he'd buy some baby clothes, but the sizes were baffling, and he wasn't about to call Aubrey with Jason prowling an aisle over.

He pushed his cart to the front of the store and was scanning items in the self-serve lane before his body registered in his mind. Mouth like cotton, heart like a hammer. Neck muscles like a vise. Had he been smart or stupid just now? He held the last can of formula over the scanner and turned it until the beam caught the UPC. Swiped his smooth new credit card and bagged the formula. He'd throw the diapers in the truck.

Only a few lanes over, Jason and J.R. stood in line. J.R. waved, but Marcus pretended not to see. Maybe he should have tried to concoct a story. A friend's sister, a girlfriend going to a baby shower ... No, dang it. Jason had no right to interrogate him. Outside the fact that he *was* guilty of multiple felonies. Daily felonies.

His neck ached. His head would soon.

Half a dozen people clustered around the automatic doors, including the store greeter. Murmurs drifted from the group. Somebody walked past the motion sensor, and the doors opened outward into the chilled night.

"What's going on?" Marcus said.

The teenage greeter tugged his blue vest and shifted on spindly legs. His eyes darted from Marcus to whatever spectacle unfolded outside. "It sounds like a terrorist. We're not sure if we should call the cops, or the con-cops, or what."

The group included two more teen boys, an older woman, and a guy around Marcus's age. They shuffled steps forward, steps back, trying to angle a view outside while staying clear of the window. Marcus pushed his cart past them, through the doors.

"Dude, be careful," one of the boys called after him.

A man stood at the edge of the store's floodlights, one shoulder of his suit jacket exposed to the sleet. More gawkers stood out here, but not too close, as if he could be carrying some disease. Marcus stepped closer, into the quarantined space around him, and the man looked up with marble-pale eyes. Cataracts? But he met Marcus's gaze.

"You trying to hurt anybody?" Marcus said.

The man laughed. "Guess you'd think that, all right."

"What're you doing out here?"

"I'm sixty-nine years old, boy, and Truth's finally found me. I'm trying to share it." He could be Frank, time-lapsed twenty years.

Marcus shot a glance back at the store. Nobody from inside had dared emerge, and the group here was inching backward, letting Marcus handle the "threat." Good. He gripped the man's shoulder and steered him to one side of the doors.

"You're going to get arrested."

"Someday soon, I'm sure." He lifted his wrist to flash a silver watch that didn't look cheap. "But time's not on their side, either."

"No. Listen to me. There's—"

The doors opened behind him. "Mr. Brenner!"

God, no. Do something.

Another onlooker, probably in his forties, ventured forward. He tugged his coat collar up to shield his ears, either from the cold or from the old man's preaching. "Look, sir, I think you're confused. I don't think you know what you're saying."

"I'm saying Jesus Christ is the only way to God."

For less than a second, in his beeline to Marcus, J.R. brushed nearer to the stranger than he was to his dad. But Jason didn't need a whole second. He snatched J.R. up and swung him half around, turning his back to the man only long enough to plant J.R. against the shield of a cement pillar that held up the awning. Then he marched forward, into the man's space.

Marcus took a step, then another, toward standing between them. *Aubrey.* Claiming his own faith would condemn her, too. And maybe everyone left on his photocopied list.

Jason and the man stood face-to-face, boxers in a ring a moment before the bell.

"Want to repeat that for me?" Jason said.

"Dad—"

"Stay back!"

The man shrugged. "There's only one way to God. That's the truth. Go ahead and call the Constabulary if you want to."

"I don't have to. You're under arrest." He shifted quickly to pin the man's arms, as if he expected resistance. He didn't get any.

God, show me how to stop this.

"Brenner." Jason pulled out his cell phone with his free hand and dialed. "Take my kid inside."

The bystanders hurried in various directions toward their cars. A few dashed through the sleet unconcerned about slipping, as if the terrorist might overpower the courageous cop and come after them. J.R. peeked from behind the concrete pillar, pinching the back of his hand.

"Go on, man," Jason said.

What the kid saw or didn't see changed none of the reality. Marcus trudged to the pillar, skirting Jason widely enough that the guy wasn't in punching range. He lifted J.R. to one arm and turned his back on Jason and on the brother whose name he didn't know, the brother he hadn't saved. He shivered.

Inside the store with J.R., he waited nearly twenty minutes. The kid sat on his shoulders and peered out the window as a squad car arrived, green lights flashing. As Jason and another agent talked to the man whose nearly blind eyes didn't hesitate to meet his enemy's. As gawkers came and went.

Two teenage boys watched the whole thing and called out commentary. "Dude, they got him handcuffed."

A cheer burst up behind Marcus, applause and a few voices. Something squeezed his chest. *They'd be clapping exactly like this if that was me.*

Do something. Say something. *God, is silence what You want from me right now?* How could it be? He half turned toward them, ready. *Aubrey. And Elliott.* Outside, Jason nodded to the other agent, then crossed through the car's headlights. He said something to the prisoner before shutting the door.

J.R. steadied himself with a hand on top of Marcus's head and leaned toward the window. "That's my dad."

"Yeah."

Five was old enough. To watch, to understand, to learn. To admire. Marcus circled his hands around the small ankles that hung over his shoulders. *God, please. Save this boy.*

3 4

"Here." Three yellow boxes of diapers dropped from Marcus's arms onto the carpet at Aubrey's feet. *Thud-thud-thud*. Resting on his full tummy beside her on the couch, Elliott didn't stir. Marcus set down the rustling grocery bag of canned formula more carefully. "Sorry—I could've woke him up."

"You couldn't, actually," Aubrey said. "Not like that, anyway."

Confusion pulled at his mouth.

"Elliott is deaf. Remember?"

"Oh," Marcus said. "Right."

Aubrey bent to lift a can from the bag. Like the diaper boxes, this label flaunted a name brand. With iron, DHA, ARA, choline, calcium …

Marcus stood over her, too still. The hands at his sides curled a bit.

"This is perfect," Aubrey said. "It's more than perfect. Thank you."

His head didn't jerk in a brief nod. In fact, his neck didn't move. At all. "Okay."

"I appreciate it."

His eyes caught on the book in her lap, one finger holding her place.

"I didn't think you'd mind," she said.

"No, it's okay."

After a moment, before Aubrey's next words could form, he turned toward the kitchen. His eyes hadn't tried to incinerate her, so that stiffness wasn't anger.

Aubrey's hand drifted over her son's fuzzy green sleeper. "Be right back." She froze at the turning of a corner that would obscure Elliott, then forced her feet to keep going. Marcus stood before the running microwave. Whatever was in there didn't look like food. Taciturn was his default, but this was extreme. "Is Lee safe?"

"No."

"I mean, obviously not, if she actually—did she? Take him herself?"

"Yeah." Marcus could have been a photograph of himself, motionless for the rest of time.

"But she's safe for now, right? They don't know who did it?"

The microwave beeped as its final ten seconds began to count down. Marcus pulled the door open and tugged out a plastic pack of blue gel. CLOSE DOOR AND PRESS START scrolled across the microwave's glowing display.

He turned to head for the hallway, gel pack draped over one hand. "I'll be in the basement."

"Marcus."

He paused, finally turned when the silence loitered.

"Are you in pain?"

"I'm okay." Off to the basement again.

"So okay you can't turn your head?"

"It's nothing."

If only, for once, she could do something for him. The desire hardened into a decision. Aubrey trailed him to the basement door, then slipped around him and planted herself in front of it. "This happens often, doesn't it? Starts with a headache, turns into a stiff neck?"

"Aubrey. Move."

"There are things you can do for it."

"I know." He emphasized the gel pack with a jerk.

"Have you ever had a massage?"

"What?"

"I mean, by a professional." Her cheeks warmed for no reason.

"You're a professional?"

"No, not exactly, but I work—worked—for a chiropractor, and we had massage therapists working there. I picked up some things."

He brushed past her.

Aubrey snaked out an arm to bar his way. "I even worked trigger points sometimes. I might be able to help. Unless you'd rather take a painkiller."

"I don't need drugs. Or anything."

"I'm not talking about a full-body massage. Just your neck, to loosen it up. I've seen it work for people before."

He could maneuver past her easily, even remove her from his way, but he didn't. His eyes leaked a blend of weariness and pain, more than he must realize she could see. Aubrey held his gaze.

"Okay," he said.

Before he could retract that, she headed for the living room. Marcus followed, but his ravenous strides had lost their appetite.

"Have a seat." Aubrey fluttered a hand at the couch as if it were a chair in Dr. O's waiting room. Marcus sank down one cushion from Elliott. She rounded the couch to stand behind him ... and her hands froze to her sides. She swallowed and nearly choked—silently, thank goodness. Her hands settled on each side of Marcus's neck, and her thumbs explored for knots. His neck was a mass of them, small, malicious fists of gritted muscle.

Aubrey's thumb found a site of extra tension on the left side and pressed harder. "Does it hurt when I do that?"

"It's okay," he said.

Her hands followed the tightness downward, across the bulk of his shoulders, and discovered an entire colony of knots.

"Do you get spasms?" she said.

"Sometimes."

"Marcus, you need to see a therapist, really. This has to be incredibly painful."

"It's—" His voice splintered as she dug a few knuckles into his left shoulder.

"If you tell me it's 'okay' one more time, I'm going to shake you."

His head dropped forward as if too heavy to hold up. Progress. A few minutes ago, he couldn't have moved his neck that far.

"Breathe," Aubrey said. "Deeply and slowly."

Over the next ten minutes, she pressed with her thumbs, her knuckles. She dug her elbow into the worst of the shoulder knots until Marcus's breathing roughened, then kept digging for a slow count of ten. She kneaded with the heels of her hands when her thumbs wore out. At some point, the tension broke from his body, like a glacier splitting from a mountain and sliding away.

"Okay," she said quietly, when most of the knots had released their grip. "How does it feel now?"

His lungs filled slowly. His shoulders rose with the breath, and Aubrey's hands rose with his shoulders.

"Marcus?"

"Thanks," he whispered.

Her hands should move away now, but they nestled closer to one another, on each side of his neck, and rubbed a gentle rhythm. Her words emerged on a soft curl of air. "Why do you live with this? It's not that hard to treat."

"Lee says …" He still barely exceeded a whisper. "Everybody's body carries stress … in its own way. Some people get ulcers. Or have panic attacks. Or can't sleep. I get headaches. Not going to kill me."

"She told you not to do anything about this?"

"No, just … that it's nothing serious."

The silent minutes weren't uncomfortable. Only after a few of them did Aubrey notice their heaviness. *Stress* seemed an inadequate description. Should she ignore it, ask about it, offer a distraction? "So, about that film book. I'm guessing the spine is in mint condition because you didn't finish it."

No response.

"And I get why. Kind of dull."

He gave a quiet sigh. "Lee got it for me. Long time ago."

Aubrey dug two knuckles into a stubborn shoulder knot. "She thought you'd want to read about movies, because you watch them?"

"Yeah."

"You know, you might like reading fiction besides *Treasure Island*. You obviously like all kinds of stories. You've got everything from *Citizen Kane* to James Bond."

"That's different."

"So is Lee still trying to turn you into a reader?"

"Not as long as I don't make her watch James Bond."

Maybe her giggle shoved the next words out, or maybe it was the bend of his neck beneath her thumbs. "She, um, mentioned that you two aren't together."

The delay could have been Aubrey's imagination. "We aren't."

"You love her."

His head lifted slowly, like a weight on a pulley. Did he know he was now leaning into her hands? "Yeah."

"Does she know?"

Marcus nodded, a slow, loose movement.

"Well, contrary to the stereotypes, sometimes the woman's the dense one. Sometimes you practically have to propose before she gets it."

His breath rose in his shoulders with careful measurement, then left his body all at once. "I have."

She'd misunderstood. She must have. "You've what?"

"Proposed."

"And … what did she say?"

"No."

"But why?" Lee couldn't be a fool of that magnitude, unless her intelligence, her self-assuredness, wove a blindfold over the eyes of her heart. She'd scorned this man's devotion? She believed he wasn't good enough for her? But it didn't fit. She'd also turned herself into a criminal to rid his house of another woman.

"She's not ready," Marcus said.

"But—"

"We're friends. Until she is."

"Not ready for what, being in love?" Had Lee actually asked him that? "When does she expect to be 'ready'?"

His shoulders shifted under Aubrey's hands. Yeah, she wasn't doing a great job neutralizing her tone. "There are things … It's not that simple."

"Sure it is. She must be nuts."

"You don't know her."

So much for helping him relax. But Aubrey knew more than Marcus thought she did. Or maybe not.

"Aubrey … Lee's not playing with me. She doesn't do games. When—if—her feelings change, I'll know."

From the far side of the couch, Elliott bent a dimpled elbow and huffed a waking baby breath. Marcus's head turned toward her son. His hand crept over the cushion to enclose Elliott's foot. "Did he get sick?"

What? "Oh, the deafness? No, he was born with it. It's a recessive gene, so I have to carry it. Brett, too."

"It's not your fault," he said, as if her self-blame had leaked into her statement of fact.

"Brett and I … we weren't a one-time thing, you know. I'd tell him 'no more,' and I'd hold to it for … awhile, it varied. But never for long."

"That's not why he can't hear."

Are you sure? A tear rushed for escape, then a few more. She swiped at her cheeks, stepped back when the heel of her hand found several drops on his T-shirt. "Wow, I'm literally crying on your shoulder."

"'S … 'kay."

Aubrey padded around the couch and bent down to face him. "Marcus."

His eyes were half closed. At the sudden nearness of her voice, they opened again, but the sleepy mist didn't leave them.

"You're exhausted. Lie down and go to sleep."

"Have to … work."

She lifted Elliott from the couch and eased him down to the carpet, then seized Marcus's arm before he could struggle to his feet. A sigh eased from him as his eyes closed.

"Good night," Aubrey whispered.

"It's good he has you. Elliott."

"I try. I guess that's all any parent does."

"But you'll try at ..." His breathing slowed. "... The right things."

His left hand found hers with his eyes still shut, enfolded it in rough warmth. Oh. She tried to ease away, but he held on. Heat crept up her arm. One-handed, she covered him with the afghan and tugged it up to his chin. A few minutes later, his chest rose and fell in calm cadence, and they both let go.

3 5

Red lights circling on one wall, then the other, through the window. EMT with paddles. An electric *zap* that accomplished nothing. Body on the kitchen tile, sheet pulled up. *"That's my mom."* Nobody listening except to glare with disgust. What had he done? *"Bring her back! That's my mom. You bring her back!"*

Awake. His whole body convulsed with a gasp that yanked him mercifully from the dream. Something soft buried one hand. He tossed it off. Oh, the afghan. And distant warbling. Aubrey.

"If that mockingbird don't sing, Mama's gonna buy you a diamond ring ... which makes no sense. Why would I buy you a diamond ring?"

He must not yell in his sleep. Good to know. He sat up but let his breathing slow before facing her. She must have covered him last night. The fatigue had hit him so fast, even their conversation blurred now.

He tested his muscles, and his neck turned easily. His shoulders didn't try to tighten. His feet touched the floor as Aubrey entered the living room with Elliott on one arm, facing over her shoulder.

"I'm afraid I misjudged you." The glow of humor emphasized the dark flecks in her eyes. "I assumed you were one of those wagon-train-trail-guide sleepers, with one eye and ear open for hostile Indians or buffalo stampedes."

"Oh," Marcus said. He felt his mouth twitch.

"I have to say, Marcus, you'd be completely worthless in a buffalo stampede. You'd sleep right through it."

Yeah, probably. "Thanks. For last night."

"How does it feel now?"

"Good."

Her lips curved into a slice of satisfaction. "I'm glad it helped you."

"What time is it?"

"It's Sunday."

He twisted to read the time on the cable box and stifled a wince. A massage couldn't mend the stupid gash in his back. The glowing numbers propelled his body upright: 8:52.

"Please tell me you're not working today," Aubrey said.

"I was asleep for …"

"About eleven hours, because you needed it. I figured I'd wake you up if the house caught fire or something. Or I'd try to, anyway."

Eleven hours was ridiculous. Marcus headed for the shower.

"So you do have to work?"

He turned back. Her hand rested on Elliott's back, and she looked different today, not so hollow. Maybe a mother was filled up inside when her baby was close to her. *God, Lee should've had the choice to have this.*

And … okay. Maybe he could wish for the choice, too. J.R.'s weight on his shoulders last night had felt warm and simple and right. But he'd never make a child with a woman that wasn't Lee, so that was that.

"Marcus?"

He had to hold in a sigh. "No, not working. Just delivering something."

"No schedule?"

"Not really."

She smiled as her baby nestled against her shoulder. "Perfect. I'm going to try flipping eggs."

"Okay."

"Oh, and I cleaned up the blood."

"Blood?"

"In your truck, on the seat."

His feet shifted. "You didn't have to do that."

"I didn't mind, really. Anyway, it dried first, so it still looks pretty obvious. We should've scrubbed it out right away."

"Yeah," he said. "Well. Thanks."

After his shower, he found Aubrey in the kitchen. One arm cradled Elliott, and the other hand gripped the spatula. A golden pool of yolk sizzled in the skillet along with the whitening eggs.

"I broke them," Aubrey said without turning. "Just like I said I would."

"They'll still taste good."

"I think you're an optimist."

"They look okay. And you've only got one hand."

"Very true." She rested the spatula against the skillet's edge and swiveled toward Marcus. "Hold him a minute, I want to get the last one right."

"I—"

"Don't tell me you've never held a baby before."

Had he? In his lifetime, maybe, but no specific memory emerged. This wasn't the same as scooping up a sturdy five-year-old. Aubrey's arms offered Elliott anyway. A tiny head lay in the crook of his arm. A tiny body settled against his, warm and breakable.

"Okay." Aubrey had already turned back to her eggs. "Here we go. One out of four, that's not so much to ask."

Elliott's mouth opened like a red flower. His head rolled sideways, face toward Marcus's chest. Discontented noises lurched from him. Some people compared a baby's cries to a kitten's mew or a puppy's whine, but they were wrong. Elliott's whimpers were the complaints of a little defenseless person.

"He doesn't like me," Marcus said.

"It's not that. He just can't see me." Aubrey paused with the spatula half under her last egg. "Face him this way."

Marcus did, and Elliott's cries rocketed to screams. "Aubrey, he doesn't like me."

"You're new to him, and you're not soft enough." She slid the spatula the rest of the way and rushed the turn. Yolk trickled and hissed. "Dang."

She abandoned the spatula and held out her arms. As soon as Elliott rested there, the screams dwindled to muttering gasps.

"Not soft enough?" Marcus said.

"You know, women tend to have somewhat cushy arms, while yours are more—I mean, men's are more—um, solid. Anyway, I've been thinking, and we have to talk."

"Okay." Mentioning her blush would only deepen it, and already her cheeks almost matched her red sweater. He picked up the clean plate that waited on the counter, dug Aubrey's eggs from the skillet, and deposited them onto the plate.

"I'm not a freeloader," she said.

"I know."

"The kindness of strangers is one thing, but really, Marcus—"

"Not strangers, family."

She sighed. "Anyway, there's no end in sight, and babies are incredibly expensive. And we're not safe for each other. If you're out on one of your midnight missions and get arrested, I will, too, and Elliott—and if they somehow find me here, same thing, they'll take us all."

Midnight missions. She made him sound successful. He blinked away the flash of last night, the elderly man ducking into the Constabulary car. Elliott gurgled into Aubrey's shoulder, as if to ward off the quiet. But he couldn't know when her fountain of words bubbled and when it dried up.

Marcus could not let them down. "There's still Ohio."

"I knew you'd offer that, and I can't ever repay you." Her hand landed on his arm like a butterfly. The same hand that had cared enough to unlock the gnashing teeth from his neck and shoulders.

"We're even," he said.

"Hardly." Her eyes caught her perching hand, and it drew away. "When can you take us?"

"Where'll you stay?"

"I don't know. Probably"—her chin tucked, and her voice all but lost itself—"I'll have to get a job somehow, but probably a shelter, for a while."

Cold crept into him. That had never been the picture in his head. Or had he ever fully pictured Aubrey in another state? Getting Elliott back had been his only objective since meeting her. "No."

"Admit it—it's safer than your house. I can be indefinitely anonymous. I never made national news, and state Constabularies hardly ever work together. That's why you take people over the state line in the first place, right?"

"Aubrey," he said.

"It's the only thing left. You don't plan to help me raise my son, do you? Put him through college? Because he is going to college."

"Aubrey."

"It's time, Marcus."

"You don't belong in some place with junkies and hookers and crazy people and … and … drunks." She could go hungry. She could get sick, Elliott could get sick. Pneumonia hit you when you were worn out, Lee had told him once. Aubrey could get hurt, robbed, stripped by somebody who wanted her Wal-Mart sweater. Raped. He wasn't taking her to Ohio.

"So you have another plan, then?"

Not yet. He had to build one. Soon. Now.

Aubrey picked up the plate and ambled to the table. "Let's eat my mangled eggs."

After breakfast, Marcus switched on the radio, and they cleaned the kitchen. A federally funded research group made national news with the "disconcerting" statistic that up to 52 percent of non-Christian Americans knew of—and still failed to report—someone practicing Christianity.

When the radio voice began its loop, tension released its grip on the air. In local news, Jason was still squashing the story of Elliott's disappearance. Maybe Lee really was safe, but he needed some way to guarantee that. His brain pawed for ideas. He should ask Aubrey to help him load the table into his truck, then leave now for Chuck and Belinda's. He needed the wind in his windows while the road's yellow lines added up, mile on mile. He needed a way to protect Lee, and a way to protect Aubrey, something she'd agree to. As she scrubbed the sink—did she do that every day?—Marcus's phone vibrated. He picked it up from the table. Lee.

"Hi," he said. Wasn't she working?

"Hello. Two of my coworkers have a bet, and I told them you could settle it."

"Okay ..."

"I'm weary of listening to them."

"Sure," he said, picturing it now. His mouth curved.

"Did Grace Kelly star in *Vertigo*?"

"Kim Novak."

Her voice distanced from the phone. "Kim Novak." The cheer and the moan reached Marcus's ears with equal volume. No wonder Lee had decided to end the debate.

Questions filled his mouth, but he couldn't ask them. Had she noticed any strange cars near her house this morning? Had anybody eyed her too long in a hospital corridor?

"Thank you for sharing your expertise," Lee said.

"Sure. How's work going?"

"My coworkers' propensity for drama has been the greatest challenge of the day." Laughter reached Marcus through the phone.

Good. If she'd noticed anything suspicious, she'd have found a way to tell him.

"I've never seen this film," she said. "It could be intriguing, given their description."

Lee and *Vertigo*? "I could bring it over. But you'll hate it."

"Why? It sounds like an intelligent film."

"You'll hate everybody in it."

"Let me judge that. And I still have sundae ingredients."

Well, no turning that down. "Tomorrow? Around seven?"

"Fine."

"Okay," he said, and she hung up.

Aubrey had migrated to the living room. She sat at one end of the couch. Elliott drank from a bottle swirled in green and blue dinosaurs.

"Aubrey, could you—"

The doorbell froze every muscle in his body and widened Aubrey's eyes. He barreled to the front door's spy hole. Indy beat him there, loudly promising to dismember whoever had the nerve to invade her porch. The glimpse of a graying head and an artificially blonde one made him sigh. Chuck and Belinda. Ignorant and harmless. He darted back to Aubrey.

"Bedroom closet."

Before the second word, she sprang to her feet, keeping the bottle to Elliott's lips. She vanished into his room and shut the door. The car seat and boxes of diapers already hid there. A few cans of formula might lurk in a cabinet, but Chuck and Belinda had no reason to ransack his kitchen. After this, though, nothing could remain in an obvious place. They could have been agents.

"Down." He half raised his arm and snapped it to his side. Indy yipped the last word, then sat. Marcus swallowed, opened the door, and feigned surprise. "Hi."

"We were in the area, sugar, and we wondered how you were going to load up our big old table by yourself. And Chuck remembered your address, from when he came by to look at that other furniture. My heavens, that's a big dog."

Belinda marched past him, and her husband followed.

Chuck glanced back as Marcus locked the door. "Figured it'd be okay to drop in."

"It's okay," Marcus said. It would be, if his closet were empty. He followed his guests. Indy cast him a pricked-ear look of question, then padded along behind him. He wouldn't be out of her sight as long as the intruders stuck around.

"I could make you some coffee," Belinda said.

"Pearl, the man can make his own coffee in his own kitchen."

She sniffed the air like a Pomeranian trying to be a bloodhound. "But you've already got some gourmet blend brewing."

"Yeah." Marcus jerked a nod toward the steaming carafe.

"This place looks spotless, Marcus. Why, it's clean enough to suspect a woman's influence, I think." She laughed.

"Now you've gone and embarrassed him," Chuck said.

"Oh, I haven't, either."

"Sure you have, look at his face."

"Sugar, that's a compliment. Most men can't even see the dirt, much less clean it up."

God, they're so ignorant. Thank You. "Well," Marcus said.

"I'll change the subject, how's that?" Belinda said. The radio news, still on the same loop, repeated the latest statistics of Constabulary success, despite the uncooperative 52 percent. She shook her head. "They sure know how to make it sound good, running off with people's freedom."

"It's their job to make it sound good," Chuck said.

"I'd resign, then." Her glower at the radio seemed to blame the knobs and speakers. "If I couldn't make a difference, I'd resign."

"Yup, you would."

They didn't know what they were saying. Marcus wished they'd go back to their kitchen remarks.

"The folks who stand up to them, I wish I could shake their hands," Belinda said. "Makes me want to do something myself."

"Enough." Chuck thrust a thumb into his belt loop.

"Marcus isn't going to turn me in, Chuck, not with all his own illegal philosophies."

"I know that," Chuck said to Marcus, and the thumb yanked the belt loop. "I'm just saying."

"Yeah," Marcus said.

"Well, then, do you mind?" Belinda shut off the radio, then patted his kitchen table. "Did you make this, too?"

"Yeah. I did."

She ambled toward the living room. Marcus's neck tightened in defiance of Aubrey's massage. Did Belinda plan to give herself a complete tour?

"The end table and all this in here?" She waved at the table in the center of the room, at the TV stand.

Marcus nodded.

"What a talent."

"You wouldn't know it from Belinda," Chuck said, "but we've got a mile-long to-do list today, so let's load up that table."

"Sure." Marcus led him to the garage.

Chuck stood in the truck bed and guided the table into a careful tilt, then leveled it, while Marcus hefted most of the weight from the garage floor. He couldn't have managed the task by himself, not given the annoying condition of his back, and not without damaging the table. And if he'd enlisted Aubrey's help, Chuck would have asked him how he'd loaded the table alone.

Reborn caution settled onto his shoulders. Aubrey could not exist. In any way whatsoever.

"You sure this thing's solid?" Chuck said after Marcus checked and rechecked each rope knot.

"Yeah."

"I'd hate for you to lose it after all the work you did."

"I won't lose it."

"She's really looking forward to getting her dining room all set for the holidays. She talks about it every day."

Marcus nodded.

"Better go get her. She'll be ogling every piece of furniture you've got." Chuck grinned.

Marcus forced a smile and followed him back ... to the empty kitchen. And the empty living room. She really was showing herself the entire house.

"Probably in the bathroom," Chuck said. "You know how women are past fifty or so. Then again, maybe you don't, but she'll be right back."

Marcus refilled his coffee mug and paced. *God, don't let her be exploring.*

3 6

Breathe. Don't hold him too tightly, or he'll cry. Let him squirm a little, but keep the nipple in his mouth. *Oh, Jesus, please, please, I don't know who's there, but please, blind them, keep them away from this closet door. Make them as deaf as my baby—my breathing is so loud right now.*

Stone had replaced Marcus's jaw. His eyes had blazed with something she couldn't name, not fear but not relief, either. Had his look through the peephole shown him uniforms the color of smoke? Agent Young and Agent Partyka?

She knelt in a closet next to a stack of diapers. This wasn't hiding. *Oh, God. Oh, God.*

Elliott writhed in her arms, kicked and flailed. One soft hand thumped against the wall. Aubrey bent over him and gulped her breaths, held onto each one as if it were her last before a dive into a million miles of water. Her son's head turned to one side. He spit out the nipple. No, no no no, Elliott, no—

He whimpered, half a lungful of sound, half frustrated with his gasping, sweating mother. She shoved the nipple back between his gums. He arched his back and spit it out again, and the protest used more air this time, more noise, more frustration.

The doorknob turned.

God, save me, oh please, God help me God help me God help me.

A female silhouette, widest at the hips. She leaned in, flipped the light switch, and gasped.

"Oh, my." The voice lilted with Southern vowels. No uniform. Jeans and an apricot sweater.

Nothing to say, nothing to do, nowhere to hide or run.

"Does Marcus know you're—oh, I'm guessing he does. Stand up, you can come on out. I'm Belinda. You don't need to hide from me."

No words were safe. Elliott wriggled and swiveled his head away from the bottle and wailed.

In seconds, Marcus erupted through the bedroom doorway. Belinda absorbed his glare and barely withered.

"Now, Marcus, I wasn't snooping. I heard that baby fussing through the furnace vent. It's right smack between the bathroom and the closet."

"You need to go," Marcus said.

"Sugar," Belinda said to Aubrey, "is it Constabulary y'all are hiding from? It is, isn't it?"

"Now." Marcus stepped forward as if he would he forcibly remove her from his house, this woman with shining eyes and a grandmotherly heart and determination to soothe the nightmare.

An older man stepped through the doorway behind him, about Marcus's size minus the shoulders, plus a hint of extra belly. "What the—?"

"He's harboring people," Belinda said. "Long-term, if there's more baby supplies around here than what's in that closet."

"It's not long-term," Aubrey said. Marcus flicked a scorching glare toward her, though he had to see she'd only tried to minimize this. As if anything could.

The man stared, first at Aubrey, then at Elliott. The unkind astonishment in his eyes and the burning in Marcus's propped Aubrey to her feet.

"I'm sorry." The words inched out of her mouth toward the rock Marcus had become.

He shook his head and addressed the strangers. "Leave."

"Marcus," Belinda said. "You don't really think we'd turn you in."

"Now."

The man stepped around Marcus and hooked a thumb in his belt loop. "You're that Weston woman."

"No, I'm not."

"Oh, come on. You match the description, and you've got a baby."

The couple turned to gape at Marcus, suddenly similar in their shock.

"The kid's with the Constabulary," the man said. "What'd you do, kidnap him back?"

"Now, Chuck, don't go making accu—"

"I'll make whatever I want to. Besides he's not denying—"

"Leave." Marcus's voice clipped their prattle short.

Silence. Aubrey's eyes drew the line from Marcus's gaze to Chuck's. An inane image of an Old West shootout flashed through her head. This wasn't funny. Maybe she was closer to hysterics than she thought.

Chuck's beefy hand roosted on his wife's back and nudged her toward the door. Belinda gazed over her shoulder with a compassion that nearly flattened Aubrey.

"However you got here, sugar, you take care, and the little one, too."

Thank you, Aubrey tried to say, but her lips were too stiff.

"And when your time's up here, if you need a place, we've got plenty of room."

Marcus herded Chuck and Belinda from the room. The wall didn't let Aubrey collapse, so she slid down its cool smoothness until she sat on the floor. *Don't drop Elliott.*

Minutes later, Marcus returned. "They're gone."

Aubrey couldn't nod any more than she could speak.

"Here." His hand offered support for her to stand.

If she couldn't nod, did he really think she could reach for his hand?

"Aubrey?"

"I think ... I need ... a minute."

He dropped to his knees. "You're shaking."

"Next time ... tell me it's not con-cops."

"Oh."

"A couple more words, that's all I needed. 'Bedroom closet, but you're not going to be arrested, not in the next ten seconds, anyway.'"

His left hand gripped his neck. The fingers rubbed and clenched, but he was fine. Aubrey was learning his signals, not that she'd ever tell him how obvious he was. Holding his neck was a habit. Digging his knuckles in was a reaction to pain.

"I'm sorry."

"It's over," she said. "But it's not. He's going to report us."

"No."

"He was appalled."

"That's just Chuck."

"You have to take me to Ohio, right away."

"Aubrey. If he had to, Chuck would take somebody in as fast as Belinda would. The rest is just what he does."

Elliott gurgled, and Aubrey dropped her eyes from Marcus's. Maybe he was right. He didn't seem to trust blindly. "I still have to get to Ohio."

Marcus stood and reached down again, and she grasped the warmth of his hand and hoisted herself up. The earthquake in her legs had stopped.

"I've got to deliver that table," he said. "And I'll be out tonight."

"You're avoiding the subject."

"No. Just … still finding another way."

What other way was there? But the stone wall was back, and Aubrey couldn't move him.

37

Anywhere but a bar. His first step inside battered his senses—cigarette smoke, grease, sweat, babbling and laughing and arguing, a hockey game on the TV, bodies pressed too close until he broke through into a clear space. And alcohol, washing all of it.

Lee's eyes had apologized when she told him where Sam wanted to meet. Marcus had reassured her. He shouldn't have. Sam had suggested it, not insisted. Marcus could have changed the location. But this was the safest of public places to exchange secrets. The noise level submerged your words until they dissolved forever. The low lighting hid you, if you wanted to be hidden. Everybody clutched his own purpose for being here, and if you ignored the other guy's purpose, you didn't exist. Besides, a few months ago, he could have handled this place without a problem. Had to make sure he still could.

He held Lee's description before him in his mind and scanned the bar. Tall, lean, black. Close-cropped, graying hair. Probably wearing a short-sleeved polo even in December. There. The corner table. Sam nodded to him. Lee must have shared Marcus's description too.

Marcus brushed between clusters of kids that shouldn't be here. A paper banner hung from one of the booth tables, enormous red letters and a foaming mug graphic. *"Happy 21, Alex!"*

He slid into Sam's booth. This was the man who'd known Lee longer than he had, who managed the wealth Kirk's death had left her. This was a man Marcus could trust. But he still had to ask.

"Why are you doing this?"

The man's dark eyes sized Marcus up. His voice came deep as a movie preview voiceover. "From what I can tell, I'm saving your sorry hind parts."

Marcus didn't have to see his own face to know what Sam could read there. The annoyance had to be printed across his forehead.

"She warned me not to say it like that. Said if I wanted to help you, I had to turn it around, make it look like you were helping me."

Marcus's hands fisted under the table.

"But this is how I figure it." Sam flattened both hands on the table, long, musician's hands, lighter brown around the nails. "If I want you to trust me, I don't spin things. So here it is. I told Lee about a month ago I was quitting, going back to finance. I'm the pro-verbial disillusioned soldier, seen too much to believe in the mission. Then two days ago, she says I can't quit. My position's too valuable, the information I can get to. And she tells me about you—that you're trying to fight this, single-handedly. We'll talk about your stupidity in a minute."

Marcus shifted forward.

Sam lifted a hand, palm out, and his voice fell to a whisper. "I ask her what she wants, and she says, 'I want Elliott Weston.'"

The words left his mouth without any regard in the same tone he'd use to say, "This film is not yet rated."

"So you set it up," Marcus said.

"Not quite. First, I tried to talk her out of it. But—you already know this—any friend of Lee's isn't going to disregard her choices."

When her choices put her on the Constabulary's Most Wanted list, they should be disregarded all over the place. Marcus should slug this idiot.

"I don't like how it worked out either, man," Sam said.

"You're the one that worked it out."

"You're the one that got her all hell-bent to do it."

Enough words. Sam was taller than he was, and the muscles of his arms ran tight as rope from wrist up into sleeves, but Marcus could take him. He swallowed the impulse. The whiskey-choked air was getting into him like a toxic smoke. Unrolling the tight, hidden coil of the worst in him. Sam was an ally, and he was right about at least one thing. Marcus had driven things to where they were now. If only he'd realized she'd go this far.

Sam's fingers drummed the table. "Here's what I can do for you—names, addresses, and dates for the warrants. Sometimes they're not acted on right away, maybe wait a few days, if we think we can get more evidence by waiting. But usually, it's within twenty-four hours."

Marcus nodded. His copied sheets would be current for only so long. The Constabulary probably identified new suspects every day.

"Obviously, I know you have Weston," Sam said. "Who else?"

Marcus shook his head. "I warn them. Or move them. I don't keep them."

"Why her?"

"She had nowhere else."

"And how've you been finding the others?"

"A list."

"From?"

Marcus shook his head. No reason to tell the whole story.

Sam's scowl only lasted a moment. "And you move them where?"

Marcus's voice lowered. "Ohio. Sometimes."

"You know? How'd you find out?"

"What?"

"Oh … You were just using common sense, then." He waved off any interruption before Marcus could say a word. "There's quite the covert fight waging in Ohio right now, almost across the entire state. Of course, media's hushing the story. People here might get inspired, try to emulate them."

A server with dyed-red hair strode up to their table and set a bottle of beer in front of Sam. Marcus drew in a deep breath and let it out as she turned to him.

"Hi there, what'll it be?"

Shot of whiskey, fire down the throat, warmth spreading all the way to the fingers—"Nothing, thanks."

She nodded and disappeared, and Sam took a long sip of beer. Marcus should've asked for coffee, but no. Coffee was separate from this place.

"What do you mean, covert fight?"

"Essentially what you're doing, but they've got a small army working on it. And they're not the only state making waves. Michigan's kind of disappointing in comparison. We've got wind of a little network up in the Thumb, but most of our state is resistance-free."

Constabularies did communicate. They knew what other states were dealing with. Maybe the federal government was feeding them information, planning to coordinate them. Marcus leaned against the vinyl seat and shifted to avoid the sore spot on his back. He'd let Sam finish before questioning him.

"Anyway, as far as Ohio goes, you didn't know how good your thinking was. Hold off on that awhile, though. There's a theory Weston's no longer … missing anything, which would be a good time to run. The state line's crawling right now."

Definitely no homeless shelter, then. The danger collided with a sort of relief.

"Now, as for the rest of our suspects. How much can you remember at one time?" Sam said.

Did he mean names? Addresses? "Numbers stick in my head pretty good."

"That's a plus." Sam stretched his legs under the table until his black loafers peeked out on Marcus's side, ankles crossed. "Your guest really messed things up for them, with the media attention. Some of the higher-ups are in a frenzy to publicly throw her behind bars."

"Well, what've you got?" This meeting had to give him more than a promise of future information.

Sam tapped his temple with one long finger. "Eidetic memory, also known as photographic."

He was serious?

"I've got three for now."

Three addresses. Good. Marcus opened his wallet. What could he—there, the receipt for the diapers and formula. Sam leaned back and stretched his right arm. His fingers tapped a silent beat on the table edge.

"Pen," Marcus said.

Sam lifted a pen from the pocket of his beige polo shirt and sat forward to hand it over. Marcus scribbled down each street address Sam recited. To the first, he added one to each digit of the house number. To the second, he would add two, and to the third, he'd subtract one. Not much challenge as a code, but better than writing the exact numbers. The street names left him lost, though. No way to mask those.

Sam's dark eyes tracked the pen until it hesitated before writing *Elm*. "Disguise it in another word."

Right. Mel? Lem?

"Lemming, elementary, melody …" Sam shrugged. "You'll remember it later. You just need a clue for which numbers go with which street."

"Sure," Marcus said. He wrote *Lemming*. But there was no hiding the next one, Whitetail. Anyway … "That one's on my list."

Sam tilted his head. "Who's your source?"

Marcus gazed back at him and didn't blink.

"This is what I'm talking about when I use the word *stupidity*. You're going to have to accept your allies."

Lee knew this guy. Marcus's thumb clicked the retractable pen back in, out, in. Okay. Fine. "Jason Mayweather. I'm a contractor. I did some repair work for him. And I searched his office."

"Mayweather?" Sam leaned forward and glanced at the door as if planning his escape. "You're nuts."

Marcus shrugged.

"I'm telling you, if he'd found you, he would've put a bullet in your head and five minutes later wondered how he was going to explain your corpse."

"He wasn't home. What's the last address?"

Sam gave it to him, and his brain blanked. Travis Court. No memory trick for that one.

"Varsity," Sam said. "All the letters, plus one."

Heck. "Do you play Scrabble with Lee?"

Sam chuckled, a rumble even deeper than his speaking voice. "I have, occasionally. She says we're evenly matched."

"I'm no good at it." He couldn't find the point to it, either.

"At least you admit it."

"No choice." Marcus's mouth tugged upward. "She stopped asking me to play about seven years ago."

That brought on a flash of smile, but then Sam's gray-flecked eyebrows tugged toward each other. His eyes held Marcus's for several moments of slow finger tapping. Maybe the beat of his fingers betrayed the speed of his thoughts.

"She can take care of herself, I know, but she's kind of been ... under my wing, for a lot of years."

"Okay," Marcus said.

"She said she's known you a long time, that you're trustworthy. Seems you're good for her. She needs a friend in it for the long haul."

Friend. As if Marcus had never proposed to her, as if he didn't wait for the day she was ready. As if he could simply transfer his love to somebody else if that day never came. Of course, Lee wouldn't have told Sam any of that.

Sam's fingers had stopped drumming. "You asked me why I'm doing this."

As a favor to Lee, of course, because she'd gotten it into her head that Marcus needed an ally.

"We need some shelters," Sam said, "immediately available. We'll need other contacts, too, hopefully some way to alter identities. I'll work on that, I know some people. Who can you bring into this?"

Marcus shook his head. "Nobody."

"That's not going to work."

One ally. That was Lee's deal. Sam had no right to change the terms. "I'm not going to put anybody else in danger."

"You just answered why I'm here."

What?

Sam's hands flattened again and pressed the red tabletop as if to brace himself, though he didn't stand up. "Someone has to broaden your vision, man. If I'm going to join this thing, I want it to do something, to mean something."

Marcus's work did mean something—to Aubrey, to the people on Jason's list. He was doing the best he could.

Sam shook his head. "You honestly think you can keep on with this, alone? You try to bite off more than you can chew and you'll gag on it. And when you get yourself arrested, who's in danger then?"

"I wouldn't talk."

"Everyone talks. Everyone's got a breaking point. They'll get you to yours."

"I'm not—"

"Solution? You don't get arrested." Sam's deep whisper volleyed the words without pause. "Which means you approach this thing realistically. You get Lee sent to re-education and I swear I will kill you. They target a person's vulnerabilities, and I'm not talking only about the darkness phobia. I'm telling you, if they can find out about it, they'll exploit everything that's ever happened to her—"

The rape. Marcus's gut clenched.

"—the rape," Sam said. "And the abortion."

The …

Sam's cheekbones seemed to sharpen along with his attention. "What? You thought I didn't know?"

Marcus tried to swallow without choking. The … abortion?

Sam's fingers perched in a frozen curve. "Wait … didn't *you* know?"

"There was no— She was never … there wasn't a baby."

"There was."

"No." Lee couldn't have children. She'd told him she couldn't.

"I don't know why she'd tell you about one and not the other, but I know she was pregnant. Why do you think she went to Kirk? You knew him, didn't you? You know what he did for a living."

She'd been sick. After. She'd told him. Kirk helped her. An OB-GYN could help a woman with something like that. It didn't mean there'd been a baby. There couldn't have been a baby. If there had, Lee would be a mother today. Lee would have an eleven-year-old child.

"It never even entered my head," Sam said. "That you wouldn't know."

"You're wrong."

"I'm not, Marcus. I met her when she was barely nineteen, only a year after."

"Lee wouldn't."

"She didn't want an abortion. Her father took her to Kirk's clinic, and when she refused to sign the paperwork, Kirk told him it was Lee's decision. It was almost a month later she showed up again, alone, and ..."

Marcus balled Sam's shirt in his fist and pulled his lanky form up and half over the table. "And what?"

"Her father didn't give her a choice."

Marcus shoved him. Back over the table, against the seat, head barely missing the wall. Sam regained his balance. His gaze shot around the bar. Pinned Marcus. Ordered him to sit back down.

No.

"You have any more attention grabbers up your sleeve?"

Shut up.

"Don't you breathe a word to her, Marcus. I guess I should have thought you might not know. Kirk's the one that told me."

His senses attacked. He smelled whiskey. Tasted whiskey. He had to get outside. Maybe he could breathe another scent out there.

"Are you hearing me?" Sam said.

Marcus's legs carried him toward the door. Out. Get out. Sam tailed him but didn't touch him. Which was good. Right now one finger on Marcus's shoulder would put Sam in the hospital. His body exploded into the night air and kept going. Walk. Walk. The cloud of his breath billowed and dissipated. Snowflakes drifted around him, fat and contented. His hand swiped the air once and tore through their path. They died as water on his palm and fingers.

"Marcus." Sam stalked into his line of sight and stood in his way. "Please. Don't tell her."

Don't hit him. He didn't do this, not any of this. He didn't steal from Lee or rip her apart. He didn't kill her baby.

"I'll be in touch, and you're going to hear me out. There's too much at stake for you to keep playing Lone Ranger." Sam turned and faded into the snow.

38

Marcus walked. Headlights passed on his left. Slush hid the white line of the road's shoulder. The weather seeped through his jacket and shoes. The cut in his back started to throb. He walked. Lee. Lee, hurt. By a monster with a tattooed wrist. By a black hood over her head. By another monster that called himself her father and paid more monsters to hold her down and scrape her baby from inside her while she fought them, because she did fight, because she was Lee. And a baby, not just hurt but murdered, born in a bloody pulp and thrown away.

God was here. Marcus hunched over and braced his head on his arms. *No. Get away from me.*

He had to tell Lee. She could stop hiding it from him. He could help her, somehow. Not with his words, but maybe with hers, if she could talk about it and know he would listen. His body straightened and turned around, put the traffic on his right instead. His strides lengthened. His hands curled against the cold. He shoved them into his pockets.

His truck sat waiting. Marcus got inside and started the engine. The neon lights from the bar window reflected on his windshield's layer of snow. No. He wasn't thirsty. He was going to see Lee.

The tiny paper squares in his pocket filtered through his resolve. Homes with endangered people inside, watching TV right now, or sleeping. Lee would be awake when he finished with them. He'd collect the right words to say to her as he drove to each house.

On the way to Elm Drive, the thirst hit him. Hard. He didn't need a drink, and he didn't want one, but part of his brain whispered otherwise. He wouldn't listen, that's all.

Not a light, not even a flickering TV, shone from inside the Elm house. Marcus skulked nearer. The snowflakes hadn't yet buried the dark points of grass, but he'd still leave footprints. He crept so close to the house that his jacket scraped brick. His path would be invisible from the street.

The garage was empty. The doorbell's tone reverberated on the other side of the door, then faded to silence. Marcus turned away from his sigh that hung in the frosty air.

He coasted his truck through the neighborhood and found a different route out than he'd taken in. When Travis Court gave him another empty house, he punched the steering wheel once.

Not once. He struck it again, smooth and shiny and solid enough to take the blow. *No, don't feel it.* One more house. Then Lee. He needed words.

He drove past Whitetail the first time, turned around and corrected the beginning of a skid. He'd had to notch the windshield wipers up twice since leaving the bar.

How to get up to the house? His footprints now would be like spills of dark paint on white carpet. Well, if he had to advertise, then he would. Down the sidewalk, up the driveway. Nobody suspicious would walk there. If the snow kept falling at this rate, his prints would fade to white soon anyway.

No doorbell. Marcus lifted the old knocker instead. Something hardly deserving the title of dog yapped and collided with the door. It opened half a minute later, and a woman in her thirties squinted at Marcus and wrapped her robe closer with a shiver.

"Can I help you?"

When he couldn't answer, the woman began to inch the door closed. He forced his voice to work. "Hide."

"Excuse me?"

Marcus's hand gripped the edge of the door and stopped its progress. "There's a warrant. They'll come soon."

In one blink, wide astonishment replaced the squint. "I don't know what you could possibly be talking about."

"Yeah. You do." Behind her, several feet up the hallway, stood a boy with a military cut, probably around eleven. Marcus's knuckles turned white against the blue door. "They'll take you. And him. Whether they've got evidence or not."

"Are you threatening my son?"

"I'm warning—both of you. You've got to hide."

She stopped pushing at the door. "Who are you?"

"Doesn't matter."

"It does to me."

Marcus shrugged. His feet shifted, but he couldn't leave. "Do you have someplace?"

"To hide? Yes, we do."

He waited.

"But I think I'll keep the location to myself."

Really, that was sensible. He nodded and turned.

"Sir?"

Maybe she was a waitress, because nobody called him that. He turned back and suppressed a shiver.

"Thank you for what you risked tonight."

Marcus nodded again and left the porch, trying to step where he already had. He reached his truck a few houses away and headed toward Lee.

How would he say it? The drive gave him about fifteen minutes to assemble his words. He thought he had them lined up the best way possible until he knocked on her door. He waited for her to open it, and the words in his head became like drops of water in a cupped hand, pouring between the fingers no matter how hard you squeezed them together.

Lee opened the door, and alarm for him leaped into her eyes. Her hair was damp from a shower. The navy hoodie swallowed her. Marcus lost the rest of his words.

"Marcus." She stepped aside and closed the door behind him. "What's wrong?"

Everything monsters had done to her. He had to be careful, get a grip, before he forgot himself and pulled her into his arms.

"Are you injured?"

"No."

Her eyes scanned him up and down, pausing at his hair. "You're quite wet."

"Just snow."

"Are you thirsty?"

"No." Yes. But that wasn't important. "I've got to talk to you."

"All right." She motioned him further inside. "Remove your shoes and jacket. They're only trapping the cold around you."

"No, Lee, wait. I've got to say this."

She turned back to look up at him. Concern nested between her eyebrows.

"I know."

Now the eyebrows arched, asking if he thought she could read his mind.

"About … about … the baby."

Confusion burrowed into her face for only a second before vanishing along with every other expression. She stared at him from behind a mask of ice, thicker and colder than he'd ever seen before.

"Sam thought I knew. Kirk told him, a long time ago."

No flicker, nothing at all in her eyes.

"I don't know why you didn't tell me, but … I know now."

She blinked, once.

"Lee? I—I had to say …" He stepped nearer. Her shoulders stiffened. He stood still. "I'm here. To help you."

"I do not require help."

"It's okay. To let me."

Lee turned her back and widened the space between them. Her stride was fluid as always, but her shoulders were rigid.

"Lee."

She laced her fingers behind her back, squeezed until the knuckles whitened. "I want you to leave."

He wouldn't desert her. No matter what she thought she wanted right now.

"Marcus. I said leave."

He shook his head. "I'm here now."

"I don't want you here."

"It's okay. You can talk to me about it."

Did she think if she kept her back turned long enough, he'd slip out the door and leave her alone with all that the monsters had done? Marcus crossed the room, approached her from the side.

"Lee. I'm not going anywhere. I'm here. I'm—"

"You are an intruder. Nothing more."

Her words punched the breath from his body. But she didn't believe that. She'd harbored this secret for too many years, wasn't ready to open up all at once. That was all. "You don't have to talk. I'll just—just be here."

If she'd only look at him, if she'd only—but his words weren't enough, couldn't break through her ice, couldn't pull her up from it. His left hand lifted slowly, fully in her sight. He settled it onto her shoulder.

She hit him across his face, an open-handed slap.

His hand fell to his side. She paused for eye contact. He couldn't move. She backhanded the other side of his face.

An ache started in his chest.

The ice in her eyes promised to stare him down until daybreak if he dared to stay. His feet dragged backward.

Lee ... He couldn't think.

His face stung. He blinked hard, stepped outside, closed the door behind him.

He climbed into the truck. A tear trickled down his cheek, warm as it left his eye, cool as it dripped over the heat from Lee's hand. He lowered his forehead to the cold steering wheel. He tried to talk to her, inside his head, the words he hadn't been able to hold. But even inside now, the words were gone. Everything was gone but a rawness he couldn't ease, a shortness of his breath. The tear dropped onto his thigh.

He was so ... No, he wasn't ... He was ... so ...

Thirsty.

3 9

Aubrey had never owned a dog, but she couldn't miss Indy's attempt at communication. From the kitchen, her whines and barks overlapped around her panting. *Thud.* Great, she was ramming her head against the window now.

Elliott slept in the center of the bed, undisturbed by the dog's racket. Aubrey pulled the covers down to the foot of the bed so that he lay on only the flat sheet, as safe as a crib. Then she swung her feet to the floor and barreled toward the noise.

"Okay, dog, this had better be good."

Indy's nails scrambled against the wooden sill. Her front paws dropped to the floor, and her head bumped Aubrey's leg. Then she barked and reared up to the window sill again. The yard lay beneath a quiet blanket that had finally stopped falling. The trees wore layers of lace.

Someone was out there.

Aubrey dropped to her knees next to the dog and peered over the window sill, her gaze level with Indy's.

A dark figure sat in the abundant white, knees half bent, back against the maple tree. A man. From here, he could be any man, but Indy made Aubrey's decision. If that were anyone other than Marcus, the dog would be growling death threats, not crying with worry. Aubrey went to the laundry room for her tennis shoes and the black coat, then stepped outside.

She should've tugged on some jeans, too. The cold gnawed through her pajama bottoms. Snow tried to invade her shoes. Under the tree, Marcus didn't move. If he was hurt, she was going to shake his snow-caked shoulders until some common sense snapped into his head.

She stopped beside him. Was he asleep? "Marcus."

His eyes rose to meet hers, the usual fire in them banked to barely a glow.

"You're sitting in four inches of snow."

"Get away from me."

Delirious? She hunkered down and captured his hand, and her breath snagged at its icy stiffness. "Come on, let's go in the house and get warm."

"Not cold."

"I'm cold, and I'm not going in without you."

Aubrey shuffled with bent knees around to his other side and planted herself in front of his face. Her foot bumped something half submerged in snow. Marcus's hand pinned it down before she could touch it. Glass. A bottle. Clear, rectangular. Empty far below the neck. She didn't have much experience with alcohol, but she knew the hard stuff when she saw it.

"You're ... drunk?" she said.

"I don't get drunk."

"But why, why would you—"

"Go in the house."

"I'll make a deal with you. Come inside, and I'll leave you alone."

The heat of his glare barely reached her through the veil in his eyes.

"I won't go away until you come inside."

He lurched to his feet, and she extended an arm to steady him, but he didn't need it. He didn't falter even when he bent to retrieve the bottle, but he couldn't grasp it.

"You don't need that," Aubrey said.

He straightened. "This wasn't a test."

What? "I'll bring it in for you. Your hands are too cold to pick it up."

"Don't pour it out."

The cold of the glass bit into her hand. She turned it upside-down, and the last half of the amber liquid gushed onto the snow.

"I said this wasn't a test, don't pour it out!"

He tore the bottle from her hand with a force that dragged her several steps forward. He hurled it against the trunk of the maple. Glass shattered into spears that lost themselves in the snow. Marcus whirled and charged into her space. His glare now was like an assault.

"Did you wait until you got home?" Aubrey's words stopped his advance. "Or did you start on that in the car, drinking and driving in the first blizzard of the year?"

He stormed past her, and his arm shoved into hers. The collision didn't seem intentional, but he ignored her stagger. He was headed for the house. *Thank You, God*—but her prayer broke off as she realized she wouldn't reach the door before he could slam it and lock her outside.

He didn't. She followed him in and closed the door. Indy rushed him, but he flinched from her anxious tongue. Snow drifted from his jacket, his hair, all over the rug as his feet dragged back and forth. Every inch of his jeans was soaked through. Wet white powder encrusted his shoes.

"Marcus," Aubrey said. Get him warm now, deal with his stupidity later.

Did he not hear her?

"Hey." She crossed the kitchen toward him.

He thrust out an open hand without facing her. "Don't."

"You have to take that stuff off. I know you don't feel cold, but you are."

"Shut up."

She tugged an earlobe and waited for him to stop pacing, but he didn't seem inclined to do anything else. "If I get you some clothes, will you change?"

He whirled on her, and the menacing fire licked behind his eyes again. His dog pushed her head into his hand, and Marcus's fist clipped under her chin and snapped her panting jaws together. Indy yelped and slunk backward, away from him. Marcus blinked. His hand uncurled. He stared at his dog, and his eyes lost their last bit of light.

"Marcus?" Aubrey said.

His gaze rose to her. "I'm drunk."

Aubrey nodded.

"Oh, God."

"Will you please put on something dry? If you get hypothermia, I'm going to have to wake Lee up in the—"

He stepped back. "Okay. Clothes."

He trudged to his room, and after a heartbeat of hesitation, Indy plodded after him and slipped through the half-open door. Aubrey waited.

What would possess him to intoxicate himself? He was too dependable for this. He hadn't gone out with some friends and had a few too many beers. He'd purchased a bottle of whiskey and drunk it straight, alone under a tree.

He remained in his room. She tiptoed to the door. He'd had enough time to change. Catching her spying might set him off again, but he might have collapsed from cold. Aubrey pressed against the door frame and peered around it.

Marcus knelt on the floor with his arms around his dog. Indy's tail swished back and forth as if to erase what he'd done. She squirmed in his embrace and managed a few licks of his cheeks, and he hid his face in the fur of her shoulder.

Elliott lay soft and asleep on the bed behind him, mere feet away from the sodden pile of his clothes. Aubrey stepped into the doorway and stood over Marcus.

"Do you have a problem?" she said.

He lifted his head.

"A drinking problem, that you can only hide for a week?"

He immersed his hands in Indy's fur, then pulled them back and stood.

"How often do you do this?"

He swallowed.

"Marcus, I have to know. How often?"

He didn't pace. He didn't turn away. He didn't grab his neck. "Eight years."

What …?

"Ten months. Nineteen days."

Comprehension stole the anger she tried to hold onto. He didn't do this every eight years. He *hadn't* done it in eight years, almost nine. "What happened tonight?"

He shook his head.

"Don't you have a—what're they called, a sponsor? Didn't you call him?"

"I didn't go through that."

"Then how did you quit?"

He brushed past her, charged down the hallway and back into the kitchen, then stood still as if wondering where to go next.

Trying to tug the story from him thread by thread would be useless right now. She should leave him to sleep away the haze and the anger. But her mind saw him fishtail his truck with an open bottle in the cup holder next to him, grabbing gulps at every red light, or maybe not waiting for that.

Whatever made him toss her safety aside like this had to be horrible. "Did someone get arrested? Did someone get hurt?"

Marcus's arms rose to shield his face, like a child who thought no one could see him as long as he couldn't see them. A chill slithered through Aubrey.

"Marcus ... who was it?" *Not Lee, dear God. He can't take that.*

"I'm no good to anybody."

"Of course you are. I'm sure you tried to—"

"I didn't."

Aubrey inhaled courage and stepped closer to him. "Is she ...?"

"Her heart. It stopped. And I didn't help her. Because I'm drunk and no good to anybody."

The room closed in. Aubrey clung to the counter. "Oh, no. When? Where—?"

"I heard them talking. If somebody called nine-one-one, they said. If somebody did something. She called my name. But I don't come when I'm drunk. I don't help her, I just drink and fall asleep and wake up and Mom's dead."

Mom. Years ago, he'd said. So no one had died tonight. Relief bowed Aubrey toward the counter. Marcus folded over and collapsed to his knees on the rug in front of the sink. His arms cradled his head.

"Everybody's trying to help," he whispered. "Saying sorry for your loss, saying they're sad, too. Like we've got the same feelings. But I killed her. So the feelings are for everybody else. Not for me."

"Marcus, that was a long time ago, right?"

"No family now. Nobody. Shouldn't have them."

"Tonight. What happened tonight? You didn't just fall off the wagon, something pushed you."

"Go away."

"Okay, you don't have to tell me, but something obviously happened. Go see Lee and talk to—"

He shuddered.

"You've never told her about your—problem?"

"She knows," he barely said.

"Then call her, first thing in the morning."

"Can't."

"Why not?"

"I'm an intruder. Nothing more."

"What?"

"She won't let me … She won't even try to let me."

"Let you what?"

He shook his head. His eyes were flat.

"Can I do anything to help?"

He slumped against the fridge and ducked his head to his knees. He pushed aside the hand Aubrey tried to rest on his shoulder. At last, she remembered her primary responsibility in this situation, and it wasn't Marcus.

She retreated to the bedroom, where Elliott hadn't stirred. His pale downy hair slid through her fingers. A hurricane picked up speed inside her. Chuck and Belinda weren't danger enough for Marcus's taste. He had to court the attention of the cops, too. They could have connected him to one of his warning missions, could have found or fabricated sufficient evidence to interrogate him about his beliefs. Aubrey could have been asleep in this very bed with her son when the con-cops came to the door. She curled her body around Elliott's and draped him with one arm. As if she could protect him from any of this.

"Oh, Marcus," she whispered. "How could you?"

The night felt endless. Again and again, she dozed, then woke to the scent of coffee. Once, the shatter of glass snapped her upright in bed, and Elliott squirmed and fussed at the interruption to his dream. Aubrey settled him on her chest, and the rhythm of his lungs evened and slowed.

The crash hadn't been loud enough for a window. Anyway, if Marcus decided to tear the house down brick by brick, she couldn't stop him.

Aubrey's hand lifted and lowered with Elliott's breathing for wide-awake hours. When she surrendered to the seeping sunrise and got out of bed, the kitchen held only Indy, stretched out under the table. Aubrey must have drifted again, long enough for Marcus to leave. The dog raised her nose like a toast. Aubrey knelt and stuck her head under the table. Indy sniffed the hand she extended, then favored it with one quick lick.

"Good dog," Aubrey whispered.

While Elliott slept, secure in the car seat, Aubrey dusted and vacuumed. Rooms removed, the vibrations of the vacuum's roar weren't enough to wake him. She'd slogged through nearly a chapter of film facts by 7:30, when the lock turned. Had Marcus forgotten something? Was his post-bender state too miserable to work? Muted, indefinable sounds wafted from the kitchen. The door reopened, and the screen reshut. After a few minutes, he came back inside. When the kitchen puttering resumed, Aubrey tossed the book onto the couch and headed there.

Lee stood before the open refrigerator. She wedged a pizza box between the top of the fridge and the first shelf. A back corner buckled, and Lee pulled the box out, set it on the counter, and opened it. Two slices remained, decorated with every meat topping Aubrey could think of. Lee fetched a plastic baggie from a drawer and slid the pizza inside, then returned it to the fridge.

Three of her glass bowls clustered on the counter, along with two casserole dishes and a foil-covered pie plate. Comfort food, of course, which meant Marcus had called her, after all. Good.

Lee's uninterested gaze flicked to Aubrey. Then she went back to her rearrangement of Marcus's refrigerator. She condensed almost its whole contents to the top shelf and slid her first bowl onto the middle shelf.

"Want some help?" Aubrey lifted a casserole dish to eye level. Lasagna. "Wow, still warm. Wait ... you made all this stuff this morning? How much of it is from scratch?"

Lee's back didn't turn. "All of it."

But no more than two hours had passed since he left. Even if he'd called Lee then, even if she owned five ovens, she'd lacked the time to prepare and cook this much food.

"I'm sure he'll appreciate it right now," Aubrey said. "I just don't see how ... I mean, you should be a TV chef or something."

Lee slanted her a chilly gaze. "Don't be absurd."

Aubrey handed her a bowl, then another when Lee had tucked the first between two coffee creamers. "So he called you at six in the morning? Did he tell you what happened to him?"

"You believe something happened to Marcus?"

That remote tone almost convinced her Lee didn't know. "You don't have to cover for him. After all, I was here last night."

"Please elaborate."

"I don't know the details of what upset him, but something did. Obviously."

"He said this?"

He hadn't called her. "He didn't use words, of course, but he didn't really need to. Drinking half a bottle of whiskey while sitting in a snowdrift pretty much said it all."

For an entire second, Lee froze. Her hands paused, half reaching toward Aubrey for a dish. Then her blankness hardened beyond steel. Lee took the dish and slid it onto the bottom shelf.

"You're mistaken. Marcus does not drink," Lee said.

"Not for the last eight years?"

Lee shut the fridge.

"He was drunk enough last night to tell me."

Lee scooped her keys off the counter. "I'm late for work."

"Lee, did you not hear a word I said? You have to do something. He could've wound up in the drunk tank and I could've wound up with the con-cops."

The icy eyes didn't deem her worth a glance. The fluid steps didn't hesitate on their way out the door. Aubrey surged forward, and her fingers snagged Lee's black leather jacket.

Lee's arm swung a dislodging blur of a circle, with such force that Aubrey's thumb nearly jammed backward.

Aubrey rubbed her thumb. "Are you going to call him?"

"My actions don't concern you."

"*His* actions concern me, and they concern my son."

"Because you're imposing on his life. Marcus is not your responsibility. You don't know him." Lee resumed her path to the door.

A pang for him passed through Aubrey's stomach. Lee might shove her aside, but she stepped in front of the door anyway. "I don't care how you feel about him; he's in love with you. And something's wrong. He needs help. He needs you."

Aubrey might as well have been wallpaper. Lee stepped around her and walked out the door.

4 0

The day was a parched blur. Nothing registered except the weird things. The streaky path of melting snow that dribbled from the roof of his truck down his windshield at the first red light. The knothole in a client's wood floor, nearly black at the center and framed by two half-ovals that met at the ends, a double-lidded eye that never blinked. The way every shade of gray, from clouds to concrete, was either lighter or darker, more blue or less, than Lee's eyes.

He worked. He shut the headache out as much as possible. He gulped coffee, and coffee, and coffee. How had he ever thought this rush could be enough? He tried to listen to his clients' conversations and tried not to hear them. He finished work and returned to Elm and Travis Court, last night's empty houses. Today, one sported a yard of yellow tape, and the other held a family that wouldn't listen. They pleaded with him not to come back. He drove home.

Day one. Almost nine years had collapsed under one night of weakness. He could see them lined up behind him, every day he'd said no, every day God had helped him say no. Every day Lee had stayed with him through the shaking and the needing and the wanting. All those days now huddled inside as a giant pile of rubble, dust still rising.

Driving might help. The old house, the Constabulary tracker house—he could park and walk for miles out there. He could get lost in trees and snow. He could hunker down inside the deteriorating structure and disappear. Maybe he'd come out when he was stronger.

When he could drive past a grocery store again without clinging to the steering wheel.

Running might help. The impact would jar his back, but he could handle that. His legs could pump out the mulch of his insides until he was hollow.

Woodworking might help. He'd bury himself and the thirst in his workshop, in sandpaper and hobby knife.

Marcus pulled into the garage and parked the truck. He didn't remember turning into his neighborhood or lowering his head to the steering wheel. He kneaded his forehead against it. That didn't feel so bad.

Somewhere inside an instinct still fought to call Lee. His thumb rested on speed-dial one, not the first time today, but he didn't press it.

She didn't have to come over. She didn't have to choose a movie or belittle his ice cream sundae. She didn't have to occupy space nearby or even say a word, if she would hold her phone to her ear while he held his.

Why had she never told him about the baby?

She'd told him everything that day at the park, their park, sitting beside him on the wrought iron bench, fingers knotted in her lap, meeting his eyes for a few seconds at a time, then staring at her hands. She'd said he deserved to understand why she'd really said no, and then she just … said it.

"When I was eighteen, I was raped."

She recounted specifics as if they had happened to somebody else. Attacked in a parking garage while leaving work. Her first job after retail, receptionist in a big medical building. The assailant had hit her. Might have done worse but was startled by someone coming off the elevator. Marcus could hardly listen to those details, and then she'd offered a final fact she meant to chase him away for good.

"As a result, I'm physically unable to have children."

He'd gone home and stood on his back deck for an hour, trying to stop picturing the crime, the details she hadn't said. When he couldn't, he'd split his knuckles against the porch beam, and the pain sharpened his thoughts to a single point: that monster's knuckles might have looked like this after he hit Lee.

He'd vowed two things while he tried to stop the bleeding. Someday, he would marry this girl. And he would never break the trust she'd offered him.

He hadn't known her trust had held back.

Marcus blinked away the past and closed his phone.

Praying might help.

No.

If God wanted to hear from him, He should do something. He should roll time back like an old reel-to-reel and paralyze the monsters before they could touch her. He should part this day like a sea and reach down to Lee and set her baby into her arms.

Marcus lifted his head. God said nothing. Marcus slid the key from the ignition and headed inside.

41

When Marcus returned home a little after 8:00 that evening, Aubrey migrated from the living room couch to the kitchen. He dropped his keys, kicked off his shoes, and ran a hand over his dog's head as if this day were no different than yesterday. He had to know her eyes were tracking his movements as he started the coffeemaker, but he said nothing.

"How're you doing?" she said.

He turned partway for a look that ended after about half a second. Without the glaze and the anger, his eyes were his own again, but the embers behind them didn't glow anymore. He froze with the fridge door only half open. He eased it the rest of the way, like the discoverer of some ancient treasure that had existed only in mythology, until now.

"She came by on the way to work this morning," Aubrey said.

Marcus reached into the fridge for one of the bowls, then yanked open the deli drawer instead. He threw some lunch meat and buns onto the counter and pawed around the door for condiments.

"You did call her at some point, didn't you?"

He gathered his supplies—mustard, a paper plate, and a white bun about as nutritious as the plate. A handful of iceberg lettuce from a bag, and layers of thick, dark-edged roast beef. This looked more appetizing to him than Lee's food?

"About last night," she said.

He squeezed four straight lines of mustard onto the bun.

"I feel like we should talk about it."

Roast beef piled higher and higher on the mustard tracks. "Nothing to say."

Aubrey rose and stood beside him. He mounded lettuce onto the meat, then squashed the second half of the bun onto the entire heap. He stood over his sandwich without saying a word or taking a bite.

"Marcus, I'm not judging you. I'm not judging what you did."

After a moment, his eyes flashed to hers.

"And I wanted you to know that."

"I'm an alcoholic," he said.

"You told me."

"I know. I remember. But—" He shook his head.

"But what?"

He didn't need to say a word, not with self-hatred shuttering the fire that belonged in his eyes.

"Listen, Marcus. That whole once-an-alcoholic-always-an-alcoholic thing—I don't buy into that nonsense."

"You should," he said quietly.

"You're recovered. Last night doesn't change that, and recovered means you're not one, not anymore."

He abandoned his sandwich to pace, fists tight. "It doesn't go away."

"I'm sure it doesn't, completely."

He replaced the carafe and sipped the coffee black, then gulped it. In a minute, he drained his mug and set it on the counter. His hand rested there as if too heavy to pick back up.

"Aubrey, I'm ..." His voice fell. "I don't know what's wrong with me. I didn't used to be this ... weak."

Father God, please put the words in my mouth. "You're not."

"You don't know what you're talking about."

"Marcus. Almost nine years is not weak."

His hands rose to cup his face, and the whisper oozed through his fingers. "One day."

She crossed the kitchen. This might be a bad idea, but she curled her hands around his, tugged them down, cradled their broadness. "Tomorrow will be the second day."

His face crumpled. When her arms wrapped him up, his circled in return. His shoulders heaved with one dry, silent sob. Her certainty hardened—why he hadn't taken the hurt to the woman he loved, what had to be the weapon that had ripped these holes in the first place. Why Lee had stocked his refrigerator, why he'd made a cold sandwich and ignored a homemade casserole. She tipped her head back against his shoulder and whispered up to him.

"It was really bad, wasn't it? The fight with Lee."

His head turned toward the far wall, away from her.

"Talking might help."

He shook his head. Did he know how tightly he was holding her? Did he know his irregular breathing was revealing his struggle for control? She rubbed a steady rhythm into his arm, up, down, up, down. His body curved over hers.

Step away.

Her hand moved from his arm to his back. He needed this. A minute to pull himself together.

Marcus shuddered, then sighed. His arms tightened around her. A dormant ache rose in her body.

Stop now.

She pushed his chest, gently. "Marcus."

His arms plummeted to his sides. He stepped back twice. Aubrey stood in the center of the kitchen, his warmth torn off her like a stolen coat.

"Aubrey." His voice rasped.

"That's right. Not Lee."

He closed his eyes and turned away, but not before the shame flooded his face. Aubrey circled to make him face her. More guilt was the last thing he needed. She shoved away the ache for herself. It was an embrace, nothing more, especially not to him. She and Marcus would never belong to each other, and she'd never considered otherwise, not for one heartbeat, until she'd spent a few of them in his arms. But these last few moments weren't reality.

"Look at me," she said.

His gaze flickered up to hers, then dropped to the floor.

"You love her. I knew that before, and I know it now. I don't get why, to be perfectly frank—"

That garnered eye contact. He opened his mouth, but she waved him to silence.

"I don't need to get it. The point is, we're okay."

He nodded slowly. He stared at the rug.

Aubrey rubbed her cold arm. The man needed to talk this out. "What's the worst thing right now, Marcus? Is it falling out with Lee, or what the falling out made you do?"

"It didn't."

Aubrey waited, but he stood wordless, motionless. "What didn't what?"

"Nothing made me drink. Except me."

Technically true, but hauling a rock of guilt around would only crush him, and his transgression was so ... small. Really, it was.

"Aubrey, the things you make excuses for—they're the things you don't quit."

Truth flashed in his words. She'd nursed excuses of her own with headlong diligence, excuses to cling to a darkness she'd recognized and wanted anyway—the salted velvet of Brett's skin, the two of them tangled like vigorous vines, the hungry kindling. And afterward, telling herself that she loved him too much to deny him, that she had to anchor his loyalty, that she'd marry him soon and the old sin would evaporate as soon as the action was no longer sinful.

Marcus studied her.

"It's just that there are worse things than drinking," she said. Illicit sex was probably on the same level, but other things ... weren't.

He paced again, this time as if a burden weighed him down.

"It might not feel like that to you, especially right now, but it's true. What you did was forgivable."

"Not really." He took another, firm step, and another, crossing the rug in front of her, but his strides had lost their mission.

"Yes. Really. And whatever happened to your mom—"

He froze midstride. His eyes darted to hers, stunned at her knowledge, then dimming with recollection.

Yes, Marcus, you said too much last night. "I'm sure it wasn't your fault."

"I talked to the paramedics. After, when I was—sober." His mouth tightened, and he blinked through a wince. "It was. My fault."

"There's no way to know that for sure."

"Don't."

"Marcus, I'm sure they told you, she might have died no matter what you or anybody else—"

"Don't."

Really, what was she trying to do? He'd believed for years that he'd killed his mother. She couldn't persuade him otherwise.

"I'm sorry," she said.

Marcus's gaze didn't rise from the rug.

"All I'm trying to say is that, even if you could have saved her, it's still forgivable. Everything's forgivable, almost."

Maybe the quaver in her voice made him look up from his feet.

"And I'd know, because I did the thing ... that isn't."

Some desperate throb inside *wanted* to tell him. Maybe her confession would even the ground between them again. Maybe a glimpse at her sin would help reduce the weight of his. Maybe she simply had to heave out the poison of guilt that sickened her more every day.

"They're not talking about it on the news. I guess because it would make their system look bad, but I ... I've been through it. Re-education. It's been less than a year."

He surged one step toward her, and a flame of alertness licked his eyes back to life. "Did they hurt you?"

"It doesn't matter what they did, what matters is that I told them there were multiple ways to God, that—Marcus, I said whatever they told me to say."

"You didn't believe it."

"I didn't know what I believed. I didn't know why God was letting this happen, if He'd save me from them or if He'd let them—"

"What did they do?"

The hard chair she'd sat in for days, the ache in her back, the zircon blue eyes that bored into her, and the scream, that woman's scream. Not as if someone were hurting her, but as if someone were hurting every person she loved in the world, all at the same time.

"Aubrey?"

"Nothing, they didn't do anything. But they said ..."

"What?" Marcus barked at her like Indy sensing intruders.

Her hand pressed her stomach, high where Elliott's fluttering heels had hammered some strength into her, but not enough. "Before he was born. They threatened my baby," she whispered.

His fists clenched at his sides. She had to back away from his anger, even though it burned on her behalf. She tried not to say more, but the words pushed themselves out into the heated air.

"I saw a woman there," she whispered. "I don't know what they did to her but her mind was broken. She didn't see anyone or anything. They kept her locked up and sometimes she would scream and I don't know if they did that to her or not but I couldn't take it. I'm not like Karlyn."

Marcus shifted into her sight.

She was crying. For some reason. "But don't you see, none of that really matters. If only I'd had more faith, but Janelle's right. I'm Judas."

Marcus came closer, and Aubrey tried to shove away the tears that blurred him. His warm hands cupped her shoulders. "Janelle said that?"

Aubrey clamped her lips together and sidestepped away from his grip, but he didn't release her.

"She's wrong," he said.

Aubrey shook her head. "I *did* betray Jesus, I said—"

"You said you didn't know Him. Right?"

Her face hid behind the curtain of her hair. Sobs squeezed her chest. *I'm sorry, Jesus.*

"Aubrey. It wasn't Judas that said he didn't know Jesus. It was Peter."

Peter. The story inched into her heart. He'd denied Jesus three times, and Jesus still let him be His disciple, even let him participate in the beginning of the church.

"Read it," Marcus said, hands still firm on her shoulders, holding her up. "And forget what anybody else says. Just look at what Jesus says to Peter."

"Okay," she whispered.

He stepped back. "Good."

Aubrey swiped at her cheeks. "What about you?"

"There's nothing to say. About me."

He believed in forgiveness for everybody except himself? *God, please show him how stupid that is.* Aubrey clearly couldn't.

"And Lee?" she said, because the other topic was up to God now.

"I've got to call her."

"I'll feed Elliott in your room, give you some privacy."

"No. I can't yet. I don't have … words. Yet."

"Okay." Had he wrought the damage between them, or had Lee? Or had they both yelled things yesterday that shamed them today?

He crossed to a drawer, tugged out a plastic baggie, and shoved his sandwich inside. At the refrigerator, he traded it for a casserole dish. He ran his thumb over an edge of foil, then turned on the oven.

4 2

"You don't need a new floor," Marcus said for the fifth time.

"I don't know what you expect me to do, young man. I'm not going to put up with this moldy old stuff anymore."

His hand latched onto his neck. "It's not moldy."

"No other word for it, all those ugly black spaces in between the squares. They used to be white, you know."

"It's dirty. And a little old. But the crack's mostly under the rug. And you could scrub the floor."

Penny's veined hands perched below the waistband of her cotton pants. "Scrub the floor? On my hands and knees like a spring chicken?"

"I didn't mean you, you. I meant anybody could scrub the floor."

"You see anybody around here besides me? Because if you do, I wish you'd point them out."

"Penny. I won't tear this stuff up. There's nothing wrong with it." And he'd taken enough money from her for ridiculous jobs that anybody could do.

"Then I'll find me someone who *wants* to work."

"That's—"

She marched to the kitchen, and Marcus followed. He grabbed the phone book before she could start to paw through it.

"Penny."

Her hands planted on her hips again. Her outward-poking elbows created triangles of space. "Give me that book, young man."

"I've got some grout coating in my truck. I'll leave it for you. It'll make the grout lines white again."

"But who's going to do it?"

"Anybody. Call Keith. He can have it done in half an hour. Then after four or five hours, he sponges off the extra stuff. That's all."

"And when do you expect me to drag him over here to do it? He's got a wife and two kids and his very own life."

Well, he still reserved time to throw a party every few months, to throw together a basketball game every few weeks. "He won't mind."

Penny folded her arms. "How much will you charge me? Never mind, I don't care how much, just do it."

Marcus captured the half-escaped sigh that had built throughout this day of giving estimates, putting up drywall, downing coffee, and searching for what to say to Lee.

"You honestly think Keith's going to drop everything to whiten tiles for a little old lady?"

"You're family."

The arms unfolded and drifted to rest at her sides, gradual as feathers. "You always say that word like it trumps all the rest."

The remainder of the sigh slipped out, strong enough for Penny to hear it.

"I'd like my yellow pages back now."

"I'll do it," he said.

"When do you have an opening?"

"Now."

Penny's mouth wrinkled upward in victory. "In that case, I'm making coffee."

Two mugs and forty minutes later, he squeezed the thin white goop into the last grout line. It was after 7:00 by the time he stopped Penny from trying to pay him, returned her grateful hug, and walked with her out to his truck.

"I'll sponge off the extra stuff tomorrow," he said, one hand on the door handle.

"Sounds peachy."

He opened the door but stopped with one foot up in the cab. He stepped back down. "What did they do? Secretly?"

Penny frowned up at him. "What did who do?"

"Whoever started this, taking freedom. Before I was old enough to know."

Her bony finger poked toward his truck and traced the outline of the side mirror. "It wasn't really any one thing. It was lots of things, all packed together, over lots of time. Things the courts decided, things the papers and the TV and the radio all said about certain people. Laws that got passed with little hidden things inside."

Marcus waited for explanations, for details, for anything else. She stood next to his truck and fingered the door trim. Then she turned back to face him.

"Do you know, it used to be that churches didn't pay taxes? And it used to be that there weren't any government workers— what are they called, monitors?—the ones that churches report to. It used to be, those jobs didn't even exist. See, there's perks for getting old. You know things. Thirty-two-year-olds don't realize how different the country was when they were in kindergarten."

"What about—"

"Now, listen here, I think I know why you're asking all this. But there's not an abracadabra to stop them, Marcus. There's no stopping them, not anymore, no getting the freedom back.

There's only …" She gave a faint chuckle. "Living the best life you can in the time you're set to live it."

"No," he said. "That's not all life is."

"Now, young man, one thing I won't listen to is the evangelical tripe. I lived with it from my Roy for a lot of years, and I'll tell you what I told him. When I get up there, God will ask if I loved my husband and my children, and if I tried to help people that needed it, and I'll say yes."

"That's not what God's going to ask."

"Come back tomorrow, young man, and finish my floor."

"Penny—"

"Did that sound like a suggestion? Because it sure wasn't one."

Marcus got into his truck and rolled down the window. "Tomorrow, we're talking about this."

"Nope. Subject closed for me about forty-five years ago."

She waved as he backed out of the driveway. While he drove, he listened to his voicemails.

"Hey, Marcus, it's Clay, just checking up on you." Clay's tone held no real caution, despite the heightened risk of recordings. At least he was vague.

Keith's voice was three times louder. Marcus held the phone away from his ear. "Hey, Brenner, some of us are hitting the gym court in about an hour, could use you if you're free. Don't plan to play too long, text me back or just show up."

Janelle's voice came last, full of forced cheer anybody would suspect. "Working on inventory here at the store, thought I'd catch up with you to pass the time, but you must be working too. Now don't ignore this message too long. I get obnoxious when I'm ignored. Talk to you soon, bye."

Marcus deleted the voicemails and signaled for the next turn. Straight ahead would take him home. Left would take him to Lee. The yellow arrow turned to solid red. He braked, and *Vertigo* slid forward on the seat beside him, then dropped to the floor.

Lee didn't want this rift to last. The stash in his refrigerator was her way of telling him. She knew words, but she didn't always use them. Soup and lasagna and casseroles and pie were a language as clear as the German shepherd puppy she'd presented to him three years ago, already named. *Indutiae.* Truce. They'd both needed one, after what had been said. Shouted, in his case.

"You want to keep both my friendship and your new righteousness. I need to accept this faith or my willful rebellion will taint you."

"All your perfect words don't make you right! You need to accept it so you don't go to hell!"

They needed a truce now, too.

The oncoming cars cleared. His truck forged ahead through traffic and dirty slush.

Lee talked when she was ready. He couldn't push her. But he had to, didn't he? How could he be sure what she needed?

By the time he plodded up her wet, salt-spattered walkway, Marcus's whole body clenched—neck, shoulders, hands, gut. He rapped on her door, too hard. A minute passed, another one, but he hadn't misunderstood. Lee wanted a mending.

Her eyes seemed to find his before the door opened.

"I ... came to ..." Well, to fix things, obviously. "How are you?"

"Fine," she said.

"That's ... good."

The quiet owned no warmth, no ease, nothing at all. It was dry and unattached, a dead branch between them.

"How was your day? At the hospital?"

"Fine."

"I had the tuna-noodle thing for dinner, last night. It was good."

Lee said nothing.

"Thanks," he said. "For bringing it—all of it."

"No trouble."

"I brought—" He raised *Vertigo* from his side, held it out.

Lee's gaze flicked over the movie, then cast to one side.

"But I … first, we've got to …talk."

She met his eyes again. "Yes, we do."

He shadowed her into the living room. She sat on the edge of the couch. Her jean-clad knees pressed together, and her hands rested on her thigh, one covering the other. Marcus half lowered himself to the stuffed chair before his legs pushed him back up.

"I," he said. She waited, of course, but the old, shared openness was sealed shut. He searched for a seam. "Well, I …"

"I understand that my actions last night were …"

When had Lee ever lost her words?

"I may have permanently damaged our friendship."

He opened his mouth to say no. Of course she hadn't. She couldn't. His pacing slowed as a stinging heat crept into his face.

"Marcus?"

"No. You didn't … damage. I—I mean …" Words broke against the ache, but he had to tell Lee that he forgave her, because he did. And he'd had a part in this too, trampling into her space.

If only he could hold her. She'd know, then, and he wouldn't have to talk. But she wouldn't let him hold her. Maybe ever.

"Lee … we're okay. Always."

She glanced up at him, ducked her head. The weave of her fingers loosened a little. "Thank you."

He paced some more, back and forth in front of her. He should say something.

"Marcus, to move forward, I need you to agree to certain parameters."

One hand gripped his neck. "Parameters?"

Stillness wrapped around Lee till her breathing seemed invisible. "Don't ever revisit that subject. Ever."

"What if you need to talk?"

"I am a capable judge of what requires discussion, and of what doesn't."

"Lee."

"Are you refusing the terms?"

His feet were going to eat a furrow in her plush carpet. "Terms? Friendship's not a contract."

"I'm willing to discuss friendship metaphors at length, after this is resolved."

"And that's the only way it gets resolved? You squash it all down and we pretend none of it happened."

Lee seemed to shrink into the chair. Her voice barely came. "Yes."

"No."

"I don't want to discuss … any of it." Her knuckles had gone white.

"I have to know, Lee. If there's any—"

The doorbell's two-tone interruption lingered in the air around them. Lee flashed to her feet and crossed the room. She parted two slats of the window blind, turned back toward him.

"It's the Constabulary."

4 3

No.

"The last patient on my shift was Elliott's foster mother."

"What?"

"She studied me, more than casually. I intended to tell you."

Marcus walled her from the front door.

"Marcus, move."

"No. Run. Or hide." Something. Anything but opening that door, anything but those agents slamming Lee's face, Lee's body, against the brick of her house.

"If you're reckless right now, you will worsen this."

Their hands collided, both reaching for the doorknob. Every shift of Lee's body slowed in front of his eyes, as if time struggled uphill. She had to escape them, now, while she still stood here able to escape.

"Wait out of sight," she whispered. "Appearances are vital."

"Appearances don't mean crap, they're going to—"

"You'll behave like a guardian, as if you know I'm guilty. They'll find a way to use that."

The doorbell chimed again.

"Step away. Please."

Marcus peeled himself away from the door. He backed into the hallway. The deadbolt slid and clicked. He pressed his body into a shadow. Sunlight reached halfway into the hall when Lee opened the door.

"Hello," she said.

"Lee Vaughn?"

Marcus's fingers dug into his palms. Jason.

"Yes," Lee said. "Can I help you?"

"I'm starting to think so. Agent Mayweather, MPC. What do you do for a living?"

"I'm a nurse."

"Not a social worker?"

"Excuse me?"

Marcus shifted across the hallway. The door still blocked him from Jason's sight, but no longer blocked Lee from his. Her hands hung at her sides with the ease of innocence.

"I'd like to know where you were four mornings ago," Jason said.

"Sir, I would like to know the purpose of your presence here."

"You already know that, don't you, Ms. Vaughn?"

Marcus didn't need to see Jason to know. He only needed to see Lee's small step backward. This man had pushed into her space, had threatened the deep places inside her that cringed whenever a person crowded too close. She would never retreat an inch otherwise.

Marcus rushed forward.

This was the Jason that Pamela had described—pride in the uniform, purpose in the badge on his chest, the sidearm. His blue eyes darted over Lee's shoulder and froze. "Marcus Brenner. I knew that pickup looked familiar."

"What's going on?" Marcus said.

"Why aren't you asking your girlfriend?"

"I asked you."

Jason's gaze retargeted Lee. "So? Four mornings ago?"

"I'm still awaiting an explanation," she said.

"Ms. Vaughn, you can simplify this and answer the questions, or you can get stubborn, and I'll take you in for questioning at the office."

"Are you implying that I'm a criminal suspect?"

The last two words knifed into Marcus's mask of ignorance. *Come on, say something convincing.* "That's ridiculous. A suspect for what?"

"I'll get the truth here one way or the other," Jason said to Lee, as if Marcus weren't standing there. "You get to choose how I do that."

"All right. I choose to call my lawyer."

What?

"That didn't take long." But Jason's tone reflected no note of smugness. If anything, that was frustration.

"You'll find that I'm aware of my rights, sir," Lee said.

"Including your right to hair dye."

Jason's finger brushed a glossy black strand that framed her face. Marcus's arm shot up and knocked the hand aside.

"Marcus." Lee's eyes begged him to retreat.

No way. Not again.

Already only feet away, Jason shrank the gap to inches. "You so much as breathe on me, and I'll arrest you for assault on a state officer."

Breathe on him? Marcus would break his nose. Or maybe his eye socket—longer recovery time.

"Marcus."

Shut up, Lee. She stood like iron beside him but wasn't strong enough to stop this. It wasn't her job to stop this. It was his.

"Marcus, think." She didn't look at him. Each syllable dropped passionless into the air. "Go home. Please."

No. No. No.

"You're not under arrest, Ms. Vaughn," Jason said.

"All right."

"But you do have to come with me for now."

She nodded. "May I get my purse?"

"Sure."

Marcus ground his teeth for the entire minute she took before returning, the entire minute Jason stood on her porch, close enough to knock cold with one punch. When he thought his jaw would crack, Lee emerged with her purse over one shoulder.

She arched her eyebrows, nodded to one side. *That's right, Lee, I do fill the doorway.* When he didn't move, she edged past him. Their shoulders brushed. He pressed his arms to his sides so they wouldn't scoop her off her feet and carry her somewhere safe.

She stepped from the porch toward the unmarked car, and Marcus's feet surged forward, too. Her hand, still at her side, opened toward him. *Let me go, Marcus. You must.*

No.

But his feet held their ground on the lowest porch step, even as Lee's head ducked into the car and her body bent inside and disappeared behind the door that Jason almost slammed. Even as the car took her away.

His fists trembled. His brain tried to tell him something, fought against everything he wanted to do right now. Screamed at him to think for once in his life. Think and save Lee. Think because he couldn't pull her into a shelter of himself. Couldn't beat the claws of this threat until they lost their grip.

Think.

She'd asked him to go home. He trudged to his truck and began the drive, but not because of her request. Because when it came to saving Lee, he was still powerless.

4 4

The back door crashed open, and every big and little fear of the last two weeks swooped down on Aubrey and sank in its talons. The Constabulary was finally here. Never mind Indy's pricking ears that recognized the engine of Marcus's truck as it pulled into the driveway, never mind the key in the lock seconds before the crash. No one but the Constabulary would drive a door into a wall more loudly than gunfire, and here she sat on Marcus's couch with an open Bible on her lap.

She snatched her startled, screaming baby from the couch and forgot for a moment that they'd already heard him. She dashed toward the front of the house as if they might not have it surrounded. *Run! Don't think, run!*

Before she could get farther, Marcus burst into the living room and tore through it like a massive tornado. He didn't seem to see his dog or his houseguests. He arrived and exited in the same breath. Now he was in his bedroom, now hurtling down the hall.

Aubrey's mind caught up with her senses and muzzled the terror. She rubbed Elliott's back, squatted to pick up the fallen Bible, smoothed its cover and set it on the end table. She walked through the kitchen. The door still stood open. She shut it gently and fingered the drywall edges of the small, round crater. Marcus's force had hammered the doorknob into the wall.

God, he wouldn't ... would he?

Aubrey took Elliott to the bedroom and settled him into the car seat. His wails rose in volume as she hurried from the room toward Marcus—where was Marcus?

He was pacing the living room, but his gaze darted back and forth, as if he'd never seen this room in his life.

"Marcus?"

He shook his head.

"Don't lie to me, but—please, say you haven't been drinking."

He halted. His eyes scorched her for a moment, then dismissed her. He stared at his bookshelf, at the carpet, at the closed blinds in the window. Yes, anger radiated from every taut muscle, but something else licked at him, too, something too searing to coexist with drunkenness. Marcus was sober. Sober and …

He barreled through the doorway. Aubrey gave chase.

"Where are you going?"

Down the hall, no slowing of his strides, no sign he heard her.

"What's going on?"

Through the kitchen.

"What happened?"

Toward the back door. He opened it and started into the garage, but Aubrey curled her fingers around his concrete forearm. If he wanted to leave, he'd have to drag her.

"You don't get to ignore me. Just tell me what—"

He pried off her grip and tossed her hand away like a piece of stranger's gum. Aubrey twisted to get in front of him, gripped both arms this time, and leaned all her body weight against him when he would have pushed her aside.

"Marcus, talk it out, whatever it is, say it."

"I've got to ..." His voice didn't burn her. She'd braced herself for no reason. Instead, it pitched toward something like panic. "I thought something might be ..."

"You thought something might be what?"

He shifted her grasp into his control, cupped his hands under her elbows, and moved her aside. Her heels rose a few centimeters from the floor. She scrambled to block his way again, but her frame was slighter, her strength no match. Convincing him to talk was her only chance, if she had one.

"Come on. What if I can do something to help? What if I can give you another perspective?"

By the last words, she was addressing his back, on its way to his truck.

"Where are you going?" she said.

Marcus slowly turned back to stare at her, betrayed by his hopeless eyes. He had no idea where he was going.

Aubrey stepped into the garage and shivered. "What is it?"

"I thought ..."

"Keep going."

"She was trying to tell me something. Home ... I thought ... something here would do something. But it was ..." He kneaded his shoulder and gazed around the garage, a lost wrinkle between his eyes. "It wasn't a—a message, it was just—just to go home because I can't ..."

She clung to patience for five whole seconds. "Marcus, you can't *what?*"

"Do anything!"

"About what?"

"Lee!"

Oh. But the reaction was off. This panic seemed ready to upend his whole house. "You called her? Did it not go well?"

He paced two steps and stopped, then two more and stopped again.

"Maybe she needs time to—"

"They took her."

They ... *no, Jesus, please*—"They arrested her?"

His shoulders bowed, and he stood there, too still to be Marcus. "Took. For questioning. But I don't know ..."

Aubrey dashed up the two cement stairs, back into the house. She swept past his startled dog and flew into the bedroom. Elliott was no longer screaming, but his whimper threatened to escalate when she hoisted the car seat too fast.

Marcus loomed in the doorway. "What're you—"

"What's wrong with you? Why didn't you tell me right away? We have to go somewhere. Get the diapers, get all the stuff, oh gosh ... Karlyn's Bible. I was reading about Peter, it's sitting on the table in there—"

Her lungs couldn't fill. She shouldn't have stopped running when she saw he was the one slamming the door open. She should have dashed outside and away from the snare of this place. The bare beige walls squeezed in closer.

"Aubrey," Marcus said. "Calm down."

"Move. Hurry, hurry hurry."

"Aubrey!"

A whole second passed in which they stared at each other. A whole second they should use to get away. Aubrey's hands clenched around the car seat's handle. If Elliott weren't nestled inside it, she'd ram it into Marcus until he moved out of the way.

"Ohio," she said. "Now, right now."

Marcus shook his head. "No."

"But you said—"

"The borders. They're watching. For you."

"Where, then?"

"There's nowhere else."

There had to be. She closed her eyes against his clamped jaw and forced her brain to process. Fear spiraled up into her throat, and she gulped it back down to the pit of her stomach. No screaming allowed. *Father God, if You're listening—no. I know You're listening. Please help us.* Elliott hiccupped. Big calloused hands closed around hers. She opened her eyes to the stark, strained lines of Marcus's face above her. He eased the car seat from her clammy grasp.

"I know where to go," she said.

The stone forehead wrinkled slightly.

"You said yourself they'd take us in, if they had to."

Confusion dug deeper into his face for a moment, then smoothed away. "No."

"Why not?"

"Because."

"Right, okay, thanks for enlightening me."

He thumped the car seat onto the floor, hard enough to jar an indignant whimper from Elliott.

So much talking when she should be fleeing, but she added more words. Eventually, some sentence had to convince him. "You said they're trustworthy people. They said—well, Belinda said—they're willing to help. Now's the time to take them up on it."

"I'm not dragging them into it."

"You're not. They offered. Temporarily, until I can find a way to make it on my own."

"No."

"Then I'll call a taxi."

Marcus glared.

"This isn't about your stupid atonement mission or whatever it is." She grabbed the car seat and shoved past him, into the hall. "This is about my freedom, my baby, and an invitation I'm deciding to accept, and if you—"

Reality glued her feet to the hall runner. She couldn't call a taxi. Or pay a taxi. Or tell a taxi where Chuck and Belinda lived … That book, Marcus's address book, the one she'd found when she was dusting. Did he keep a client list in there? Somehow, she had to contrive another look at that book. But knowing the route didn't provide the transportation. She could hardly steal Marcus's truck.

She could borrow it, though.

"Aubrey," he said.

Elliott squirmed. Aubrey stepped into the living room for more space, then swung the car seat from one hand to the other. Marcus followed with probing eyes, but he didn't seem to read the solution on her face. Yes, she could borrow his truck. If it was a stick shift, she'd remember that. Bulkier than her little car, sure, but she could handle it. When she arrived at Chuck and Belinda's, one of them could go pick Marcus up.

Oh, he was going to be angry.

"You won't let me go?" she said. *Final chance, Marcus.*

"You're not in jail here."

No, not jail. Not a cell, and not a room with one chair and an interrogator that circled like a shark. "But you won't take me anywhere or let me leave."

"It's not safe. To take you anywhere."

She set the car seat down, gritted her teeth, and breathed deeply. Different details colored this circumstance. Lee had been detained, not arrested. Marcus had never undergone re-education. And even in Aubrey's more drastic situation, the con-cops had waited a day to grill her about Karlyn.

On the cable box, the clock read 7:16. They wouldn't come tonight. But tomorrow … Well, by tomorrow she and Elliot would be hiding somewhere else.

"Okay," she said.

Marcus blinked.

"It's not like I have a lot of options right now."

He tilted his head, measuring her sudden compliance. Aubrey tried to glare away his suspicion. After a few moments, he jerked a nod. Then he stood. Still. His gaze drifted to the floor. The brick wall was eroding before her eyes.

"Let's pray." The words sprang from her mouth first, then sheathed her soul. Yes. She could pray. God held her in His hand, clothed her in forgiveness. She smoothed the sleeve of her red sweater, dark as communion wine. Red letters she'd found in Karlyn's Bible today jumped into her mind. *Simon, do you love Me?* Her heart nestled into her Father's palm. *Lord, You know everything. You know I sinned. You know I love You.*

4 5

Aubrey's bottom lip quivered before curving into a smile. "I know, you've probably prayed at least a hundred times by now, but ... could we together?"

The wall in the back of Marcus's mind slid forward again. God was everywhere. Except this side of the wall.

"Marcus?"

The silence had said too much. "I don't pray out loud."

"You did for Jim and Karlyn."

Yeah, when he and God had been on speaking terms.

"It's fine, I'll do the talking. All that matters is 'where two or more are gathered together.'"

"Go ahead," he said.

She hefted the car seat again and marched to the living room. Elliott kicked when she lifted him, gurgled when she supported his head against the bend of her elbow. His neck and the brief length of his body fit along her arm. She sank onto the couch without jarring him.

"Sit, Marcus."

Sit. While Lee ... "Just pray."

Aubrey's head bowed, then raised. "Lee's not a Christian."

"No." The word jabbed his chest.

She lowered her head again. "Father God."

Marcus ducked his head and stared at the carpet. *Not praying. Out loud or in my head.* But Aubrey wasn't, either. He looked up. Her body huddled over Elliott.

Her throat cleared softly. "Dear God, my Father, and Jesus. Thank You that I can talk to You, that I can—even ask for things. Right now I'm asking for help, for Lee."

The wall inside Marcus started to slide backward, narrowing the space of his fortress.

No. He shoved back. *I told You, stay away from me.*

"Please don't let the con-cops hurt her or scare her or even keep her. Make them let her go, please. And whatever reasons she's chosen to push away from You, please shine truth through those dark reasons, and pull her into Your holiness and love. Take care of Lee, Jesus. In Your name, amen."

Take care of her. Keep monsters away from her. Well, God hadn't done that yet.

"Marcus?"

He broke into a pace to hide the startled jolt. "Yeah."

"What does she believe?"

How could he pace the floor while the Constabulary had her? They might have arrested her. If Jason had touched her hair again, touched her at all again, intimidated her, crowded her, hurt her … If the room he'd put her in wasn't well lit … If they knew somehow about the baby, were using it to—

"You must think I'm unbelievably nosy," Aubrey said.

She was. His deep breath tried to ease his shoulders. "Lee …"

Elliott fussed, and Aubrey's thumb rubbed the bottom of his foot.

"Lee says Christianity doesn't fit the world. What happens in the world."

"Okay," Aubrey said, but the word was an invitation. What else was he supposed to say?

"That's all."

"What part of the world are we talking about?"

"The—well, the ... evil that happens. To people." People like eighteen-year-old Lee.

"Aha," Aubrey said. "So, God can't exist, because if He did, He'd stop all this stuff from going on."

"No. Lee believes God exists. But she doesn't ..." He shook his head, and his knuckles dug into his neck. "Doesn't trust Him. She says that if He's powerful, then He's not good. And if He's good, then He's weak."

"Which does she think it is?"

"God's powerful. But He's ... Lee believes He—well, she calls it a 'sadistic side.'"

"Have you explained it to her?"

"We've talked about it."

The desire to help lit Aubrey's face, lilted in her hopeful questions. "Have you talked about allowing evil, not causing it? That they're different?"

"Lee says, if God's powerful, then they're not different."

Quiet pushed between them, filled the room like an oppressive mist. Marcus had to go somewhere. Do something. These walls held no answers, no plans, just the same furniture standing where it had stood before Lee was taken. The same rug sprawled on the floor. The same movie collection clustered in rows—*"Shouldn't you organize them alphabetically, like a library?"* He shoved aside the memory of her voice, because memories were not all he had. Lee had not been arrested. He picked up Karlyn's Bible from the end table and headed for the bookshelf.

"You don't want to talk about this, do you?" Aubrey said.

This meant Lee's rejection of God, not the Constabulary's stealing her. But in both things, talking fixed nothing. Anyway, words didn't exist for the heaviness and the helplessness when somebody as precious as Lee slammed her life's door in God's face.

"I've talked about it," he said. "For years."

"So you've given up on her?"

"No." Could her questions get any more ridiculous? He pressed the shelf's back panel into a downward swing.

"What, then? If you haven't given up on her, why don't you still talk to her about it?"

His jaw locked, unable to explain, and not wanting to even if he could. He could never give up on Lee. He'd pray for her the rest of his life, if he had to. But at some point, he'd given up on himself. Obviously, after three years, he was never going to figure out what he could say to make a difference. He prayed sometimes that somebody else would say it. Somebody smarter than him, maybe somebody she worked with. Anybody. He lifted his Bible without disturbing the family of figurines on top and slid Karlyn's underneath with a whisper of leather. When he turned, Aubrey stood closer. Her face was a wide-open window to something he couldn't quite name, something unlocked.

"You're wrong," she said, "about Chuck and Belinda. And you're wrong about yourself."

"It's not about—"

She waved at him as if shooing a mosquito. "But you were right about something else. I read the end of John, where Jesus shows Peter that He forgives him."

That was it, the unfurling—it was peace. "Good."

"It wasn't the first time I'd read it, but ... it kind of was."

Marcus nodded. The Bible did that sometimes.

"Maybe I let ... other people ... influence how I saw Jesus. Maybe since they didn't forgive me, I thought He wouldn't either."

"God's separate from what people think."

"He is, yes," she said. "He's showing me, with Peter."

"And there's more, after that part. Peter keeps working for God. Preaching and stuff."

"Yeah." The wide pink ribbon of her lips lifted. "Maybe He'll use me like He used Karlyn, after all, to give someone the truth."

Maybe that someone would be Lee. Maybe God would give Aubrey the words Marcus didn't have. His feet kept moving, back and forth across the room, his path needing purpose. He had to do something. Lee couldn't be gone.

46

Aubrey feared Marcus would never sleep again. After they talked about forgiveness, he'd gone to the kitchen and started the coffee-maker. Then he imploded into visible anxiety. He paced like a caged bear, riled mass throwing itself into motion as if that could break down the iron bars of his helplessness. He consumed mug after mug of coffee and glared her into the ground when she asked if he was trying to stay awake for the rest of his life. But most maddeningly, he stopped talking. He spoke three words to her in three hours. When she asked him one last time to take her to Chuck and Belinda's, he said, "No." When she finally withdrew with Elliott to the bedroom, he returned her "Good night."

In case he checked on her, though he probably wouldn't waste a thought on her once she left his sight, Aubrey snuggled under the comforter. She fluffed a pillow and hoped Marcus would be too dis-tracted to notice it wasn't exactly Elliott's size. On the floor beside the bed, concealed from the doorway, she left Elliott in his car seat, ready for their journey.

The next few hours consisted of periodical scouting missions from the shadow of the hallway. She could spy most of the kitchen and half the living room from there, including the couch. Usually he paced, but one time he stood before the kitchen window, fists gritted against the trim on either side of the frame, the muscles of his arms straining, as if trying to fell the house from the inside out. She almost crossed to his side, but no. He had to believe she was asleep.

Around 3:30, she peeked from her now-comfortable shadow to find Marcus sprawled facedown on the couch, still wearing the same jeans and gray T-shirt. His left arm hung over the cushion, and his hand rested on the floor, curled like a spiral shell. Aubrey slunk nearer. His face was turned toward the back of the couch. Was he really asleep? The easy lift and lower of his shoulders convinced her. Awake, Marcus could never relax that much.

Onward, then.

She sped silently through the house. The last hours had provided ample time to hone her plan. She piled the diapers and formula, her purse, and the Wal-Mart clothes beside the back door. Then she sneaked past the couch to the bookshelf and tugged out the spiral-bound address book. Back in the kitchen, the range hood spread barely enough light to read by.

Starting at A would be logical. Aubrey picked through pages crowded with small, vertical printing in all capitals. Some of the addresses featured no city or zip code, only a house number and street name. If Chuck and Belinda's looked like that, she'd never be able to find it. Some, though, included rudimentary directions scribbled alongside them. These must be clients. *"E SIDE VAN DYKE PAST 24." "N SIDE 19 BT. SCHOENER & HAYS."* Wow. He couldn't spell.

Around S, Aubrey concluded that she'd missed them, or they weren't in the book after all, or she should have started with Z. The last thought proved correct. Her finger jumped on the page when it found them. Chuck and Belinda Vitale. They lived on Indian Trail. Why did that sound familiar? The directions in the margin indicated north and a little east … oh! Indian Trail. The abandoned house—Chuck and Belinda must be the clients who lived farther down that dirt road.

Such a God-sent situation. Chuck and Belinda lived on the near side of nowhere. Aubrey tried to retrace their route in her mind. The darkness and Marcus's breakneck driving didn't help her memory, but she knew which highway he'd stayed on for most of the drive, and she'd probably recognize the exit. She could do this.

She slid the key ring from the rack with one hand. With the other, she pressed the keys and knife together until they dug into her palm. Not a clink.

Bump. Indy stood at her hip.

The keys plummeted with a raining jingle, hit the rug with a clattering thump. Aubrey's hand clapped over her gasp. She whirled to face the couch. Indy nudged her again. Maybe it wasn't an old wives' tale that dogs could smell a person's feelings, and Indy somehow sensed her dry-mouthed adrenaline.

She crouched to retrieve the keys. Marcus's hand twitched. His breathing didn't change. Half a minute later, Aubrey dared to move, and the dog followed.

No note this time, not with a con-cop interview pressing in on his future. The impulsive, incriminating good-bye she'd left stuck to his fridge a week ago—what had he done with it? Her first escape loomed over her plans now, that desperate trade on which she'd nearly impaled her chance at freedom. But she wasn't remaking a mistake. Certainty flowed from her fingers as she pulled out the address book once more and opened it to the V page. Now, where to put it that he couldn't miss? She leaned it against the coffeemaker.

Jesus, I hope he's not too mad tomorrow. And please take care of him. And Lee. And Elliott, and Karlyn and Jim and ... She could finish the prayer now. The words wobbled, but Jesus wanted to hear them. *And me.*

She leaned down to leave a kiss on Indy's black nose. "Bye."

47

"We'll get there when we get there," Chuck said.

Marcus's scowl only spiked his headache. He should have jogged the twenty miles. Or even walked.

"And that's not going to get us there any faster."

"What?"

"All your squirming. You're worse than a worm on a hook."

Well, a worm would get there faster than Chuck's driving. His car crawled through the snow at forty miles per hour. He started coasting so far from the red lights that they turned green before he had to brake. You'd never know the guy was a lifelong Michigander. Sure, the snow was bad. It kept shifting between soft flakes and angry sleet, and the salt-truck drivers must be asleep like everybody else. But still. It was *snow*.

"She up and made off with your truck, huh?"

"Yeah." Marcus's thumb hit the window button. A gasp of icy air slid into the car.

The window slid back up. "No sense heating the outside," Chuck said.

Marcus's feet stirred. The air had to be nearing eighty-five degrees, and the persistent whiff of stale cigar smoke grated in his head. Soon he'd suffocate.

"Have to say, that girl's got real guts. It'd almost be funny, if—" Chuck shrugged. "You know."

"It's not funny." Even if everybody was safe, even if the Constabulary had never existed.

"I'm just saying, if it wasn't almost five in the morning."

Was it really ...? It was. Marcus hadn't looked at a clock before now, even when Chuck had yawned in his ear over the phone line. One fact had captured his brain: Aubrey had once again run off like some rebellious kid. With his truck this time. To rope others into danger, people who could be discovered and pushed inside a Constabulary car and erased from their life of freedom.

Lee wasn't erased. He was going to get her back.

And he was going to stop Aubrey. She'd be with the Vitales less than a morning.

"Thanks," he said to Chuck.

"Huh?"

"For coming." At 5:00 a.m. in a snowstorm. Far from the road, a barn's floodlight seemed caught in a swirling cloud. Chuck's headlights lit a sudden squall.

"I was going to tell you it could wait until a decent hour, but Belinda said you don't ask favors and it must be life and death, so ..." Chuck shrugged, then glanced at Marcus. "Then I get here and find out all she did was borrow your truck, and she's headed for our place anyway. Definitely could've waited."

No, it couldn't.

"Don't see how you noticed it was gone in the first place. Weren't you in bed?"

"I woke up," Marcus said. The headache must have dragged a moan from his sleep, because Indy had been tongue-bathing his hand before he even opened his eyes. He still didn't know what had pulled him up off the couch and into the kitchen. Not like he had a single pain pill in the house, despite Lee's countless promises through the years that he couldn't get addicted to Tylenol.

When they turned onto Indian Trail, Chuck seemed to forget that his car came with a gas pedal. At this rate, they'd reach his house around noon. A cat leaped into the road and dashed through the sleet and high-beam headlights. What had happened to the skinny striped thing with the convenient leather collar? Where was the chip now?

"I'm not really clear, Marcus ... why'd she take off in the first place?"

Because she got an idea and skipped on ahead with it, as usual. "Doesn't matter."

"I say it does."

He could say whatever he wanted.

"Look, you're the one that called asking favors. If something's going on here, I have a right to know."

Marcus let Chuck hear his sigh. "She panicked. That's all."

"Why?"

"The Constabulary have a friend of mine. For questioning. If they—if they arrest, then ..."

"Then they'll come after you?"

"Not 'come after.'" Unless they somehow caught on to his recent felony spree. "But they might come to the house. To ask about her."

"Ask about her? Nobody knows she's there."

"Not Aubrey. My friend."

Chuck braked, and the car's back end veered right, then left.

"What're you—"

"Stop sign."

"Where?"

"Up there. Can't see it yet, the blizzard's hiding it, but it's up there."

Marcus didn't bother with a response. Heat clung to him. He tugged off his gloves.

"Ice on the road now, under the snow. Real hazard."

Belinda might be tucking her new houseguests into bed. That was the hazard.

"So," Chuck said when they finally reached the stop sign. "That'd be a tough one, having to hide a baby with them at the door. I'll make sure we have a plan, just in case. But we've got so many rooms and rooms inside rooms, even a real search would miss—"

"What?" Had he jumbled his words that badly?

"It was a good call, her coming out here."

"Chuck, she's going back with me."

"Of course she's not. You just said the Constabulary could be looking at you next."

"You won't be safe."

"And she will be, back at your place? Don't be a fool, Marcus."

No single situation provided safety for all of them, so he had to choose the lesser danger. This was about damage control. Triage, Lee would call it. Aubrey was already on the wanted list. He wasn't going to expand it. The car crept forward, over a slight rise in the road, then down the gentle dip. Less than a mile to the house now.

"Look," Chuck said. "If we were going to turn anyone in, we would've done it a week ago."

"That's not what I mean." Something gleamed out in front of the car, to the left. Chrome, a bumper, jutting up from the ditch. "Stop."

"What's the—?"

"Stop!"

Marcus grabbed the door handle. He threw himself from the car while the tires were still sliding. His shoes skidded over snow-masked ice. The air snapped at his ears, his bare hands.

"Marcus, wait—"

"Aubrey!" His truck faced back the way they'd come, tilted on its side. The driver's side. "Aubrey!"

He hurdled the narrow ditch and leaned on the hood. Despite the angle, the truck was wedged tightly enough to support his weight. The frozen frame stung his hands as he scrambled up onto the leaning back end, then over the passenger door to kneel beside it. He tested the handle. Locked. His face pushed against the window. Darkness filled the cab.

"Are they okay?" Chuck approached the ditch, hunched into his black ski coat.

"Move your car," Marcus said. "Point the lights here."

"First we call an ambulance. They might—"

"No."

Chuck fished a cell phone from an inside coat pocket. "If they need a doctor—"

"No. You know what'll happen."

Sudden full knowledge entered Chuck's eyes.

"Move the car." Marcus bent down to the window again. "Aubrey!"

Why didn't she answer, push the door open, pound the window? She had to be hurt. A listless wail drifted up to him. Elliott. If one of them did need medical help ... *Lee, how will I know what to do?*

Chuck's headlights washed him in a glare that throbbed across the top of his skull and behind his eyes. Most of the light was wasted on the underside of the truck, but a dim glow permeated the cab now. Marcus pressed against the cold window again. Elliott's carrier hung securely, strapped to the seat and facing backward. Past him, Aubrey slouched against the crushed driver's door. One arm draped the steering wheel. Her hair spread over her face, loose and wild, too lively for her unconscious form.

Chuck's voice came from the lip of the ditch. "Locked?"

"And she's knocked out."

"I'll get the crowbar. You can bust that window."

"Could cut them." But it was the only way to get inside.

"Can you see their faces?"

Marcus leaned down to the window. *Move, Aubrey. Come on.* But Chuck was right. The glass would fall into her hair, not her eyes. If Marcus moved her carefully, she shouldn't be cut. The white plastic side of the baby carrier glowed in the cab's dimness, obscuring Elliott. Shielding him.

Marcus straightened. "Crowbar."

Chuck probably did try to hurry, but his steps were so cautious, all the way back to the car. Marcus should leap back over there and get the crowbar himself. *No. Wait.* Chuck crossed the icy road a little faster the second time. He reached the heavy tool out over the ditch to Marcus.

The window shattered with the crowbar's first swing, a simple give, a moment of surrendering chime. Twinkling greenish fragments of glass showered the cab's insides. Marcus lay across the side of the truck and reached through the hole.

"Don't cut yourself," Chuck said.

Great plan. His hand found the door lock and slid it as far as it would go. The passenger side always stuck a little. He withdrew his hand too fast, nearly raked it across a jagged bit of glass in the corner of the window frame. Then he gripped the door handle and leveraged all his body weight into a backward heave. The door was heavy but manageable.

"I'll give you a hand." Chuck jumped down into the ditch and hoisted himself up onto the other side.

Marcus leaned down into the cab and grasped the baby. Elliott was snug and safe, belted in and covered with a nest of sweaters. The back of Marcus's hand strayed across Elliott's face. Cold. His fingers slipped on the little buckle. If he dropped Elliott into all that glass... He stretched one hand under the baby's back and curled his fingers. Then his other thumb pressed the center of the silver buckle. Weight settled into his hand. He stretched his arm to clear the side of the carrier, then drew upward. Elliott kicked, and Marcus's arm strained. He cleared the door frame and sat up.

"I've got him," Chuck said with outstretched arms. "But you can't get her out by yourself."

"Got to." Marcus's hands burned. He clenched them, held them against his coat. Then he gripped the door frame and lowered himself feet-first into the cab.

He braced his feet on the dashboard and the seat. He tried not to grab a handhold without inspecting it for glass. At the other end of the cab, a yard away, Aubrey lay in a sea of shards.

"Aubrey? Can you hear me?"

She could have a spine injury, a neck injury. Moving her could paralyze her. You were never supposed to move an unconscious person. But Marcus had no choice. He lifted her arm over his shoulders and shifted his weight to support both of them. She wasn't heavy, just unwieldy. And cold.

"I'm getting you out," he said, in case she could hear him. "I don't think you're bleeding anywhere. That's good."

"Marcus? She okay?"

"She's cold. Is the baby cold? She's really cold."

Work faster! Come on, work faster. He raised her as smoothly as he could. Glass fragments trickled from her hair. He pressed his back against the seat, and a few pinpricks poked through his coat. He repositioned until one foot braced against the buckled driver's door. He wedged the other between the steering wheel shaft and the dashboard. Okay. Good. Surer footing. He lifted Aubrey the rest of the way, tucked her against his chest and cradled her head. Supporting the neck was important.

"Think you can get her up here?"

"We've got to be careful," Marcus said. "Her neck and her back and—"

"I'll have to set the baby down. Hold on. I'll put him in the car."

Marcus waited because he had to. He couldn't do this by himself, not with maximum safety for Aubrey. The cab was like a freezer. He sighed frost into the air.

Frost.

Aubrey's breath made no frost.

"Aubrey?" He supported her head in the crook of his arm, the way she did with Elliott, and his fingers—two fingers, no thumb, a long-ago lesson from Lee—pressed under the point of her jawbone. There was a rhythm here, a rhythm of blood, of life. He had to find it. But she was still. Everywhere, even her neck, that artery you could feel easier than the others. Aubrey was still.

"No," he said. "Aubrey. Where is it?"

His fingers moved closer to her throat, then farther from it, fumbled, pressed harder, yet she was still. No rhythm. No breath.

The truck rocked. Chuck was back. "Okay, hand her up and—"

"She's not breathing."

"What?"

Marcus gripped under her arms and lifted her through the open door. Her head flopped back. Her hair spilled across his coat sleeve. Chuck's gloves brushed his hands, securing a hold.

"You got her?" Marcus said.

"Yeah, let go."

As soon as her feet cleared the door, Marcus pulled himself up and out. Chuck had sprawled her onto the side of the truck and removed one of his gloves. His hand circled her wrist.

"You're right," he whispered. "She's—"

"Move." Marcus struggled to remember. CPR wasn't that hard. He tilted her head, lifted her chin. Airway. Breathing. And a C. It was for the chest compressions. Those were the most important, Lee had said. He found the point of Aubrey's breastbone, laced his fingers above it, and pushed. One. Two. Three—

"Marcus."

"Shut up." Four. Five.

"Feel her skin. It's been too long."

Six. Seven. Eight.

"She must've hit her head. It must've been instant."

"Shut up!" Nine. Ten.

"Even if we could get her pulse back, she hasn't had oxygen. Are you hearing me? It's been too long."

Eleven. Twelve. Thirteen. Fourteen. Fifteen. Now breathe. He sealed his mouth over her stiff, icy lips. *Come on, Aubrey. Wake up. Breathe. Move.* His fingers wove back together, pushed against her stiff chest. One. Two. Three.

"We need to get the baby to my place," Chuck said. "Come on."

Four. Five. Six.

"Marcus."

Seven.

"Marcus."

Chuck's arm blocked him, pushed him away. Marcus shoved back. Aubrey was not going to die. Arms clamped around him from behind, pinned his to his sides.

"Look," Chuck said. "Look at her."

She looked like Aubrey. Probably she heard everything they said and Chuck's words terrified her, convinced her they'd leave her alone in the cold for the Constabulary to find. She lay trapped in sleep, hair fanned around her head, one arm stretched over the edge of the truck.

"She's dead." Chuck snapped the words close to his ear. "She's dead."

"No." Marcus braced, prepared to throw Chuck over his back, off the truck, into the snow. "She isn't."

But he kept looking, and little things bled into him. Missing things. The breath, the rhythm. The always shifting creases in her forehead. The pink tinge in her cheeks that turned red when her words tumbled too fast. Her face held one color now, a color that wasn't color. She was smooth, like plastic.

"Come on, Marcus."

No. *Please, Aubrey ... come back.*

"We need to get away from here. Come on, son."

"I'm not leaving her here."

"Not like this," Chuck said. "The Constabulary would end up on my porch, and Belinda can't lie to save her life. But the ground might be too hard to bury the body."

The body. She wasn't a body, she was a person. But the person wasn't here anymore, so this was just a body. Marcus could hide it and leave it and think about the person later. He jumped down onto the snow, grasped the wrists, tugged it down off the truck. The legs flopped into the snow, and the torso bumped his shins.

"Somebody needs to go back to the kid," Chuck said.

"Go." Marcus scooped up the thing, the shell. Its knees and its neck bent over his arms.

He carried the body into the woods that stretched on this side of the ditch. Unruly brush reached for his bare hands and face, his hair. He ducked, sidestepped, then shoved through. The snap of twigs announced his intrusion. When the road was concealed, even Chuck's headlights, with nothing but the sound of the engine to guide him back, Marcus knelt in a small clearing. Snow blew in lazy circles along the ground, drifted against one tree. He lowered the body and pulled his arms back. It didn't look much like Aubrey, after all, more like a doll that was supposed to resemble her but didn't. The sleet had softened again. Flakes settled on the body's red sweater and didn't melt.

She hadn't taken Lee's coat this time.

"Aubrey," he said, and something colder than the air knifed his chest.

A twig had torn a bloodless gap in the skin of her cheek. The snow might provide a burial, but not for long. Not out here with coyotes and foxes and other animals.

"I'm sorry."

His heavy feet retraced his path to the road. He leaned inside the car. Chuck sat on the passenger's side and rocked Elliott as if he knew what he was doing.

"Screwdriver?" Marcus said.

"Got some tools in the trunk. What for?"

Marcus reached down and tugged the release lever. The trunk sprang open. Not a single car had passed them in all these minutes. The solitude had to survive till he'd finished this final task. He found a Philips in Chuck's sparse toolbox and crunched through the snow back to the truck. Cans of formula and the rest of the diaper package lay in a corner of the truck bed. He threw the stuff in Chuck's trunk first. Then he worked as fast as his cold fingers would allow—not really cold, though, not like Aubrey was cold—to remove the license plate, in case somebody found the truck before he and Chuck could return for it. They had to, right away. Chuck's tractor could haul it out of the ditch. And they had to bury the body.

He slid into the car on the driver's side and tossed the metal rectangle onto the floor. Chuck held the baby out to him.

"Good thinking," Chuck said with a nod at the license plate.

"No."

"Sure it was, covers your tracks."

"No, you hold him. I'll drive."

"I'd rather you—"

Marcus backed the car away from the ditch and cracked his window. The drive to the Vitale house was only a few minutes. Chuck kept talking until Marcus reached the twisting driveway. Then the quiet resettled, weighted like the spruce trees on either side of them, sagging with snow. Silence was good. Marcus let it shroud him and fill him up. He pictured his hands holding it, blanket soft, not warm exactly but less cold than his hands, less cold than the hole in his chest.

He parked the car. He waded through five inches of snow to the back of the house and rapped hard on the glass door. Chuck trailed somewhere behind him with Elliott. After a minute, the curtains swung aside, and light poured into Marcus's face. Belinda bounced up onto her toes and tugged the old door open wide with an anxiousness that jiggled at least her arms, if not other parts of her. She waved him and Chuck inside and hurried to shut the door.

A voice drifted quietly from the TV across the room. "And that ends the two-minute minor for interference and Detroit's now back at full strength with one and a half minutes left in the second period ..."

"Now, Marcus, I want the whole story, as fast as you can tell it—my heavens." She stared at the baby.

The whole story. She wanted words.

"Pearl," Chuck said.

Her eyes jumped from the baby in her husband's arms to Marcus, then back to Chuck. She stepped close and eased Elliott into her arms.

"This is the same baby, that young girl's baby," she said. "Where is she?"

Marcus couldn't unlock his teeth. Splinters of pain filtered from his body to his brain. His head, his neck. The spasm that clawed at his shoulders was starting to reach down into his back.

"Something's happened, Pearl." Chuck glanced at Marcus, then cupped his wife's elbow and guided her to the couch.

"Marcus." Belinda tilted her chin toward the love seat.

Maybe she was right, and he should sit. But his knees locked like his jaw.

"Chuck, what in heaven's name—"

"Aubrey Weston died tonight."

Belinda went still, but not completely still. Her pulse still beat in her neck. Her chest rose and fell. "Oh, no."

"There was an accident," Chuck said. "With Marcus's truck. She was driving here, to ask us for help, and she spun out on the ice, went off the road."

"She was … but why was she driving? Marcus, why weren't you driving?"

Belinda should stop talking. Leave the silence alone. She looked up at him, and tears washed her face. Why was she crying? What would that fix?

"Oh, son, what happened? Didn't you get her to a hospital? They might could do something, they—"

"Belinda," Chuck said.

"She was gone too fast?"

Yeah. Too fast.

"But the baby's not hurt?" Belinda rocked Elliott as if the motion could heal hidden injuries. "Marcus, you're not hurt? How could she be the only—"

"Marcus wasn't there. She took the truck, and we found it."

"But how, why, why would she be out there like that? Why wouldn't you be driving her, if she needed to come here?"

"Belinda." Chuck squeezed her arm, and the rocking ceased. "Knock it off."

"It don't make sense—"

"He look like he wants an inquisition right now?"

What Marcus didn't want was her gaze crinkling at him, warm with care, trying to view his insides. His feet thawed enough to step back.

"Heaven help us, Chuck, she was just a girl, and this poor child—"

Chuck grunted at his wife, lurched to his feet, and headed for the kitchen.

"We've got to go back," Marcus said. "Now."

Chuck nodded. "In a second."

The moment Chuck vanished through the doorway, Belinda tore the quiet into fragments too thin for Marcus to hold. "I don't understand what went on. Why was she coming here? Did you tell her to? Was there danger?"

Elliott's heels beat Belinda's arm with an alternating rhythm, and the gurgling noise didn't sound unhappy. She must be soft enough. Marcus's legs brought him closer to Belinda and her questions, closer to the little person in her arms that had just lost his mother. That would ache someday, when Elliott was old enough to understand. He wouldn't remember Aubrey. Maybe Marcus could write a letter. He'd have to describe not just her hair and her eyes and the curve of her nose, but also the funny tugging on her earlobe, the nightmare screams of fear for Elliott, the insistence that every child should be raised with books. The kindness of her massaging hands. The willingness to trade herself for the people she loved, and the peace that cloaked her when she held her baby, when she embraced the forgiveness of God.

"Marcus?" Belinda's crowing had waned to a whisper. "What happened?"

"She didn't listen to me."

"What do you mean?"

He meant what he said. She'd galloped off into the night and killed herself and left her baby. She'd left her body, and now it lay unprotected, submerging in snow.

"What did you tell her?"

"To stay." He should have hidden his keys. He should have rigged the door with some kind of alarm, something loud enough to wake even him. He shouldn't have fallen asleep at all.

"Why'd she want to leave?" Belinda said.

"I should've known she'd do this."

"Did she tell you she would?"

Of course not ... did she? "I ... don't know."

"Maybe you weren't listening to her, either."

But he had listened. She'd spouted panic, mostly. She'd said ... well, she'd demanded he take her to Chuck's. Later, they'd talked about forgiveness. She'd prayed. For Lee. If a hint of her plan had hidden in her words, he couldn't decipher it even now.

"You are utterly incapable of listening."

Maybe Lee was right. If he listened better, he might be home right now, with Aubrey furious at his thwarting of her plan.

The seal of a can cracked open as Chuck strode back into the room. A yeasty smell attacked as the beer fizzed. Marcus's headache spiked.

"Help yourself, more in the fridge," Chuck said.

The fall was too fresh. Barely on his feet again, and he was going to cave in. Again. Right now. It didn't matter, anyway. Nobody left to know.

"You don't look so hot. It'll help."

"Yeah," Marcus said.

"Well, go get one for the road, then."

His feet carried him into the kitchen. He didn't need this. He wanted it, to stop the tremors in his hands and fill up the holes inside. He didn't want this. He needed it, so he could do what had to be done. His hand closed around the refrigerator door's handle. Nobody saw.

He jerked his hand back and fled the kitchen as if distance from cans of beer could make distance from himself.

4 8

He lifted the body from the snow. He set it on the blue plastic tarp and rolled it up. He lifted it again, into the bed of the truck Chuck's tractor had hauled from the ditch. Drive. Back to Chuck's, past the driveway, past the frozen pond, over a barely cleared path into the snowy woods.

He got a shovel and started to dig.

Square blade and hard ground, not an easy combination. More muscle, more weight. Turn the ground. Break it up. Sweat and break.

"Marcus."

A corner of the blade bent down, but the ground was giving in. The hole deepened, widened, a dark mouth against the snow, a yelling mouth. Not that he heard anything, but he should. Some sound ought to be coming from somewhere, to drown the *thunk* of shovel against dirt, the clink when the blade rammed into a rock.

"That should be enough."

Of course it wasn't enough.

"Marcus. You can stop."

Stop what? Stop failing them all? No. If he could do that, a corpse wouldn't lie in the back of his truck.

Hands on the wooden handle tugged it away.

"It's deep enough."

Over the top of a gray scarf, Chuck's face peered at him. Reddened with cold and creased with worry, which was pointless, since the body was already dead.

He climbed out of the grave. Traipsed back to the truck and lifted the body again. The tarp crinkled around it. Then he was kneeling to lower it into the silent maw of dirt, then covering it up, shovelfuls of dirt raining down.

"Okay, that's all. You ready to go?"

He snapped two twigs from a bare, poking bush. Now, something to fasten them together.

"What're you doing?"

A loop of twine dangled from the shovel's wooden handle. He yanked, but it wouldn't snap, only tightened. *Come on, break.* Chuck's hands stole the shovel again. He pulled off one glove and loosened the knot of twine.

"Here. Are you making a cross?"

He had to remove his gloves, too, to tie the twigs together.

"Marcus? Are you hearing me at all?"

He knelt beside the snow-flecked mound.

"Come on, son, I need you to say something."

He pushed the cross into the ground. It broke. The two pieces dangled, then flopped apart in his hands. He held them together.

Chuck crouched beside him. "Don't worry about it. Come on, we need to go."

Not until this was fixed.

"Marcus."

The more he pushed the twigs together, the more their edges frayed. The fit was ruined now. Even glue would leave them ragged at the break, if he had glue.

Chuck scooted nearer, in front of him now. "Marcus, it's time to go. Let me have that."

His hands curled around the twigs. One of them punctured his palm, but he couldn't let go. Chuck's fingers pried at his, grasped his wrist. It wasn't a wrestling match or a tug-of-war but both, and then the cross fell into the snow and Marcus struck out at something. No give when his punches landed, just an explosion in his knuckles, and finally that dark mouth he'd filled with a body, filled with dirt, wasn't silent anymore. It yelled now. For the body it had swallowed tonight and every other person ever failed by his uselessness.

He yelled until he was empty. Until his fists drooped and bled into the snow.

His forehead leaned against smooth birch bark. He shivered.

"Are you with me, son?"

Marcus lifted his head and remembered. Oh, no. But Chuck's face wasn't a pulp of punches.

Chuck's mouth twitched. "I know what you're thinking, but in fifty-five years, I did learn how to duck. When you missed me, you lit into that tree. Let me see your hands."

Marcus raised them from the snow. The throbbing in his left hand pulled a hiss through his teeth.

"Easy does it. I tried to stop you, but by then you didn't know I was here." Chuck cradled Marcus's hand in both of his and squinted. "Not enough light out here. Does it feel busted?"

He shook his head, though maybe it did.

"Come on up to the house."

49

When Belinda met them at the door with Elliott in the crook of one arm, Marcus's hands clenched and widened the splits in his knuckles. A drop of blood spattered to the gray rug. Belinda stared down at it, then at Marcus's hands. She cupped a hand over Elliott's eyes.

"Stay here, Pearl. I'll fix him up."

Chuck's hand weighted Marcus's shoulder, shepherded him into the bathroom that seemed even smaller with its dark blue walls. "Blood makes her woozy. Hold your hand under the light there."

Marcus pushed up his coat sleeve, flexed his fingers, blinked the wince away. "I'll just go home."

"And patch yourself up one-handed?"

Not like he hadn't done it before. Or tried to, anyway.

"Stand still." Chuck dug through a drawer of Band-Aids and bug spray. He held up a spool of white medical tape. "Great stuff. All-purpose."

"I can take care of—"

"You're not driving that truck on the roads, either, or didn't you notice it's totaled?"

Marcus thrust his hand under the faucet. It throbbed in the icy stream, then numbed a little. Water swirled down the drain, first red, then pink. Yeah, this looked familiar, but it wasn't as bad as the last time he'd tried to beat up a piece of wood, when the water stayed red for twelve minutes. After a while, Chuck shut the water off and snagged a towel from the chrome wall rack.

"It was an accident, Marcus." Chuck dabbed his hand dry and ignored the blood now spotting the pale blue towel. "But you're thinking about pitching a tent on the side of a mountain somewhere and never coming back."

Not a bad idea. Chuck pulled a length of medical tape and bit off the end. Lee would lecture him for half an hour about lack of sanitation. A smile twitched for release. A burning filled Marcus's chest.

"But what would that accomplish, son? You tell me." Chuck stretched first one length of tape, then another, over Marcus's knuckles. "Well?"

Marcus's teeth clenched, half to stifle the gasp when the tape tugged at raw skin. Blood soaked through, but didn't seep around it. Lee would say that was good.

"See, in the big picture, hiding yourself away is nothing but selfish. Pretty clear there are a lot of folks that need you to—"

"Nobody needs me." The words ricocheted off the mirror and close walls.

Chuck pressed the last piece of tape to Marcus's hand, stood back, and hooked a thumb through his empty belt loop. "Look what you've done so far."

"You don't know what I've done." He brushed past Chuck, into the hallway.

That same hand fell onto his shoulder again, held him still.

Leave me alone. "Some mountain would be better. For everybody. I'm just going to keep on—"

Chuck held out his hands, palms up, and spoke quietly for the first time since Marcus had met him. "Okay, son. Okay."

Oh. Marcus had been shouting. He stalked toward the door. The ache in his chest didn't need witnesses, especially if he broke down and started hitting things again. He passed Belinda in the kitchen, but he couldn't look at her. His right hand fumbled the lock on the sliding glass door.

"Marcus," Chuck said.

His hand stilled on the lock. *Let me go.*

"That's it, then? You're writing yourself off?"

His arms remembered the weight of Aubrey's body. The rest of him remembered the cluster of powerless paramedics, Mom stretched out on the kitchen floor, mouth open and eyes shut.

"Everyone's done something they can't take back, son."

"Have you killed anybody?" Marcus threw the words at Chuck without turning around.

The silence behind him pressed at his back. His hand flipped the lock easily this time, though his limbs weighed him down. Time to escape the prying, the caring.

"Yes," Chuck said.

Yes what? Wait … Marcus faced him. Chuck's face was calm, but his arms crossed like a barricade. Behind him, still holding Elliott, Belinda stared at her husband. One hand covered her mouth.

"Vehicular manslaughter," Chuck said. "Broad daylight, the week after New Year's, coming up on twenty-seven years ago."

"Chuck." Belinda rocked the baby as she approached him. "You don't have to—"

"Yes, I do, woman. Make us some coffee."

"No." Marcus stepped further into the room. "No coffee, but …"

Chuck led him to the living room and sank into one of the paisley-upholstered chairs. Marcus perched on the edge of the other one. His feet still wanted to walk out the door. But the ache inside wanted something else.

A slow sigh eased from Chuck as he leaned back. "Sunny day, the streets just looked wet. She was twelve years old, out walking the puppy she got for Christmas."

"And you ... hit her?"

"We had a little car, rear-wheel drive, wimpy little thing. Slid right through a stop sign, spun out, jumped up on the sidewalk."

Marcus pushed to his feet, paced the length of the room. He had no right to know the things Chuck carried, and this sounded like the heaviest of them all.

"Her name was Payton. She died in the hospital the next day."

"Why are you telling me?"

"Know what I did after that girl died? The same thing you're getting ready to do. Decided I didn't deserve anyone's concern. Told Belinda to find herself a husband that didn't kill kids."

Chuck scrubbed at his face, and another sigh poured out.

Marcus's feet stalled at the mantel, and his fingers rubbed the gold frame of a wedding photo. Chuck, his hair solid black. Belinda, her frame slimmer but her smile unchanged.

"I treated her bad, Marcus. I treated everyone bad, but Belinda ... I said some really crappy things. And she stuck by me. Until I came through to the other side."

"What's ... what's on the other side?"

"Deciding that there's something more important than hating yourself."

Marcus picked up the wedding photo, and the rounded edge of the frame dug into his fingers. "It's not that, it's ..."

"My marriage was worth more, Marcus. My family was worth more. I'm betting you've got people that are worth more. And even if you didn't, this mission of yours—you wallow and hide for a year like I did, and dozens of people will end up behind bars that you could've helped."

An hour ago, Marcus would've thrown the picture at Chuck's head. Now he clutched it in both raw hands, staring down as if the beaming bride and groom knew something he didn't.

"I can't pay for what I did." Still leaning back against the chair, Chuck eyed him on a downward angle. "All I can do is take the acceptance that people gave me anyway. That Belinda gave me."

"You don't have to pay for it." The words barely hit a whisper, but they crumbled the fortress inside. God was here, had never left. Stiff legs carried him to the other chair and lowered him into it. *God, is that what I'm doing? Paying for ... everything?*

"With Jesus, there's nothing left to pay." The memory of Frank's voice burned behind Marcus's eyes. He knew that already. He blinked hard, swiped at his dry face, rubbed his thumb over the picture frame's decorative ridges.

Chuck scowled his confusion.

"God has to pay for it," Marcus said. But even this? Failure at the thing God had given him to do?

Frank would say yes. Would tell him anything else cheapened the payment Jesus made.

Chuck grunted, shifted in his seat. "Well, I don't know about God. But I know that if you keep making yourself pay, you're going to hurt more people than just you."

The nod came stiffly. The burden of the last two days bowled him over. *I know You want me to keep up this fight. Am I doing it wrong?* The weight didn't disintegrate or even become lighter. He breathed beneath it, raised his head, leaned back against the chair, closed his eyes. So heavy. But he had to carry it. *Jesus, I don't feel strong enough. Make me stronger. Show me the right way to protect them all.*

And help me stop trying to pay.

When he opened his eyes, Chuck glowered at him.

"I should go," Marcus said.

"You ready for that yet?"

"I'll call a taxi." Somebody to drive him wherever the heck he asked. He'd prayed. But the weakness still weighed him down.

"It's no bother, driving you home."

Taxi was better. Nobody would know or care if he stopped and … "I'm okay."

"If you're sure."

"Yeah." He surged to his feet, dug out his phone. Searched and found a number, listened to the line ring. A cold fist squeezed his gut.

"Red Cab, how can I help you?"

He closed the phone.

Chuck stepped around him, stood in front of him with arms crossed and a creased frown.

"Chuck, I …" His head ducked, chin to chest. *God. Please help.*

"What's going on?"

Would it be okay? To tell him? "I … if you could … I can't …"

"Spit it out, son."

He spoke to the burgundy flecks in the carpet. "I need you. To drive me. Please."

"I told you that's no problem."

"If you don't, I'll go and—and drink. And I can't drink. I'm—I'm—"

A warm hand clapped his back. "How about some coffee?"

The brewing scent he'd failed to notice before wrapped around him, an embrace that thawed him inside. "Please. Yeah."

Belinda leaned into the living room. "How are we doing in here?"

"He's going to stick around for some of your gourmet hazelnut. Then I'll take him home."

A smile flitted into her eyes. "Nothing but gourmet for you, son."

5 0

Marcus hunched into his coat and rubbed his arms. He'd parked the rental in the adjacent parking lot. In a few more minutes, he'd have to head to his first client's house. The store opened at 9:00, and now it was almost 8:30. Janelle should have shown up by now.

No. She hadn't been arrested. She was just running late.

Her pink Volkswagen—"strawberry," she called it—skidded into the parking lot as he was stomping his feet for the last time, counting down one more minute before leaving. She shuffled over the ice to the door, bundled like a little kid in her purple coat, blue ski mittens, white scarf, and a yellow wool hat that covered her salt-and-pepper hair all the way to her ears. A moment after she disappeared inside, light shone at the crack in the door.

Marcus stepped out from under the naked oak tree and crossed the parking lot. His work shoes slid on the ice. His gloved hand flailed a moment before steadying against the side of the building. He pushed the door, and it actually opened. A bell tinkled over his head.

Janelle's voice rose from behind the counter. "We don't open until nine."

"You should lock the door," Marcus said.

Her head popped into view. "Marcus!"

"Why don't you lock the door?" She'd get herself robbed, or worse.

"What's the point? I'll be—" She rushed around the counter, still wearing her mittens and coat, and tried to smother him in a quick but hearty hug. "—Unlocking it in twenty minutes anyway, and I'll be alone with customers all day long, and oh my goodness what on earth are you doing here?"

"I can't stay." She released him, and he turned both steel bolts on the door.

"Really, the lock's not—"

"No customers till I'm gone." He headed for the back room, and she followed.

"Is everything okay? Have you decided to come back to us?"

He turned the storeroom knob—she didn't lock this at night?—and walked down the stairs. He switched on the lone bare bulb. His throat tightened. The hours he'd spent here wrapped him up in a blanket of memory. Huddling with the others, sitting on this cold floor, talking about truth and life, listening to Abe's quiet, level voice, to all their voices as they talked to God.

"It's not the same without you," Janelle said.

"There's two things that I came for."

"Okay."

Marcus reached into the inside pocket of his coat. He'd wavered over which Bible to give her, Jim's or Karlyn's. In the end, Karlyn's had fit into his coat, and Jim's hadn't. He brought out the small burgundy book and offered it to her, but she didn't take it.

"Is that …?" she whispered.

"It's Karlyn's. They'd both want you to have it."

"Oh, Marcus, oh …" Her hand, still mitten-clad, hovered over it. She pulled off her mittens, and they dropped to the floor. Then her hands settled together on the leather cover.

"Janelle. Here." Marcus guided her hands around it. "It's yours."

"I have a Bible?"

He nodded.

A small cry burst from her, then tears that coursed down her cheeks. She clutched the book to her chest and bent over it. Under his hand, her shoulder quivered with sobs. She cried until Marcus wondered when she would stop. The tears dried gradually, and then she looked up at him.

"I'll never, ever be able to thank you, much less repay you."

He shook his head. "It's not a debt."

Her hands tightened around the Bible. "I'll never give this up, Marcus. No matter what they do."

She should know how Aubrey found this Bible in Karlyn's locker, years before Marcus or Janelle knew them. She should know Aubrey was gone, like Karlyn but not like Karlyn at all. But he couldn't say it.

"Janelle, I ... there's the second thing too."

"What is it?"

He gently shifted her to face him. Her eyes glistened with tears and gratitude and trust. "You might not see me anymore."

Her lip wobbled. "But, Marcus, you—"

"You've got to tell them, tell Clay and everybody. If I can come, I will, but you can't call me anymore. Ever."

"Wh-why?" she whispered.

"Because."

A tear squeezed from her eye. "You'll come to the wedding, won't you? Phil and Felice, they'd be so happy."

"No."

"Just the wedding? Just this one last thing?"

Cracks widened inside him. "I can't."

Her gaze fell to the Bible, and her hand caressed its cover. She lifted her head again, hurt and confusion replaced with fear and knowledge. "You're fighting them. Aren't you?"

"Janelle. Don't."

"How else could you possibly have a criminal's Bible? You're in danger, so you're staying away, to protect the rest of us."

"They can't know," he said.

"You don't think they'll figure it out?"

"If—if they do, then okay. But you can't tell them. Please."

More tears dripped down her face. "If that's what you want."

"Thanks." He jogged up the stairs, opened the door. After he'd gone two steps toward the front of the store, Janelle grabbed him in a hug.

"I'm so glad God made you part of my life," she said against his coat, "even for a little while."

His eyes burned. He hugged her back, squeezed her shoulder, stepped away. "I ... you ... all of you—"

A smile curved her lips. "I'm glad. That we matter to you, as much as you matter to us."

He nodded and crossed to the door.

"Wait, one second." Janelle disappeared into the storeroom. After a minute, she reemerged to follow him to the front door, the Bible vanished from her hands. He'd bet she'd be locking that storage door after today.

He didn't pause on his way out the door and across the parking lot. They'd said everything they could. At the edge of the lot, something tugged him to turn around. Janelle stood framed in the door, that ridiculous cracked door. She raised a hand and waved. Marcus turned back around and crunched through the ice-topped snow. His breath frosted the air and disappeared. Would he ever see his own breath again without remembering how Aubrey's wasn't there?

Two streets over, as he started the truck, his phone vibrated in his pocket. If Janelle was calling him, he was going to— But he didn't know this number.

"Hello," he said.

"Marcus."

"Lee." Both his hands gripped the phone. He trembled. "Are you—?"

"I'm all right. Listen to me." And then she stopped talking. How could he listen if she stopped talking?

"I'm listening," he said.

"All right. Obviously, there's insufficient evidence to hold me further. I'm being released. I wanted you to know as soon as possible."

Somebody could hear her side of this, maybe his, too. "Okay. Good. I'll come get you."

"That's not necessary. I've already called a cab. I'll talk to you later today."

"No."

"Marc—"

"Cancel the cab. I'm coming." Silence invaded, but she wouldn't win this. "Lee, cancel it."

"All right." Her voice had lost a layer of its ice.

"Are you at the Schoenherr building?"

"Yes."

"I'll be there in ten minutes."

Thanks to the rental's tendency to fishtail and the fear of being pulled over, the drive actually took fifteen. Marcus found a parking spot marked "Visitor" and crunched up the salt-spattered walkway. He pushed through the revolving door into a small, sparse lobby with wheel-spoke corridors leading away. An oak desk stretched along one wall. Marcus approached the gray-haired woman perched behind it. She stared at him like a hawk ready to catch a mouse. He wouldn't be surprised if even clerks here had been trained to read crime on a person's face. A few weeks ago, nobody could read more in his eyes than the misdemeanor of being a Christian. Now, she could scroll down a whole list of felonies, from his forehead to his chin.

"What exactly can I do for you?"

"I'm picking up a friend."

"Fancy that." She stabbed a manicured talon toward one of the hallways. "They'll probably be waiting there on the right."

"Thanks."

The hallway opened like the jaws of a snake. Why hadn't Lee waited for him at the door? His gut tightened with every step. No doorways appeared on the right. Somebody opened the next door on the left and stepped into Marcus's path.

Marcus halted as Jason turned. He didn't try to hide the look that sized Marcus up.

"She called for a ride?" Jason said.

Marcus nodded. Close enough.

Jason nodded back. Quiet settled, but he didn't move aside.

Act innocent. Marcus stepped forward. "Somebody said she's down this way."

"She's brilliant, you know. We're releasing her, her lawyer's ready to file a suit, and all the time she's guilty as—" He shook his head.

"No," Marcus said. "She isn't."

"Tell me one thing."

Marcus shrugged.

"How does a dirt clod like you end up with a woman like that?"

Enough. Marcus pushed past him. Get Lee and get out. His feet propelled him toward the first doorway on the right.

"Brenner," Jason said from close behind him. "I'm not stupid."

Keep walking.

But Jason kept pace. "Buying diapers? You knew she had that kid. All I'm left wondering is if you knew who the kid was."

"You don't know what you're talking about."

"I'm going to prove that Lee is guilty of kidnapping. She's going to be locked up for the next twenty years, with guards that don't give a crap and cellmates who'll get a real kick out of her educated vocabulary and her rigid personal space."

Marcus whirled. Charged. Reached for a handful of suit coat. No. Don't. *This is what he wants.* His hand jerked back empty, dropped to his side, but his fist still strained the blood-stained tape over his knuckles. He turned his back on Jason and headed for the doorway.

"Don't get comfortable," Jason said.

Marcus crossed the threshold.

She *had* waited for him by the doors. A wide glass pair of them stood across the room. Sunlight glared from outside, magnified by the snow. Lee sat in a chair that faced the whole room, backed against a wall. Her attention flicked toward the movement of his entrance, then fixed on him. Dusky circles sat under her eyes. Had they kept her up all night?

She stood as he reached her. "Marcus."

"You're okay? What did they—?"

"I would like to leave."

Of course. She'd been imprisoned for the last twelve hours.

Twelve hours. That was all. Aubrey had been alive less than a day ago.

He motioned Lee in front of him and shepherded her through the doors, hands clenched at his sides. She shivered once as they walked. He led her to the pickup truck and opened the passenger door.

"What's this?"

"Rental."

"Where is your truck?"

"Totaled."

Lee studied him as if she hadn't seen him in years. "Last night? Were you injured? Your hands are—"

"Get in."

They drove a few minutes before she spoke. "What happened?"

"I—Lee, I'll tell you … everything, but I … You talk first. What made them let you go?"

For a minute, she gazed at his hand as if trying to see the injury through the tape. Then she sighed. "Their only real evidence was my physical resemblance to the sketch. The foster mother attempted to identify me in a lineup, but she was less certain than she'd been in the hospital, under the stress of receiving sutures in her arm. She's also African-American, and cross-racial testimony is considered less reliable. After the lineup, they were unable to obtain a warrant for my house."

Something like hope barreled toward him. "So what will they do now?"

"Unless new evidence surfaces, nothing. I have no motive for involvement, no connection to the child's mother. I have no alibi for the time of the kidnapping, but I do have proof I worked a double shift at the hospital the day and night before. That I would be sleeping at home is reasonable."

"Lee, are you saying … it's over?"

"Agent Mayweather doubtlessly intends to watch me. But yes."

"It's—" The back wheels skidded. She was free, and he was going to kill her in a car wreck.

"Pull over, Marcus."

"Just some ice." Ice that had sent his truck into a ditch. Ice that had stolen Aubrey.

Feelings swamped his chest. They'd been doing that too often since this morning, when he'd sipped coffee at the new dining table with Chuck and Belinda. *Don't feel it.* But he had to. He couldn't make it stop.

"Marcus. Please."

He signaled, turned into the next lot, and parked.

"At my house, Mayweather recognized you," Lee said.

"I contracted for him a couple times. Handyman stuff."

Surprise rippled over her face, but she nodded and turned to face the window.

"He knew about the hair dye," Marcus said. "Even though you darkened it back."

"He speculated based on the fact I didn't fully match the description."

Yeah. Okay. Marcus tried to picture her with bleached hair, but it just didn't fit. "You said you were wearing makeup, too?"

"And Goodwill was happy to take the electric yellow suit."

A smile tugged at his face. "You should've taken a picture."

She smiled and stretched her legs under the dashboard, then settled back in her seat. But their last conversation hung like smoke around them. He waited, but Lee said nothing.

"You're sure you're okay?" he said.

"I am."

"Nobody did anything to you?"

"The lawyer's presence diffused the situation. I'm all right, Marcus." Her head turned slightly to gaze out the windshield. Lines of weariness pulled at her profile. But she was here. Free. Safe, from this. God had chosen to save her, and maybe from other things too, maybe soon. *Thank You.*

"Good," he said.

"What about you?"

"I couldn't get you back. But now you are."

She turned to meet his eyes. "You seem wounded."

"It's nothing. It didn't bleed very long."

"The incompetent attempt to treat it looks disturbingly familiar. But I wasn't referring to your hand."

He had to tell her, needed to, couldn't, didn't want to. Lee allowed minutes to fade away without words, without movement. She wouldn't ask again. She'd let him choose to say it, or not. They sat in the truck till it started to get cold. Marcus turned the key and cranked the heat on high, then let her gaze hold his.

"Today's day three," he said.

The hands in her lap parted. The fingers laced together.

"And ... it's ..." He pushed out the rest of the words. "Hard, but I'm getting back up again."

She nodded, and a moment stretched, then snapped. "I had a role in this."

"You were right that I don't listen. I didn't listen to—"

Lee arched her eyebrows, but then the curiosity drained from her eyes. Something else filled them, something that knew more than he'd said. "You're not all right."

"No," he whispered. Words crept from the hole inside him, up into his mouth. There they were, waiting. *Aubrey's gone. I tried, Lee. CPR. Maybe you could've brought her back. But I don't think so.*

"When you're ready, please allow me to help."

He nodded. His mouth opened to say the words, but he swallowed each bitter syllable back down, and other words poured instead. "We ... when we talked, before, you said ..."

She stiffened instantly. She seemed to lean away from him, closer to the truck door.

"I want to help too. With—what happened. To you. But I ... you're right. I don't know what you need."

Her voice sliced quietly but without ice. "I don't need assistance with the past."

Didn't she? *God, I don't know what to do.*

"Please trust me in this," she said.

Her eyes weren't hiding behind a cold mask. Maybe she was okay. "If you do need to talk, or anything, you'll tell me?"

She nodded.

"I'm here."

"I know. Thank you." Her fingers relaxed.

If he reached for her hands, pulled them close, they would clench. They would pull away. The moment she'd looked at him as more than a patient, more than a friend—maybe he'd seen what he wanted to see. He put the truck in gear and pulled out onto the road.

"Come over. Tonight. We'll eat the lasagna." Maybe then he'd be able to talk.

Lee's forehead furrowed. "You wouldn't prefer my house for a discussion?"

Oh. Of course. "There's ... nobody at my place now. Just me."

"Is this connected to the loss of your truck?"

The road seemed to narrow. Marcus focused on the patch of wet blacktop up ahead, kept the truck moving toward it.

"Is Aubrey responsible for the accident? Is she with the Constabulary?"

"No."

"Where else could she find a haven, especially with an infant?"

"I-I'll tell you. But I have to get the words."

Lee turned to look out the window. "All right."

Marcus inhaled the silence around them, weighted but still easier to breathe than air clogged with endless words, trying to heal and tearing more things open. The pounding in his head settled to a vague throb, not hard to ignore. His hands slowly eased on the wheel.

"I'm not going to stop," he said quietly.

Lee continued to face the window. "I assume you're referring to your resistance movement."

The words seemed too impressive for skulking around yards and knocking on doors to offer warnings. But a fugitive's child hid this morning in the home of strangers. An arrested woman's Bible hid in a free woman's storeroom.

"I've got to do this."

"I didn't expect otherwise."

"But you're staying out of it."

Lee shifted to face him again, her eyes like lakes under sunshine. "That was the agreement."

"Okay."

Marcus coasted through a nearly red light, straight ahead when a right turn would have chopped ten minutes off the drive to Lee's.

She slid a glance at him, then leaned back against the seat and closed her eyes. Well, this road was pretty straight. He'd keep track of it in his peripheral vision. Lee's eyelashes feathered over her cheekbones. Her hair drifted against the back of the seat and bared her neck. Soft. He didn't have to hold her to know. Silence eased alongside them and warmed the spaces that didn't need words.

EPILOGUE

Marcus didn't last an hour into the film. Before Stewart and Novak shared their first kiss, Lee's peripheral vision caught the twitching of his hands. He was a limp mass, shoulders tilted back against the couch, head lolled to one side. She should perhaps wake him before that pose stiffened his neck, but the exhausted lines had eased from around his eyes, and she didn't wish to bring them back.

Her own eyelids felt swollen with needed sleep, but she could not allow herself to drift. The last thing either of them needed was for Marcus to witness a flashback nightmare. He wasn't even aware they occurred. She stretched her legs, pointed her toes, and yawned. She curled deeper into the stuffed chair and attempted to refocus on the film. Marcus was right about one thing: these characters deserved no pity.

The second incarnation of Novak turned out to be no more tolerable than the first. Willingness to throw one's identity aside for a man was hardly a laudable trait.

Identity. To distract herself from the characters that deserved everything they got, Lee studied Novak's two looks. Very different, but she wore both well. Lee's own recent attempt at makeup had been purposely more dramatic. She had cringed at her reflection, especially the lipstick, some hue between crimson and fuchsia and designated "Garish," so aptly that Lee couldn't help choosing it. She'd set out for the foster home aware of the possible consequences, yet not truly prepared when they knocked on her door in the form of Agent Mayweather.

She'd sat in the Constabulary office for an entire night, waiting for the emergence of handcuffs, the uttering of Miranda rights. Yes, the guilty—even the unremorseful—often escaped justice, sometimes even after an interrogation by law enforcement; but this escape seemed unlikely for herself.

And then, abruptly, she *had* escaped. Whether Lee had her own impassive face, that insufferable lipstick, her lawyer, an unreliable witness, or all of the above to thank—she didn't care.

Stewart and Novak began to yell at each other. Lee lowered the volume and darted a glance at the couch, but their outburst hadn't wakened Marcus. Perhaps nothing would, now, until morning. That would be best for him.

But no, as "The End" filled the screen, Marcus's right hand jerked against the cushion. A gasp distorted his whimper.

"Aubrey," he said.

Oh.

Lee crossed her arms. The room had grown chilly over the last two hours. He jolted forward, and his gaze shot around the room. In search of Aubrey?

"Marcus," Lee said.

The eyes that found hers held confusion, then recollection as they sprang to the TV. "Oh ... I ... missed the end."

"And the middle."

"Sorry. What did you think?"

"They were all insufferable. I don't see why you own it."

He rolled his shoulders, not a shrug but an attempt to loosen them. "Jimmy Stewart, I guess. And Hitchcock. But I never watch it."

"You could have mentioned that fact."

"Hey. I said you'd hate it." His mouth should curve, tried to and failed.

"Was your dream unpleasant?"

His gaze tore away. Not unpleasant at all, then? Too pleasant to verbalize?

Comprehension dripped into her mind. Here it was, the issue of which he couldn't speak.

"Your concern for my feelings is unnecessary," Lee said. More sensible to open this topic, like a clean incision. If she didn't, it would continue to fester.

"What?"

"You are ... exploring possibilities with her?" Aubrey could give him a normal, healthy relationship. Most likely, she could think about intimacy without almost throwing up. He'd given Lee a decade to overcome herself. It was time for him to reach for someone else.

Aubrey could give him children.

Lee's chest throbbed. She curled her fingers against her palm, trying to squeeze the stubborn life out of the part of herself that wondered how thick his hair would be between her fingers, how broad his palms would be against hers.

He was staring at her. "Lee ... what're you talking about?"

"You spoke her name as you woke up."

His face filled with shock, then with something she couldn't name; he turned away too quickly. He lurched to his feet, shuffled the few steps to the low table, and pawed for the remote. For Lee, he switched the table lamp to a brighter setting before turning off the television. Then he stood in the center of the room, too still.

"Marcus, obviously, I want you to find ..."

Happiness? Distress more accurately described the bow of his massive shoulders.

"I hope you intended to tell me," she said. "As a friend, I should be informed of—"

"Aubrey's dead."

The dull words trapped time and Lee's breath, then released both at once. "Are you certain?"

Was that a nod, or did his head simply duck to his chest?

"If she's vanished, there may be other—"

"I found it. Her. The body."

In his home? She hadn't been ill. So she *was* party to the loss of his truck, and perished in the accident?

Marcus straightened and crossed the width of the living room, then slowly turned and paced back, likely unaware of his own movement.

"Where is your truck? Can the Constabulary link you to the accident? To her, to ... Is the child dead as well?"

"No. Hiding. With some people. And it's in the woods. The truck. And everything. It's all in the woods." His words dropped toward the floor, sluggish like a concussion victim's, heavy like the treading of his feet.

"Marcus, look at me."

When he finally did, his eyes held something that didn't belong there, something that drained his essence.

"Surely there were witnesses," she said. "A car accident always involves—"

"It was a dirt road, nobody saw. Everything's hidden."

"Everything, including the body?"

"She laid there. Until we found her."

"We?"

"Me. And Chuck."

Was he working with someone else, then, after his vehement refusal of Sam's assistance? "Would it be possible for you to start at the beginning?"

"She's dead."

"I need you to elaborate."

Several times, Lee nearly allowed him to terminate the story. He struggled for every phrase. Halfway through, his pacing feet stopped midstride, and he sank onto the couch. She had no right to demand that he speak of this, but she had no choice, either. He might have overlooked a danger to himself.

Finally, long minutes later, he lifted his head. Lamplight caught the sheen of his eyes. "Lee? Do you think she ... hurt?"

"No. She was likely unconscious." Cerebral hemorrhage was more detail than he needed.

Marcus bent double, stared at the carpet. "She's buried in the woods, behind Chuck's house. No stone or cross or ... just in a tarp, wrapped up, in the ground. She should have a grave. She shouldn't be dead."

No, she shouldn't be dead, not with an infant to care for. Yet he would continue to trust the God that had permitted her to die. The God that might as well have swatted Marcus's truck into the ditch and crushed it with an omnipotent finger.

"I know it's here," he whispered. "The plan. I know I can't screw it up, but—but I did. She's dead because ... if I just would've ... sooner."

"Sooner what?"

"Listened. To people. But I didn't and now she's ..." A minute passed, then another. His hands curled up and surely pulled the raw skin, which she'd rewrapped with gauze before they started the movie. But he didn't wince, merely sat, stonelike.

Lee stretched her feet to the floor and sat forward but couldn't tug his gaze to hers. "Do you believe yourself capable of defeating the Constabulary single-handedly?"

"No." The word snapped quietly.

"Do you believe they can be defeated?"

"They've got to be."

"Then allies are a necessity."

"Lee, I know. I've got some now. But she's still dead." He stood and trudged to the kitchen.

Minutes later, he wandered back to the couch but did not sit. Steam wafted from the mug that both his hands encircled as if seeking warmth. Lee folded herself further into the chair and rested her chin on her knees. He might choose to speak, or he might not. Regardless, she would stay. If he wished her to leave, he would say so.

"I've been thinking," he said quietly. "I know she had family. I should try to—"

"No."

"I wouldn't meet with them. I'd send a message. Or something."

"The risk is too great, Marcus. They would search for the child, as well as someone to blame. Either search might lead to you."

Marcus gazed into the mug he had yet to sip from. "Somebody should know."

"You know," Lee said.

"I met her a week ago. Somebody should do something for her, somebody that mattered to her."

"That's not possible."

He slammed the mug down. Coffee sloshed onto the glass coaster, which might have just cracked.

"Your attempt to memorialize her holds no meaning for her. You'd be doing it for yourself, prioritizing the dead before the living who still seek a haven."

He nodded. His face crumpled before he turned toward the wall. His promise to safeguard Aubrey lay across his bent shoulders, a yoke like a mountain.

All of this on day three. "You're thirsty. Right now."

He ducked his head.

"Marcus."

"I ... can't talk anymore."

Her hand felt again what she'd done to him only days ago, the stunned yield in the turn of his jaw, first against her palm, then against the back of her hand. She'd known exactly how to break him down. What sort of person did that?

He reclaimed his mug from the end table and sank back onto the couch. The thumb of his bandaged hand rubbed the mug's handle. He'd split it almost exactly along the old scar, consistent even when breaking down. At least this time, he'd volunteered to let her rewrap it.

"I'd have gone to the hospital. If it got bad."

"Since when would you rather face a hospital than me?"

"You'd just told me someone ... did that ... to you. And then I got mad and started hitting things. If you knew, you might think ... I could hit you, too."

Lee blinked away the old memory, the moment she'd finally understood him. Trusted him. Did he still trust her? He sipped his coffee, and the mug trembled when he set it back down. She should take his hand.

No. She shouldn't. She couldn't.

He gazed at the table, and his shoulders quaked, once. Lee opened her palm and ordered her hand to reach out, to enfold his callused fist or curve around his shoulder, to give him this small thing after all he'd given her. To say in a way that meant more to him than words, *Marcus, I . . .* But her hands remained still, both of them in her lap, one clenched, one open.

"Lee?"

"Yes?"

"Thanks. For knowing. And staying."

She laced together the fingers of the hands that couldn't touch him. "You're welcome."

ACKNOWLEDGMENTS

So many people are traveling life's journey with me and taking part in my author's journey in unique, precious ways. Thank you …

To my first writer's group, for friendship and memories. To Heather MacLeod for telling me who my main characters were and getting me to spill sleepover spoilers because you needed to know *now*. To Jocelyn Floyd for MIBFTRO, Marcus-love, and meteors. To Melodie Lange for finding romance in pancakes. I go on record to say yes, all of you were right about everything.

To Rachel Hauck and Susan May Warren for encouragement and affirmation when I was an uncertain newbie at a retreat in February 2011, for praying over me and believing I *would* be published.

To Hannah Jacobsen for keeping the red binder.

To the Best Crit Group Ever (trademark pending)—Edie Melson, Erynn Newman, Jessica Keller, and Charity Tinnin. For support as I stepped onto the publication road and invaluable crit comments including "huh??"

To Jessica Keller (again) for the Team Marcus shirt and for expressing more excitement than I can.

To Charity Tinnin (again) for character therapy, hours of phone chats, and dragging me off my ledges. For loving Marcus and Lee even though you'd slap them in real life, and for being my friend.

To Andrea Taft for physician assistant expertise ("she should clean that again to avoid osteomyelitis"), for unsolicited story-related texts ("Marcus would like this coffee"), for impatience to hold this book in your hands, and for being my friend.

To Jessica Kirkland, my amazing and extroverted agent, for tearing this manuscript apart, for freaking me out with your fire hose of ideas, and for pushing me and this story to be our best.

To the David C Cook digital team and editor Jon Woodhams, for dedication to excellence.

To my siblings, Joshua, Andrew, and Emma, for being your awesome selves and loving me, and especially to my sister Emily, for being the best sister a writer could ask for. You know all the reasons why.

To my parents, Bill and Patti, for love and encouragement and Christ-like examples. To Dad for thinking I'm a genius and telling me the obvious goal here should be the *New York Times* best seller list. To Mom for home schooling and reality checks, and for texting me when the book made you cry.

Lastly and above all, to the Creator God Who gave me an inner fire to create, the Father God Who loves me more than I could ever love these fictional children of mine, the righteous God and King Who left His throne to come down here and pay for unrighteousness. Dear Lord, receive glory from my little offering.